On one of those gusts came a cry of anguish

that sliced the heart of Mather Wyndon, a scream of pain and fear from a voice that he knew well.

He drew out his sword and used it to lead the way through the tangle of branch and snow, pushing out into the frigid air, trying to orient himself and determine the direction of Bradwarden's howl. The wind was from the northeast still, and it had carried Bradwarden's cry, so Mather set out that way, circumventing Dundalis, the smoke of the many chimneys thick in the air. Soon he found a path cut through the drifts—by goblins, he knew, though he could hardly see on this dark night. He didn't dare light a torch, fearing to make himself a target, but he understood his disadvantage here. Goblins were creatures of caves and deep tunnels. They could see much better in the dark than even an elven-trained ranger.

Mather was not surprised when he came through one large drift and caught a flicker of movement to the side, a missile flying straight for him.

He sent his energy into Tempest, and the sword flared with angry light. He brought the blade whipping about, intercepting the hurled spear and knocking it harmlessly aside, and then slashed back, deflecting a second.

The third got through…

—from "Mather's Blood," by R. A. Salvatore

D1603468

THE PLANET STORIES LIBRARY

STRANGE ADVENTURES ON OTHER WORLDS

AVAILABLE MONTHLY EXCLUSIVELY FROM PLANET STORIES!

FOR AUTHOR BIOS AND SYNOPSES,
VISIT PAIZO.COM/PLANETSTORIES

Planet Stories is a division of Paizo Publishing, LLC
2700 Richards Road, Suite 201
Bellevue, WA 98005

PLANET STORIES is a trademark of Paizo Publishing, LLC

Visit us online at paizo.com/planetstories

Printed in China

Planet Stories #14, *Worlds of Their Own*, edited by James Lowder
First Printing August 2008

10 9 8 7 6 5 4 3 2 1   2008

Worlds of
Their Own

edited by James Lowder

Cover by Daren Bader

PLANET STORIES
Seattle
Erik Mona, Publisher

ACKNOWLEDGEMENTS

"Mather's Blood" by R. A. Salvatore, © 1998 by R. A. Salvatore. First published in *Dragon* magazine #252, October 1998. Reprinted by permission of the author.

"Keeping Score" by Michael A. Stackpole, © 2000 by Michael A. Stackpole. First published in *Guardsmen of Tomorrow*, edited by Martin H. Greenberg and Larry Segriff; DAW. Reprinted by permission of the author.

"The Oaths of Gods" by Nancy Virginia Varian, © 2005, 2008 by Nancy Virginia Varian. First published in a slightly different form in *Lords of Swords*, edited by Daniel E. Blackston; Pitch Black Books. Reprinted by permission of the author.

"The Doom of Swords" by Greg Stolze, © 2007, 2008 by Greg Stolze. First published as an audio podcast at www.gregstolze.com, August 2007. Published by permission of the author.

"Catch of the Day" by Jeff Grubb, © 2001 by Jeff Grubb. First published in *Oceans of Magic*, edited by Brian M. Thomsen and Martin H. Greenberg; DAW. Reprinted by permission of the author.

"Ghosts of Love" by Steven Savile, © 2007, 2008 by Steven Savile. First published in a slightly different form in *Touched by Wonder*, edited by Jackie Gamber; Meadowhawk Press. Reprinted by permission of the author.

"The Wisdom of Nightingales" by Richard E. Dansky, © 2002 by Richard E. Dansky. First published in *Stillwaters Journal*, September 2002. Reprinted by permission of the author.

"The Guardian of the Dawn" by William King, © 2005 by William King. First published in *Flashing Swords* #1, January 2005. Reprinted by permission of the author.

"How Fear Came to Ornath" by Ed Greenwood, © 1982, 2008 by Ed Greenwood. First published in a slightly different form as "Sky Pirates of Shiningstorm" in *Magic Casements*, edited by Hailey Greene and A. C. Paquette; Trumpet Press. Reprinted by permission of the author.

TABLE OF CONTENTS

THE LAST WORD MATTERS

BY JAMES LOWDER

If you write in a shared world long enough, some eager young editor will eventually inform you that you don't understand a character you created back when that wielder of the red pen was still playpen-bound. He may be right. A novel or comic book or roleplaying game supplement contracted to another writer could have leveled your particular patch of imaginary landscape or transformed your dashing young hero into a sniveling back-stabber. You might have had a plan for your inventions, back when you first gave them life on paper, but that doesn't matter. The world's owner has the final say, and the plots envisioned by that publisher or estate or multinational corporation trump the lowly writer's plans every time.

From the owner's perspective, this arrangement makes perfect sense. A lot of effort and money go into developing an intellectual property, or IP, so it's important that the various products tied to that IP support its carefully constructed brand identity. If audiences love the ethnically diverse starship crew immortalized in two obscenely popular summer movies, an animated cable series, and a line of action figures, why allow a single novel to sour that adoration by depicting the sophisticated and erudite captain as an illiterate, xenophobic rube and the ultra-logical science officer as the victim of a lifelong and irrational fear of technology? Even if those concepts make for an interesting story, they undermine the public's perception of the characters and damage the marketing push for the third summer blockbuster and the associated computer game tie-ins and Happy Meal toys. The only way the IP owner can guarantee that no individual project subverts the brand in this way is to maintain final approval over everything everyone does with the property.

The constraints this sort of arrangement can place on creativity are obvious and have prompted critics such as John Clute to savage the idea of shared world fiction. As Clute puts it in a 1989 essay (reprinted in 1995's *Look at the Evidence*), the author involved in such a project is "a tenant farmer, he sows what Bwana tells him to sow, and he does not reap. Nor does he *make things up*. For the franchise owners who have hired him, any attempt by the sharecropper to look upon the world and *make it new* would be to violate their property rights. Originality is theft."

To be certain, some shared world assignments begin with an editor handing a wordsmith a plot and an established cast, seeds for the workman to sow across a carefully pre-furrowed field, but not always. With roleplaying-game-related fiction in particular, writers frequently direct the adventures of characters they invent and detail huge areas of the setting, places heretofore undefined or sketched with only the broadest of strokes in a game supplement. This affords a writer a very good chance to make the work personal and to craft a novel or story that displays a unique perspective and voice. Originality here can be welcomed, even rewarded, particularly within settings that are structured to grow and incorporate new ideas.

The ideal situation arises when a writer envisions a story that is not artificially constrained by the IP's boundaries. If the editors running a shared world line are particularly enlightened, they've created slots in the publishing schedule for just such projects. They encourage authors to submit stories that do not shake the entire universe or upset the cosmology, but rather explore individual characters or discreet corners of the setting. These elements can be developed or destroyed as the author sees fit, without recasting the entire brand. Many of the most popular shared world characters, such as the dark elf adventurer Drizzt Do'Urden, are the result of this kind of arrangement, where a writer grafts something new onto a setting and is allowed to cultivate that material over time.

Allowed is the operative word in that description, and it highlights the peril of shared world projects that encourage originality. To succeed in these assignments, a writer must invest creative capital and go beyond the role of workman to contribute something novel to the franchise. Little surprise, then, that an author would feel attached, even protective of such contributions, or come to view his role as something more than a sharecropper. Yet the writer has no formal claim to those creations and can develop them only so long as the IP's owner permits it. He has the responsibility for growing the world, but few, if any, creative rights.

Given the conflicting goals and expectations, a clash is inevitable. Not every book or story will lead to a conflict, but authors who write in a shared world for more than a few books will find themselves at odds with the IP owner eventually. The disagreement might arise over a plotline the writer wants to pursue but the IP owner doesn't favor, or just changes made to a manuscript, since most shared world contracts don't even allow the author final say over punctuation or word choice. A writer might object to the way in which the world's owner permits a signature character to be used in a licensed product—a pre-painted miniature assembled by child labor or an embarrassingly cheesy T-shirt or, most often, a novel or story written by someone else.

Changes in editorial staff can also precipitate a row, as the new editors assert themselves by redefining characters, recasting the line's metaplot, or simply bringing in favored writers and marginalizing others. These sorts of power shifts occur all the time in publishing, but a shared world writer faces additional risks from such inevitabilities. Unlike an author who controls his own copyrights, the franchise writer cannot pack up his characters and take them elsewhere. If an editor decides the storyline a writer has been cultivating for a decade is done, it's done. If an author's characters are re-assigned to another writer, their creator can only hope their new (and equally temporary) master will treat them kindly.

The editors are not the villains here. No, the lot of a shared world editor is a hell all its own. The job consists of all the typical editorial duties, with the additional Augean task of coordinating a setting's complex and contradictory continuity. Under ludicrously tight deadlines, they must encourage writers to craft the best, most inventive stories possible, even as they keep a tight enough rein on the freelancers to prevent anyone from destabilizing the IP. Factor in the demands of subsidiary projects connected to the setting—roleplaying games, comics, computer games, other novels and stories, even movies and TV shows—along with the aesthetic and ethical concerns, and you get a calculus that would make Einstein's eyes bleed.

But the shared world editor has one distinct advantage. He's an agent of the IP owner, so he gets the last word in every argument with the author.

So why would a writer bother with a shared world project? What's the allure?

Despite popular misconceptions, the money for most franchise books is not all that great. Some writers can make a steady income if they work quickly, meet their deadlines, and avoid all conflicts with the IP owner over content, but that pace is hard to maintain for long. Fame isn't really a lure, either. Most franchises are careful to keep the creators' identities secondary to the brand. For years, TSR even refused to put authors' names on the spines of its successful Dragonlance and Forgotten Realms books in hopes of encouraging readers to remain loyal to the line over the people crafting the individual titles.

For many, the chance to be part of a pop culture franchise justifies the often dubious working conditions. It can be a thrill to put words into the mouth of an iconic character you've followed for years, to choreograph a battle of wits between Batman and the Joker or a lightsaber duel between Luke Skywalker and Darth Vader. Or, better yet, create a new character with whom those internationally famous figures can trade blows or quips.

Shared world franchises, especially those that encompass feature films and TV series, also boast large established audiences, much larger than the one books alone attract. This means the chance to showcase your writing chops to new readers—a lot of them. While some fans pay little attention to the writer's name on a shared world book, others can be very supportive. More than a decade after I last wrote a story set in the Forgotten Realms, I still receive letters and e-mail from Realms buffs. A healthy number of those readers have kept up with my creator-owned projects, as well.

There's another community aspect to working in a franchise that can't be dismissed lightly: professional camaraderie. I count many of the authors, editors, and artists with whom I've worked on shared world projects as friends and respected colleagues; several are represented in this anthology. Writing is a rather secluding pursuit, so participating in the artistic network that grows up around a shared world can be refreshing. In fact, under the right conditions, working in a franchise can be an experiment in collaborative storytelling. The best, most creatively dynamic shared worlds, such as Thieves' World and Wild Cards, are structured around that concept of collaboration. The contracts they utilize formalize the author's status as something more like a partner, correcting at least somewhat the lopsided balance of power between creator and IP owner. This helps these projects take the form of literary jam sessions. Like jazz musicians trading eights, the writers are inspired by the expressions of the other artists on stage, but are encouraged to articulate an individual vision, too.

In many ways, the modern franchise novel market is the successor to the pulps, structured around a mode of production where oppressive deadlines and myopically market-driven editorial policies maximize the chance that any individual work will be tediously predictable. However, crafting interesting, even inspired stories under those conditions is not impossible. Just take a look at the work of pulp veterans Clark Ashton Smith or Cornell Woolrich, H. P. Lovecraft or C. L. Moore (some of whose best fiction has already seen reprint in the Planet Stories line), to say nothing of such writers as Tennessee Williams and Upton Sinclair who graduated from the pulps to mainstream success.

The vantage of history will reveal which, if any, of the writers toiling in shared worlds today will make names for themselves beyond their franchise releases, and which of those novels and

THE LAST WORD MATTERS

stories will maintain any sort of readership. In the meantime, even forming a meaningful assessment of those authors' shared world titles can prove rather tricky. It's a simple enough matter to review a work as a whole, to catalog its merits or failings based upon whatever critical standards you want to employ, but discussing the writer's individual contributions to that work places you on unstable ground. Thanks to the way in which any individual project might be put together, the wildly variable amount of aesthetic input a writer could have, it's difficult to untangle that creator's contribution from the existing franchise content, the influence of fellow "sharecroppers," even the impact of editors and other IP continuity coordinators. Only by comparing an author's shared world fiction with the stories he crafts outside the confines of the franchise can a critical baseline be established.

Which brings us, at long last, to the anthology you hold in your hands.

The stories presented herein take place, as the book's title suggests, in worlds created and controlled by the participating writers. The tales were crafted without a weather eye cast toward some distant franchise owner nervously tensed against the creative liberties that might be taken with his IP. The authors had no worries that someone else might be tasked with undoing or contradicting whatever changes these stories wrought to their characters or setting. They applied their passion and their skill, and told the fantasy and SF adventure tales they wanted to tell. Sometimes their style or theme dovetails nicely with the author's franchise work. Other times they are surprising departures. But the stories all depict worlds for which the original author has final say, a fact that places the burden for each work's success or failure squarely on the shoulders of that author.

They accept that burden gladly. It's a small enough price to pay for the chance to finally have the last word.

James Lowder
New Berlin, WI
May, 2008

Worlds of
Their Own

R. A. Salvatore

R. A. Salvatore began writing shortly after receiving his Bachelor of Science degree in Communications/Media from Fitchburg State College. Salvatore's first published novel, *The Crystal Shard* (1988), became the first volume of the acclaimed Icewind Dale Trilogy and introduced an enormously popular character, the dark elf Drizzt Do'Urden. Since that time, Salvatore has published numerous novels for each of his signature multi-volume series, including the Dark Elf Trilogy, Paths of Darkness, and the Cleric Quintet, as well as creator-owned series with Warner Aspect (the Crimson Shadow series), Del Rey (the Chronicles of Ynis Aielle), and Ace (the Spearwielder's Tales). With over 11 million books sold in the U.S. alone, and nearly four dozen books to his credit, many of them bestsellers, Salvatore has become one of the most important figures in modern epic fantasy. He is currently working with 38 Studios, LLC as "creator of worlds" for their first game project.

"Mather's Blood" is set in the world of Corona, home to Salvatore's DemonWars saga. The first novels exploring Corona were published by Del Rey, beginning with The Demon Awakens (1997). Six additional Del Rey releases followed. The series moved to Tor in 2007 with a reprint of The Highwayman (originally published by CDS in 2004) and the original novel The Ancient in 2008; the Tor volumes are part of the Saga of the First King, a four-book series that chronicles Corona's early history. The setting has also inspired four roleplaying game sourcebooks, published by Fast Forward in 2003, and several comic book series, most recently from Devil's Due.

In a 2006 interview with the Flames Rising website (www.flamesrising.com), Salvatore laid out his thoughts on writing in the Forgotten Realms shared world:

"This isn't my playground (I still think of it as Ed Greenwood's), and I'm just thrilled to be able to participate. It can get frustrating, particularly when some other material, of which I had no knowledge, contradicts what's in my work, but my editor explained it best. He considers each author's work to be like a campaign the author is playing in the Forgotten Realms.

"The upside of it all, of course, is that I get to play off the ideas of people like Ed and Gary Gygax and all the rest. I get to stand on the shoulders of giants.... The challenges are usually greatly overwhelmed by the pleasure of the creative environment."

MATHER'S BLOOD

BY R. A. SALVATORE

"OH, BUT YOU'RE a quick one!" Mather Wyndon cried out, leaping a fallen log and cutting a fast turn about a sharp bend in the trail. He spotted the creature he was pursuing, an ugly and smelly goblin, far ahead, scrambling up a steep hill and over a wall of piled rocks.

The large man lowered his head and started straight on, but he stopped fast at the sound of a cry to his right. He cut behind a tree, grabbing its solid trunk to help break his momentum, and pivoted about, his fine elvish blade glowing with an eager white light.

Out of the brush came the second goblin, running wild, running scared, holding its crude spear—no more than a sharpened stick, really—out wide in one hand, in no position to throw or to stab.

The creature wasn't up for any fight, anyway, Mather understood as soon as he saw its features, twisted into an expression of the sheerest fright. That was the secret of fighting goblins, the seasoned ranger knew. Catch them by surprise, and the cowardly beasts would scatter, all semblance of defense thrown aside. Mather smiled as a second creature burst out behind the goblin, a huge beast with the lower body of a horse supporting the upper body of a man: a centaur, five hundred pounds of muscle, and this one, Bradwarden by name, was merely a boy, Mather knew.

A boy, but an impressive sight no less!

Hardly slowing, howling with glee, the young centaur ran up the goblin's back, trampled the ugly thing down into the dirt. Then, as he came up above its head, he lifted his hind legs and stomped down hard, splattering the goblin's skull.

Mather didn't see it; having all faith in his half-equine companion, the elven-trained ranger was already in pursuit of the first goblin, running hard up the ascent, then leaping atop the stone wall, and then leaping far from it with graceful, fluid movements. Mather was closer to fifty years of age than to forty, but he moved with the agility of a far younger man. Though he had spent the majority of his life in the harsh climate of the Timberlands, serving as silent protector for the folk of the two small towns in the region, Dundalis and Weedy Meadow, he felt few aches in his old bones and muscles.

From the top of the ridge, Mather saw spread before him a familiar vale of man-height spruce trees, triangular green dots among a field of white, ankle-deep caribou moss. And there was the running goblin—and indeed it was a quick one!—scrambling along, cutting sharp corners about the trees, stumbling often, and half the time turning right around in a circle as it tried to keep its bearings in this vale where all the trees looked the same.

Down went Mather in a rush. The goblin spotted him and squeaked pitifully, then ran in a straight line away, to the south, and up another slope. As it neared the top, the foliage changed back to deciduous trees, small growth and scrub. The goblin slipped into one tangle of birch and peered back anxiously.

"If you're waiting for your friend, you'll be waiting a long time, I fear," came a voice behind the goblin. Mather's voice.

The creature shrieked and scrambled out of the birch, one step ahead of the ranger, one step ahead of that deadly blade. The goblin went around a large trunk, but Mather was the quicker, coming around the other way, cutting off the escape. The goblin lifted its club and, forced to fight, tried to assume a defensive posture.

Mather's blade swerved left, then right, and the goblin's club moved with it, in line to block.

But Mather knew *bi'nelle dasada*, the elven sword dance, and the goblin did not. The side-to-side movements were naught but feints, for this fighting style, so unlike all the others of the day, focused on movements forward and back. His lead foot perpendicular to his trailing, bracing foot, his front knee bent and his weight out over it, Mather waved the blade again, and then, before the goblin could recognize the move, before it could react with the club, before it could even blink, Mather's elven blade, Tempest, stabbed forward, seeming to pull all of his body, extending, extending, past the goblin's meager defenses, through the goblin's torso, to crack hard against the tree trunk behind the creature.

Mather let go of the blade.

The goblin did not fall, even as the last life left it, held firmly in place by the embedded sword.

Mather glanced to the south, down the slope to the tiny village of Dundalis, nestled in the vale beyond. The day was early and bitterly cold, and none of the folk were about, though Mather could see the glow of morning fires through several windows. They wouldn't see him, though, and wouldn't know what he had done here this morn. They knew nothing of goblins, these farmers and woodcutters. Indeed, goblins were rare in these parts; these three were the first the ranger had seen in several years. But that only made them doubly dangerous to the unsuspecting folk of Dundalis, Mather realized. Goblins were not so difficult an enemy when they were caught by surprise, as Mather and Bradwarden had done. They were cowardly creatures, and purely selfish. Thus, when surprised, they would simply scatter. But if they got the upper hand, if they ever found Mather and Bradwarden's camp instead of the other way around, then the ranger and the centaur would indeed find a difficult fight on their hands. And if the goblins ever managed an ambush on the sleepy village of Dundalis....

Mather shook the unsettling images away, but not before wondering if he should try, at least, to better educate and thus prepare the folk of the village for that grim possibility. The notion merely brought a chuckle to his lips. The folk would never listen. To them, goblins were but fireside tales. Mather looked at the dead creature. Perhaps he should bring it and its companions into the town to show them. Perhaps....

No, the ranger realized. That was not his place, and the ramifications of such an action could be disastrous—everything from scaring half the folk back to the civilized southland to bringing an army up from Palmaris, a force that would despoil all of this nearly pristine land.

Let the folk remain oblivious. And of the ranger, their secret protector, let the folk continue their perception of him as a mad hermit, an eccentric woodsman, to be shunned whenever he ventured among them.

Better that way, Mather thought. He was performing as the elves had trained him. As he had learned all those years in the elven homeland of Caer'alfar, he did not take his satisfaction in accolades. Mather's strength came from within.

He grasped Tempest in both hands and yanked it free, then wiped the shining blade on the ragged clothes of the fallen goblin. He grabbed the ugly little creature with one hand and went down to the north, back into the pine vale, dragging the goblin behind him. By the time he found Bradwarden, the centaur had the other two goblins the pair had killed this day piled with a mound of sticks and dead branches, ready to burn.

"The first kill was mine," Bradwarden insisted later that night, while he and Mather feasted on venison stew.

"The goblin's blood stained Tempest," Mather answered, though his tone showed that he hardly cared for the credit.

"Ah, but it was me arrow that sent the thing sprawlin' to the ground," the centaur reasoned with a big slurp to catch a piece of meat that slipped out the corner of his mouth. He wasn't successful, though, and the venison hit the ground. Bradwarden, with hardly a thought, scooped it right up and popped it back into his mouth. "And lyin' there, as it was, ye're finding an easy time killin' the thing. Too easy, I'm thinking, and so the kill's me own to claim."

"I will split the kill with you," Mather said. "A goblin and a half for each of us this day."

The centaur stopped chewing and eyed the ranger unblinkingly. "Two for me and one for yerself," he argued.

Mather couldn't suppress a smile. He had known Bradwarden for nearly five years now, and the young centaur's overblown sense of pride and wild spirit had been a true amusement to him for all that time. Bradwarden was just into his thirties, which equated to the same stage as a human teenager. Oh, how he acted the part!

"Take two for yourself, then," Mather teased. "After all these years, it seems appropriate that you finally best me in something, even if it is but a minor battle with a trio of weakling goblins, a trio I'd have had an easier time killing myself."

Bradwarden recognized a challenge when he heard one. He dropped his bowl of venison stew—but cupped it as it hit the ground, catching a substantial part of the spillage and rushing it right back to his waiting mouth. He nodded his chin in the direction of a tree stump at the side of the small encampment.

Mather smiled and shook his head. "You'll only get angrier," he remarked, but the centaur was already on his way. With a feigned sigh of resignation, Mather climbed to his feet and rolled up his right sleeve, then took his place opposite Bradwarden and planted his elbow on the stump.

They clasped hands, and the centaur began to pull immediately, gaining a quick advantage. But Mather, the muscles of the forearm bulging with strength from all the years he had spent squeezing the milk stones to make the elvish wine, locked his arm in place and turned his wrist over the young centaur's. Within a matter of seconds, Mather understood that he would win and he flashed a smug smile at his straining companion. The ranger figured that he would enjoy the victories while he could, for his strength was on the wane, while Bradwarden was twice Mather's weight, but the centaur would likely gain that much again within a couple more years. Even now, so young, the centaur could best almost any human at arm wrestling, though his human arms were undeniably his weakest assets.

But Mather Wyndon wasn't just any human, was a ranger, was, in fact, the epitome of what a human warrior might achieve in body and soul. Slowly but surely, the centaur's arm slid back and down toward the tree stump.

Bradwarden's eyes went wide in apparent shock as he looked over Mather's shoulder. The ranger, expecting a goblin spear to be flying for his back, glanced around—and the centaur pulled hard, nearly yanking Mather's elbow out of joint, and slammed the ranger's hand down on the tree stump.

With a howl of pain and outrage, Mather, realizing the ruse, spun back on Bradwarden, and now it was the centaur wearing the smug smile. "Two for me and one for yerself," the centaur said. "And now ye're beaten again." And then he was off, spinning and bucking to ward off Mather's rush, then galloping across the encampment and into the forest.

Laughing all the way, Mather followed him as far as the edge of the camp. "Have your victories, then!" he shouted. "I've got the stew, and that makes me the winner!"

"And what would you know of any victories?" came a melodic voice from behind, a voice like the tinkling of sweet bells, of the drift of perfect harmony on summer breezes through a forest. At first, Mather stood as if turned to stone, stunned that someone, anyone, had been able to sneak up on him so. As he considered that voice, that familiar voice, he came to recognize the truth, and his smile was genuine and wide indeed when he turned about to face the speaker.

She sat on the lowest branch of a tree at the side of the camp, her delicate legs dangling and crossed, her nearly translucent wings fluttering behind her. "Blood of Alturias," she said derisively, a taunt Mather Wyndon had heard so many times, a reference to a deceased distant cousin, one who had been an elven-trained ranger long before him, one who this particular elf, Tuntun by name, had apparently considered far more worthy of the training than she had Mather.

"Tuntun, my dear old friend," he said dryly, feigning resignation, though it was obvious that he was overjoyed to see the elf.

"Never that," the elf replied.

"My mentor, then," Mather replied.

"Hardly."

"My teacher, then," Mather agreed.

"Unfortunately," came the curt response, but Mather understood the joke behind it. Tuntun had been, perhaps, his most critical instructor in his years with the elves, and, despite that she weighed nowhere near to a hundred pounds, had bested him many times in sparring matches. Keen of wit and of skill, the delicate elf had put more than a few bruises on Mather Wyndon, body and pride!

"What brings Tuntun so far from Caer'alfar?" Mather asked. "And does she come alone?"

"Would she need any escort in these lands full of bumbling, stupid humans?" the elf replied.

Mather bowed, granting her that. Indeed, he knew that Tuntun could pass all the way through the human lands and back again, stealing food wherever she chose, sleeping wherever she decided was most comfortable, without being spotted once by anybody.

"And why am I so blessed with your visit?" the ranger asked.

Tuntun half-jumped, half-flew down from her perch, going at once to the cauldron and sniffing it, then curling her features in obvious disgust.

"Were you just curious as to how I was getting along?" Mather pressed. "It has been three years, at least, since I have seen you or any of the Touel'alfar."

"That is the joy of training rangers," the unrelenting Tuntun went on. "Once we are done with them, we send them back to their own kind and do not have to smell them again."

Mather let it go with a chuckle. He knew that behind the gruff words and constant insults, Tuntun, perhaps more than any of the other elves, truly cared for him. Tuntun, though, had always equated any show of the softer emotions with weakness, and both of them understood that weakness could quickly spell disaster for one working as a ranger.

"And yet, here you are," Mather said, his smile as unrelenting as Tuntun's insults, "come to share my meal and my company."

"Come with news," Tuntun corrected. "And to see how you fare with the child of Andos and Dervia," she added, referring to Bradwarden's parents, whom Mather had never met.

"Bradwarden grows stronger each day," Mather replied, and even as he spoke, as if on cue, a beautiful, haunting music drifted on the breeze. "And his piping improves," the ranger added.

Despite her demeanor, Tuntun smiled at the sound of the centaur's distant music, a wondrous tune indeed, and nodded her approval. "He has his mother's gift for song, and his father's strength."

"A fine companion," Mather agreed. He sat down and picked up his stew, then, and Tuntun did likewise, lifting Bradwarden's abandoned bowl. Neither spoke for a long while, both just enjoyed their meal and the continuing melody of Bradwarden's piping.

"I am returning to Caer'alfar," the elf explained much later on, after Mather had told her of his most recent exploits in the region, including the fight that day with the goblin trio. "I meant to go this very night and should not have veered from my path to speak with you. Too long have I been away."

"But you did come, and with news, so you said," Mather replied.

"Do you remember when you were a child?"

"When Tuntun used to stop me from eating my meals hot, or even warm?" Mather returned with a grin.

"Before that," the elf replied in all seriousness.

Mather stared at her hand. He had been only a few years old when the elves had taken him in, rescued him from a mauling by a bear, nurtured him back to health and then trained him as a ranger. He didn't remember the bear attack, just the elves' retelling of it. Try as he might, he could remember nothing of the time before that, other than small, uncapturable images.

"You had family," Tuntun explained.

Mather nodded.

"Younger siblings, and a brother who was born some years after you left them," Tuntun went on.

Mather shrugged, hardly remembering.

"His name is Olwan," Tuntun explained. "Olwan Wyndon. I thought you should be told."

"Why? And why now?"

"Because Olwan has decided to make the Timberlands his home," Tuntun explained. "You will know him when you see him, for there is indeed a resemblance. He rides north with his family and two other wagons, headed for the settlement called Dundalis."

"This late in the season?" Mather asked incredulously, for few ventured north of Caer Tinella after the beginning of the ninth month, and here they were, halfway through the eleventh, and those who knew the region somewhat surprised that winter had not yet begun in earnest. It was not wise to be caught on the road during the Timberlands winter.

"I said he was your brother," Tuntun replied dryly. "I did not say that he was intelligent. They are on the road, two days yet from the town, and a storm is growing in the west."

Mather didn't reply, didn't blink.

"I thought you should know," Tuntun said again, and she rose up and straightened her clothes.

"And am I to tell him, this Olwan, who I am?"

Tuntun looked at the man as though she did not understand the question.

"About my life?" Mather asked. "About who I am? That we are brothers?"

Tuntun held her hands out and scrunched up her delicate face. "That choice is Mather's," she explained. "We gave you gifts: your life, your training, your elven title, Riverhawk. But we did not take your tongue in payment, nor your free will. Mather will do as Mather chooses."

"To tell him that I was trained by elves?" the ranger asked.

"He will think you crazy, as do all the others, no doubt," Tuntun said with a laugh. "We have found that the Alpinadoran bar-

barians to the north and the To-gai horsemen to the south have oft been accepting of rangers, but the men of the central lands, the kingdom you call Honce-the-Bear, so smug in their foolish religion, so superior in their war machines and great cities, have little tolerance for such childish tales. Tell Olwan your brother what you will, or tell him nothing at all. That, you may find, could prove the easier course."

"They'll not make the towns before it breaks," Bradwarden said to Mather, the two of them watching the caravan of three wagons trudging along the northern road. They were still ten miles south of Dundalis, half a day's travel, and Mather knew that the centaur spoke truly. Tuntun had returned to him before the dawn, warning of an impending storm, a big one, and also warning him that she had seen quite a bit of goblin sign in the region. Apparently, the three Mather and Bradwarden had killed were not the whole of the group.

Mather had not disagreed with either grim prediction. He, too, had noted signs of the impending storm, and of the goblins, and all of this with his brother making slow time along the road from the south.

So Mather had come out, and Bradwarden with him, to watch over the caravan. When he looked to the western sky, dark clouds gathering like some invading enemy, and when he felt the bite of the increasing northeastern wind through layers of clothing, he thought it a good thing indeed that he had not waited for their arrival about Dundalis.

"I cannot go down to them," Bradwarden remarked. "Whatever ye're thinkin' ye might do to help them through the storm, ye'll be doin' alone."

Mather nodded his understanding and agreement. "And with the weather worsening, I fear that Dundalis might become a target for the desperate goblins," he said. "So go back and look over the town. Find Tuntun, if she is still about, and make sure that you keep a watch."

With a nod, the centaur galloped away. Mather continued shadowing the caravan, silently debating whether he should go down to help them construct some kind of shelter or whether he should just hope. Another hour, another couple of miles, meandered by.

The first few snowflakes drifted down; the wind's bite increased.

And then it hit, as if the sky itself had simply torn apart, dumping its contents earthward. What had been a gentle flurry became, in mere seconds, a driving blizzard of wind-whipped, stinging snow. Mather continued to watch the wagons, nodding his approval of the skill shown by the lead driver, the man bunching his cloak against the cold and forcing the team on.

Another mile slipped past slowly. By then, three inches of snow covered the trail.

"You can get there," Mather said quietly, urging the wagons on, for now they slowed and men scrambled together, likely discussing the possibility of stopping to wait out the storm. But they were southerners—likely not one of them had ever before been north of Palmaris, which was some three hundred miles away— and they couldn't appreciate the fury of a Timberlands snowstorm. If they circled their wagons now and huddled against the storm, they might find themselves stuck out here, with no help coming from Dundalis, or anywhere else, for many days, even weeks.

Winter would only get rougher. They'd never survive.

Mather pulled the cowl of his cloak low, as much to hide his face as to ward the cold, and rushed down to join the group. "Are you looking for Dundalis?" he asked in greeting as he approached, yelling loudly so that the men could hear him, though they were but a dozen feet from him.

"Dundalis, or any place to hide from the storm," said the lead driver, a large and strong man, a man who, as Tuntun had said, bore some resemblance to Mather Wyndon.

"Dundalis is your only choice," Mather replied, running up to grab the bridle of one of the horses. "You've got five miles to go."

"We'll not make it," another man cried.

"You have to make it," Mather replied sternly. "Even if you must desert the wagons and follow me on foot."

"But all our possessions—" the man started.

Mather cut him off and looked directly at Olwan as he spoke. "To stay out here is to die," he explained. "So tie your wagons together, front to back, and drive your teams—and drive them hard."

"I can hardly see the road before us," Olwan replied.

"I will guide you." As Mather finished, a haunting melody came up about them, music carried on, and cutting through, the howling wind.

"And what is that?" the stubborn man on the second wagon yelled.

"Another guide," Mather replied, silently applauding Brad-warden, understanding that the centaur was using the music to help Mather keep his bearings.

On they went, against the driving snow, against the howling, stinging wind. Mather, his body numb from the cold, pulled the lead horses along, kicking through the piling snow. Several hours passed, and still they were a mile away, and now the snow was a foot deep all about them and before them, and the afternoon was fast giving way to evening.

It grew colder, the wind only increased, and the snow did not relent.

Mather hardly knew where he was, the snow stealing land-marks. He plodded on, yanking at the reluctant horses, and then he found that he was not alone, that his brother, with equal de-termination, was beside him, pulling hard.

"How far?" Olwan yelled. Mather hardly heard him.

The ranger glanced around, searching, searching, for some-thing, for anything that would give him some indication. Then he saw a tree, and he knew that tree, and he recognized that they had but one climb to go, a few hundred yards and no more. But it would be a difficult climb, and by the time they capped the last ridge, darkness would be deep about them.

They fought and scrambled for every foot of ground. At one point, the trailing wagon slipped off the trail and hooked on a tree root. They thought they would have to cut it free, but stubborn Mather, now thinking of this storm as an enemy, would not surrender anything. He went behind the wagon and grabbed it with hands that could hardly feel, and with strength beyond that of nearly any living man, he began to lift.

And then he was not alone, Olwan beside him, setting his legs and his back and hauling with all of his strength, and somehow, impossibly, the two brought the wheel over the root and shoved the wagon back onto the trail.

Mather glanced at Olwan, at his brother, at the strength of the man's body and the determination on his face. He wondered then what feats they two might accomplish together, allowed himself to fantasize about the two of them hunting goblins in concert. Perhaps he could give to Olwan some of the gifts the Touel'alfar had given to him. Perhaps he could tutor the man on the ways of the forest and the fighting styles that would elevate him above other warriors.

But that was for another day, Mather promptly reminded himself as Olwan returned his gaze and smiled.

"We did well together," the man said, voice strong and resonant.

Mather smiled in reply. "But we've a ways yet to go," he reminded, and they each went right back to work, urging on the horses, pulling hard the wagons, and somehow, against the odds and against the fury of the storm, they crested the ridge and rolled and slid into Dundalis proper. Mather pointed out the common house.

"You will be welcomed there," he assured Olwan.

"Are you not accompanying us?" the man asked incredulously.

"This is not my place, though the folk here are friendly enough to those who come in peace," the ranger replied.

"Where, then, will you be?" Olwan asked. "Which house?"

"None in town."

"Surely you don't mean to go back out in this storm!"

"I am safe enough," Mather assured him, and with a smile and a pat on the man's arm, the ranger started away.

"And what is your name?" Olwan called after him.

Mather almost answered, but then considered the possible implications of revealing a name that might be familiar to Olwan Wyndon. All of the townsfolk knew him merely as "the dirty hunter," so that is what he replied. With a smile to assure Olwan once again that all was well with him, he melted into the snowstorm.

And what an entrance winter had made! Snow piled and piled, blown into drifts twice the height of a man, whipping and stinging so ferociously that Mather could hardly see a line of towering pine trees, though they were barely twenty yards away. He crawled under one large specimen, its branches wide, the lower ones pushed right down to the ground by the heavy snow. With numb fingers, he fumbled in his pack for kindling and flint and steel. Soon he had a small fire going. He wouldn't get much sleep this night, he realized, for he had to keep the fire burning and had to tend it constantly to ensure that it did not ignite the tree about him.

But that was his way, his calling, and as his hands began to thaw and to hurt, he accepted that, too, as the lot of a ranger. He would spend the night here, and in the morning, would dig himself out and perhaps go to Dundalis and speak with his brother.

Perhaps.

The snow continued that night but lightened, and the wind died away at last to a few remnant gusts. On one of those gusts came a cry of anguish that sliced the heart of Mather Wyndon, a scream of pain and fear from a voice that he knew well.

He drew out his sword and used it to lead the way through the tangle of branch and snow, pushing out into the frigid air, trying to orient himself and determine the direction of Bradwarden's howl. The wind was from the northeast still, and it had carried Bradwarden's cry, so Mather set out that way, circumventing Dundalis, the smoke of the many chimneys thick in the air. Soon he found a path cut through the drifts—by goblins, he knew, though he could hardly see on this dark night. He didn't dare light a torch, fearing to make himself a target, but he understood his disadvantage here. Goblins were creatures of caves and deep tunnels. They could see much better in the dark than even an elven-trained ranger.

Mather was not surprised when he came through one large drift and caught a flicker of movement to the side, a missile flying straight for him.

He sent his energy into Tempest, and the sword flared with angry light. He brought the blade whipping about, intercepting the hurled spear and knocking it harmlessly aside, and then slashed back, deflecting a second.

The third got through.

In the brutal cold, Mather hardly felt the impact, but he knew it was bad, for the spear had caught him in the side, under the ribs, its tip driving front to back. When he grasped at the bleeding wound, grabbing the shaft to steady it, for every twitch sent a wave of agony rolling through him, he felt the slick point of the weapon sticking out of his back.

He hardly realized that he was lying down now, on his back in the snow, staring up at the descending flakes, and suddenly, so very, very cold.

Movement nearby, the goblins rushing in for the kill, brought him back to his senses, made him understand that death was imminent.

But not now, Mather determined. Not like this. With a growl, he snapped apart the spear shaft just above the wound entrance and fought away the surge of blackness that threatened to engulf him. Growling still, teeth clenched in sheer determination, he closed his hand upon Tempest and lay very still, waiting, waiting.

Three goblins came upon him, laughing and hooting, and then howling in surprise as Mather sprang up at them like a cornered wolverine. He whipped and stabbed Tempest in a furious flurry, hardly bothering to aim, and when his sword flew above the closest ducking creature, leaving it an opening on his left side, he simply punched out his free hand with all his strength, connecting solidly on the goblin's jaw and launching it to the snow.

Mather let his rage take him, knowing that if he stopped and considered his movements, if he played out this fight with insight and thoughtfulness, his pain might overwhelm him. Thus, he was surprised mere seconds later to find that all three goblins were down, two dead and the third groaning. Mather moved for that one, thinking to make it tell him where he could find Bradwarden, but then he heard the centaur cry out again and marked the direction well.

He killed the goblin with a clean stroke.

And then he fell to his knees, the waves of pain buckling him, the dark and cold weakness creeping into his every joint. He looked down at the bloody spear stump. He wanted to pull it out, but understood that the barbs would take half his belly with it. He wanted to push it through and knew that soon he would have to, but he understood that to extract that point now would be fatal, for he would likely bleed to death before he ever found help.

He looked back in the direction of Dundalis, peaceful, oblivious Dundalis. Not so far away, he thought, and he realized that he could make it there, and that someone there would tend him, his brother, perhaps.

Bradwarden cried out again, and Mather took his first steps... away from Dundalis.

Half blind with pain, his limbs numb with cold, he plowed on. His blood came thick in his mouth, that sickly sweet taste promising death.

He spat it out.

Purely focused, beyond pain and weakness, he knew where he was and could guess easily enough from the direction of Bradwarden's cry where the goblins would be. On he went, refusing to surrender to the pain and the cold, refusing to die. He tried to pick his path carefully but wound up having to burst right through snowdrifts, the wet stuff only increasing the cold's grip on him. But on he went, and some time later, he saw a campfire, and then, as he neared, saw the silhouettes of several goblins, and one large form, balled in a net and hanging above the camp, above the fire.

He could only pray that he was not too late.

The goblins had their eyes turned to Bradwarden, the centaur squirming in the heat and smoke as flames licked at him.

And then Mather was among them, and one, and then another, fell dead to Tempest's mighty cut.

The others did not flee, though, as goblins often did, for they outnumbered this obviously wounded man seven to one, and in this snow and in this cold, they had nowhere to run. On they came, howling and hooting.

A feinted slice, a turn of the wrist and a straight-ahead stab, and Tempest took down another.

Mather backhanded away a club strike from the right, but a third goblin, running right over its dying companion, thrust with its spear, inside the ranger's defenses. A quick retraction of the sword severed the spear shaft even as the point dug into Mather's shoulder, but the goblin thrust took the strength from his arm.

Quick to improvise, Mather simply grabbed up the sword in his left hand and stabbed the goblin in the face, then brought the weapon about powerfully to take a club from an attacker at his left. The ranger pivoted to square up with the creature. With a roar of defiance against the blackness that edged his faltering vision, he brought the sword up in an arc and then down diagonally atop the goblin's shoulder, so powerfully that the enchanted silver blade slashed through he creature's collarbone, down through its spine, cracking ribs apart and tearing flesh. Another growl and Mather rolled about, the fine blade finishing the cut, exiting the goblin's other side and dropping the two bloody pieces to the snow.

But four other goblins were about him in a frenzy, two whacking at him with clubs and the others stabbing him with spears.

He connected with one, or thought he had, but took a thump on the back of his head that sent his thoughts spinning, that brought the darkness closer... too close.

And then Mather knew. He could not win this time. Through blurry eyes, he saw the goblin before him slump into the snow, but he took no comfort, for another spear found him, digging into his hip.

He knew that Bradwarden would die if he went down, reminded himself of that pointedly, and that thought alone kept him on his feet. He blocked a spear thrust but was hit again on the side of the head. He staggered away, somehow managing to hold his footing.

But now one eye was closed, and darkness crept at the edges of his other eye, narrowing and blurring his vision to the point where he could not even see his enemies, could see nothing at all except the pinpoint of light that was the goblin's fire.

Mather made for that light.

The goblins pursued, hooting and howling, stabbing and smacking the defenseless man through every step.

But on he went, determinedly putting one foot in front of the other, stepping, stepping, feeling no pain, pushing it away, burying it under the mantle of responsibility, as a ranger and a friend. He hardly saw the light now, but heard the crackle of the fire and knew he was close.

He was hit again, on the back of the head; the blackness swallowed him.

He felt himself falling, falling, thought of Olwan and the times they would not share, and he thought of Bradwarden.

Mather roared one last defiant roar and forced himself to stand straight and tall. He swung about, the slicing Tempest forcing the goblins back and that buying him the time he needed to turn again to the fire, to look above it, and using more memory than vision, to aim his cut.

He felt the sword bite at the supporting rope, felt the rush of weight as Bradwarden dropped before him, brushing him and throwing him to the ground.

Then, from somewhere far away, he heard the centaur's outraged roar, heard the goblins' shrieks of fear, heard the trample of hooves, the cries of pain.

And then he knew… peace. A cool blackness.

It all came back to Mather in that last fleeting moment, memories of his childhood before the Touel'alfar, his times with Tuntun and the other elves, his days silently protecting Dundalis and Weedy Meadow, unappreciated, but hardly caring.

Doing as he had been trained to do, acting the role of ranger, and of friend.

As he had this night.

Olwan Wyndon, his wife, and their infant son, Elbryan, slept peacefully that night in Dundalis, they and their companion family, the Aults, warmly welcomed by the folk. Listening to the wind howling futilely against the solid common house walls, the rhythmic breathing of his loved one, Olwan knew he had found his home, a place where his child could grow strong and straight.

He didn't know that he had lost a brother that night, didn't know that any goblins had been about, didn't know that any goblins even existed.

It would stay that way for Olwan, and for all the folk of Dundalis—save the very old, who remembered goblins—for more than a decade.

Following the trail of carnage, Tuntun found a tearful Bradwarden piling stones on Mather's cold body the next morning.

"It's the only place," the centaur explained, referring to the thick and well-tended grove about them, a special place for Mather, where the trees had blocked much of the snow. "Riverhawk's place, for all time."

"Blood of Alturias," Tuntun spat, using the insult as a shield against emotions that threatened to overwhelm her. How many times had she said that to Mather over the years?

And how many times must she watch a friend, a ranger, die? There were never more than six rangers at any one time, but Tuntun had lived for centuries and had witnessed so many of them put into the cold ground. None had hurt more than this one, hurt more than Mather, the boy she had personally trained, whom she had cultivated into so fine and strong a man. She thought about her own mortality then, the long, long years in the life of an elf, and, ironically, a smile crept across her delicate features.

"A man might live but a day's worth of life in an entire year," she said to Bradwarden. "Or a year's worth in a single day. River-hawk had a long life."

Michael A. Stackpole

Michael A. Stackpole is an award-winning novelist, editor, screenwriter, graphic novelist, podcaster, and game and computer game designer; his first game design appeared in 1978, his first novel in 1988. Stackpole is best known for his eight Star Wars novels, including *I, Jedi* (1998), and his work in the BattleTech universe. His fantasy work includes *Once a Hero* (1994), *Talion: Revenant* (1997), the DragonCrown War series, and the Age of Discovery series. The final book in that set, *The New World*, appeared in mass market paperback in July of 2008. In 2008 he also had the singular honor of having an asteroid named after him. In his spare time, he enjoys playing indoor soccer, dancing, and spending a lot of time in Second Life.

"Keeping Score" is set in Stackpole's Purgatory Station universe. He got the idea for creating the world while reading a volume of Arthur Train's legal stories featuring Ephraim Tutt, which were all published in the first half of the 20th century. "I said to myself that it's too bad that you can't write stories like this anymore, and within five minutes had figured out exactly how it could be done." The Purgatory Station stories are set in a universe that has a great diversity of life and conflict. The setting has become a perfect place to examine a variety of issues and maintain some perspective, which is how science fiction functions best. The other Purgatory Station stories are available online at Stackpole's website, www.stormwolf.com.

Stackpole sees "Keeping Score" as a lot like his shared world work: "It has action, strong characters, humor, and a nice twist at the end," he explains. "The only real difference is that when writing in a shared universe, I have to work around things that some moron tossed in there. In this case, the moron is me. Working on your own material does bring with it an added sense of continuity. I can always write more stories set in any universe I've created, while the same is not always true in a shared universe. While I don't find working on one type of story preferable to the other, having the option to go back to the well does add something to the job."

KEEPING SCORE

BY MICHAEL A. STACKPOLE

THE AMBUSH SEARED scarlet light through the mauve jungle. Sara had felt it coming a heartbeat before beams flicked out— things had gotten *too* quiet for a second. The enemy fire manifested as full shafts of light instantly linking shooter and target, then snapping off, since light traveled far too fast for even the most augmented eyes to see it as tiny bolts. Ruby spears stabbed down from high branches, or slanted in from around the boles of trees, here and there, as the Zsytzii warriors shifted impossibly fast through the jungle.

Sara cut left and spun, slamming her back against the trunk of a tree. Her body armor absorbed most of the impact and she continued to spin, then dropped to a knee on the far side of the tree and brought her LNT-87 carbine up. The green crosshairs on her combat glasses tracked along with the weapon's muzzle, showing her where it was pointed. The top barrel stabbed red back at the ambushers, burning little holes through broad leaves and striping trunks with carbonized scars. Fire gouted from the lower barrel as chemical explosives launched clouds of little flechettes at the unseen attackers.

To her right Captain Patrick Kelloch, the fire team's leader, laid down a pattern of raking fire that covered their right flank while she concentrated on the left. Flechettes shredded leaves and vaporized plump, purple *lotla* fruit. She thought she saw a black shadow splashed with green, and hoped one fewer laser was targeted back at her, but the Zsytzii were harder to hit than she'd ever found in virtsims.

Bragb Bissik, the team's heavy-weapons specialist, stepped into the gap between the two human warriors. Underslung on his massive right forearm were the eight spinning rotary-barrels of the Gatling-style Bouganshi laser cannon. Into each barrel was fed a small lasing cell, consisting of a chemical reagent that released a lot of energy really fast. The cell converted that energy into coherent light of great power and intensity that blazed for almost a second once the reaction had been started. The cannon whined as the barrels spun. The red beams slashed in an arc, nipping branches from trees and burning fire into the jungle's upper reaches.

The weapon spat the smoking lasing cells out into a pile at the hulking Bouganshi's feet. The brilliant red beams bathed him in bloody highlight. Hulking and broad-shouldered, the Bouganshi could have been a demon from any number of human pantheons, and Sara hoped the Zeez would find him purely terrifying.

As Bragb's fire raked the higher branches, two beams stabbed out from the ground to hit the Bouganshi's broad chest. Sara shifted her fire right, intersecting it with Kell's assault on the origin point of one of those beams. A purple wall of foliage disappeared in a cloud of smoke and mist. Something screamed, then something screeched, barely heard above the thunder of the fire team's weapons. Red beams winked off from the Zsytzii line, then never appeared again.

Kell raised a hand. "Hold fire. They've run, I'm thinking."

Sara remained in her crouch as burned leaves fluttered down and smoldering twigs peppered the ground. "Makes no sense for them to run. They had us."

"Close." The Bouganshi slapped with a three-fingered hand at the smoking black scars on his purple and gray, camouflaged body armor. "Heat, no crust."

She checked her armor and saw a couple of dark furrows melted in it. "Likewise, toasted, not burned."

"Better than I was expecting." His azure eyes bright, Kell gave her a nod. "Bit different than simming, it is, isn't it?"

Sara tucked a wisp of blond hair back up under her helmet. "In sim they're relentless. They never break off like this."

"That's because, lass, you're using Qian simware. Much as they hate the Zeez, they grant them a bit more honor than in reality." Kell thumbed a clip free of his 87 and slapped a new one home.

"For an honorable kill, you need an honorable foe. Only simZeez act that way."

Sara Mirke frowned. "I'm not clear on your meaning, Captain."

"Qian like order in their Commonwealth, hate mystery and hate dishonor. They don't like to acknowledge they exist. Quirky, our masters." Kell rose and waved the others forward. "Let's see what we got."

Still covering the left flank, she moved out in Kell's wake. Bragb came behind, watching their rear. They went up a slight slope and over the splintered remains of underbrush. On the other side of the crest the land sloped down into a tree-choked ravine, through which ran a small stream. Halfway down the hillside a body lay against a tree, twisted against itself, with a gray-green rope of intestines pointing back uphill.

Kell nodded. "One less to play with."

"Too bad it wasn't the Primary."

A gruff chuckle humphed from the Bouganshi's throat. "Too much Qian virtsim."

"Better to take the juniors first, Sara." Kell knelt by the body, emphasizing just how small the black-furred Zsytzii was. In life it would have looked like a crossbreeding between a chimp and a wildcat, with tufted ears rising high. It had a long black tail that Sara knew was not prehensile, though she checked herself on that assumption. *Most of the stuff I know comes from virtsim, so is subject to that Qian programmer bias.* The closed eyes should have been rather large, the closed mouth should have had nasty fangs, and the hands should have ended in savage claws, but as nearly as she could see they remained sheathed.

She shivered. The dead creature looked like nothing so much as a schoolchild dressed up in some elaborate costume. "It's like we're making war on children."

"More so than you know." Kell produced a knife from a boot-sheath, turned the Zsytzii's head to the left, and cut up along the neck and behind the ear. He exposed the skull and dug out a small, cylindrical device that had been inserted into a hole behind the right ear. The thing trailed two wires. "The Primary will be severing the link, but intel will want it."

Sara looked away from the body and busied herself plucking a stray flechette from a tree. "We continue on the patrol, or head back?"

"We push on." Kell smiled over at Bragb, who reciprocated, exposing a mouth full of serrated white teeth. "We're ahead in the game, and they need to know that."

"I'm not sure I understand."

"I know, lass, which is why you're out here with us." Kell waved the Bouganshi forward. "Take point, I'll get the rear. We'll let Lieutenant Mirke continue her learning experience."

"Point." The Bouganshi hefted his weapon and marched along the ridgeline, then down into the game trail they'd been following before the Zsytzii had hit them. Bragb moved off at a pace that Sara thought was less than prudent and when she turned back to complain to Kell, she saw he'd slung his LNT by the strap over his right shoulder.

"This has got to be a game because you two are playing by rules I don't understand."

"War's not really a game, at least, not from the Qian point of view. Same can't be said of the Zeez, which is why the Qian hate them so much." Kell tipped his helmet back, exposing a lock of brown hair pasted to his forehead. "You know the Zeez only allow males to act as warriors, and that males come in two flavors. Juniors are born five or so to a litter, along with a Primary. They're augmented these days so the Primary can give them direct orders but, for all intents and purposes, the little hoppers are the mental equivalents of five year olds. The juniors can remember a command or two and carry them out, but without the Primary, they're very limited."

"I know, which is why killing the Primary is so important."

"That depends, Sara. If you're killing the Primary right after he's given his brothers an order to get some sleep, well then, well done and more of it. If, instead, he's just told them it's time to kill the enemy, and he's been a bit vague on defining *enemy*, you have little homicidal beasties roaming about."

"Omni-cidal, Kell." The Bouganshi glanced back, flashing a white curve of grin. "If understanding of Terran is correct."

"I'm corrected, Bragb." The team's leader smiled easily. "The Zsytzii seem to have a view about this conflict with the Qian Commonwealth that isn't quite clear to the Qian. Being as how the Zeez are augmented, fight differently, and have an annoying habit of being hard to kill, the Qian really want little to do with them."

"Which is why we're here." Sara sighed. The Qian Commonwealth had approached Mankind at a period when Men had only moved to a few of the other planets in the solar system. The Qian took humans in through something of a protectorate program, giving them faster-than-light travel—which they suggested humanity would eventually discover—and integrated them into their galaxies-spanning empire. Humanity contributed what it could, and some of the better exports were soldiers. A few were even seconded to the elite Qian Star Guards, with all of them serving in the Blackstar Company.

As Kell had explained as they were inbound to the world Lyrptod, the *Zmnyl-gar qert-dra*, as the Blackstars were known in Qian, had a name that could be read two ways. The black star emblazoned on the shoulders of their armor was an emblem feared in the Commonwealth, but in Qian the name could also be read to mean *black hole*. Recruits for that unit came mostly from Ward worlds, and while the Qian used them to show those worlds that they valued their contributions, there was little doubt that the Blackstars were held in contempt by their Qian commanders.

Qian pride concerning their warrior tradition contributed heavily to this view, and was the source of Sara being tossed into a mission before she even had time to unpack her belongings from the trip to join her unit. While Qian workers and the female leaders were all heavily augmented, Qian warriors were not. They were bred true and quite formidable, with those belonging to the Guards being of the highest caliber.

Sara, on the other hand, was what was colloquially referred to on Terra as a "graft." Genetic engineering on Terra had eliminated genetic disease, but environmental factors and spontaneous mutations meant children were still born with defects. These children were sold to corporations, which then treated them and trained them, selling their contracts to companies or governments that needed their skills. Nastoyashii Corporation had used her in its Rota program, making her into a warrior. Test scores short-listed her for liaison with the Commonwealth and landed her the place in the Blackstars.

"Well, we're here, lass, because we're expected to handle this problem with some delicacy." Kell laughed lightly, a sound that seemed natural within the violet jungle.

Lyrptod, when surveyed initially, had fallen into the Ward world class. The humanoid indigs had a tech level equivalent to the settlers who formed the United States, though explosives development had not occurred yet. They lived in a theocracy that preached pacifism and salvation from the stars, so when the Qian came down they were welcomed. The Commonwealth quarantined the world, which was located back a bit from the Zsytzii frontier, leaving it open only to scientific teams studying the flora and fauna.

No one was quite certain when the Zeez inserted a team, but scattered sightings were reported back to the Commonwealth. Kell and his team were dispatched to Lyrptod to figure out why the Zeez were there, while their insertion ship, the *Chzrin*, orbited the planet. They'd established a base camp in the vicinity of a number of sightings and engaged in patrols for a week without incident.

Given the nature of the world, and its location, the Zsytzii presence posed little threat to the Commonwealth, but the nature of interstellar warfare demanded some sort of response. Because space had few natural features that barred hyperspace travel, frontiers didn't really exist. The only way you could hit an enemy was to land on a world where you knew he had a presence. Learning why the Zeez were in Lyrptod could help determine other potential targets, or if they would be coming back in force. If so, scattered forces could be gathered to hurt them.

"Delicacy, yes, sir." She resisted the temptation to sling her weapon over her shoulder. "I know it's a natural preserve. I'm surprised you didn't have us collect up our shells."

"Saw you getting that flechette, lass. Good enough for me, though the skulls and their think-team would probably like more policing of the battlefield." He stretched his arms out to the sides and let his gloved fingers play over velvety ferns. "The point about the Zeez and war being a game for them is this: a lot of their objectives don't seem to make a lot of sense for the Qian. For example, why they would send a team here is baffling, so we get to deal with it. I'm not thinking we're going to be finding out what they're up to, and the Qian wouldn't understand it if we did. We get rid of them and we'll have done our job."

Sara rolled the flechette needle between her fingers and thumb. "You're not expecting another ambush right now because of why, then?"

"It's the focus thing: the juniors handle a couple orders at a time. Shifting them between attack and run modes takes a bit of transition, which is why they tend not to retreat." He jerked a thumb back toward the ambush site. "In past incidents they've fired upon indigs in the jungle, driving them off. I'm thinking their current orders are such that they engage briefly and scarper. There may be one out there watching us, but they're not going to hit us, not right now. We killed one of them, so that will take a new plan, and the Primary will be wanting to think on it a while."

"I understand the logic, but is that a safe assumption to make?"

"I hope so, lass." Kell winked at her. "Since I'm last in line here, likely I'll be the one they fry first."

Up ahead the Bouganshi crouched at a point about ten meters back from where the trail opened onto a meadow. The stream that had been running through the ravine to their right bled down and out into a marshy area on the edge of a lake. The grasses in the meadow rose to hip height and had gone from a lavender to a bright golden color, contrasting beautifully with the lush purple jungle and violet-tinged waters of the lake.

Sara took that whole vista in with a glance, then focused on a tree near the lake edge. She felt fairly certain, based on its dark gray trunk, that it was dead, but the branches were not bare, clawing at the sky. Instead they were covered with blue foliage, iridescent in nature, which fluttered with a breeze that neither rippled the water nor rustled the grasses.

She smiled. "That tree is covered with butterflies."

"Or the nearest evolutionary equivalent, yes."

Bragb cast a glance back at Kell. "Not fair. To you, if it lives in water, it is a 'trout.'"

The team leader sniffed and raised his chin. "Fish are noble creatures, not bugs. Evolution being what it is, there are plenty of fish around. Probably some in that lake."

Sara chuckled lightly. "Can we go down there?"

The Bouganshi nodded. "Seems safe."

"Sure. If they're watching us, give them something to watch." Kell came up and sidled around Bragb, then led the way down the trail. It wound its way down a steep hillside, then along a high patch of ground that bordered the swamp. Nearing the lake he slowed and looked for a dry path toward the shore.

"Bragb, you watch our backtrail. Lieutenant, if you want, you can recon the bugtree."

"And you will survey the trout population?" Sara shook her head as she pushed the flechette through the strap on her LNT-87, keeping the steel needle in place. "And then come back here fishing some time?"

Kell crouched at the shore and peered into the murky water for a moment, then turned to look at her. "Lieutenant, if you'd done the study of Lyrptod—"

"If I'd had the *time* to study the data—"

"—you'd know there is nothing of commercial value to exploit here, and you'd know that taking wildlife without a study-permit is quite illegal." He shrugged. "Of course, an informal scientific survey, well, now, that couldn't be consi—"

The water boiled in rush of bubbles as a huge, mottled gray and purple creature lunged up and out at Kell. Its leathery flesh, though glistening with water, had the same armor plates grown into it as the Bouganshi's skin did. The beast's mouth flashed open, white peg teeth contrasting with light blue flesh, then snapped down. The creature caught Kell by surprise, closing its mouth over him, leaving his legs kicking and arms waving as it raised its maw and tried to choke him down.

Sara's carbine came up instantly and she emptied a clip at the beast. She sprayed her fire over the water, aiming at its midsection, churning the water into froth, but not stopping the monster from sliding back beneath the surface. Her empty clip hit the ground and another had been slapped home in an eyeblink, which was just enough time for her to realize gunfire wasn't going to stop the thing.

Before she could cast her weapon aside, Bragb came at a sprint and hurled himself into the lake. With a glittering silver, crook-bladed knife in one hand, and freed of his cannon and its bulky ammo pack, the hulking alien splashed down noisily, spraying water everywhere. He sank from sight for a second. Then his right hand rose with the dagger and fell. Once, twice, then too many times for her to count. A black stain filled the water. The creature's flat tail lashed, breaking the surface, before Bragb rose up, gasping. Water cascaded from him, then he went down again.

A heartbeat later he came up and coughed, once, hard, then struggled to the shore. He had the creature's tail in one hand and dragged the thing from the lake. Ragged gashes had been opened along its twelve-meter-long spine—not all of them made by the knife—and the rhythmic little gnashing of its teeth indicated it wasn't quite dead yet.

That didn't stop the Bouganshi, who contemptuously spat out a hunk of green meat. Bragb flipped the creature onto its back, then stabbed his knife in near the hindmost of the three pairs of legs and cut along up toward the middle. The wound gaped and verdant guts came pouring out, along with the distended gray sack that was the monster's stomach. Another slash opened it. The Bouganshi reached in and dragged Kell from the stomach, sliding his slime-covered body onto the golden grasses.

Sara dropped to her knees and swiped a hand across Kell's lips, then opened his mouth, cleared it with a finger, and lifted up on his neck to open his airway. She pinched his nose shut, then covered his mouth with hers and breathed. One breath, two, and a third. She shook off a glove and felt his throat for a pulse.

He had one, good and strong. She started to breathe for him again, but he pushed her away, rolled onto his side, and puked. He sucked in a loud noisy breath, then coughed and vomited again. He tried to come up on all fours, but abandoned the effort and stayed down on his right side.

"You okay, sir? Anything broken? Bragb?"

Kell weakly waved a hand.

The Bouganshi, sitting with his knees drawn up against his chest, shook his head. "Fine." He stared at the dark stains on his knife, then glanced at the dead monster and nodded to himself. "Tastes foul."

Sara swallowed a comment about how she would have thought it would have tasted like chicken, uncertain if Bragb's command of Terran would have let him follow the pun. She retreated to her carbine, picked it up and turned to face back toward the woods. "Nothing from the jungle."

"Good. Last thing I'm wanting to be hearing is Zsytzii laughter." Kell rolled onto his belly and came up on his elbows. "My helmet must still be in there. Be a good lad and fetch it for me, will you, Bragb?"

"Fetched you. On your own for equipment."

Kell sighed. "Guess I won't smell any worse for digging around in there, eh?" He heaved himself up and knelt for a moment, swaying slightly. "And thanks to the both of you for saving me.

When it bit, it crushed my armor down, costing me my wind. Not that there was much to breathe in there anyway."

He crawled over to the creature and reached a hand into the slit through which he had emerged. He felt around, then smiled and pulled out a thirty-centimeter-long finned thing. "See, they do have trout here."

Bragb snorted a laugh, leaning away as Kell flung the fish out into the lake. "Bolts food whole, lets it digest. Such creatures exist on Bougan."

"On Terra they're known as crocodiles." Sara smiled as one of the butterflies landed by the barrel of her weapon. "Stories tell of their stomachs being full of undigested junk."

"I'm thinking I'll ignore that insult, thank you." Kell winked at her. His helmet came free with a wet sucking sound. He turned it over and a slime soup of fish, his combat glasses, and a tangled clump of fibers drained down into a puddle. He looked down at it and his smile abruptly died. "This isn't good, not at all."

She frowned. "What's the matter?"

"I'll be able to tell for sure back at camp, but I'm thinking this knot of wires here, it's Zsytzii in nature." He spat to the side. "Seems I wasn't the only Xeno this beastie welcomed to Lyrptod. Unless I miss my guess, the last was the Primary leading our little team of Zeez.

The hike back to their base camp was remarkable in only one way. While Bragb and Sara were both quite content to have Kell at the back of their formation because of his stench, the butterflies must have thought the crocslime was pure ambrosia. They fluttered and flickered at him, trailing in his wake like ion exhaust from a fighter. With each fern frond that brushed him a few of the insects would stop and feast on the transferred slime. Kell wiped off as much of it as he could, casting leaves aside to distract them. Even so, by the time they had reached the camp, two dozen still orbited him like little moons.

Their base camp was nothing worthy of holoing home about. They'd established it on a little wooded knoll, stringing a tarp between trees to make a clear area. They'd set up a couple of small camp tables, their perimeter warning gear, a radio, and some simple scientific gear. All of it was very compact, and any serious analysis would require liaising with the scientific teams to the north. Still, the camp was dry and had access to a nearby stream for water, so it suited their needs very well.

While Kell stripped naked and cleaned himself up as best he could, Bragb studied the wire harness taken from the beast, as well as the device sliced from the Zsytzii junior they'd killed. As best he could determine, the two devices seemed to be of similar manufacture, apparently confirming Kell's guess as to the source of the wire from the monster's gullet.

Sara established contact with the xenobiological survey team to see if they'd had any more Zsytzii sightings in their area. She passed on the story of their encounter with the lake croc, as well as the attraction of the butterflies to the slime. The person at the other end of the radio link seemed less than impressed with the reportage, noted they'd seen no Zeez and that they'd taken enough samples of the lake monsters and butterflies to last scholars several lifetimes.

Sara switched the radio off as Kell emerged from the camp shower they'd set up. "The Nobel Committee says it didn't see anything z-ish today. They weren't interested by our adventures, either."

He shrugged and pulled a dark jumpsuit from his rucksack, then tossed his towel at the flock of butterflies on his armor. "I'm thinking it's a pity the Primary didn't make it out of the belly of the beast. We'd just have to follow the butterflies to the Zeez lair."

"Yeah, well, about that—to hear the scientists talk, the 'bluewings' are not true butterflies, but just gaudy maggotflies. If we go back to the Zee body or the lake monster, it'll be flyblown and alive with larvae." Sitting back, she wove a flechette end over end from index finger to pinkie and back again easily. "I could hear the disgust pouring through the airwaves when I called them butterflies. They have to think we're just ambulatory laser-artillery."

"They're assuming ignorance because of our calling."

"I know, and I don't like it. Don't like being judged because of what folks assume I am."

"Being a graft, you get a fair amount of that, do you?" Kell pulled on the fresh jumpsuit, then batted at one persistent bluewing. "Look at this one, would you? Go on with you. I'm not dead."

With a fluid economy Sara came up and out of the chair. She stabbed out with the flechette, piercing the bluewing through the thorax. The insect's wings flapped a couple more times, slowing down, then froze in place. Its feet clutched at the needle and its antennae curled in.

Kell had jerked back, but well after she'd stabbed the bug. "Damn, you *are* fast."

"Part of being a graft." She smiled slightly and returned to her seat, holding the bluewing up to study. "When I was a little girl, I used to collect bugs. Always dreamed about discovering some new species or something and having it named after me. All of us in the Rota program knew what we were being made into, but we all had other interests. The company tolerated it and even encouraged it in case war wasn't a 'growth market sector.'"

Kell laughed and the Bouganshi smiled. "Little chance of that, I'm thinking. If you're wanting to add that one to your collection, we might could be able to smuggle it off-world for you."

She frowned. "If I still had the collection, it would be very tempting. It would be interesting to have something unique. Problem is, I'd have to Mona Lisa it."

Bragb scratched the side of his domed head. "That expression is unknown."

Kell raked fingers back through his brown hair. "Famous painting on Earth. It was stolen back a century ago, never recovered. It's assumed to be in the hands of a private collector. He can't be showing it to anyone, or letting anyone know he has it, since the reward for its recovery is huge now."

Sara nodded. "Worse yet, and you know it will happen since the skulls are pulling samples from here, a black market for these things will grow among collectors. There will be bluewing poachers coming down. Next time we come back we'll be fighting folks who did what I just did."

"Reflexes like yours applied to the problem, and I'm thinking Bragb and I will just sit back and keep score."

The Bouganshi smiled coldly. "Might hunt lake monsters. Know the bait they like."

Kell arched an eyebrow at him. "And I'd be thinking, were I you, about what eat them beasts, since you're just a pair of legs shy of being taken as one."

Bragb paled slightly. He frowned and narrowed his dark eyes. "Worth consideration."

"It is, but I'm thinking we'd all be better served if we turn our minds loose on the problem of finding the Zeez." Kell folded his arms across his chest. "We did okay today, but they could get lucky in a series of running ambushes."

The Bouganshi pressed his fingers together deliberately. "They are not protecting the Primary. What else do they need to hide? Their camp? A recovery craft?"

"Could be one in the same, it could." Kell smiled slowly. "And recovering one of them would put us in possession of something as unique as Sara's bluewing. I think, tomorrow, we head out on the same patrol, starting at the lake and working backward. See where we run into them, and see if our contact points can let us triangulate back to their base."

"Sounds like a plan, sir." Sara stabbed the flechette into the tree to which they'd tied the tarp. "Plots on the other sightings don't have a pattern, but the Primary probably saw to that. If they'll come out and play, we can probably follow them home."

"Good enough." Kell picked up his towel again and shoed bluewings away from his armor. "I'll take first watch so I can clean up this armor and patch it. Bragb, you'll go next, and you're the anchor, Sara. We'll see sunrise over that lake."

The Bouganshi smiled. "You just wish to see if trout will be hitting at insects."

"She has her hobby, I have mine." The man laughed. "Rack out now, morning will come much too soon."

Dawn broke over the lake, and Kell's trout were hitting the surface hard. Bluewings, in swiftly diminishing numbers, lay on the water and were scattered around in the marsh. Sara knelt on one knee to get a closer look and found dozens of them mashed into the mud by little feet. A few discarded flechettes likewise had been worked into the mud. Of the lake croc there was no clear sign, though lots of crushed grasses and more footprints suggested it had been dragged off into the jungle.

Sara frowned. "Wonder what the bluewings did to offend the juniors."

Kell, crouched well away from the shore, shook his head as he scanned the Zsytzii backtrail. "No lasers used. Wasn't war against them, I'm thinking. Something else."

"Captain, take a look at this." Bragb stood next to the dead tree and pointed at a splash of blue. Sara and Kell both approached. Two bluewings had been stabbed through the thorax, one on top of the other, then pinned to the tree with a flechette. "The junior had to be moving that needle very fast."

Kell tipped his helmet back on his head. "Faster than even Sara here. Don't be jealous, lass."

She glanced over at him, but before she could snap off a retort, a throbbing pulsed from the rainforest. The three of them came around, weapons raised, and watched a small, disk-shaped ship rise from the jungle. The rate of climb could best be described as slow, but the ship remained stable in flight and moved upward at a steady pace.

Kell immediately keyed his radio. "Ground Lead to *Chzrin*. We have a Zsytzii craft coming up."

"*Chzrin* copies ground report. Zsytzii warship has just appeared in the solar system, headed this way. Tschai Mriap says we can burn your upcoming ship, but then will be destroyed by the warship." The Qian communications officer delivered the information flatly, with no inflection and no indication of personal involvement in the unfolding events. "He says five minutes go/ no-go on the burn. Your mission, your choice."

Kell closed his eyes. "Stand by, *Chzrin*." He pointed his carbine at the Zeez ship and triggered the laser. The red beam tagged the ship, but did nothing to it. "They're leaving, so do we assume they are retreating and let them go, saving the Qian ship, or have they accomplished their mission, in which case we can't let them go? Input?"

The Bouganshi growled for a second or two. "Have to assume they accomplished their mission, whatever it was. The Zeez will burn *Chzrin* then come down. Has to be done."

"Sara?"

Something odd here. She glanced at the bluewings pinned to the tree. *This is the key, I know it.*

"Sara?"

A smile blossomed on her face. "Of course, yes, they accomplished their mission."

"That's what I'm thinking, too." Kell shrugged uneasily. "Gotta burn them."

"No, no, no you don't. Let them go." Sara turned away from the tree. "Let them go. It will do more harm than good."

Kell frowned. "You've got two minutes to explain."

"It's all right here—the dead bluewings, the flechettes, the two pinned to the tree." She opened her arms. "You're thinking about stuff from an adult point of view, but the juniors, they aren't adults. They are treating this like a game, and they've won. Think about it. They scouted our scientific teams. They saw them taking samples, but the Primary probably recognized what was going on and was able to put those things in proper perspective.

"The juniors, though, once he died, only had orders to avoid detection and to study us. The Zsytzii mission here was the same as ours, to see what the enemy was doing on this planet. Face it, it has no obvious value, yet is quarantined. They suspect we're hiding something here."

Kell narrowed his blue eyes. "You're saying they think we're here to harvest bluewings?"

"Makes no sense to an adult, but to a child? We killed one of them, *then* killed the monster that killed their Primary. That got their attention, made us important in their eyes." She pointed at the two bluewings pinned together. "One saw me stab *one* out of the air. They got *two*, just to show who was better. The other needles here show other attempts. It was a kid's game, and just as we scored against them yesterday, getting two with one needle, that beats us today."

Bragb squatted on his heels. "So juniors are carrying a lake monster and bluewings. They think we came for them."

Kell smiled. "And the Zeez will spend time and resources trying to figure out why we want them."

"And when they can't, they'll be back with another survey team, or something more, and we'll know they're coming." Sara smiled. "The Zeez may not be trout, but chances are they'll be swallowing that bait whole, and be back to be caught."

"Ground lead to *Chzrin*. You'll be wanting to move our ride home out of the way. Let the warship get its little craft."

"Copy, ground." The barest hint of relief threaded through the Qian's voice. "Running now. We will return, with help."

"Copy, *Chzrin*." Kell slowly smiled. "We'll have to check the Zeez camp, see what they left, then wait for our lift home."

"If taskforce comes back, could take days to organize." The Bouganshi squatted, resting a hand on the hilt of his knife. "Perhaps the Zeez will land more teams and give us something to do."

"I think I'd prefer they didn't." Sara smiled at Bragb. "Not that I'd want to ruin your fun."

"I'm agreeing with Sara there." Kell dropped to one knee and fingered a bluewing out of the muck. "Having been swallowed by a monster, I'd be content with some peace. And given as how them trout seem to be liking these bluewings, we won't be lacking for something to do."

"Fishing never struck me as the sort of thing Qian Star Guards would do." Sara arched an eyebrow at Kell. "Won't our commander take a dim view of our spending our time that way?"

"He will indeed, lass." Kell laughed. "And that will make it even that much more fun."

Nancy Virginia Varian

Nancy Virginia Varian (who until 2005 wrote as Nancy Varian Berberick) has been telling the stories of the Dwarf skald Garroc and his human foster-son Hinthan since the 1987 publication of "A Tale at Rilling's Inn" in *Amazing*. The story was not intended to go further than it did, one of the two protagonists being fated to suicide and possibly soon to meet that doom. Nonetheless, it wasn't long before the skald came back with other tales to tell about himself and his foster-son, stories from before the shadow of doom fell over them. And so "Between Lightning and Thunder" soon followed in *Dragon* magazine #138 (1988) and "Cairn and Pyre" turned up in the May 1989 issue of *Amazing*.

A period of time passed while Nancy concentrated on writing the Dragonlance novel *Stormblade* (1988) and her novel *The Jewels of Elvish* (1989). During that time she continued to work on her own short stories and regularly contributed to the popular *Dragonlance Tales* anthologies. All the while, the idea of writing a novel about Garroc and Hinthan haunted her. After much research Nancy created the full setting for the novel (and all future short stories in the series). Enchanted by the ancient poem *Beowulf*, Nancy found a home for Garroc and Hinthan in a highly mythologized Britain in the early seventh century. Ace published *Shadow of the Seventh Moon* and *The Panther's Hoard* in 1991 and 1994.

Since then Nancy has written *A Child of Elvish* (1992) and five more novels in the Dragonlance universe. She's also translated several poems from Old English and continued to write short stories, some in the Dragonlance universe and many more in the "Nancy-verse." Some of those other stories, such as "Tal's Tale," from *Adventures of Sword & Sorcery* #4 (1987), and "Hel's Daughter," from the anthology *Legends of the Pendragon* (2002), are drawn from Norse legend and mythology.

As for Garroc and Hinthan, the skald still comes around, still has stories to tell. In 1998 the short story "Scatheling" was published in the UK in *Odyssey* and then republished in 2002 in the US in *Black Gate*. The story you're about to read, "The Oaths of Gods," was originally published by Pitch Black, in the anthology *Lords of Swords* (2005). It is the most recent in the ongoing series of Garroc's tales. Will it be the last?

Not likely.

THE OATHS OF GODS

BY NANCY VIRGINIA VARIAN

FOEMEN OR FRIENDS, all men knew my cyning Erich Halfdan's son as the War Hawk.

Long-lived Dwarfs like me, mann-cynn like you, be they the wild Welshmen over the western border or our own Angles or Seaxe, they know him. In the lands north of the Humber where you find many Cristens and very few Dwarfs, they tell tales of Erich the War Hawk of the marches. Even the boy king Oswiu, propped up by his Cristen priests and lately prodded by them to go warring into Erich's lands—he knew Halfdan's brave son.

Sunset of the day when Hinthan and I were but a morning's walk from home, Rilling, and the cyning's hall, priest-driven Oswiu was back behind his walls at Eoforwic. We were abroad on Erich's bidding, taking news ahead of the army to his wife and young son that the war was for now stilled.

In that louring hour… me, I didn't know my cyning when I saw him, so beaten and bloody he was.

Hinthan did, and the knowing wrenched grief out of him in a sound so raw with rage it frightened the ravens from the murderer's tree.

Hanged at the crossroad, as murderers are, the battle-king had come home before us.

Beyond the roads the river Rill ran noisy, the clear water changed to dun by the rains of a week. Storm-light flashed, flinging Erich's lifeless body into pale light, for the space of a breath showing us how he'd bled before he died. He wore no mail shirt, his boots had been taken from him and the fine shirt of bleached woolcloth his fair wife had woven. Rain washed away his blood, his wounds gaped, pale-lipped.

Darkness, and then again lightning. Hinthan's face shone pale as bone above his black beard, his gray eyes glinted like sword-iron when he looked at me. Sweating on that chill night, breathing hard, he said, "Foster-father, what do you hear?"

What ghost, what voice, what last groaning breath? He did not ask easily. Men call me Ghost-Skald, though Hinthan never did. He'd known since he was a boy that I heard the voices of the dead; boy and man, he was never at peace with it.

A gathering of ravens, wind whining low across the road like a dog slinking, these I heard, just as he did, but no ghost, no sound of our cyning.

Grimly, I said, "Wherever Erich has gone, youngling, he is gone."

I, his skald, had spoken no word at his pyre, as I had at his father's; gone, and I'd made no praise song for Erich's son to learn.

The dangerous sky growled. Hinthan shook his hard fist at the night and the storm, shouting, "Woden Oath-breaker!"

The wind sprang, Erich's body rocked on the tree. They'd tied his hands behind his back, and then his hobbled ankles to the rope binding his wrists. Thus twisted, the corpse turned a little, this way and that, and the ravens returned.

"Boy mine," I said, in the old way, "what promise do you think the Raven God ever makes to those who follow him? Only one: die in his cause, and he will welcome you into his hall."

Welcomed, the battle-slain will be at his side at the end of all days, fighting in the army of the light. Die otherwise, and join Hel's war band when the earth breaks and the sea drains and all the stars are wrenched from the sky. A man hanged for murder does not die in Woden's cause. That one is Hel's. Hinthan knew it. I am the skald who taught him about gods and their ways.

Cold, he said, "Erich murdered no one."

He said it from faith; in faith, I believed it. Someone had killed Erich and left the body at the murderer's crossed roads to speak a lie.

The ravens shifted from foot to foot; one, the tallest, stretched black wings wide, dark eye brooding. The sky flashed again. The nearness of lightning lifted the hair on my arms, on the back of my neck.

A shadow fell aslant the crossed roads, dark on the dead man hanging.

Hinthan turned sharply. Like silver fire, light slid along the blade of his swift-drawn sword, glinted from the ruby eyes of the dragon that made the sword's grip. None stood behind us to cast the shadow, and yet the shadow lay. Hinthan shook his head, thinking his eyes mistook. He turned back to the corpse. Draca, his sword's name, Erich's gift to him, and with that dragon sword Hinthan cut the ropes binding Erich's hands and feet while I stood ready to ease our murdered cyning to earth.

Again, lighting. Again, the shadow fallen on Hinthan and me and the dead man. Wind grew stronger, the branches of the gallows tree clacked and clattered together.

In me where the voices of the dead speak arose a storm of wolfish howling and ravenous shrieking. From down the sky a voice cried: "A sword age! An axe age!"

Hinthan gripped his sword, two-handed and ready to strike. Me, I held still; I knew the voice of the god who, long years before, thought it was a good idea to let me hear the dead speaking.

"A wolf age," god-Woden said from where he stood on the road. His voice dropped as to threaten. His blue cloak lifted in the wind. He wore no mail shirt, bore no weapon. He didn't have to; he knew how he would die, and knew who would kill him. Fate had woven the story for him long years before.

"A wind age," I answered. "And brother will fall upon brother, father will kill son."

"The Dwarfs will groan," he snarled. Wind tugged at his white beard, his one good eye glittered like ice. "Those sages of the rocky walls will stand before the doors of their barrows and moan for the fate of the gods."

His lips moved, a snake of a smile.

"Tell me, Skald Garroc: why are you here by a murderer's corpse?'

There is no love between the Raven God and Dwarfs. He has cursed my kindred, doomed his Firstborn and with his magic changed us so that we know the number of our generations, and in each live thrice the length of mankind's fullest number. Six generations he'd left us, and mine the last, for he has stolen my strong sons and robbed me of my fair daughters. Woden Doomsayer. I could look him in the eye and not fear he would see how little I loved him. What worse could he do to me than he has already done?

"Tell me, O God of the Hanged, why are you here speaking the Ragnarok beside a murdered man?"

"Why speak the Ragnarok," Woden mocked, "why speak of the Fate of Gods? Tell me, Garroc Grimwulf's son, do you think your fate—" he jerked his head at Hinthan "—and his aren't tied to mine?"

The sky pulsed with pale light. In the black pupil of the god's eye I saw my foster-son reflected, dark-haired warrior, young and strong, sword gripped and ready. Again I heard wolves and again ravens, the heralds of the dead. Woden laughed. Hinthan's hand shook, but he did not drop his sword, and he did not flee, not him. He took a long step and stood beside me, ready to defend.

The dead man on his rope jerked and danced in a wind rising wild.

Garroc!

I heard my name, cried in two voices, one Hinthan's and another hoarse as a storm crow's.

Hinthan leapt for the gallows mound; I jerked around to find Woden. He was gone. When I looked back, I saw Erich Halfdan's son standing at the foot of the gallows tree. Dead, yet he moved, taking a stumbling step. He wore his rope around his neck, the length of it dangling. His eye-sockets glared empty, rain matted his golden hair and beard. He lifted his hand to me, his mouth opened, his blue lips moved. My name staggered out of a hanged man's mouth and the voice was no ghost's cold whisper. The voice was Woden's.

"Follow," the dead thing said before it fell over in a heap of arms and legs.

Long and low, a wolf's howl unwound the night.

A storm of sleet drove down, slashing, shining in sudden lightning. Hinthan cried warning as the sky flashed wildly. The last burst of lightning flared so brightly that for long moments afterward we stood blind.

Sight came back to us slowly, and when it did we stood where no living wight ever does.

Again, I heard my name, Hinthan's voice thick and rough. I couldn't see him, for all around me was a swirling haze that was not fog or smoke. Cold in the lungs, that mist, like thin, bitter ice. Hinthan called again; now I thought I saw him, a tall darkness against the haze. I used his voice to guide me, walking nearly blind until I felt his hand grip my shoulder. The warmth of his grip, living flesh, changed things and now I could see, for the mist had fallen, sunk down to the stony ground so it drifted only a little around our feet.

"It stinks here," he muttered. It did, like old bones and moldy earth, barrow-stench. "Garroc, where are we?"

"Helgardh," I said. "Come here on the sleet storm."

Around us dark figures drifted, shrouded in shadow. All had walked out the doors of their barrows, risen on the smoke of their pyres to go out from Midgardh and into Helgardh. Shuffling along the misty road, they looked neither right nor left; no one looked back. There was nothing to look forward to but long, cold sleep.

"Do you hear them, Garroc?"

I nodded; all the voices of the groaning dead. I answered his question before he asked. "We won't find Erich here. He's already got to where he's going."

He asked me how I knew.

"Living or dead, I'll know his voice if he wants to speak. Yet, I think Erich is the reason we're here, youngling. We are in Hel's

Garden but it wasn't Hel called us into this place. The Raven God sent us."

He quickened. "To fetch Erich back?"

I looked again at the dead, one after another traveling on the Hel-way. "It's hard to know. But I think if Hel has him, she won't give him back. Woden has tried before now to have a soul brought back from here."

Baldur, the dead god.

Baldur, Woden's son, the brightest of all gods, killed in long years gone, when the nine worlds were young. Allfather sent to have him back, murdered Baldur, but Hel had invoked the old oaths between gods having to do with sharing out the dead. And they are the ties that hold the worlds together, oaths; made by mortals or gods, they must be honored.

"You call Woden oath-breaker, boy mine, but of all things he is, Allfather isn't that."

Hinthan's eyes looked like gray ice. "He is worse. He left his son to Hel." Yet, standing where living men don't go, honing a grudge against the god who had been well served by our cyning and had not shielded him from a shameful death, Hinthan was grimly practical. "If we can fetch no one home from here, Garroc, what did Woden put us here to do?"

On his words, like an echo, a lorn howl followed, Woden crying the way.

Hinthan had his sword half out of its sheath, but when I settled my axe in the sheath on my back he let be. Against whom would he threaten harm or death in Hel's land?

"Woden guides," I said.

He touched the grip of the dragon sword, Erich's good gift. "Woden guides," he said bitterly. "Maybe fools follow."

He said so, but he turned and walked along the roadside with me, following the voice of the wolf in the wake of the dead.

It is strange, the light in Hel's land. It shifts, as shadow in the worlds where sun shines down, sometimes swirling across the darkness or throbbing in the sky like the pulse of spilling blood.

In that moving light, we followed the old gray wolf until we came to a bridge arching across a racing white river, Howler. Gods named it Gjöll Bridge. Thatched with gold, glittering ruddy in the red light of Helgardh, the bridge made a mighty span across the river that runs through all the worlds.

The cry of the god-wolf echoed, the red sky flashed, pulsing like a heartbeat, then fell still again.

Long and strong as iron that bridge, woven by giants in a far land, made of whiskers from the dread Fenris wolf, Hel's own brother. Upon Gjöll Bridge stood a maiden of bone, her head a skull, her body like that of a wolf-stripped corpse. Módgudr, her name, Death's Warden. She was girt with filled sword belt, clothed in a mail shirt red as blood under that evil sky.

"Ho! You're too ruddy and full of flesh for these lands, Garroc Grimwulf's son! What sets your foot on Gjöll Bridge?" Her hollow glance slipped past me, a gleam in the skull-deep. Her jaws gaped and clattered, the bone-woman laughing as she said, "You cannot pass unless you have an errand to Hel."

Hinthan looked at her narrowly. "If you know our names, you know our errand. Stand aside."

"His name I know," Módgudr said, tipping her head at me. "Garroc Grimwulf's son, Garroc Ghost-Skald. But yours, youngster?" She shrugged, a rattling gesture. "That's a pretty sword you carry, but has it killed enough men for me to know who you are? Maybe it sent one or two into the arms of valkyries to be rapt away to old Woden, but no one knows your name in the halls of the dead, young son. You come in good company, though." The bridge keeper cocked her bright, sharp hips at Hinthan. "The wardens of the dead, we all know your foster-father. So come ahead if you will."

Gjöll Bridge was long to see, stretching out over the foaming river, but it didn't seem long to walk. We took only two steps past Módgudr when around us the mist changed from bloody red to the green of sickness, rot and wretched ending. We stood at Hel's reeking doorstep, outside the gates of Sleet-Cold, her hall like a Frost Giant's mountain fastness. The groan of grinding ice filled the air, rime whitened Hinthan's young beard and pulled at my own. The mighty gates swung wide. We entered a hall delved from the heart of an ice mountain.

Icicles hung from the ceiling, some as thick around as oaks, others thin as spears. I looked around and saw no high seat, no sign that a goddess lived here, Hel feasting her army of the dead. But the place smelled of old bones and rotting grave clothes, and in the corners the shadows had the look of dark veils moving to someone's breathing.

Hel was there, Death hidden in the darkness.

The floor beneath our feet gleamed black as winter night, the walls—Hinthan whispered a startled oath—the walls were thick, and yet when we looked closely, we saw through them, the way you can see through an iced-over stream, past the freezing to living water below.

"Look," Hinthan said, wiping his hand across the wall and making what we saw beyond clearer. "Garroc, there are people."

There were gods.

Shadows far at the end of the hall shifted, Hel laughing silently.

I went closer, and it wasn't the cold in the place made me shiver. The thick wall seemed to hold a great hall within its frozen grasp. Columns of ice rose from the floor as though to uphold a roof. All was not still there. A long-limbed man sat in a gilded high seat all the wood of which was writ round with runes. Sat—no, drooped, as though he were ill or burdened with care. All in golden, the man, yellow hair and beard, bands of rune-marked gold around his arms, rings of gold on his fingers. Beside him stood a woman whose long, shining hair was the color of moonlight and spilling to her heels. As gold adorned the man, the woman wore silver; and she wore jewels of pale blue and watery green.

My heart tightened, aching suddenly. In that icy hall was dead Baldur, Woden's murdered son, Hel's captive until all worlds end in Ragnarok's rage; and there was Nanna, the goddess, his wife. For love she'd held him to her breast as the funeral pyre blazed, for love followed him into Hel's land.

"Faithful queen," Hinthan whispered.

Faithful queen, she is that, and Baldur the proof that of all things a man can name Woden, oath-breaker is not one. Hinthan, who had come upon our cyning hanged, Erich named murderer at a crossroad, had nothing to say about that.

Daughter of the Moon, pale goddess, Nanna lifted her hand to stroke Baldur's brow. Like a fall of moonlight, that motion, and graceful her fingers when they touched him. Baldur turned his face to her hand, she caressed his cheek. Hinthan looked away. So I have seen him do when the light is about to leave the eyes of a dying man.

Upon the icy wall fell god-Woden's long shadow.

Hinthan's blade sang free of its sheath. An iron-eyed wolf stood before us, so tall the beast that his head was as high as Hinthan's shoulder. His shaggy pelt shining in the wan light, Woden One-Eyed growled, then drew dark lips back from gleaming fangs, unsheathed a deadly smile.

"Welcome," said the god-wolf, the word coming from the throat of the beast and echoing behind us as though from the throat of a man.

And then beside me no one stood. I turned toward the back of the hall and the breathing darkness of shadows.

The wolf was gone and Woden laughed.

"No need to fret about your foster-son," he drawled. He leaned on his staff and pointed to the wall behind me.

Nanna, the pale goddess, extended her arm, gestured with her hand as though to summon. Hinthan stood before her, and the dead god Baldur sat up straighter in his tall-backed seat.

"He's in good company," Woden said, the father who could not free his own son from Hel's grasp. "He's a proud youngster, that one of yours, Ghost-Skald. Fine, strong son of mann-cynn, learned his lessons well from you, skald and warrior."

In the shadows a voice hissed laughter.

Woden did not bother to look, and I did my best not to show him how Hel's laughter made me shudder.

His voice rough with threat, Woden said, "It looks like you've stolen a son for yourself from right out of fate's hands, Dwarf."

Quick, I turned from him, expecting to see the shadow of a sword over Hinthan's head.

But in the ice chamber, Baldur rose, a lord greeting his guest, and his lady wife put a silver-chased drinking horn into Hinthan's hand. It seemed to me, watching through the thickness of ice, that the horn spilled drops of light when Hinthan tipped it to drink, there in the company of the dead, the Lord of the Sun and the Daughter of the Moon.

"Baldur's tomb," Woden said. He sneered. "And Nanna's folly. But probably not Hinthan's barrow. He's no one's fair-gotten man, not mine nor Hel's. Not now anyway."

So he said in Hel's cold hall and the shadows where the Woman of the Dead watched seemed to thicken.

"Tell me," I said to the god, "if I am not dead, if Hinthan isn't, why are we here?"

His brow darkened, his eye grew stormy. "Better to say neither of you is dead *yet*, Dwarf."

"You threaten, Allfather?"

"When do I not?" He shrugged. "Except when I promise. I'll make you a promise now, Ghost-Skald. Get me what I want, and you and your foster-son will have nothing to fear from me." Again, he shrugged. "And help if it's mine to give."

"Why would it not be?"

His eye gleamed balefully. "None of us is in golden Valhall, Ghost-Skald—not you, not me; not your foster son and not your lord Erich. If I had help to give in this cave of the dead, do you think my own son would be here, bound to Hel?"

I didn't think so. I did think that whatever he needed, god-Woden couldn't get it by himself. And so I asked him what he wanted.

"I want what is mine. Hel has lately added two men to her army, your lord Erich and the man his foes say he murdered. She has no right to both. We have sworn oaths and if she thinks I don't know when a man of mine is missing, she has grown foolish."

I didn't count on that; neither did Woden.

He lifted a hand and turned back the patch that covered the place where his left eye used to be. A pit lined by scars, the barren place like a rune to speak of the thing sacrificed. I wanted to look away. I could not. The darkness there held me fast, and in the emptiness where a god's eye had been, I saw a thing that had happened. Men crept across a bloody field, two leading three horses. They stepped over the bodies, ignoring most, only now and then pouncing on some weapon or jewel left by the reavers of the dead. There wasn't much of that. Prowling, they stopped at likely prey, scattering feasting ravens, until at last they stopped and one of the shadow-goers looked up to the sky. The smoke off the killing field stirred before a breeze, letting the sickle moon slip through.

The sickle moon! Hinthan and I had left Erich's army on the dark night of the moon. There had been no battle then, the priest's boy Oswiu had been chased back behind his walls.

He had come out again.

Wan light shone drear on the bloodied links of a dented mail-shirt. That broken byrnie had failed its promise, it had not kept my cyning safe. In Woden's vision, Erich lay in his gore, and around him lay the men he'd killed in battle.

Woden's voice shivered the vision: *He is mine*! And I watched Erich's body taken up from the battleground, stolen and brought to the crossroad where Hinthan and I had found him. A lanky, pocked-faced man was their master, ordering the others to strip him of his mail shirt. They kept his weapons for themselves and hung him on the tree for all to believe our brave battle-king died a murderer.

"Hel stole him after that," Woden said. The shadows at the end of the hall shifted, seemed to thicken. Muscles tightened between my shoulders, hair lifted on my arms. Woden paid no mind to shadows. "Loki's daughter came sneaking and took him away to her icy halls."

As she had taken Baldur, but she had no right to Erich.

"This one, I will have back. A name has been put to the man he's blamed for killing. Ranulf Wulf's son is dead, aye, but not by the hand of your cyning. Yet they are saying now, even in his own hall, that Erich was hanged for murder."

And I knew his wife was weeping, his little son in danger, while dark-minded men up and down the land sharpened their swords and talked about who would capture Erich's queen and rule in the War Hawk's hall.

"Bring the murderer to Hel, skald. Then see how things work out."

He lifted his fist and of his magic there rose around me a storm of howling and icy wind that sucked the breath from my lungs. I heard my name called—as I'd heard it when first Hinthan and I had come into Hel's land.

Garroc!

When I breathed again, I stood in a hall ablaze with the light of torches, and Hinthan leaned against one of the broad oaken doors, a tankard of ale in his hand and looking like he'd been invited to the feast.

The air was thick with the smell of leather and sweat, of spilling ale and meat roasting in the long fire pit. I drew breath to speak, but Hinthan stilled me with a glance. He nodded past me to a red-haired girl balancing a laden tray on her hip. She flashed her eyes at him; to me, with pretty respect, she said, *"Hal wes þu, ealdor,"* and offered me the hospitality of the hall.

I took the offered cup and thanked her. Hinthan watched her away then drawled, "Not the same hall I was in a while ago." He drank deeply then wiped his mouth with the back of his hand. "Where are we now?"

"I don't know yet. But wherever we are, Hel let us go and Woden put us here."

"Woden put us in Hel's land, too," he said, his lean smile humorless. "I talked to a dead god and his dead wife, you talked to the Raven God, and here we are." He finished the ale in a long gulp. "Where is here?"

I looked around us. "North of where we were last time we weren't with Hel. Listen."

Hinthan cocked his head, then heard what I had when the serving girl wished me good health. In that hall they spoke as folk from across the Humber do, clipping their words as though impatient to have done with speech. That's how they speak where the Cristen priests rule. We were in the land of the boy king Oswiu.

For all that, I felt easier than I had in Hel's hall, glad to have Hinthan back from his visit with dead gods. My voice low, I told him what I had learned from Woden.

"Do you trust him, Garroc?"

"I have to."

"I don't. Not anymore." He fingered the grip of his sword, red Draca, the gift of our dead cyning. Bitterly, he spat, "Never again."

But he trusted me, that I knew looking at him. He always had.

The noise in the hall rose and fell, the way it does when drink is flowing and the trenchers are always full. I had a feeling that two or three of those I'd glimpsed in a god's eye would be here. I looked for them among the feasters. None of those at feast were Dwarfs. These were Cristen lands, they didn't like the earthborn here. We saw only mann-cynn. They filled the place to the doors, shouting, boasting, howling challenge one to another. The ale flowed in frothy streams, the wine like blood on a battleground.

Still, Woden had put us here and Hel had not prevented. If Hinthan did not, I trusted that enough to know we'd find the one who killed Ranulf Wulf's son.

"There," Hinthan said, nudging me with his elbow.

Two came into the hall from the far door, a man and a woman in close conversation. Torchlight showed the man's pox-scarred face. The woman he spoke with stood as tall as he; her iron-gray hair hung down her back in two thick braids.

I knew her, and now I knew just where we were, for Ardyth Aefentid was the wife of the man Erich was said to have murdered, the daughter of a clan of wolves who dwelt in a borderland of their own making, their holding standing between Erich's marches and Humberland. In the fighting between Erich and priest-ridden Humberland, Ardyth Aefentid's kin turned one way or another, depending on where they saw gain. Most times gain lay in keeping still and picking off what they could from the dead when armies fell back from the killing ground.

I told Hinthan the woman's name, and I said, "Ranulf was her husband. That one with her is Caelin, her brother. No one in this hall was Erich's friend."

It looked like Erich and the priests across the Humber had done Ardyth a good turn. Her man was dead—never in battle, that one—and her brother had put the blame on one who had no hand in the killing.

Hinthan elbowed me again. I looked where he did. Two little boys laughed and tumbled with the dogs in the rushes, the sons who would inherit their murdered father's hall and holding.

"Her sons?"

I shook my head. "Her husband's."

Two boys not got in Ardyth's bed, and sons not the less. Their portion of their dead father's lands and goods would be that of any rightful son—and they were the only sons.

Ardyth looked at the boys, then away. Their uncle took a deep cup of ale from the red-haired serving woman.

"They won't live the night out," Hinthan muttered. In the torchlight his gray eyes glittered. "Their kin stink like ravens."

Ardyth looked up and it was as though she heard us. She turned her head, her pale eyes met mine. All the distance of the high-raftered hall lay between us; still, I felt her glance. Eyes on me, she spoke to her brother, who leaned closer to hear her.

Caelin left his sister and headed for the door. Before I could tell him to, Hinthan slipped out into the night. Wherever Caelin went he would have a tall, lean shadow behind him.

Head high, the lady of the hall went between the boards, speaking with one and then another of her guests, all the while her eye on me. I waited, and when she stood before me, I took my axe and grounded it. Two things she might know from that gesture:

I offered the weapon in the peace of her hall, or no one would challenge me without speaking to the axe first.

"Be welcome," she murmured. That greeting was not so pretty as her servant's. The hard glint in her eyes told me she understood what my axe said and did not much care. "We don't see many strangers on this moor."

"It's a far place, lady."

The laughter of her stepsons skirled up through the rumble of men's voices. One of the dogs nipped another, the smaller boy scrambled back but his brother stood his ground. He would have nothing of dog fights, that one. He scolded off both hounds and when they were gone he took a dive at his brother, tumbling him down into the rushes again, laughing.

Someone flung open the far doors, stumbling out to empty himself of ale, one way or another. Another came in, and he was Caelin. I didn't turn to the door behind me, but I listened. I heard no footstep, familiar or otherwise. Nor clash of iron, nor wan whisper of any man dying. Hinthan was still out there, let those who came upon him take care of themselves.

"Dwarf," Ardyth Aefentid said, "I think I must know you."

"It might be. I've known these borderlands since before they laid the foundation of this hall. I come and go."

She did not pretend to hide her cold smile. "They don't much like Dwarfs here. New priests with their new god are changing things, eh? Whose bidding takes you into such hard places?"

"I go where Erich Halfdan's son bids, and I come back when he tells me to. Your husband knew that."

She didn't flinch at the mention of murdered Ranulf or the man hung to take the blame. "Well, I will not invite bad luck into the hall by turning a poet out of it, be he Dwarf or otherwise. Come in, Erichskald, and share meat with us."

The name from her lips caught hard at me, stopping my breath. I saw my cyning again as I had last, hanged for a murderer at the crossroad, feeding ravens and fit for the scorn of any who passed.

Ardyth looked at me keenly. She knew me, indeed. I let her see nothing.

I glanced past her and didn't see the boys. Then I heard them, and a moment later saw them, one under each arm of the pretty serving woman, all three laughing as she toted them toward the door.

"They never listen to anyone but her," said their father's widow. Her look reminded me of Woden then, canny and cold. "For that, I should be grateful. They're a handful since… well, their father…" She let the thought die away as though it were too difficult to frame in words. My silence told her she needn't have bothered.

"Come, guest, and eat."

Her words were proper, her eyes like iron, and behind me stood two men, both weaponed with fine swords. Neither had unsheathed, yet.

I followed Ardyth of the Evening into the hall while her two wardens remained at the door. Folk turned on the benches for they saw I'd come with weapon in hand. One stood, a burly fellow with fists like hammers and hair the color of fire. Taller than most mann-cynn, he looked like a tree rooted there. He sat when his lady gestured.

"No doubt my folk would like to hear what word you bring, friend Dwarf. We have heard rumor that your lord didn't come home from his battle with the bold boy in the north."

Someone snickered, another laughed aloud. In the shadows and the smoky rafters I heard rustling and thought of a raven's dark wings, but the only eyes I saw up there were the golden eyes of hawks waiting to swoop down for scraps.

Low-hanging smoke stirred near the south door. Caelin was gone again from the hall. So, too, were his nephews and the red-haired serving girl. As there were armed men at the north door, so now did men move to stand guard at the south.

"Erichskald," said Ardyth.

One of the men at the door shifted from foot to foot. The other stood suddenly straight. They closed hands on their weapons in the moment a scream tore through the night, high and terrified. Came another, and the sound of men cursing. One voice I knew! Hinthan damned men to Hel and Woden both with every clash of his iron against the blade of a foe.

It was no hard thing to fight to the door. Ardyth's border-skulkers hadn't seen a battleground in long months; I'd just come off one, none the worse for it. It wasn't so hard to cut the legs from under the yellow-bearded man who got in my way, or break the skull of one of the watchers at the door.

Harder, though, to see what lay beyond that door in the moonlight and the mist just then rising.

Her berry-blue gown turned black with her blood, the serving girl lay dead with the youngest of Ranulf's boys in her arms. Still struggling, the boy, and screaming as his uncle's sword flashed down to kill him.

His brother dashed toward them, shouting "Sighere!" but got no farther than the end of Hinthan's arm. Then he saw the serving woman was dead.

"*Mother!*"

The boy struggled against restraint with no luck. Hinthan held him hard, then thrust the child behind him as Caelin and two others left the bodies of mother and son like wolves scenting other prey.

Wolves. I heard wolves. On the moor I heard their lustful howling as I took the arm off one of Caelin's men, left another screaming in the river of his blood. Pale mist rose around the dead, and rising it darkened to the same red tinge as that in Helgardh.

"Hinthan! Take the boy out of here!"

He turned aside Caelin's sword thrust, keeping himself between the iron and dead Ranulf's son. Sweat ran on his face, glistened in his black beard. Gray eyes alight, a storm of wrath, he growled, "I won't leave you—"

"Go! I made a deal with the god. Trust that and go!"

Trust Woden, trust Hel.

He looked at me and my blood ran like ice melt.

Just that way do you look at the dead.

I turned to see Ardyth Aefentid parting the folk in her dooryard as though they were wheat to bend before her.

Like one of Woden's shield maidens, that one; a chooser of the slain. She had wound her braids around her head and they looked like a helm. In her hand, a gold-hilted sword.

"Hinthan, *go!*"

And Ardyth, knowing where my mind was, struck first. I knew I couldn't match her strike. Cursing luck, Woden, and Hel, my eyes were still on her when something whistled past me, cold and flashing. Hinthan's sword, flung with all his might, took Ardyth Aefentid through the throat and pinned her up to the wall.

Hinthan gripped my shoulder. Over his hand, through it, I felt another, and that grip was like a raven's taloned claw as Woden took me back.

It wasn't Woden I found waiting for me. It was the Daughter of the Moon, Baldur's grieving wife. She sat on a bench of whitest stone, her back against the wall of a cave whose mouth was closed by ice.

Soft, she said, "Welcome, Erichskald. This isn't Hel's hall and it isn't Midgardh. It's a place we can talk."

The sky held no light but that of the dimming, but there was other light to see. The ice that closed the cave breathed with a red glow, as though the sun lay trapped there.

The wife sat outside the prison of the dead god, Baldur her husband. She looked at me and her eyes were as deep as the night sky. She said she was sent to greet me, but not by Woden.

"He is done with you now. My husband sends me. He bids me remind you of something his father said: 'You cannot steal a son from fate.'"

Hair lifted on the back of my neck. "Where is Hinthan?"

Nanna lowered her eyes, her fingers traced the shape of runes embroidered in silver on her gown. When she looked at me again, she said, "You got what you wanted, skald, and Woden did, too. Erich Halfdan's son sits in Woden's golden hall tonight. And Hel, she's sated. She has Ranulf Wulf's son, and the one who killed Ranulf's boy and his leman." Long pale fingers stroked the runes. "Hel got those, and more besides."

Her silvery hair like a cloak of moonlight moving, Nanna leaned back against the ice. The light behind the frozen gate touched her cheek with gold. "The oaths of gods are strange things, Erichskald. We weave them, and we never break them."

The light behind the goddess's back pulsed more slowly. Ravens rustled somewhere just out of sight, a wolf moaned low.

"But we pay a little to loosen a bond now and then."

Cold, cold, I said, "What do you pay?"

She stood, tall and graceful as the fall of light. "What we have to."

"Lady, tell me. Where is Hinthan?"

But she said, "Listen, here is a thing I know: when he put his son on the funeral pyre, Woden whispered in his ear and no one knows what words he spoke. Now here is another thing I know, and it was Baldur who told it to me. *Love is stronger than death, nor can the grave destroy it*." She smiled a little. "I don't say the two are the same, Baldur's words the echo of Woden's, though... Well, I tell you these things because you must remember them."

Nanna lifted her hand, she traced figures in the air. Where her finger passed, runes hung silvery in the twilight and then vanished. When the last one fell, she was gone.

Then, as though from a great distance, someone spoke my name, and his voice was low, his tone guarded.

I was no longer in the company of the goddess.

"Garroc," Hinthan said.

"You cannot steal a son from fate."

So said the Daughter of the Moon outside the prison of Baldur the Dead.

Hinthan sat beside the body of hanged Erich on the bank of the Rill. He'd found a horse somewhere. It stood tied to a willow's trunk cropping grass. He sat still as stone, my foster-son, my youngling. Nothing moved but the horse's sweeping tail and an iron-blue dragonfly dancing above the water.

Hinthan had taken Erich from the gallows tree and washed his body clean. He'd made a resting place of his own outspread cloak, and he'd turned a corner of it up over the cyning's face to hide the harm ravens had done. The storm-washed blue sky reflected on the face of the river.

"Hinthan."

He nodded, to say he'd heard me.

I went closer, carefully. For I knew him, had known him boy and man. Something hurt, and he didn't want me to see. "We should bring him home."

Again, he nodded.

I offered what I knew, what I thought perhaps he didn't. "It's all right with Erich now."

At last he spoke, and his voice sounded rough and ragged. "Yes, everything's all right. Erich's son has no father; the last child of Ranulf Wulf's son is kinless. Across the border in the north—" he laughed bitterly "—a boy plays at being cyning while his priests become warlords. But, yes, if you are Woden Faith-Breaker, old Battle-Father who loves nothing more than strife and killing—" he spat "—everything's all right now."

Hinthan turned then, and the sight of him stopped the words in my throat. Once black as night, his young beard was changed; a swathe of white marred it, as though frost had traced the hair along the right side of his jaw and frozen the color from just that place. He looked at me through narrowed eyes, head back and wary.

"Did Woden tell you that gods don't break oaths, but sometimes they'll pay to loosen the bond?"

"Not Woden," I said.

Something flickered in his eyes. "Who?"

"Nanna."

His lips twisted in a bitter smile, the light gone. "Did she tell you everyone's happy—Woden and Hel and—?"

My belly turned sickly. "And me."

"Well. Might be, but maybe gods don't know everything, eh?"

"Hinthan—"

He shook his head. "No matter what gods say, you don't look so happy, Garroc. They made some trades, those two gods. Hel gave up Erich, but she wanted more for that than she was owed."

Greedy Death!

I heard his words as though from a far distance, muffled by the thundering of my heart. He told me that if Hel were to give up Erich, she must have one or the other of us—Hinthan or me—in his place. Not now, with luck not soon, but finally.

And so, at the end of all days, when the nine worlds break apart and gods go to war... one of us would fight the dark, the other battle the light.

"So, the old liar made the deal," Hinthan said. "He made it—" He laughed, a short, sharp bark. "He proposed it before anyone called us to Helgardh."

Hinthan got to his feet and bent to turn up one side of his cloak over Erich's body and then the other. The day was growing old. *We must take our lord home*, I thought. Hinthan lifted Erich's body and gently placed him face down over the horse's back. He looked at me, one flashing glance; in his eyes I saw the boy I'd raised, not the man who had fought in battles beside me. But only for a moment, and the boy was gone.

"After the killing in Ardyth's hall, I did not go where you went, Garroc. But I did talk to a goddess." He put his hand to his belt, and then I saw he'd got a new sword to take the place of Draca, lost in the killing of Ardyth. He lifted it from the sheath, it shone in the light bright and clean.

Hinthan said its name was Ice.

"Hel's gift. She said: 'I get one of you. It's going to happen, no matter what you will. But you've served gods well tonight, so I'll put it to you and your foster-father and you two can choose....'"

But he'd made the choice himself, as she'd known he would. Hel gave him a sword for the one he'd lost.

He said no more. He took the horse's reins and we began the long walk home to Rilling in empty silence.

"You cannot steal a son from fate."

So said Woden, who had stolen every son and daughter from the race of Dwarfs. So said the god who couldn't steal back his own son from Hel, and knew he'd already bargained away mine.

But a brighter goddess had said something else, and I held Nanna's words close in my heart, even as I felt the world around me changing, the boy I'd loved and raised slipping away.

"Love is stronger than death, nor can the grave destroy it."

Above in the washed sky, a glossy-winged raven flew, its mocking cry marring the sleepy silence. It alighted on the high branch of a willow. Swift, Hinthan let go the reins, nocked an arrow to bowstring, and let fly.

The raven screeched, flew up on staggering wings, then plunged, dead before it hit the ground. Hinthan wiped the storm-crow's blood from his cheek with the back of his hand and walked on, cloaked in the long purple shadows at the end of the day.

Laughter hissed in those shadows and I saw her, the Woman of the Dead, as she glided silently beside Hinthan. Flesh white as corpses, eyes black as graves, she looked over her shoulder and laughed again.

At me.

Greg Stolze

The bulk of Greg Stolze's work has been in the area of roleplaying games, contributing to or authoring over 80 books for numerous companies. He's well known for co-creating the setting of the game Unknown Armies (1998), an occult universe governed by a form of spiritual democracy. In Unknown Armies, humanity is ultimately responsible for everything that happens to it—a terrifying prospect, to be sure.

Stolze has contributed to the largest and best-known shared universe, the Cthulhu Mythos, through short pieces in the Delta Green collections *Alien Intelligence* (1998) and *Dark Theaters* (2001). In both, an FBI pathologist skirts the edges of transforming encounters between unknowable entities and mundane law enforcement officers. He has also written for "Naperville Unwound" in a local newspaper (a sort of all-over-the-place comic soap opera; realistic fiction, no less!), and both iterations of White Wolf's World of Darkness. For the old version, he wrote 2003's Trilogy of the Fallen (*Ashes and Angel Wings*, *The Seven Deadlies*, and *The Wreckage of Paradise*). Later, he got to write from the perspective of Lucifer, both in the two-part story "Right and Wrong" (2004) and in the setting-ending *Days of Fire* (2003), which he approached as if he'd been handed the setting and told, "You can play with all the toys in the box. Break 'em if you want to." In the relaunched World of Darkness he continued his habit of presenting eloquent philosophies of evil, through the voices of religious fanatic vampire Solomon Birch and, in *Rites of the Dragon* (2004), Count Dracula himself.

Since 2007, Stolze has concentrated on expanding the continents of Heluso and Milonda, the setting for his fantasy game Reign. "The Doom of Swords" spans two of its cultures, illuminating their historical antagonism. A blend of untidy commonality and megascale magic weirdness, Heluso and Milonda are expanded upon and illustrated online. Start at www.gregstolze.com to find more. There's a lot there.

One interesting element of Heluso and Milonda's development is the amount of fan feedback from which it benefits. Since the material is released in small chunks and paid for by fans directly, their requests and ideas have a specific and rapid impact on what gets developed and how. Stolze's methods of interacting with his audience have been examined in *Wired* magazine and *Business 2.0*. Answering to readers directly is an interesting change, he finds, from working with an editor. Fan input is generally more passionate and sometimes more coherent. It must be said in their defense, however, that the editors usually have better punctuation.

THE DOOM OF SWORDS

BY GREG STOLZE

IT WAS A hot day, and raining, and their donkey was sick. No one would choose to walk far in those conditions, but the three men were walking nonetheless.

"How about a story, then?" asked the young one, whose shoulders were broad and who carried the largest pack.

"Surely you jest," said the handsome one. The donkey raised its tail and relieved itself in a stinking torrent, as it had been doing with terrible frequency. It let out a piteous bray, as it did each time. The handsome man curled his lip, as he did each time.

"It's your job, isn't it?"

"My job is to tell tales, sing songs, read and write documents, and provide the blessings of literate society for money. Do you have any money? Hmm? Been holding out on us?"

"Tell a damn story," said the third man, the old one. He kept darting nervous glances at the animal. "It is a long way to the next town, and I want to make it before that beast collapses. A story to cut the miles. Do so."

With a sigh and another lip curl, the handsome man agreed.

"Many years ago," he said, "Before the Empire arose, there was a child born in the Western Marches. His name was Rook, and he was the son of a mighty warlord. In those days, the Western Marches stood alone against Dindavara, but the Dindavarans themselves were broken into squabbling families with no strong hand to guide them.

"Rook grew to be of surpassing size and strength, and he, too, grasped the broad blade of war against his neighbors. Rook's father was known as a cruel soldier, and stingy with his love. To every appearance, Rook was destined to be a beast of a man as well. He grew to adulthood hunting through the woods, break-

—87—

ing through the ice-crust on streams to bathe, and carrying slain deer back home on his shoulders.

"One day as he was traveling through the woods he met a woman who had strayed off from a picnic and become lost. It was many hours before they reached settled roads again, and no one knows what was said or unsaid in that time. Her name was Robin and she was plain, but the warlord's son called upon her and visited her and, in time, they were wed.

"While Rook was growing up in the harsh woodlands, twins were born across the border in Dindavara. They were identical in every way, and their names were Shai and Guai. They were of noble birth, and fair of face, and while their father was away at the wars their mother immersed them in affection and acceded to their every whim.

"When the twins were ten years old, Guai fell from a tall wall that he had been forbidden to climb, and when he landed he bit through his tongue. After that, he was always thick-worded and said little. Instead, he dedicated himself to mastering the sword.

"This was his great flaw. Because eloquence had become difficult for him, he gave up on it.

"Shai, on the other hand, fell far behind his brother in the art of the blade but was soon renowned for his quick wit, charming demeanor, and splendidness of speech. As he grew, he proved equally adept at the arts of debate and seduction, which were rather more developed in Dindavara at that time than they are presently.

"This was Shai's great flaw. Because speech came easily to him, he studied little else."

"Stay a moment," said the young man, who to this point had been listening in silence. "Guai's failure is that he didn't learn to speak well and Shai's was that he did? That doesn't make any sense."

"No," said the old man, "it does if you are a Dindavaran who sees virtue in battering straight through a wall even when there is a perfectly good door. More than once I have watched a Dindavaran march straight to disaster, lured by the promise of adversity. What makes no sense is the notion of Dindavaran seduction. They are the biggest prudes I have ever met."

"It was long ago," the storyteller said, glaring. "Do you want to hear this or not?"

"Sorry, sorry. Go on."

The donkey shat. The teller grimaced, then continued.

"In time, Rook became the warlord and showed more cunning and restraint than his father. He even agreed to negotiate with his rivals, and so it was that the twins Guai and Shai came to his castle to see if some treaty could be made. All might have gone well, but for a curious thing. After Rook and Robin had married, she became beautiful.

"At first it seemed only the natural health and happiness of a girl in love, but time worked upon her wonderfully. As the other women her age became fat and slack, Robin's slenderness filled out pleasingly; the maturity that set lines and fatigue upon them gave her an air of tranquility and insight. When Rook assumed his father's seat, she was a beauty, and by the time Shai and Guai came to call, she was breathtaking.

"Shai immediately turned his every effort to luring her into infidelity. In this he succeeded."

"What?" the old man said. "What strange diplomat would do something so crass and directly stupid? He could not offend his host more if he seduced Rook's mother!"

"Oh, and I suppose your dramatic success at diplomacy gives you keen insight?"

The old man looked away. He had once been a praised and pampered retainer, but his own lusts had set him upon the wanderer's path again, at an age when most men were sitting content by the fire, having their sore feet rubbed.

"You forget that Shai had never been denied anything in his life, had never suffered from his excesses."

"Unlike his brother," said the youth, before a sharp look silenced him.

"Shai acted from arrogance, assuming he could humiliate Rook undetected, and perhaps also from craft. There is much one can learn about a man and his intentions, if his wife is in the proper mood." The storyteller preened a bit as he said this, and the others rolled their eyes, but it was undeniable that their companion possessed a face of excessive refinement.

"I just can't believe she'd be untrue to him, after he saved her in the woods," said the youth. "And besides, he loved her even before she was beautiful. Doesn't that count for anything?"

"If certain people would stop interrupting me, perhaps the story would make that clear. Hmm? Anyone else have any questions? Comments? Well then…"

"Robin's great flaw was this: Having grown up plain, she was not prepared for the ardent attentions of a fair-featured man, armed with all the charms and tricks of a courtly seducer. She permitted herself to be flattered, and then praised, and then consented to see him alone, and then met him alone in secret, and then agreed to a single kiss, and by then the romance of being desired was so overwhelming that she could not stop at one kiss. They met rarely, and in the haste of secrecy, but all that was to Shai's advantage. Had he been constrained to court her openly, she might well have become bored with him. But perfumed by intrigue, she was intoxicated.

"Shai bragged of his conquest to only one person, his brother. Guai, as usual, said nothing. But he brooded.

"Guai the warrior had heard many tales of his twin's romantic feats and had few of his own to compare. A deep and abiding envy had been slowly growing within him, and seeing the lovely Robin fall so readily into his brother's arms brought it to full and vicious flower. Working in secret, Guai sent a message to Robin, penned like his brother's hand, requesting an assignation. When Robin arrived, expecting Shai, she quickly found herself couched with Guai, his brother, instead. Both were unclothed and entwined before she whispered, 'Tell me I'm beautiful' and got no reply. Guai had none of the gentleness and patience of his brother. A more experienced woman would have stayed calm, perhaps, but Robin screamed, and her scream brought both her husband and her lover running.

"Rook was armed, of course. He carried a blade as long as I am tall, notched from great use. The Dindavaran twins had two slender swords each, one long and one short."

"Which style?" the old man asked. Though foreign to Dindavara, he carried paired swords himself. They were trophies, taken after killing his previous employer.

"What?"

"Which style of swordplay did the brothers employ?"

"I don't know."

"Let him tell the story!" said the youth.

"Seeing bare steel, Guai's instincts preserved him. He rolled aside and reached for his own weapons, and even his quickness would have availed him nothing had Rook not paused, aghast, seeing the shocking evidence of his wife's treachery. He stirred from his surprise when Shai lunged at him, but though the sweet-voiced brother's weapon was light, he was still slower than the great man's blade. With one crashing blow, Rook blocked and shattered the offending sword. He would have killed Shai with his backswing had Guai not flung himself between them, his body as naked as his weapons, which slid toward his betrayed host with the speed of striking serpents.

"Rook was one man with one sword against two men with three, but his soldiers were coming up the steps close behind. Guai pressed the attack while his twin slammed the door, but again Rook's weighty blow left an attacker holding only a broken hilt.

"Rook had his choice of the twins then, and there is much discussion of his decision. One enemy was clearly the offender, but also the superior fighter. The other, with his back briefly turned, was vulnerable and was also attempting to change the conditions of the battle. Perhaps it was his tactician's instincts, but Rook swung his sword up between Shai's legs, shearing through his hip bone and out the side of his body."

"That is a hard cut to make," the old man said professionally. "Even if you know the Doom of Swords."

"Excuse me?"

"The Doom of Swords. That is probably what Rook used to break their weapons. Even in ancient times, Dindavaran blades would not snap easily."

"Can you teach me that?" the young man asked.

The old man shook his head. "I have seen it a few times, but never learned it. Besides, it demands a heavy blade to work, and I have not the frame for it. You could probably—"

"Excuse me," the storyteller repeated. "I thought the two of you had begged and pestered for a story?"

"Apologies."

"Having dispatched Shai with one strike, Rook turned to Guai and swung, to cut him down like grain. Guai, the great swordsman, leaped over the incoming blade and rolled to his feet, clutching his brother's sword. With a short blade in either hand, he countered Rook's next thrust, and the thrust after, and then two cuts. This exchange happened in the time it took Robin to scream and Rook's soldiers to run five steps up the stairwell. When the guards burst through the door, Guai flung himself out the window, crashing twenty feet down onto the roof of the stables below.

"Rook rushed to the window and stared down as the Dindavaran fled. 'I've killed you!' he cried. 'Your soul died the moment you ran!' A few of his soldiers fired arrows and others gave chase, but the gates had been opened as a sign of friendship. Guai escaped across the border clad in a stolen horse blanket.

"The Western Marcher turned the force of his fury to the battlefield, flinging himself at the enemy like a rabid bear. He fought from the front and was inexorable. When he raised his blade he was like a mountain, and when he brought it down it slew all on whom its shadow had fallen. He pressed the attack through that winter, and for a year more, and for a year after that. Rook won every battle at which he was present, for even the vaunted Dindavaran courage turned weak at the sight of him, at the sound of his roar.

"Three years after, Rook was encamped in the ashes of Shai and Guai's family estate. An army of routed defenders sheltered in a nearby forest, and Rook planned to chase them down in the morning when the light was good. But he heard a murmur from his picket guards, and a messenger came saying, 'An enemy appears, clad like a ghost, calling you to face him. He says he is Guai the swordsman! Shall we fire upon him?'

"Rook narrowed his eyes and said, 'No.'

"Soon Rook's soldiers watched as he strode out to meet the challenge. It was indeed Guai, but with his hair long and disarrayed, in the fashion of a Dindavaran in mourning. He was clad in a white funeral shroud and carried two swords. One was his own. The other was his brother's.

"'I thought you had slunk off, to wither in a living grave of cowardice,' Rook rumbled. 'Has your captured dignity called you back to face me?'

"'I am dead indeed,' Guai replied, 'and I can fear death no longer. The first year after you killed my brother, I went to the river valleys. There I stood waist-deep in the icy rivers of spring, practicing movement on slippery rocks and against the rushing of water. In that way I became swift of foot. Then I spent a year with the sword-saint of the mountain. Every day we would start at the bottom and fight our way up to the top. In the morning, he stood above and I fought uphill. During the heat of the day, side by side. As the sun dimmed, I crouched as he stabbed from below me. Then we descended to sleep and start again the next day. I fought thus every day for a year, until I could defend and strike from every direction. On the last day of the year, I slew him on the peak to keep the secrets private, for me alone. I have burned all mercy out from my soul. I am untouchable. I cannot be stopped.'"

"'Such a long speech,' Rook said. 'All I've done with those years is slaughter untold scores of your countrymen.' Then he turned and said, 'Bring forth my wife.'"

"When Robin appeared, Guai's eyes widened, for she was now the ashes of her onetime beauty. Rook had taken her with him, and after every battle they walked together among the dead. 'This is your doing,' he said, every time.

"That was Rook's great failing. He did not hate her enough to kill her, nor love her enough to forgive.

"When Rook saw Guai's mouth go weak, he launched his attack."

"A good trick, using the woman," the old man said approvingly. It earned him a conflicted glance from his young student.

"That's it," said the storyteller. "I'm done! You ask for a tale to pass the miles and then chatter like magpies throughout! If you can't listen with respect, then I will speak no longer!"

"But who won?" asked the young man.

"If you like talking so much, you tell the story!"

"I don't know it!"

"They both died," the old man said.

"You've heard it?" asked the storyteller.

"No. But it's hard to survive against a skilled man willing to die for your blood. I'd guess one was killed instantly and the other succumbed after a couple days. That's often how it goes."

"So both of them lost," the youth said. "What a sad story."

"No, both of them won," said the old man. "It's a tragic story."

They walked on in melancholy silence, broken only by splashing and groaning from the donkey. They had gone a quarter mile before any of them realized the rain had stopped. When it had ceased, none of them could say. Then there was a break in the trees, and the young man said, "Look! Chimneys with smoke!"

"You can see that?" The old man squinted.

"If we hurry, we'll make it before the light fails."

"Well, old girl," asked the old man, "you have one more trot left in you?"

"Doesn't anyone want to know what happened to Robin?" asked the storyteller.

Jeff Grubb

Jeff Grubb has spent most of his career building worlds. He was one of the co-creators of both the Dragonlance and Forgotten Realms fantasy settings, with such creations as Spelljammer and Al-Qadim along the way. He has mapped the planes of existence, roamed the intricate halls of the mighty Marvel Universe, and even contributed to the World of Warcraft. He is currently indulging his world-building talents working for computer game companies, such as the popular Guild Wars setting from ArenaNet.

Grubb says about this tale: "My stories and my worlds sometimes start with a single image. In the case of the world of 'Catch of the Day,' the inspiring image was a cartoon by Winsor McCay, the cartoonist who gave us Little Nemo and Gertie the Dinosaur. It was an editorial cartoon, titled 'Men Will Live on Mountaintops,' and portrayed a huge pile of early 20th-century skyscrapers dominating a mountain peak, with airships cruising overhead.

"While intended to be a vision of a progressive future, the drawing begs the question: Why would mankind have to live on mountaintops? From there, the concept of a world wrapped in hostile clouds evolved. The 'good' races were driven up to the mountains, and the rest of the world wrapped in a hellish, Venus-like landscape, with those trapped beneath mutated into monstrous forms.

"The world was initially conceived to serve as a roleplaying game setting, and it solved a problem I'd run into before. Everyone likes the idea of ships in fantasy adventure games, but they had one big drawback—it was a long swim back when your ship got sunk. With ships sailing atop the clouds, it was a bit of a fall (solved initially with parachutes, but later with the belts made of floatwood), but still you could find your own way home.

"As things turned out, the RPG setting idea was scrapped in favor of another proposal, and the world was put back onto my mental shelf. As the years passed, I would take it down, dust it off, trim up a few concepts, and put it back. It was during this time that Margaret Weis introduced me to the works of Patrick O'Brian, whose Jack Aubrey series so brilliantly captured the spirit of the age of wooden ships and iron men. And I saw that, while the fantasy version of my world had its limitations, one set in the later age of fighting sail had great promise, and the story spun itself out easily.

"Such is the nature of creativity, whether as part of a group or as an individual. Ideas will lie in wait for years before finding their perfect place."

CATCH OF THE DAY

BY JEFF GRUBB

*Therefore will we not fear, though the earth be removed, and though
the mountains be carried into the midst of the sea.*
—Psalms 46:2

OLD EUSTES, PERCHED up at the peak of the mainsail, spotted
scholar August Gold first, and let out a sea-cry to warn the rest
of the *Antigiam*'s crew.

"The new bird has arrived!" he bellowed with leathery lungs.
"Tell the captain!"

"What sort of bird be he?" responded the ship's master, her
round face turned skyward.

"Paycock, by the looks of 'im," shouted Eustes, not diminishing his volume in the least. "With a long tail as well."

Indeed the ship's master had to agree with the wizened lookout
as she saw the new arrival striding down the broad granite stairs
of Calendonia Harbor. This newcomer was a flashy bird, all right,
his buff coat still single in color and as yet unstained by the elements, and his trousers ironed with creases that could cut cold
butter. His face was smooth, but narrow, partially concealed by
pince-nez spectacles, and the neatness of his outfit was spoiled
by the casual disarray of his hair, its short brown spikes jutting
to every direction of the compass and a few new points as well.

In his wake the newcomer towed a veritable army of bearers,
each carrying an overstuffed crate or trunk. Two bore spools of
rope, and two more carried what looked like small anchors.

The ship's master ran her heavy fingers through her graying
hair and sent one of the deckboys below for the captain. She
hoped the arrival of this peacock, this passenger, would at last
calm the captain's obvious feelings of ill ease. For the past three
months since taking command, "Black Cat" Meridan had acted

as if she expected the roof to fall in on her. Perhaps this would dispel those worries.

For his part, the peacock, August Gold, paused and inhaled the mist-laden air. The *Antigiam* was berthed right where the harbormaster said it would be, past the two xebecs and just before the drydocks. The xebecs and the *Antigiam* rocked gently at their moorings, their hulls half-sunk into the heavy clouds that supported them.

Indeed, the day was perfect; there were only light striations of overclouds moving like a schoolteacher's scrawl over a deeper blue vault, steadily rolling on a northern breeze. The real cloudscape, the stuff that man sailed upon, was a thick blanket surrounding the mountain peak that was Calendonia. It looked solid and heavy and thick enough to eat with a spoon.

He knew that if he continued down the mountainside, he would pass through and fall under the shadows of those clouds, into the dimly lit world of foothills and valleys that rarely saw light.

That was the world below, the world of lightning-storms and bitter rains, the world where man used to live (if the old tales were true), where all manner of fantastic beasts once dwelled. Unicorns. Elves. And most of all, dragons.

Now, August Gold, newly minted researcher of the newly minted College of History and Mythology, looked upon the ship that would carry him to that land.

The *Antigiam* was a small ship, almost a skimmer, and was dwarfed by the heavier, slowly rocking xebecs along the quay. It was narrow, and fitted with an outrigger, a secondary spar of floatwood lying along the ship's left side.

August pursed his lips for a moment. *Not left, port.* The *Antigiam* had a *port*-mounted outrigger. Despite a second in atmospherics at University, August knew little of sailing itself, and most of what he did know came out of several small digests that were packed away with the rest of his library.

August, his retainers in a slow train behind him, paced up the gangplank. He was met at the top by a thick-bodied, gray-haired woman, wearing the torc of a freewoman. He gave a crisp University bow.

"August Gold, reporting to the *Antigiam*," he said, then added uncertainly, "permission to come aboard."

"Sandotter, Master of the *Antigiam*," said the woman, and August's hand drifted to his vest pocket. "You'll be wanting to give those papers to the captain. I'm only the master—I take the ship where the captain tells me. She's the commander of this vessel."

August noted the slight stress on the word *she*, a testing of the waters, a hard look to see if he would flinch. Some men reacted to the old-fashioned notion of freewomen badly, and there were those within the Commonwealth Chambers seeking to phase them out. It was a touchy political issue.

August, for his part, merely bowed slightly and said, "My humble mistake. And our captain is…?"

"That would be me," said a tall, imposing woman by August's right shoulder. He had not heard her approach. She had a well-formed face and deeply set eyes, eyes that in another place and time could be considered "laughing." But not here, on the deck of her vessel. Here she was the commander, and her hair was a thick black mane that framed her strong features like smoke.

"Jemmapolis Meridan," she said, extending a hand, "Captain of the *Antigiam*. You must be Scholar Gold."

"Just Mister Gold, if you please," said August.

The captain took the oilskin folder, breaking the blue leaded seal with the offhanded ease of someone who had dealt with Admiralty orders all her life.

She scowled at the orders for a long moment, and the entire ship seemed to fall silent. Indeed, the entire world seemed to wait.

Then she snapped, "Madam Sandotter!"

"Captain?"

"Are we ready to sail?"

"Awaiting your orders, ma'am."

"Cast away, then, and make a heading past the Deep Rocks, bearing south by southeast."

"South by..." the ship's master paused for a moment. "That's Church waters. You mean we're..."

"Yes," said Jemma Meridan. "We're bound for the Holy Sea."

"It's the most dangerous patch of ocean in this misbegotten world," said Captain Meridan, slapping the rolled orders in one hand. "Exactly why are we going there? These orders fail to elaborate."

They were in the forward quarters set aside for the scholar, a tight space even before Gold's arrival. Now it was loaded with the crates, barrels, two small anchors, two huge rolls of rope (*Bringing rope and anchors onto a ship?* she thought; *what was the scholar thinking?*), and books (*Far too many of these...*). Meridan was used to cramped quarters, but this was tight even by naval standards.

Gold leaned back, and almost lost balance from his perch on the back of a sea chest. Meridan stifled a chortle.

"It all breaks down to a question of history, a question of the old tales," he said, recovering and readjusting his spectacles. "A question of dragons."

Despite herself, Meridan grimaced. Scratch a scholar and find a nostalgic, one pining for the supposed golden age when the world was not wrapped in eternal clouds, cloaked save for a few mountain islands and plateaus. A time of heroes, it was said, a time when mankind sailed on water, not on the cloudscape canopy.

She confined herself to a brief, "Dragons are a myth," and looked at her green-ink instructions again, as if to seek out some overlooked illumination. They remained maddeningly unclear.

"Myths have their basis in truth," said August, "and it is the scholar's job to find that truth."

And the captain's job to haul you about while you search, thought Meridan, but she only nodded and said, "And the particular truth you seek is dragons."

"There are numerous legends of the great beasts," said August. "Check your Horatio, check your Aubrey. Check all of your great historians..."

"Poets," said Meridan.

"Poets, as well," nodded August. "Visionaries of their times. They speak of dragons that flew through the sky, defying all science and magic, breathing fire and raining destruction down from above."

"And you want to *find* these creatures?" said Meridan.

"If anything survived the deluge and devastation," said August, "if anything survived the Times Before, it would be them. Huge creatures they were, resistant to storm and lightning alike. They fought over their territories like ancient barons, often to the death. Only the bravest and most fortunate survived them."

Now the scholar's face was animated, and his features positively glowing beneath his spectacles. *Not only a nostalgic*, thought Meridan, *but a would-be poet, as well*.

"In deed," said Meridan, making it two words, then repeating, "and you want to find these creatures?"

"Of course," said Gold. "My thesis depends on it."

"And all this..." Meridan pointed to the collection of chests.

"Some notebooks, some research texts," said August. "A lot of cable. About a mile's worth, hemp wound with steel strands for strength. Lanterns. Anchors, of course, with sharpened blades. And replacements, of course."

Meridan was impressed. She said, "And you think the dragons would be...?"

"Before the Deluge, the area we are making for was a broad, rich plain, filled with herds of wild beasts. Perfect hunting grounds. If the dragons survived, they would be there."

"That 'broad, rich plain' is now under nearly a mile of cloud cover," said Captain Meridan.

"Which is why we haven't found them so far," nodded August.

"It is also territory claimed by the Holy Church. They're quite prickly about Commonwealth ships in general, and scholars in particular." *And me most of all*, she added to herself.

August Gold's face fell only a trifle. "I was informed that you knew your business, Captain," said the scholar. "When I made the request three months ago—"

"Three months ago?" said Meridan. "How long have you been planning this little expedition?"

"Why, this type of research, these resources, take years to work up through the hierarchy," said August. "Three months ago I finally received the full grant, and requested through the Admiralty board for a fast ship and a fearless captain. I was informed that Black Cat Meridan was the best choice. I'm sorry, have I offended?"

Jemma Meridan tried to erase the frown from her features. "No, of course not," she began to explain, but then young Smith appeared at the hatch, saying the harbormaster had signaled. "I'm needed on deck, Scholar... Mister Gold. Please stow your gear, as best you can, and join me when you are available."

Calendonia was the last of the Commonwealth ports to the southeast, hard on the bookbanging thunderheads of the Holy Sea. From the small quarterdeck of the *Antigiam*, Meridan saw the harbor now drop away, the low mountains of the headland becoming a muddy purplish shadow only broken by the beam of the jetty's lighthouse.

The *Antigiam* cut a nice figure, reaching a point abaft the beam with only its mainsail unfurled, lanteen-rigged in the southern style. There was no need for the sternmast yet, nor the spankers, not until they had lost the landbreeze entirely. In the ship's wake, the clouds beneath churned in two lines—a wide one for the main hull, and a thin, pencil-like scrawl of the outrigger.

Three months, thought Jemma. That fit exactly with the commission from Lord Simon, unexpected and unhoped for. There were more than enough captains without ships dogging the halls of the Admiralty, and Jemma had earned both cheers and jealous stares when it was reported in the *Gazetteer*. Few captains get a posting after losing a ship. And Jemma had lost two.

The nickname Black Cat did not come from her hair, but from her run of luck.

But here she was, back at the helm once more. *This August Gold must have pull. In deed.*

She had had three months of message-carrying and hunting phantom pirates. Of training the crew. When she had gotten her, the *Antigiam* had its share of malingers, impressed mountain men, and deck lawyers, but over time and with the incessant rhythm of the life on the clouds they had been whipped into a reasonable shape.

What they sorely lacked was gunnery. She had but two cannon, a squat flight-gun in the stern and a chaser in the bow. Still, with only three rounds of powder on board, it was a dumb show drill, shorn of real shot, and she was unsure how the crew would perform under fire. Not that it would matter—if they ran into anything larger than a holy hymn-boat, they would have to run.

There was a flurry of japing laughter on the main deck, and Meridan snapped back to the real world. Mister Gold had apparently arrived on deck.

The scholar was costumed as a tortoise, carrying a curved board strapped to his back and a similarly huge plank over his chest. Additional shards of wood were strapped to his forearms and thighs. His spectacles were covered with heavy lenses set into a broad leather band that encircled his head.

Old Eustes was nearly cataleptic in his delight at the sight of the scholar, and Knorri and Gunnar were busy slapping each other on the back in convulsives. Even Crossgreves, the sour-pussed purser that counted every gram of gunpowder like it was gold, cracked a smile.

"What," said August Gold, looking as proper as man can be when dressed like a shelled reptile, "is so funny?"

"What is the meaning of this, Mister Gold, disturbing my crew like this?" said Meridan.

August thumped the front of his chest. "Floatwood, Captain. The same as in the seam of your hulls. Fine grain, I was informed by the salesman."

August's statement of his wooden armor's provenance sent Eustes and the others into further paroxysms of laughter.

"The finer the grain, the better the floatation," continued August.

"Have you had the chance to test your…" Meridan tried not to crack a grin, "suit?"

"I was unpacking and thought there was no time like the present."

"In deed," said the captain, adding sharply, "Mister Gunnar, what is the sounding?"

At the sound of her demand, Gunnar stopped in mid-chortle. "Ten fathoms, by the pilot's chart."

"Then play out fifty feet of rope," said Meridan. "Mister Knorri, please secure Mister Gold's… outfit… securely."

The wide-shouldered Norlander worker quickly fit August with a firm harness, lashed at the back.

"What is all this?" asked August.

"An experiment," said the captain. "As any scholar would know. Mister Gunnar, Mister Knorri?"

"Aye, Captain?"

"Throw our guest overboard, please."

August Gold let out a squawk as each of the sailors grabbed him under an arm and pulled him to the port side. Without a pause or even a grunt on their part they heaved the shouting scholar over the side.

He hit the clouds and disappeared, leaving a hole like a cannonball through the canopy and a lingering scream. The line played out behind.

"Slow that line!" snapped the captain, "I don't want to hang him! Easy now. There. Hold him at fifty." A slow count to ten, then, "Haul him back up."

The angry scholar turned toward the captain, and for the first time Meridan saw the fury contained within the slender man. It lasted only an instant, but it was there, a very unscholarly passion.

Quickly August composed his features and said, "You knew."

"I suspected," said the captain. "Often the gaudier the armor, the less protection it offers."

"I should have guessed," said August. "Often the flashiest relic of the past is really some huckster's trick. It never occurred to me that someone would lie about floatwood."

"It's better to find out now, as opposed to later," said Meridan. "Mister Crossgreves?"

"Aye?" said the purser.

"Fit Mister Gold with a proper belt of floatwood. I'd say two spans should do it. Enough to keep him aloft." The purser knitted his brows together at the thought of opening something else of his precious stores, but nodded.

"And, Mister Gold?" the captain added toward the scholar's back.

"Yes?" said August, and the captain caught another flicker of lightning beneath that brow.

"I would like to invite you to dinner tonight," said the captain. "Unless you have other plans?"

"No other plans," said August Gold. "I will be there."

Wine soothes many ills, reflected August Gold, *and washes away much embarrassment.*

Captain Jemma Meridan served a fine table, and it had only benefited from their recent stay in port. A half-boar, laid out on wild rice seasoned with currants and apples, dominated the small table. In addition, Crossgreves had laid in some very fine bottles of an Eastern Bloodwine, and didn't even seem perturbed as the captain opened the third one of the evening.

The quarters were tight, but no more than at a scholar's dorm. And indeed, August's stomach responded quite easily to the rocking motion of the clouds beneath the ship's hull. In the tiny gunroom were Gold, Crossgreves, Mister Baker the master's mate, and Sandotter, as well as Young Smith, doing the serving.

And the captain, of course, her broad shoulders rising above her compatriots'. The *Antigiam* was a small ship, but even so, as captain it was her duty to lead the conversation.

"Eat up," she encouraged, "for it will be rice pudding and jerky for the next week, and after that we'll be down to normal fare—bangers and mash."

"And weevil-biscuit and water, if we stay out too long," noted Crossgreves, and August had little doubt that the purser knew to the minute when that instant would be.

The topics wavered with the wine. Meridan would tolerate no talk of national politics at the table, but there was enough with stories from port, of prizes taken against the Ruq and the various sizes of Churchships. Meridan commented on the apparent superiority of the *Antigiam*'s rigging, though its own strength put horrible stress on the ship's frame. Burrows, the ship's carpenter, was continually complaining.

"Antigiam," said August. "That was a hero's name, of course."

"It is named after another ship," said the captain. "The first was the discoverer of Thunder's Cove and set aflame at the Battle of the Dunne."

"Aye, but before that," said August. "Before the Deluge."

Meridan shook her head, but August pressed on. "Antigiam was a hero, back in those days; in a suit of glittering armor he battled against the hordes of darkness. He alone defended the Khelson Pass against the unliving forces of an ancient necromancer, and when they found his body after four days of battle, it was surrounded by a mound of bones twenty feet high."

"You said 'found his body,'" said Sandotter. "So I take it he didn't survive the experience."

"He did not," said Mister Gold. "But his legend lived on, such that the *Antigiam* was named after him."

"Fable," said Meridan. "Saga. Epic poetry."

"Lost fact," countered August. "I take it you do not believe in the Lost Times?"

"If you challenge me to deny that man once lived beneath these clouds, I will defer to your greater knowledge. But if you ask me if I am a nostalgic, longing for the past, the answer, I'm afraid, is no."

"I confess surprise," said August. "I always thought of captains as romantics at heart."

"We captains are pragmatics," said Meridan. "You have to be, to survive away from the safe shores of the peaks. You cannot long for the past, I'm afraid, so I leave it to the poets."

"And historians," said August evenly. "So tell me, Captain, what do you think happened to the world? How did it get like this?"

"It doesn't matter much, does it?" said the captain. "The world is as it is, and we just have to live in it."

"I always heard," said Baker, "that there was a crystal heart at the center of the world, and someone broke it and released a cloud that wrapped around the globe."

"Nay, you're daft," said Crossgreves. "They had too much hoojoo. Too much magic. That caused the world to cloud over."

"You're both wrong," added Sandotter. "It just started raining one day and forgot to stop. It's just simple natural processes."

The captain, pouring herself another mug of wine, asked, "So, Mister Gold, how *did* the world come to be wrapped in clouds?"

"No one knows," said August Gold. "But *I* think someone killed a god."

There was a silence for a moment around the table, then everyone broke out at once. All except Meridan.

"Really," said Sandotter, with a giggle.

"Now *that's* daft," said Crossgreves. "Begging your pardon, Scholar."

"It would explain why the Churchmen act like they have a wasp up their kirtles," said Baker, "if somebody killed God."

"Not God," corrected August. "A god. There were many such powerful beings once, the old tales say. Only some being of that magnitude could cause it to start raining and *keep* raining for a hundred years, wrapping the world in a blanket of clouds such that the only survivors had to hike up the mountaintops and start again. And only killing such a being could release such power."

Crossgreves snorted, but Baker and Sandotter nodded.

"Have you proof of your gods?" asked Meridan.

"No. I don't even have proof of my dragons yet," said August.

"I've been meaning to ask, Mister Gold," said Meridan. "Tell me, how *do* you intend to prove the existence of your fabled dragons?"

"Why, Captain, I thought you had figured it out, looking at my equipment," said August Gold calmly. "I intend to go fishing for them."

"Bait," said August, holding up a blackened vial stoppered in wax. Meridan saw something gelatinous ooze within the glass walls.

They were in the hold of the ship, around the deadman's hatch. On a water-sailing boat a hole in the bottom would be suicide, but beneath the *Antigiam*'s hull were only thick clouds. The deadman's hatch was traditionally used to consign the bodies from the ship into the clouds beneath.

The three of them, Meridan, Gold, and Baker, now clustered around the open deadman's hatch. Beneath them there were only the reddish clouds. August had set up a great spool of his wired rope alongside the hatch, with a second spool next to it.

They were three weeks into the voyage, well into the bangers and mash stage, and would not have to "hit the biscuit" for another two weeks. Twice they'd had to run before a storm, and three times spotted sails on the horizon and fled before discovery. Now, however, a thick mist rose in the morning, providing more than enough cover for the *Antigiam* to drift, its sails furled, for August Gold's experiment.

"Enough for two tries," said August. "I attempted to get a sample from another museum, but the curator was... well, let's say that we had words, and I queered my chances."

"And in that glass is...?" said Meridan.

"Dragon's Blood," said August, "or at least what we think is Dragon's Blood. It may be another hoax, like the floatwood armor." He reddened for a moment, then pressed on: "But the provenance is good, in this case, at least."

"Don't Dragon's Blood prove there were dragons?" said Baker.

"Doesn't," corrected August, "and it proves there *were* dragons, but not that there *are* dragons."

"And this will prove it how?" asked the captain.

"The old tales, the 'fables,' say that dragons were very territorial creatures," said August, "such that the smell of another dragon in their territory would bring them out for combat."

"Sounds like the Churchmen," said Baker with a grin.

"But this blood is ancient," noted Meridan. "Surely even a reptile won't be brought up by cold blood."

"Which is why I created this," said August Gold, pulling out a lanternlike device. "This censer will vaporize the blood into a fine mist, which should be carried by the undercloud currents. If there's a dragon here in the Holy Sea, we'll find it."

"A large if," said the captain.

"A large dragon," countered the scholar.

After another twenty minutes of fiddling, August poured a small bit of the fluid into the lantern's porous mantle, and set it aflame. The mantle guttered for a moment, then sprang to life, and a rich, sanguine odor permeated the hold.

Meridan's eyes watered, and Baker held his nose, but August acted like he was sniffing a fine wine. He shut the door of the censer, clipped the lantern to the sharpened flukes of one of his great anchors, and dropped the entire collection through the hatch. Baker stood at the spool, the crank in hand.

"Carefully lower it now," said August, fishing out a notebook and pen, "and call out the measurements as they pass."

Long moments passed, broken only by Baker's regular chanting as the wire-wound rope unspooled. A hundred feet to clear the cloud canopy. Then two hundred. Then three hundred. Six hundred. At nine hundred the scholar said, "Hold."

Meridan looked at them—the scholar hunched over the deadman's hatch, the master's mate gripping the crank. A long moment passed. The musky fumes had cleared out of the hold now, though Meridan had no doubts that they were steaming away far below them.

Five minutes passed. At last Meridan said, "In deed. I don't think your dragon's at home."

That's when the ship's line went taut and the entire hull shook.

"Snag?" said Meridan.

"Depth by the pilot's chart?" said August.

"Nearly a mile," said the captain. No, she realized, it wasn't a snag.

Then whatever it was at the far end of the line pulled. And Baker was flung forward into a bulkhead from the sudden jerk on the spool.

"The crank!" shouted Meridan. "Grab the crank!"

But it was already too late. The creature at the far end of the line dove like a trout taking the bait, unspooling the line behind it. The crank whipped around now, almost a blur, a heavy club threatening to break the fingers of anyone who attempted to grab it. The wire-wound rope began to smoke from the friction of its unplaying.

Captain Meridan realized what would happen when they reached the end of the rope. She ran to the deck hatch and bellowed upward. "Make sail! Spread the cloth!"

"How much, Captain?" came the reply.

"All of it!" shouted the captain. "Every sheet and spanker."

Overhead they could hear the clatter of feet running to unfurl every inch of sail. The captain went forward in the hold. Through the bones of the ship she could feel it straining already as it gathered the wind within its sails and surged forward.

For his part, August could only watch the rope unspool, the line nothing more than a blur. Surely whatever it was at the other end would abandon the bait with the heavy line behind it. Surely…

But no, the last of the line, firmly secured to the heart of the spool itself, unleashed, and pulled tight.

The entire ship gave a heavy shudder, the wind above pulling one way, the creature on the line the other. Even August could feel it now, the tension carried through the rope and into the ship itself.

Then, above, more shouting. The ship was not making any progress. Indeed, it was starting to slip backward through the clouds, leaving its wake ahead of it.

Worse yet, the stern was starting to dip deeper into the clouds themselves.

August Gold was frozen until the captain returned, an axe in hand, and took it to the rope. The rope, strengthened by the wire wrapped around it, refused to part despite her best efforts.

Above, more shouts, something about the mainmast.

Meridan wheeled to August and snapped, "Tell them to drop the sails. Just drop the rigging!"

August stared at her goggle-eyed.

"The tension is too much. The mainmast is splintering!"

August staggered off to the deck hatch and bellowed up the captain's order. There was more scuffling of feet, followed by a great thunderous crash as the main boom landed on the deck above them.

When August turned back he saw that the captain had abandoned attacking the rope and was taking out the spool's mounting instead. The heavy chips of wood flew in all directions as the spool splintered, but still it refused to part from its mounting.

August stumbled back to the deadman's hatch. They were almost through the cloud cover now, and the reddish darkness of the land spread beneath them. It was illuminated by lightning storms, far below. Despite himself, August gripped the belt of floatwood that he had been fitted with, and hoped that this one worked.

The cable itself drifted like a silver line, drawn with a ruler, straight astern. And there, at the limits of his vision, was something hooked to its end.

Something indistinct in this twilight realm, but incredibly large.

Finally there was the shriek of wood giving way and the shattered spool uprooted itself from the deck. The smashed disks of the spool flickered briefly, and then they were gone.

The *Antigiam* surged upward like a cork, and August was knocked from his feet again. There were shouts of panic from above, and the ship rocked precariously to the starboard, its outrigger raised high in the open air. Then another sway as it stabilized.

Meridan pressed past him. August checked on Baker, to find the young man knocked out, his breathing ragged, then staggered upward to follow the captain.

When he got to the deck, the captain was already talking to Burrows the carpenter, a young lady who said everything in a loud, Scolven accent. He clearly caught: "Nearly splintered as it wah-ess. Can't tay-eck full sail."

The captain cursed, and August said, "Mister Baker's been knocked out. It might be a concussion."

Meridan turned toward him, her face filled with thunder. "We have no doctor. Can you address it?"

August's jaw flopped open a moment, then he said, "I have some basic physiology."

"Do what you can," said the captain. "I'm going to take us back to port."

"Port?" said August, startled. "We can't go back now. We're on the verge of discovering something amazing!"

"We have discovered something that can drag this ship to the bottom of the cloudscape," said Meridan. "You can go back to the ministry and get a more suitable ship. This one is done."

"I still have Dragon's Blood," started August, "and another spool. I brought replacements. We can't return as long as there are options available."

Meridan turned to say something, but the words came from far aloft. "Sail ho!"

Immediately the captain craned her neck upward, the scholar forgotten. "Position?"

East by northeast, said the watch, and Meridan was up the ladder for the quarterdeck. As she passed, she snapped to August, "Scholar, I think we're suddenly out of options."

The rising mist had served to conceal the *Antigiam*, but had concealed their pursuer as well. Now, as the fog burned off, it was large enough on the horizon to see clearly without a lens. Meridan brought it under her glass and cursed loudly.

"Church?" asked August.

"A Holy Tomebook of a ship," said the captain. "Not a Bible, one of the big ones, but big enough. And it has the weather gauge on us."

"Meaning?"

"When we turn, it can turn to follow us more easily. Madam Sandotter!"

"Ma'am!"

"Haul that sail off the deck and heave to!"

"Captain, that last stunt nearly shattered the mast," said Crossgreves, Burrows in tow. "If we rig it up full, it could splinter clear through."

"Then spread cloth halfway," said Meridan, "and get the stern-mast and spanker rigged. We're going to need all the speed we can muster."

August said, "We have guns."

Meridan shook her head. "We have two small chasers that can't be brought to bear at the same time. A crew that hasn't fired live ammunition since we commissioned. A Tomebook-class ship has at least a dozen guns to a side, likely."

Around them the ship's master was shouting at the crewmen, as every bit of sail that could safely be spread was issued. Even so, the mainmast creaked dangerously in the wind.

On the horizon, the Churchship drew larger. August could see it had three masts. And stacks of embroidered sail.

"If they catch us—" started August, then stopped, and started again. "The Church does not care for scholars."

"It does not care for much of anyone," said Captain Meridan in a clipped tone. "Look at the forward mast. It flies a Brother's pennant, you see. That ship has a single-sex crew. Those are always nasty fighters, and they particularly don't care for mixed crews."

"So they'll catch us and…?"

"Kill us. The Church is very imaginative when making martyrs. Do you have a knife?"

August blinked. "Surely you don't think we should kill ourselves rather than—"

Meridan waved him silent. "You'll need a knife once you go overboard. The trick is to whittle away a bit of your floatwood spans at a time until you can settle to the ground. Then it's a long walk back, but it's better than the Church."

August looked at Meridan, and from her gray pallor it was as if she *was* discussing suicide. And indeed, for a captain to discuss losing her ship, it was.

August looked around. Surely the crew must have realized the hopelessness of the situation. Yet they were all at their posts, nursing as much speed out of the *Antigiam* as they could, pressing her until the mainmast made its squawking complaints, then easing off quickly.

The sails on the horizon loomed larger. There was a puff of smoke from one of the guns, and a few moments later, the sound of rolling thunder crossed the cloudtops. The crew did not seem to notice it.

"Finding range," said Meridan. "That means no powerful priest on board. But still they'll find and splinter us. Prepare to abandon ship!" Her pallor was now that of a ghost.

"Captain, no!" said August, suddenly.

"I know you don't want to lose your books," said Meridan. "But it's them or our lives."

"No. I mean we can escape if we work up a distraction."

"Distraction? In this cloudscape? Can you whistle up a Commonwealth Man-o-War, or a Dwarven Siege-Barge?"

"I can whistle up something," said August Gold. "If you can sail."

To the captain of the Churchship, the Commonwealth vessel made a sudden, fatal mistake. The Commonwealth captain should have spread full sail and trusted to the winds to let the lighter ship escape. Instead, the intruder kept its main sail half-banked, allowing the larger ship to close further. Then, in panic, it jerked to port, trying to sail across the bow of the Tomebook.

Had the Commonwealth ship possessed any real guns, the Churchship could have countered by turning itself. But the Tomebook was sufficiently powerful to maintain its course, cross the "T" behind the *Antigiam*, and unload a hellish broadside against it. At that range the long 24s would reduce the *Antigiam* to splinters.

On the quarterdeck, Jemma Meridan shouted as three crewmen manhandled the stern chaser into a rough firing position. The angle was still horrible, but it was enough to unload one ball before the Churchship crossed behind them. Time enough to keep the Church's full attention on the *Antigiam*.

In the hold, at the deadman's hatch, Carpenter Burrows had rigged up the other spool of wire rope. This time, however, it fastened to the deck with a single beam, and the woodworker gripped it with both hands. Baker held a dark-stained rag against his bloodied head as he watched August lash several splints of floatwood to the second lanternlike censer's sides. With sure, deft motions, the scholar then filled the lantern with the last of the Dragon's Blood.

"Will it work?" managed the master's mate.

"It will have to," said August through thin, bloodless lips. "Otherwise it will be a long walk home."

The scholar lit the mantle of the lantern, and blew on it so it would catch. Baker shuddered as the warm, musky scent permeated the hold once again. Without another word he dropped the floatwood-bound lantern out of the hatch. Supported by the floatwood, the lantern bounced along the bottom of the ship, and then was clear, dragged behind them, along the tops of the clouds.

"It's away," said August softly.

"*It's awe-ay*," bellowed Burrows, and Baker clutched the rag tighter to his throbbing head.

"It's away," said Meridan. "Let's keep their attention. Fire at will, Mister Knorri."

The hulking crewman stuck his tongue out of the corner of his mouth as he touched the burning taper to the slow match fuse. There was a flare, and the gun jumped. The angle was not good enough yet, and the clouds fifty feet in front of the Churchship's bow rose in a rough plume.

They could hear the cheers of the Churchship—they knew the *Antigiam* would not get another shot from the flight-gun before they had it under its own broadside. A hymn broke out on board the enemy ship, an anthem of smiting the godless ranging over the choppy cloudtops.

Meridan could see the Churchship clearly. It was called the *St. Guthrie*, and was fitted out in the rich trappings of a Tomebook with many sanctioned kills. Pennants draped from its spinnaker showed all of its actions and captures. The gun crews were huddled on the port side with their slow matches, waiting for the command.

And Meridan saw the *Guthrie's* commander standing on the sterncastle, his tall helmet glittering in the sun, his robes flowing backward. The helmet gave a small dip, a bit of salute to a fellow captain, and the rich sleeve raised to give the broadside order.

And then the sun went out. More accurately, a shadow fell upon both the *Antigiam* and the *St. Guthrie*, as something rose on the far side of the Churchship.

It was huge, boiling out of the clouds like a nascent island, covered with barbed shields that Meridan realized were no more than scales. Its eyes were half the size of the *Antigiam* itself and beamed with their own yellow radiance. It maw was larger than the Tomebook.

And that maw was open. Its jaws were lined with innumerable teeth the color of stained ivory, as long as jollyboat oars and curved inward. Catfishlike tendrils jutted from the mouth. Then Meridan realized these were not whiskers, but rather rope, bound with metal wire, fixed with August's hooks.

Those aboard the *St. Guthrie* had time to react, to shout out, and for the quick-minded and truly devout, to pray before that gaping maw beat down upon the Churchboat. The mainmast snapped at once under the assault as it descended upon the ship, dragging it under with a single, graceful move.

Meridan, Knorri, and Sandotter stared as the huge island-fish dived now, taking the church vessel with it. Its scales flashed in the sun like the shields of a long-lost legion, showering the area with prismatic sparks.

"Cut away!" shouted August, now halfway up the deckhatch.

"*Cutting awaa-ey!*" sang Burrows, pulling the timber support away from the spinning spool. The entire assembly pitched forward, and like the first spool, was gone.

August Gold made it to the deck only in time to see the last of a scaled tail, an appendage the size of a scholar's tower, flick upward and submerge. The clouds roiled for a moment, and then were still.

"What happened?" said August. "What did you see?"

Meridan turned to the scholar and blinked, her eyes still wide as platters. "I saw our salvation, and a very good reason to get out of here. Sandotter!"

"Yes, ma'am!"

"Full sails as we can manage for home! And get Burrows to look for a decent splint for the mainmast! I don't want to be here when our friend comes looking for dessert!"

The great beast seemed content with its sacrifice, and did not resurface. By the end of the day, they were two hundred miles closer to home and scheduled to reach it before getting to the weevil-biscuit stage.

Crossgreves had acquiesced to breaking out the last of the Bloodwine vintage on board, and August, Burrows (replacing the ailing Baker), Sandotter, and the purser were once more in the gunroom. The captain was strangely silent, but August made up for it with his complaints.

"I cannot believe that I missed it!" he fumed, his irritation fading only slightly with every glass.

"You have the descriptions of most of those on deck," said Sandotter philosophically.

"Yes, descriptions that grow with each telling," said the scholar. "Big as a house. As two houses. As the Commonwealth House. And eyes that were beacons. No, huge slabs of amber. No, liquid fire. Pah!" He waved an empty mug at Young Smith, who brought the ewer.

"And you saw a bit of it yourself," noted Crossgreves.

"Only the tail!" said August. "Only the last bit of the tail." He let out a long, protracted sigh. "At least I've proved that 'here be dragons,' eh?"

"Not necessarily," said Captain Jemma Meridan softly.

Eyebrows around the table raised, and August said, "Surely, Captain, you cannot deny your own eyes! Something rose to the bait we cast out behind the Churchship and took it to the bottom of the clouds! You don't deny that!"

"I don't deny it. Oh, I'm no denier of reality," said Meridan. "I just express doubt that what we saw was one of your old-fashioned *dragons*."

Sandotter swirled the dregs in her mug and said, "What else could it be?"

"I'm just saying it's not necessarily a dragon," said the captain. "What if it is something else? Something that, perhaps, ate all of the dragons after the Deluge."

August Gold blinked. "A dracovore? No, it couldn't... but yes, there's no proof that it isn't." The scholar managed a weak smile. "I guess we'll have to go back again and look for firm proof after all."

The captain chuckled and said, "I have no desire to meet again anything that could eat a dragon. And now we've given it a taste of cloudships as well. No, I think we should avoid the Holy Sea for a while to come, and let the Holy Church deal with this particular devilfish. In deed."

Steven Savile

Thera, the backdrop to Steven Savile's dark fantasy "Ghosts of Love," was conceived in public—that is to say, it spiraled out of a conversation between Savile and Tim Powers on a panel at Hypericon in Nashville, Tennessee in 2006. The notion was simple enough: What happens to Fantasy Land after the character who is fated to save it decides to stay at home instead? It was an off-the-cuff remark and led to several roundabout discussions about the young heroes of Narnia and The Dark Is Rising being too frightened, or too safe, or just plain too young to do what was needed, and conversely, about old men regretting the fact that, when push came to shove, they didn't have the courage to save the world.

The first Thera story, "The Song Her Heart Sang," was published in *The Solaris Book of New Fantasy*, edited by George Mann, in 2007. Of all things, it was a love story about a blind girl and a boy who liked to tell her all about the world she could not see. It was followed that same year by "Ghosts of Love," which first appeared in the anthology *Touched By Wonder*, edited by Jackie Gamber for Meadowhawk Press, the proceeds of which were donated to Breast Cancer Research and Awareness. A third tale, "Night of Falling Stars," was published in *Orson Scott Card's Intergalactic Medicine Show* in 2007.

Savile co-edited *Elemental* (2006) for Tor, collected the horror stories of Fritz Leiber for Midnight House (*Black Gondolier and Other Stories* in 2000 and *Smoke Ghost and Other Apparitions* in 2001), and most recently helmed the shared world tribute to classic monster movies, *Monster Noir*, forthcoming from Bad Moon Books in December 2008. He has written extensively in shared worlds, including four novels in Games Workshop's Warhammer Fantasy line: *Inheritance*, *Dominion*, and *Retribution*, which were collected in 2008 as *Vampire Wars*, and the stand-alone novel, *Curse of the Necrarch* (2008). He has adapted comic strips into novel form with *Sláine the Exile* (2006) and *Sláine the Defiler* (2007), and written original novels tied in with popular television shows, including Doctor Who, Torchwood, Stargate SG-1, and Primeval. His short fiction can be found in such anthologies as *Daikaiju! 3* (2007) and the upcoming releases *City Fantastic*, *Blood Lite*, and *Bits of the Dead*. Savile's in-depth study of 50 years' worth of genre television, *Fantastic TV*, was recently published by Plexus. Other non-fiction work has appeared in the Horror Writers Association guide *On Writing Horror* (2006) and in *Hobby Games: The 100 Best* (2007). He's been a runner-up for the British Fantasy Award, nominated for the inaugural Scribe Award for tie-in fiction, and won the Writers of the Future Award.

GHOSTS OF LOVE

BY STEVEN SAVILE

GHOSTS WALKED IN Atynia Brennus's shadow.

They had been with him since the bloody battlefield of Saltash Fields, dogging his every step. By turns they mocked and pleaded with him. He walked in search of peace; it was a simple right, but with every new mile their voices had grown increasingly incessant. They would not let him forget. The worst of it was that they had trusted him. They had been his friends.

Friends abandoned.

Friends unavenged.

Their fate did not sit well with Atynia, but that was his burden. He was an old man now, tired and ready to settle. He had lived the best of his life in anger, a blade in his hand and a sneer on his lips as enemies fell to his steel. He took no pride in the killing. It was what he did. Some had a gift for words, others could paint prettily. Atynia had a gift for death. When he happened to catch a glimpse of his reflection these days, he saw a monster looking back. Somehow he had ceased to be the hero of his own life; that knowledge brought an intimate pain with it.

The black breath of the sirocco blew in his face. It was thick with dust and sand from the desert as it swept along the streets of Kalatha. He never ceased to marvel at the city's beauty. Approaching along the Pearl Road it appeared as though the rising spires were fashioned from iridescent glass. They coruscated in the baking sun, blinding flashes reflecting from every conceivable angle as the fire moved slowly through the sky. The truth of the illusion lay in the fact that the façades were faced with a whisper-thin layer of pearl that caught and refracted the sun, and at night bathed the city in silver moonglow.

In the chill of a gathering twilight he heard the first frantic cries of a baby being born. It was the most natural sound in the world, at once utterly desolate and yet so full of hope. He wanted to bang down the new mother's door and tell her of all the woes she had just brought into existence for the sake of a few minutes' lust. Atynia walked on, concentrating on the scrape of his heels on the cobbled street, reducing the world around him to sounds.

It saved his life.

A tavern sign groaned in the wind.

A cat's claws clicked across the hard-baked clay of the baker's roof.

The streaked glass in the windows all around him ticked as it cooled.

And in the heart of those everyday sounds, a tightly controlled *snick* that was so completely out of place and yet so intimately familiar to Atynia: the sound of a crossbow bolt dropping into place.

Instinctively he threw himself to his left, going down hard. Atynia was slower now than he had been in his youth. A fraction of a second slower and the feathered shaft would have thumped into his back, squarely between his shoulderblades. Instead, he came up in a tight crouch, his hand moving to the throwing dirk in his boot sheath, in time to see the bolt sail over his shoulder and skitter off the stones harmlessly.

He drew and threw in one smooth motion. Age betrayed his hand. The dirk tumbled end over end, low, rather than sailing true, and hammered into the crossbowman's thigh. The blade tore through the muscle and buried itself deep, slicing through the thick artery in a spray of blood. His attacker screamed in pain; the man's leg locked and betrayed him as he lurched forward a step. He hit the cobbles, the crossbow clattering away, out of reach of his clawing fingers.

Atynia rose slowly, every muscle trembling as the adrenal rush pumped through him. He walked back to where the dying man lay, bleeding out. His eyes had glazed over in agony. He was barely a boy. Then Atynia recognized his would-be killer. They had broken bread together only hours before. The boy had been full of questions and admiration for the old warrior. He had talked of his dreams, of his hope to serve with the Immortals in their fight against the Imacian heathens. There had been so much passion in him, such fire. Atynia knelt, covering the boy's mouth with his hand and pinching his nostrils shut. It took less than a minute to suffocate him.

"Foolish boy. Stupid, foolish boy. We shared a table, lad. We broke bread and supped that damned sour slop they had the cheek to call wine. We shared stories. For a while we were friends. Why did you have to go and do that? Why did you have to go and get yourself killed? I promised myself I was done with death, and you made me break my word." Atynia stood, his old bones groaning. *Who will mourn for the boy*? he wondered. It was a melancholy thought. He did not dwell on it for long.

Atynia looked behind him, knowing that the ranks of his ghosts had swollen, another soul lost to their number. It was the high cost of living his life: people came looking to prove themselves, desperate to bring him down, when all he wanted was peace. He craved solitude as other men craved excitement. All he got was mournful, resentful shades trailing in his wake.

"I am getting too old for this," he said to the dead boy's corpse, leaning in to close the blindly staring eyes. "But you, you had so much life left to live and you threw it all away." He spoke to the body, not the phantasm in the crowd behind him, the ghosts only he could see and hear. Then Atynia said a soft prayer over the corpse and walked away.

It was beyond dusk as Atynia walked the last mile down to the Narrows, a warren of dilapidated housing down by the harbor. The cerulean sky turned the night melancholy. The remnants of the floating fish market were drifting away, the various flat-bottomed pontoons returning to the docks, the merchants, stinking of salt water and fish oils, busily cleaning themselves with lye, soaping up vigorously. Few of the merchants in this part of Kalatha were what they seemed; some claimed to be priests of the various fabricated deities meant to terrify the unwashed masses, others worshiped themselves, their mysterious benefactor the great god coin. They sold all commodities, including flesh, whether through slavery or prostitution.

The noise of the market ebbed and flowed around Atynia like the tide itself. A single silver star glimmered through the dust. The chlorine-reek of the salt sea stung his nostrils. Black water lapped against the stonework at the edge of the dock. He was in a foul temper by the time he found the whitewashed tenement in the warren of warehouses, whorehouses, and taverns that crowded in around the harbor. It was an utterly unremarkable building, to all intents and purposes identical to its neighbors and to twenty more hovels like it along both sides of the alley.

But it was home.

Dust devils swirled and curled along the street. The entire cramped maze of alleys and side streets choked on the wheezing wind, the dusty-hot breath of the dying day, coming in off the Pearl Road. The world was angry, and it worried Atynia. He was a superstitious man; he liked to believe that fear of omens had served him well. Certainly he was old enough to fool himself into believing that to be true.

He banged on the door and waited.

When no one came running he banged again, long and slow, his thumps resounding through the brickwork of the house. He didn't stop until he heard the sound of the bolt being shot. The door opened a crack.

"Whatever yer sellin' we don't want none. Now get gone."

"Not even if it is forgiveness?" Atynia said, half-expecting the door to slam in his face as soon as the old woman recognized his voice. "What is it they say—you can never come home?"

"You? You've got some nerve showin' yer face around here, Atynia Brennus."

"One thing I never lacked was nerve, Jayden. I came for Danyell."

"Well, yer too late. She ain't here any more." The woman peered around the edge of the door. Her hair was wire-gray and hung in lank, greasy ringlets. She had something smeared on her chin—food—and thick hairs sprouting from her top lip. Anger belied her frailty. "Go! You ain't wanted."

"Where can I find her, little mother?"

"Don't you call me that, don't you dare!"

"I just want to see my wife. Is that too much to ask?"

"Why couldn't you have come a year—two years ago? Why now? Why after all this time? Yer arm gone? You too old and tired to stand alone, toe-to-toe with old man Death?" She didn't leave him a breath in which to answer before she barked: "Or did you come to appease yer guilt? Well, you'll have to live with it, warrior, that and so much more."

Something about the way she said it sent a smooth-sided stone of fear sinking into his gut. "Where is she?"

"Gone where you can't hurt her no more. She begged you not to walk out, not to go back to yer precious Immortals and throw yerself into another man's damned war. She pleaded with you. And still you went."

"It was my job."

"It was yer excuse, you mean. You can't lie to me, Atynia Brennus. I know you too well. You reveled in the violence, the killin'. You were good at it. It made you feel whole."

"I served my people."

"'I served my people,'" she mimicked cruelly, parroting his words back at him. They sounded hollow in his ears, almost like the ghosts' murmuring. "And in doin' so you betrayed yer wife. Danyell was with child! She begged you to stay because she couldn't stand to lose you, and you slammed the door in her face. Do you know what that did to her? Can you even begin to imagine?" The old woman shook her head again, more in despair than anger. "Yer not welcome here. There is nothin' in this house for you. Nothin' for me, now, thanks to you. So just go. Leave me in peace."

His head was reeling. One word stuck in his mind: *child*. Danyell had been pregnant. He looked down at his feet, hating himself all the more. He hadn't known. She hadn't told him. How could he have been expected to know? *Would it have made any difference?* he wondered bitterly.

"How can I find Danyell? I'll make it up to her. To them."

"You can die. That's the only way yer goin' to find her now. But I doubt her shade will be there to greet you. She hated you in the end. You did that to her. You made my sweet, sweet girl hate so much she took her own life. She couldn't live with the constant fear of not knowin', and the sickenin' knowledge that when it came right down to it, you just didn't care about her. You wanted to feel blood on your face. On your hands. You wanted to stand proudly over yer dead. Well, you won. You killed her, as well. So go. Just go and leave me alone."

She closed the door on him and he didn't try to stop her. Atynia stood for a long moment on his mother-in-law's stoop. The dust eddied around his feet. He had lived with ghosts for so long now, lying to himself that Danyell would be his salvation, that he would come home and fall into her arms and everything would be all right. But it would never be all right again.

He walked night and day through the streets of Kalatha, lost in a haze of grief and guilt. And anger. Anger at himself, at his brother-soldiers, at the Imacians, but even more so at Danyell. He had been a father and never even known it, or had almost been. That was somehow worse.

Atynia sat alone on the water's edge, his feet trailing in the black water as it churned around his ankles. He had loved her with all of his heart—still did—but it hadn't been enough. Not for him and not for her. The cruelest irony of them all was that he had come home now, that he had failed his sword brothers, turned his back and come home in search of solitude and shelter, a place away from all of the violence and killing… and death waited for him on his own doorstep.

Could he die? Did he have it in him to make that kind of sacrifice to find her?

He didn't, and he knew it. He was one of nature's survivors. He clung to life too fiercely.

Atynia found his mind wandering. What would it feel like to have a small, warm hand slip into his, to know it was his son or daughter walking at his side? He would never be able to answer that. The simplest of pleasures a father ought to experience would never be his. The loss tore at him. To be so touched by wonder, to feel life beating close instead of snuffing it out....

Instead of being surrounded by ghosts.

The old warrior lost himself to the grief, began drinking. Two days turned into three, turned into a week. There was no relief in it, no end to the constant haranguing of his shades. And he lived in dread of hearing a new voice, one that would cut right to the core of his being: Danyell's. But he never heard it. Never saw her. If her ghost was there, it was lost in the murmuring press of all the others.

"How do you silence the dead?" he asked the man slouched beside him at the pitted and stained bar of the Strangled Vine. Atynia's mouth was stale with alcohol and the ferrous tang of iron itching at the back of his throat.

The other drinker simply looked at him as though he were mad and returned to the contemplation of his tankard. He had no answer for Atynia. But the voices did:

Go back to the fighting...

Join us...

Avenge us, Atynia...

Die with us, Brother...

We were friends once, weren't we? Prove it...

And so they went on, whispering insidiously in his ear night and day, until he could stand it no more. The drink didn't silence them; it only served to give them strength.

Atynia left the tavern and slept his drunk off in the gutter behind the whorehouse, with its endless stream of pox-riddled doxies and sailors eager to buy some affection by the half-hour. He had an overturned cart of rotten cabbages for a pillow, a filthy tarpaulin for a blanket.

People mostly left him alone, just another drunk stewing in his own mess. They didn't see the Immortal he had been, only the broken man he was. He awoke beside a crust of vomit, the money gone from his purse. He couldn't bring himself to care about the coins.

He didn't know what to do. It was a frightening feeling. All his life he had been in control. He had acted in surety. He had been part of something powerful, strong, righteous. Now he was alone. The Immortals had proved all too mortal. His own personal vanity had been humbled. Every single certainty had been shorn from him.

As he struggled to stand he knew only one thing: drinking himself to death wasn't the answer.

He leaned against the wall, needing it for support.

How desperate are you? he thought, though the voice inside his mind wasn't his own. There was nothing familiar or comforting about it as it planted the seed: *You need a raveler.*

The very idea of it was repugnant, putting his life in the hands of one of those freaks. But he had heard talk among the men, rumors that they had certain *gifts*. Olin, normally so rational, so grounded, insisted the ravelers could talk to the dead, drawing the threads of their spirits back from the endless fields so that they might speak once more with the voice of the living.

Perhaps that was the way to make the ghosts listen to him, to make them leave him alone. Perhaps he could just quiet them enough that he might hear the one voice he longed for now more than he feared it....

The thought of hearing Danyell again, of speaking to her so that they could make their peace and part forever, was almost too much for him to bear. He slumped back to the dirty cobbles, his head in his hands, and wept.

Come to me, Atynia Brennus, the insidious voice crooned. *Let your love lead you to my door. She will be waiting for you. Let that be my gift to you.*

How desperate are you? Atynia thought, and this time he owned the voice inside his head. He had no desire to admit his need. Desperate men were capable of great wrongs in the name of their desires. Calling on a shaper was one thing, but to submit to the foul attentions of a raveler? It went against every ingrained instinct the old man possessed.

The difference between the two was subtle but the ramifications of that difference were shocking—from what little he understood of the matter. A shaper was capable of manipulating the stuff of the universe, binding the disparate elements that made up the world into something wondrous. A raveler, on the other hand, was by nature destructive, his gift unraveling and manipulating the ties that linked spirit to flesh. It was a dark art, there was no denying that, but there was a sweet seduction to its promise.

Come to me, Atynia Brennus, the voice suggested, and before he realized he was doing it, Atynia was following his feet through the dank streets, listening for anything that might betray a raveler's presence.

After a time, a wraith of a man, cadaverous and crooked, shuffled toward him, leaning heavily on a twisted rowan staff. A sad smile bared broken and yellowed teeth. His eyes were bound with a dirty rag, though whether he was truly blind was impossible to tell. A rusted manacle hung from his left wrist, links of chain dragging low enough to scrape the cobbles. It was the mortal chain of his existence, marking him as a raveler. That single iron band and its earthing chain were more than mere decoration, Atynia knew; they served to join the raveler's spirit to his flesh long past the bounds of his natural life. They shackled the wearer's soul to the mortal plane.

Do not fear me, warrior, and do not scream, the raveler whispered inside his mind. Atynia watched the man's lips; they did not so much as twitch.

"What would you have of me?" the old warrior asked aloud.

Nothing you would not give freely and willingly. I would have the dead that follow you, those guilts that weigh you down, real or imagined. In return, I offer one last tilt at love.

"Love," Atynia said, drawing a curious look from a weathered maiden scrubbing at the stoop of a nearby tenement. She smiled at him as though he had meant the word for her ears alone. It reminded him of another smile, another woman on another stoop, in another time.

Do we have a bargain, man of swords and ash? Do you accept my terms?

"I do," Atynia vowed, sealing the pact.

It was nothing more than a vague prickling sensation at first, as though a goose had walked over his grave somewhere in the unknowable future, but it spread quickly. As he stepped forward the air around him fell away like yesterday's rose petals, colors slightly faded as they spun lazily away from him. The chorus of ghosts quieted. The warrior looked back and saw the raveler's broken-toothed grin widen.

And for the space between heartbeats Atynia Brennus thought his foolishness had undone him, but it wasn't his own flesh that was unraveling, it was the doorway behind the woman with her scrub brush. The buckled wood peeled away grain by grain, sloughing off its solidity.

He looked from the doorway to the woman to the raveler. The blind man nodded.

Take the first step to seal the bargain, Atynia Brennus. Your woman waits beyond the door.

"Will I be able to return?"

Will you want to?

He did not know. All he knew was that he wanted to take that first step, that he wanted to pass beyond the miraculous door and take Danyell in his arms once more, to beg her forgiveness and to be the husband he had never managed to be in life. Why would he want to return to a life without her?

He took the first step.

The bargain is struck. Enjoy your moment, Atynia Brennus. I will claim your dead now so that they do not mar your reunion. The raveler chuckled mirthlessly inside the warrior's head.

The woman on the stoop stopped her scrubbing and looked up to smile at him. The smile froze on her face. Atynia followed the direction of her horrified gaze to see the raveler's chain dancing erratically in the air, sparks chasing up and down its length.

Come to me, Immortals! Let me show you the meaning of death so that you might wonder at your arrogance!

The raveler strode past Atynia, into his army of ghosts, the harsh iron of his wildly swinging chain corroding the essence of his dead, until all that remained were foggy memories and mis-remembered guilts. The attack left Atynia feeling disoriented. Whether the shades had been real or imagined, it did not matter to the warrior; they were his burden and he had borne them for a long time. It was the curse of the survivor. Had Olin or Gant or any of the others left Saltash Fields alive, they would have carried the dead with them, or so Atynia believed. Such was the nature of the curse.

Not once did the ghosts scream or cry out as the chain bit into them, not even as they lost shape and form, scattered and then swallowed by the rusty iron links.

And for the first time in years Atynia Brennus was alone and felt that way.

It took him a moment to realize there was blood on his shirt, a wound in his side where the raveler had stuck him. It was barely a scratch, but it burned fiercely, betraying the poison that laced it.

What are you waiting for, man, forgiveness? They have left you. That has to be enough. You only have so much life remaining. Go claim your love before the doorway fails and she is lost to you forever.

"Are they truly gone?"

They are.

"Where? What have you done with them?"

A little late to concern yourself with their fate, Atynia Brennus. They are gone. Content yourself with that. Now, go. The threads are binding. Soon the door will be just a door and you will be lying dead in a dirty street, one more of Kalatha's victims.

The old warrior nodded curtly and rushed up the step, almost tripping over the woman's skirts in his hurry to be past her. He threw himself through the open doorway. The shock of the transition between the physical and the spiritual was savage. Mortality clawed through his veins, a feeling akin to nothing he had ever felt—not any wound, not any heady delight. His skin burned. His eyes itched. His heart raced, using up his life frantically, just to be done with it so he would be free to join Danyell. It was the poison, he knew.

With his flesh on fire, Atynia stepped out into an impossible landscape. His first impression was that he had passed between life and death into his own personal hell, tricked by the raveler into sacrificing what remained of his life—and he couldn't bring himself to care. If this place was Death's domain, it was not such a bad place to be. And then he saw the tree: only it wasn't a tree, it was a river rising into the sky, so high into the heavens the water froze into ice, the ice forming coruscating branches that reached out across the otherwise empty landscape. It was huge, a league high, the span of its icy branches dozens more leagues wide. But the true wonder was at its base, where the trunk was not frozen. There the river rose, climbing like a waterfall in reverse. Atynia smiled. He had spent his life in trenches and on killing fields. There was something soothing about the idea of an afterlife filled with such beauty. If he was in hell, at least it was glorious.

He didn't see the woman beneath the ice tree until he was much closer. He couldn't make out her features—he didn't need to, his heart sang at the sight of her.

His legs tangled even as he ran down the gentle lee of the hill, desperate to be with her.

"I waited for you," Danyell said as Atynia fell at her feet.

"I came home," the old man said through the pain. "I came back for you, but you were already gone."

"And you found me like I always knew you would. Yet it is not your time, my love."

"I am here," he objected, clutching at her hand as she tenderly stroked his cheek.

"You cannot stay. There is more fighting left in your life."

Atynia swallowed back the pain. "You are wrong, Dani. I am through fighting. My flesh is undone. Poison worms its way into my heart and there is nothing you can do to stop it. My body is failing. This blood upon my shirt is my own."

The woman who was the love of Atynia's life pushed her hand into the water as it streamed upward into the sky, turning it and turning it again. For a moment the old warrior thought he saw faces pressing out through the liquid's glassy surface. Danyell touched her wet hand to his wound and he felt the coldness spread throughout him, as though the blood in his veins were turning to ice. He focused his gaze on her. She was beautiful, more beautiful than he had remembered. It was as though here, in death, her skin wore the loveliness of her soul. She was luminescent. He could not bear to stop looking at her, drinking her in.

"You found me once, my love. You will find me again, when it is time," she soothed. Her hand was wet with his blood now as she lifted it to his face.

"Please, don't leave me. Not now. Not now that I have found you."

"I have never left you, Atynia Brennus. Not once." There was no accusation in her words, only love. "But you must leave me again. Look for me in the rain when it falls, in the sun when it shines, in the rainbow that gathers when the two come together."

"Did I not love you enough?"

She did not answer that question. Instead, she took a delicate chain from around her throat and pressed the stone setting into his hand. He had given her that necklace when they first met. Dani had called the necklace The Song Her Heart Sang, because he had sung to her that first night, when he'd given it to her to seal their love. The warrior had no singing voice to speak of, could not charm the birds from the trees with his crooning, could not even carry a tune particularly well. He smiled now, remembering his embarrassment, as he felt the stone's warmth against the cold of his skin. Finally he closed his eyes. The full memory came back to him with perfect clarity, as though the necklace itself somehow remembered.

And then he knew: "I never loved you enough. I never loved you enough to stay home and be your husband."

"You loved me enough to come home," Danyell soothed. "You loved me enough to die for me. Love is a gift given, not one taken. Just promise to come back to me." Saltwater tears ran down her cheeks.

Atynia reached up for his wife, but she wasn't there. He opened his eyes. She was above him, standing, her flesh losing substance. "Come back to me," she whispered, and then rose, a ghost twining around the great ice tree before merging with it.

Atynia stared at the tree for a long time, at the faces pressing out of its watery trunk. At Danyell's face.

Only it was the washerwoman's face and the tree had faded, the doorway become just a door again. He lay at the foot of the stairs, his blood mingling with the suds of her water.

In his hand he clutched the stone, The Song Her Heart Sang.

"I will come home, I promise," the old warrior said.

"Not yet, you won't," the washerwoman tutted, her voice uncannily like Danyell's. For a moment Atynia thought he was still there, still beneath the wondrous tree; it was a beautiful moment.

He tried to smile. It hurt. Atynia closed his eyes against the pain for a moment, letting the woman's words wash over him.

"The man who attacked you took off on his heels, a real coward, but Marten took off after him. He won't get far. You just rest here a minute, then we'll get you inside and see to your wound. A few days in bed and you'll be good as new, you mark my words."

"No need," Atynia managed, his voice hoarse with the pain, though whether he meant no need to tend his wounds or no need to chase the raveler even he didn't know. The old warrior struggled to look around. A fresh wave of pain threatened to swallow him. His vision blurred, the buildings crowding in around him, swaying with the tilt of his head. The raveler was indeed gone, as were his ghosts. Atynia sank back to the cobbles, his heart beating erratically in his chest.

Not all of them, he thought, savoring the icy cold of the stone in his clenched fist. It felt for all the world as though he were holding her hand in his, all the distance between them gone. Atynia lost himself in memories of Danyell and that night when he sang his heart out for her.

Lying there in the street, he no longer felt alone.

There were some ghosts, Atynia Brennus realized, he had no wish to be free of.

Richard E. Dansky

A complete and deliberate departure from Richard E. Dansky's grimmer and more baroque work on White Wolf's World of Darkness, "The Wisdom of Nightingales" was originally composed as a birthday present for the daughter of a friend. It served admirably in that purpose, but the character of Sir Henry Jackdaw made such a forceful impression that it became immediately clear that more tales of his adventures were there, waiting to be told. None of the further adventures of Sir Henry have yet appeared in print, though he swears that's just because he's biding his time.

On the subject of shared world writing, Dansky notes: "Writing in someone else's world offers more opportunities than one might think. With the sides of the sandbox and the rules of the world already established, you don't have to spend time and energy on setting up the universe, and can instead dive right into character and story. That sort of running head start can be a huge help, especially if you want to avoid having the Extensive Exposition Fairy chewing up your word count from the get-go."

Dansky spent four years in-house at White Wolf as a line developer for such games as Wraith: The Oblivion (1996), Vampire: The Dark Ages (1996), and Kindred of the East (1998). He contributed to well over a hundred books for White Wolf as writer or developer, including *Charnel Houses of Europe: The Shoah* (1997) and *The Guide to the Camarilla* (1999). Dansky also published four tie-in novels with White Wolf: *Clan Novel Lasombra* for Vampire in 1999 and the Trilogy of the Second Age for Exalted in 2001 and 2002. More recently, he has been working as the Manager of Design for Red Storm Entertainment and the Central Clancy Writer for Ubisoft, contributing to such games as *Rainbow Six: 3* (2004), *Splinter Cell: Double Agent*, and *Dark Messiah of Might & Magic* (both 2006). His most recent fiction was his debut original novel, *Firefly Rain* (2008), for Wizards of the Coast's Discoveries imprint. You can find him online at www.snowbirdgothic.com.

THE WISDOM OF NIGHTINGALES

BY RICHARD E. DANSKY

ONCE UPON A time, in a land far to the north and west of wherever you happen to be, there lived a princess named Amber. Now, Amber was never quite certain what she was the princess of, but since she always was referred to as Princess Amber (especially in story introductions like this one), she figured that she had the job and might as well get used to it.

The princess lived in a tower miles away from anyone else. The tower was made of ice that an evil sorcerer had conjured from the mountains to the north, and he had cast spells on it so that it would never melt. It was two hundred feet high, and its sides were as smooth and slippery as glass. There were only four windows in the tower, and they were all on the top floor, where the princess lived. The tower had no doors, however, and so Amber was trapped inside. She had explored every inch of her prison, from top to bottom, and had never been able to find a way out.

Now, the evil magician (whose name was Marcos, and who had a long black beard that he used to tie into braids when he was feeling fidgety) had stolen Princess Amber from her mother when she was very small, for no reason that anyone could discern. Wise old men in the village would wag their beards (which did not have braids in them) and mutter something about curses and vengeance and so forth, but generally it was agreed that one too many spells had addled Marcos's brain and that he was just a generally unpleasant sort of person anyway.

When he had kidnapped Princess Amber, Marcos had made sure that the tower he imprisoned her in was full of all sorts of wonderful things. It was stuffed to the seams with toys for her to play with and clothes for her to try on, with books for her to read and delicacies for her to eat. Every morning, when the princess awoke, she would wander down the ice steps to the foot of the tower, where a magnificent breakfast had mysteriously appeared, full of her favorite foods. At noon, a covered tray containing a delicious lunch would materialize on her windowsill, and at suppertime, a sumptuous meal would appear wherever she happened to be. But she was never allowed to see any other children, and she was never allowed to leave.

Now, the only human beings who knew where the Tower of Ice was were the princess (who knew exactly where it was because her toes were cold most of the time) and Marcos. All around it were green hills, occasionally dotted by dandelions when the weather was warm, and by drifts of snow when it wasn't. There were no villages nearby, however. No houses or castles or even roads. On clear days the princess could look south and see a thin trail of chimney smoke twisting its way into the sky, but she never saw a human face except in the pictures in her books, and she never heard a human voice except her own. She had everything a princess could ask for, but still she was very lonely.

The princess's loneliness did not go unnoticed, however. While other people could never find the Tower of Ice, there were other eyes in the world in those days, and some of the sharpest belonged to the members of the Court of the Birds. It was Sir Henry Jackdaw who first noticed the tower, on his way back from plucking a snowberry from the top of the highest mountain in the northlands, and who brought the matter to the attention of the court as a whole. When he had done so, a terrible hullabaloo broke out. Some of the birds said that they should leave well enough alone, because the princess was a human child and none of their business. Some said that they should whittle away the tower with their beaks, because surely the princess could not have done something so terrible as to deserve to be caged like that. And some just loved to argue, and so the screeching and squawking and yammering and tweeting got louder and louder until not a bird among them could hear himself think.

And suddenly, when the debate was at its loudest and most vehement, and when the estimable Sir Henry Jackdaw himself was ready to challenge the ever-cheeky Baronet Mervyn Sparrow to a duel, a very quiet voice could be heard. It was the voice of Terrence, who was a nightingale and the King of the Birds' court minstrel, and he was much loved by the other birds.

"I shall go see this tower," said Terrence, "and I shall see the girl who lives within, and then we shall discuss the matter further." And since all of the other birds held Terrence in such high regard, they fell silent, and as one flew away. Only Sir Henry Jackdaw remained, and he bowed.

"Excellently spoken, Terrence old chap," he said. "Now how's this for a plan: I'll fly with you to the tower—it's a terrible long way, it is, and Heaven knows you might get lost or eaten by a hungry cloud or some such along the way—and let you make your roost there. Then, in a month, I'll come back for you and bring you home. That should be plenty of time for you to make up your mind, would you say?"

Terrence nodded and stretched his wings. "A most excellent plan, Sir Henry. Let us fly!" And away they went, with the setting sun on their left and the first shy stars of the night on their right.

It took three days and three nights for Sir Henry and Terrence to find their way back to Amber's tower. They arrived at sunset on the third day and saw the princess leaning over the railing of her balcony. She was singing, and the wind that always swirled around the tower caught her hair and made it dance around her face.

"That's her," Sir Henry whispered (unnecessarily, as they were still a good quarter mile away from the tower, and Amber couldn't understand the language of the birds in any case). "Poor thing, to have a voice like that and to be caged."

"I'll make my own judgments," said Terrence. "Thank you, Sir Henry."

"Hmmph," said Sir Henry, and flew back home.

For the next month, Terrence observed the princess in the tower. He watched her at play and when she slept. He heard her singing, and he listened to her read stories to herself from the great library that Marcos had left for her. And sometimes, late at night, he just perched on the railing of her balcony and listened to the sounds her dreams made—for nightingales can hear dreams, which is why they know the saddest and loveliest songs of all of the birds.

At the end of the month Sir Henry returned, full of bluster and bravado. "I say, Terrence old chap, had enough of this place yet? Worms and crabapples, man, you look like you've frozen your toes off! Come back home with me and we'll get you patched up in a jiff! Tut, tut!" And then, in a much quieter voice, he added, "So, what do you think?"

Terrence just shook his head. "I think something very strange."

And so it was that before the Court of the Birds, Terrence said something that had never been said before. He told the other birds of what he had seen, and heard, and what Amber had dreamed, and then he told them that they should teach her the language of the birds, so that she wouldn't be lonely any more.

Never before had such a clamor been heard in the Court of the Birds. Wise old owls hooted and hollered and said they'd never heard of such a thing. The eager young robins of the King's Royal Guard, crack archers all, swore that they'd defend the princess to the death and would fight anyone who'd deny her this gift. Such a shouting and squawking had not been heard in years.

Finally, the King of the Birds, who was a great golden eagle with wings wide enough to cover the night sky, spoke. "You ask a great deal, Terrence," he said. "But for you, we are willing to set aside our ancient ways" (the King of the Birds always called himself "we," and no matter how silly it sounded, no other birds would dare to argue) "and see the girl is taught." At this there was much cheering, but the King of the Birds held up his wing for silence. Instantly, there was a hush. "Such gifts come with a price, however. Since you request this boon, Terrence, you must pay that price.

"You are hereby charged with teaching this princess the songs of the birds, our histories, legends, customs, rites and rituals. You must teach her the proper forms of address for the lowliest thrush and the most honorable and learned heron, and you must make her swear never to reveal our secrets.

"Now, for the coin's other face. This is your doom: to have your boon granted. You cannot ask such a thing and expect it to come to you without cost, as free as the spring breeze. If you choose to do this thing, you are pronounced exile, never to return to this court until the day the princess leaves her tower." Then the King of the Birds lowered his beak slightly, and said in a softer voice, "You may, of course, choose to abandon your errand and remain here instead." For the King of the Birds was truly fond of Terrence, and had no wish to banish him, but he could not bring himself to revoke the sentence he had pronounced.

"Your Majesty is very gracious," said Terrence, and bowed. The king bowed in return, an honor never granted to any other bird, and then, as the assembled hosts of the court gasped, Terrence flew off, alone.

Princess Amber was counting the colors of the sunset when the nightingale first perched on her finger. She had gotten up to three hundred and twelve (not counting a particular shade of red she wasn't certain hadn't been caused by a passing cloud) when the bird flew up, bold as brass, and landed on her finger. She noticed that he was gentle with his claws, and that he looked her in the eye with a very serious expression.

"I'm sorry, Mister Nightingale," she said (for she had studied all the birds of the air and was quite proud that she knew what he was), "but you can't stay here. It's much too cold for you, and I don't have any birdseed. Though I am quite glad you came to visit me."

"The pleasure," said Terrence, "is mine, Princess."

Now, an ordinary little girl might have fainted at hearing a bird speak. She might scream, or insist that she was hearing things, or otherwise get herself quite upset for no reason at all. But Princess Amber was most certainly not an ordinary little girl. She was a princess, for one thing, and she was very brave, for another. So she merely looked at Terrence and corrected him. "Princess Amber," she said.

"Ah. Of course. A gem among your kind." Terrence did the same hopping little bow he had performed for the king (which was a great honor, though the princess did not know it) and shifted his feet, so as not to pinch her finger. "My name is Terrence, and I have been charged by the King of the Birds with a most wondrous and terrible task, in which your assistance is dreadfully necessary."

"Oh?" said Amber. "How can I help you, Terrence?"

Terrence straightened himself up and cleared his throat. "His Most Beneficent and Raptorous Majesty has instructed me, his court minstrel, to instruct you in the language of the birds. To do so, however, I must charge you never, on pain of having all the birds of the air as your sworn enemies, to reveal what I teach you. Do you so swear?"

Amber looked down at Terrence and giggled. "Why are you talking like that?"

"Err, umm." Terrence found himself at a loss for words. "Well," he finally said, "it seemed important to sound important, and... oh, never mind. Let me start again. My name is Terrence, and I'm here to teach you the language of the birds so you can talk to us and not be lonely. You can't tell anyone, though, or I'll get in a great deal of trouble. Now, would you like to learn?"

And Princess Amber, being very careful not to displace the nightingale on her finger, did a curtsey and said, "I would be honored."

Terrence looked extremely pleased with himself. "Right. No time like the present, then. Repeat after me." And with that, he sang, and in seconds, Princess Amber was singing with him.

Word of Terrence's audacity and exile had spread like wildfire from the Court of the Birds. Every sparrow sang of it, every peacock whispered the tale and tut-tutted behind a fan of feathers. And so it was that, very shortly, Princess Amber began receiving visitors on the wind. Every morning, evening, and afternoon

RICHARD E. DANSKY

birds presented themselves to her, and she was always gracious
and charming to them. They would tell her stories of the places
they'd seen and the news of the wide world, and in return she
would read to them from her library. Even the King of the Birds
visited one day, and Terrence fussed and fretted and eventually
hid, but Princess Amber was regal and charming, and eventually
His Raptorous Majesty bowed to her, as well.

Princess Amber became known as the Princess of the Air, and
of all the birds who visited her, only her friend Terrence could
sing as sweetly as she. She became friends with a great many
birds. Sir Henry Jackdaw would always make a point of visiting and telling her of his latest exploits. He told her of the time
he outwitted the Great Steam Dragon of Antioch by having it fly
into a cloud and lose track of itself, and of the time he walked a
hundred miles pretending to have a broken wing so as to lure a
hungry werewolf away from a poor farmer's cottage. Other birds
brought her flowers, which she wove in garlands for her hair, or
gems. And these things, which her friends had brought her, she
treasured more than all the things that Marcos had provided.

But there was one bird who did not love Princess Amber. The
short-tempered Baronet Mervyn Sparrow was jealous. He was
jealous that Sir Henry had grown more popular as a result of
finding the tower, and he was jealous that Terrence was much
loved in exile. So he brooded on his jealousy, and eventually he
hatched a terrible plan.

Before dawn, on the second-shortest day of the year, Sir Mervyn
flew south, to where he'd heard an ancient buzzard say that the
sorcerer Marcos the Rambunctious dwelt. For nine nights he
flew, sleeping by day, until at last the twisted ramparts of the
sorcerer's castle appeared. There was but one window, and Sir
Mervyn flew boldly through it.

Inside, the sorcerer's palace was dark. Mervyn could see nothing. He looked left, looked right, and then suddenly felt cold talons seize him.

"What have we here? A little morsel?"

Sir Mervyn twisted to see his captor. It was a gargoyle, with a leering face and long, sharp claws. The monster hung by its toes from the windowframe, and it had reached down and caught Sir Mervyn like a spider catching a slow-moving fly.

"Unhand me, sirrah," said Sir Mervyn. "I am a knight of the Court of the Birds, and I am here to see your master!"

"His master," said a voice from the shadows, "is here." And with that, Marcos the Rambunctious strode into the room. He was tall and thin, and his hair made a half-circle around the back of his head. He wore black robes inscribed with sigils that danced and moved, and his fingers were never still. "What do you have to say to me, Sir Bird?"

"I have an offer," Mervyn replied, though he was frightened.

"Is he offering to become lunch, master?" asked the gargoyle.

"Hush," said Marcos. "You haven't eaten since you were turned to stone. But you, my little bird, had best make me a very interesting proposition, or I may yet allow Grigory to test his appetites."

And so it was that Sir Mervyn outlined his plan. He would teach Marcos the language of the birds (for up until this point, they had been conversing in people-speech, which all birds know but disdain as unmusical) and then fly back to the king, claiming Princess Amber had betrayed her promise. As a result, Terrence would suffer some terrible fate, and Princess Amber (whom Mervyn had never visited) would lose all of her friends, and he would be regarded as a hero for having brought the treachery to light. As for Marcos, he would now know the language of the birds, and be free to converse with them as he chose.

"Very interesting," said Marcos, and pulled the shutter across his window so that Mervyn could not fly away without... further discussion.

A season later, Sir Mervyn returned to the Court of the Birds, his very voice all a-flutter. "Your Majesty, Your Majesty!" he called, "I have grave news! Treachery!"

The King of the Birds leaned forward. "Indeed, Sir Mervyn? Tell me of this horrible crime."

Sir Mervyn hopped onto the ceremonial Branch of Telling, and panted a bit (for it had been a long flight). "Your Majesty," he finally began.

"He said that already," whispered Sir Henry very loudly, to general laughter. Sir Mervyn glared at him, and began again.

"Your Majesty, I have proof that the human girl Amber has betrayed us! I was flying far south of here, in a land of ash and metal, and I heard a human man address me in our own tongue! It was the sorcerer, Marcos the Rambunctious, and he had learned the secrets of our songs. Curious as to how he had accomplished this feat, I risked great personal danger and flew into his palace. There, I discovered the truth—he had been taught by the human girl. She dwells in his tower, and as thanks for all his kindnesses, she gave him our most precious gift!"

"Nonsense!" called Sir Henry.

"Vile slander!" called another bird. And once again chaos raged back and forth, until the King of the Birds called a stop to it.

"We shall see," he decreed, "the truth of this matter. We shall visit this Marcos, and we shall visit once again Princess Amber, and we shall render our judgment. And if Princess Amber has betrayed us, never more shall a bird speak to her and Terrence shall die."

Far off in her tower, Princess Amber knew nothing of this. She had just received some wonderful news. A sprightly magpie of her acquaintance, named Jackalyn, had found a small palace far away, and in it she had found a beautiful and wise queen who ruled her land kindly and well, but who mourned a daughter who had been stolen from her long ago. And Jackalyn described the rooms of the palace, and they stirred long-buried memories that haunted Amber's dreams. So Princess Amber asked her friend to return to the palace, and to tell her what she saw of the woman whom the princess knew was her mother.

Thus it was that Amber's trusted friends flew back and forth, to bring Amber the latest tales of her mother. They sang to Amber the songs her mother sang, they told her about the judgments she rendered and the mercy she showed, and about the smallest details of life in the palace. But Princess Amber remembered her promise and did not ask the birds to bring her mother a message. Instead, she was thankful for her friends' gift of stories.

The next morning, the King of the Birds and all his court flew south, to meet with Marcos. He flew over the twisted landscape and saw preparations for war. Men with swords marched to and fro, and things that were not quite men lurked in shadows, hungrily. And at the very heart of the desolation stood the castle of Marcos the Rambunctious, who wished to be known as Marcos the Conqueror.

When the King of the Birds flew into view, Marcos greeted him courteously and spun him a gossamer net of lies. It had been Princess Amber, he said, who taught him the language of birds, on one of his many visits to the tower. For Princess Amber, it seemed, was his daughter.

The King of the Birds listened to Marcos's tale with great deliberation. Then, with a great rushing of wings, he flew north toward the tower, there to pronounce his sentence. All unseen, on wings of stone, Grigory the gargoyle flew behind him.

Meanwhile, Princess Amber had begun to grow sad. The tales her friends brought back of her mother's land were grimmer with each passing day. Ruffians and monsters harried the borders, driving back the soldiers of the queen. And on the shields of the evil men who fought was the symbol of a mocking, black tower. One particularly clever magpie managed to dip her bill in ink and sketch the sign on a piece of the princess's carefully hoarded paper, and the princess gasped. There could be no doubt: the tower the bird had drawn was the mirror image of her own.

It was a day later that the King of the Birds arrived at the Tower of Ice. His face was stern, and his voice was terrible. "Terrence," he commanded, "Show thyself to thy king!"

"Yes, Your Majesty?" replied the nightingale. "This is an unexpected—"

"Silence!" the king thundered. "You shall answer our questions, and otherwise you shall not speak. Did you, in fact, teach this human girl our language?"

"Of course, Your Majesty." Terrence was puzzled. "I did so at your command."

"You will answer only the questions that are put to you." The king's anger was terrible. "Did you not make the girl promise that she would never reveal our secrets to another human?"

"I did, Your Majesty. And she has not done so. She has not seen—"

"Another word, Terrence, and I will give you to the vultures for their sport. Do you understand me?"

At this precise moment Princess Amber emerged from her chamber and saw the King of the Birds on her balcony. She curtseyed.

The King of the Birds cocked his head at her. "Young woman, you have been accused of a terrible crime."

Princess Amber was astonished. "What crime could I have committed, Your Majesty? Surely I have been a good friend to your people."

"That remains to be seen. I have been told by your father—"

"My father?" she said, forgetting for a moment that she was interrupting a king, though truth be told she wouldn't much have cared either way.

"Ahem. Your father, the great and noble sorcerer Marcos. He has told me that you shared with him our secret. If you have, then Terrence must pay the ultimate price for your misdeed. Now, Princess, speak truly: Have you broken your vow?"

Just then there was a great commotion behind the king, and who should emerge but Sir Henry Jackdaw. In one talon was the struggling Grigory, and in the other was Sir Mervyn.

"Unhand me, coward! I'll fight you!" shouted Sir Mervyn. Grigory just snarled.

"Here are your real traitors, Your Majesty," Sir Henry spat. "I caught them plotting in the distance. Sir Mervyn taught the human our speech, and this creature is his spy!"

The King of the Birds turned, and great was his anger. "Then, Sir Mervyn, as you have broken our law, you and your strange friend must die. Prepare yourselves."

"No!" All heads turned, for never before had anyone dared gainsay the king. It was Princess Amber, and she spoke in the language of the birds. "Your Majesty, I never broke my promise to you, but still the fault here is mine. Were it not for me, these poor wretches would not have conspired. I ask you to spare them, that they might repair their evil."

The king coughed with surprise. "Why are you talking like that?" he said very quietly, and Princess Amber blushed. More loudly, he said, "Very well. As you have proven yourself a true friend of the Court of the Birds, Princess Amber, I grant your wish. And we shall take flight against the forces of Marcos the Rambunctious, he who would be a conqueror, and rout them. None may lie to the King of the Birds and boast of the fact."

"You, little monster," he then said to Grigory, "shall stay with me, as a jester. Amuse me, and you will be treated well. Betray me, and great shall be my wrath. And as for you..." He fixed Sir Mervyn with a deadly glare, and the sparrow trembled.

"I will take charge of him, if it pleases Your Majesty," said the princess.

"Very well," said the king. "I remand him to you. He is your prisoner, to do with as you will."

"Then I release him," said Princess Amber. "But I ask him to remain here, and try to learn to be my friend—and Terrence's, as well."

Then another murmur swept through the crowd of birds, for they had never seen mercy before. But those birds who had witnessed the far-away queen knew that her wisdom and justice had passed to her daughter, as well.

"Then all is settled," said the king, and he prepared to take flight.

"Not all," said the princess. "Your Majesty, all of this trouble was caused because Terrence didn't want me to be lonely. And now I'm not. He has been the best friend and most wonderful teacher I could imagine. But humans should not know the language of birds. See what trouble it's caused for you? No, as much as I love this, it cannot continue. Not if it would cause harm to come to Terrence, or any of my other friends."

"So you are asking me to take away your gift?" said the King of the Birds, amazed. "Never before has such a boon been granted, and now you refuse it? I cannot imagine the sheer temerity!"

"Nevertheless, it is what I want—for the sake of my friends."

The King of the Birds bowed his head. "Very well," he said, and prepared to speak the magic words that would steal the gift of tongues from the princess. Just then, however, Terrence spoke.

"Your Majesty," he said, "I think I have an idea."

The king ruffled his neck feathers, as he was unused to being interrupted. "Yes, Terrence?" he said, very slowly.

Terrence hopped over to the king and whispered in his ear for a moment. And then, if eagles can be said to smile, the king smiled.

"You are right, Princess Amber," he said. "A human girl should not know our language. But a gift given at the king's command should not be refused, and more importantly, your friends love you as much as you love them. Therefore, I—ahem, *we*—have made a royal decision. Where are my magicians?"

Two portly owls waddled forth. "Here, Your Majesty," they said in unison. "What is your command?"

"This girl sings our songs. This cannot be. Therefore, she should no longer be a girl. Do you not agree?"

And at this, Princess Amber's heart leapt within her, for she wanted more than anything to be free of the Tower of Ice and to see her mother. The owls chuckled and nodded and hemmed and hawed, and finally the shorter and fatter one said, "We can make this so, Your Majesty."

"Very good," he said. "Do you wish it also, Princess Amber?" he asked.

"Oh, I do," she said in a whisper. "Please."

The owls worked their ancient magic then, and the princess found herself shrinking and growing feathers. As she did so, she heard a kindly voice ask, "What sort of bird shall you be?"

With her last smile, she said, "A nightingale."

Now, Princess Amber's story does not end there. It is sung of by birds to this day how she flew with the king's army, and how they routed the brigands and monsters. Sir Mervyn fought bravely and well, but was slain in the last and greatest battle. His last words were a request for forgiveness, and to call Terrence a friend. Amber's mother, the queen, then ruled the lands that had belong to Marcos, and under her care they bloomed once again. Marcos was driven from his castle by three shrieking ravens, who let him neither sleep nor eat until he had fled far to the south, and his keep was torn down. The Tower of Ice remained standing as a marvel of the world, but only the birds continued to visit it, for it had once housed their friend. Grigory the gargoyle grew fond of serving the King of the Birds, who acquired the habit of sharpening his beak on his jester's nose. The king learned to laugh, and Grigory learned that Marcos's dark and evil ways were not those he would willingly choose. Jackalyn and Sir Henry found that they had much in common, and they took turns courting one another, much to their friends' amusement.

And on summer evenings, the queen of a newly healed land would sit in her garden and listen to the songs of the nightingales, who so often came to see her.

William King

Born in Stranraer, Scotland in 1959, William King went off to Edinburgh University in 1977 to study English. Once there, he discovered the age-old student distractions of beer, wild parties, wilder women, and probably worst of all, Dungeons & Dragons. So ended a glittering educational career and began a 25-year obsession with gaming which, fortunately for King, was to stand him in good stead for his eventual profession. He went to work for Games Workshop in 1989 and has been working for them off and on ever since. Somewhere in the past dozen years, he also found the time to produce an awarding-winning game, script a few comics, and start his own company, though he is currently concentrating solely on his fiction.

The majority of King's novels have belonged to the Warhammer fantasy series and Warhammer 40,000 science-fiction series. He's best known as the creator of the most (or should that be, least?) successful Trollslayer in the history of the Warhammer universe, Gotrek Gurnisson, and his poet-companion, Felix Jaeger. The Gotrek and Felix series kicked off with *Trollslayer* (1999) and continued with *Skavenslayer, Daemonslayer, Dragonslayer, Beastslayer,* and *Vampireslayer,* all of which have been collected in omnibus form by Black Library. The latest Gotrek and Felix book is 2003's *Giantslayer.* King is also the author of a series of Warhammer 40,000 novels focused on the Space Wolves, the most recent being *Wolfblade* (2003). His creator-owned Terrarch Trilogy, beginning with *Death's Angels* (2006), has seen print in German, Czech, and Spanish.

As King explained in an interview with the Sword & Sorcery website (www. swordandsorcery.org), the creative process behind the setting for "The Guardian of the Dawn" was unusual for him. "I normally write huge 'bibles' for books I am thinking of writing. I think it comes from my years of working in the game industry. I work out the world in enormous detail, with maps, and histories, and background sketches of everything from city-states to major personalities. It can take up a great deal of time, and an awful lot of the work does not get used. For my last book, *Death's Angels,* I wrote about 50,000 words of background, and a lot of that never got used. I was sitting around thinking there has to be an easier way than this of building a world, and I thought of what Howard and Moorcock and a lot of others had done, which was to develop their worlds by writing short stories. *Why not give that a try?* I thought. So I sketched out the background quite vaguely by my standards and set out to write some stories that would explore it from the inside. 'The Guardian of the Dawn' was the first result."

THE GUARDIAN OF THE DAWN

BY WILLIAM KING

"OPEN THE DOOR," Kormak yelled. Blood seeped through his shirt, the wound in his side hurt, and he was dizzy from all the witchroot he had chewed for the pain. He needed to get inside soon. It was almost twilight and this, of all nights, was no time to be abroad.

He glanced back toward the darkening woods. At least there was no sign of his pursuers on the road. They were most likely safe indoors, hiding behind Elder Signs, praying to the Sun to keep them safe from the terrors of the dark.

"Go away!" The voice from within was deep and rough, the accent that of a peasant farmer.

"You would turn away a fellow man on the night of the full moon?" Kormak said. "The Holy Sun will turn his face from your crops. Your cattle will be barren."

"How do I know you are a man? It is twilight and we have had trouble with the Children of the Moon." That would certainly explain the suspicion in the man's voice, Kormak thought. This land was close to the marches of the world where the Old Ones still disputed the borders with men.

"If I were a moondog would I be able to stand on the Elder Sign worked on your doorstone?" Kormak asked. It was just as well they could not see his blood dripping onto the crude five-pointed star. It was the worst of omens.

"He does not sound like one of *them*, Father," said another voice, lighter and less gruff than the first. There was a sound of cuffing and a cry of pain.

"What would you know about such things, boy? *They* can sound like anything they want."

"Are you going to open this door or must I kick it in?" Kormak felt ashamed at making the threat but he needed to get inside to have a look at his wound. He needed to get his horse into a protected stable, too. It must be rested, if tomorrow he was to outdistance the men who wanted to hang him for the murder of the Mayor of Sturmgarde!

"Recite the Sun's Prayer!" shouted the man. It was an old superstition that the Moon's Children could not recite those words. Kormak had reason to know it was not true, but now did not seem the time to share that knowledge. He spoke the words he had learned as a small child over thirty years ago.

The door swung open.

"Get in quickly," said a voice. Kormak debated a moment whether he should draw his sword. The people inside might be armed and inclined to mischief. On the other hand, he saw no need to frighten them any more than he was going to. No lowlander was ever thrilled to see a dark-haired highlander come through his door, especially at twilight. Memories of the old wars were long.

He stepped into the gloomy fire-lit interior. Straw covered the floor. He ducked his head to avoid low beams. The place smelled of the pigs and dogs and humans huddled there.

Kormak saw a man of medium height, middle-aged, burly and yellow-bearded. Behind the farmer was a woman, plump, face weather-lined. There was a boy, not past his thirteenth year, presumably the one who had spoken, and a girl, maybe five years younger, most likely his sister. Beside the window was another man, in his twenties, the eldest son or perhaps the wife's younger brother. He held a pitchfork in his hand and he looked nervous enough to use it. The man who had opened the door had a heavy club. Kormak moved to give himself a clear space in case of trouble.

"Easy," he said. "I mean you no harm. The Holy Sun smile upon you." He ducked his head and made the Solar Sign, keeping his eye on the men the whole time, not wanting to take a blow as he bowed.

The men relaxed a little. They had feared a monster. They had found a big man, garbed like every other landless mercenary, a sword on his back, blood seeping through a dirty linen shirt and dripping from the thick leather jerkin. "See to my horse and I will pay you copper." He pulled a coin from his flat purse, letting them see how empty it was. No sense in giving them reason to murder him in the night.

The oldest of the men nodded to the boy. "Do it. We will keep an eye on the stranger."

The boy headed through the door, torn by curiosity about what would happen next, a desire to stay and help his father in case of trouble, and fear of going out into the gathering gloom.

"Do it!" the father said. The boy jumped to obey.

"You are bleeding," said the girl. She sounded concerned.

"Bandits on the road," Kormak lied, too smoothly for his own liking. He had become too well practiced at lying. "I took a wound but managed to cut my way free. My horse all but foundered carrying me here."

"You look more like a bandit than their victim," said the eldest son, half-defiant, half-afraid, from his place of safety by the window.

"I am a soldier," said Kormak, hiding the greater lie in the lesser truth. In one sense he was a soldier. He just fought in a different war from the one these people would think of.

"A lot of you on the road these days," said the farmer. "Now that the wars in the East have ended. Sometimes I wonder if it had not been better if the orcs had overrun us. They could not commit more robberies or killings than our own so-called defenders."

It was always the same, Kormak thought. When the threat was there, people cheered and threw roses and called you a hero. When the threat was gone, they forgot and called you a bandit.

"You know nothing of orcs if you can say that," said Kormak.

"And you do?" said the younger man. There was the sneer again, but there was something else there, as well. Fear, most likely. Or perhaps envy. Many a boy had left his farm to go fight in the wars, but many had stayed behind and doubted their courage ever since.

"I do. If the greenskins were here, they would not leave your house standing, they would burn it...."

"Men would do the same, and they would do worse to our women...."

"Aye, cruel men might. But they would not take you for their herds."

"Dead is dead," said the eldest man. "It does not matter how it happens."

You've never seen an orc herd, Kormak was about to say, but the will to argue spilled out of him. Why should he inflict tales of such horrors on these people? They had troubles enough of their own. They lived with fear all their lives, saw the barons take more than their share of crops in taxes, and were unable to raise their voice in protest. They had lived in terror of bandits and of the Children of the Moon coming by night. Why add to the burden of their fears?

"You're right," Kormak said. "And I would be a fool to argue."

That took them off guard. He suspected they were not used to politeness from the likes of him. "May I take a seat by your fire? I must see to my wound."

The old man nodded. Kormak went to the fire and opened his shirt. He propped his scabbard against the hearth, making sure the blade was in easy reach and everybody knew it. The poultice he had bandaged in place earlier, before the pursuit had become obvious, formed a bloody crust. He chipped it away with his knife. The wound wept a little blood but looked clean and shallow.

He took the needle and the catgut from his pouch and began heating the point in the fire. When it was red-hot he let it cool. If he'd had wine he would have set the needle in it, but he did not. The family watched him silently, fascinated by the actions.

He pinched torn flesh together with thumb and forefinger and set to work. The needle goes in, he told himself, gritting his teeth. The needle comes out. It took him some time to finish but was easier than he had thought. The bitter witchroot he had chewed earlier was still in his system.

At least he had done something right today, he thought, and slumped wearily in the chair, stretching out his long legs. Things had gone very wrong back in Sturmgarde.

"That hurt like a bishop's stomach after a banquet," Kormak said.

The woman took the hint. She ladled out some broth into a wooden bowl from the cauldron on the fire and brought it over. He watched her warily, in case she suddenly cast its scalding contents into his face. He had seen men die from making simpler mistakes than letting their guard down with people like these. He did not intend that it should happen to him.

She made no sudden moves and presented the bowl to him with a small curtsey. He accepted it with thanks, and his shame grew when she returned with a small loaf. He had forced his way into these people's home and made them fear him, and they were treating him with more courtesy than he had any right to expect.

How had it come to this? he wondered. These were the people he was supposed to protect.

Then again, when he had taken his vows he had never expected to be hunted for murder either. Life had seemed so much simpler when he was a lad. He had thought he was going to be a hero. He had been a fool then, just like he had been a fool today when he had almost been killed performing what should have been a routine execution.

That thought brought the guilt back. Killing the man had been only right. The Mayor of Sturmgarde had sold his soul to the Shadow and unleashed monsters by night to slay his enemies and secure his wealth. The townsfolk had not known it, of course, for he had been clever and hid his evil well. The man was powerful and had rich friends in very high places, and the Order's position in the King's favor was precarious enough these days so the judgment had to be passed in secret.

It should have been a simple, clean kill but he had made the mistake of taking his eyes off the Mayor when the eight-year-old had wandered into the room to show her father her new doll and found him standing with a stranger's blade at his throat. The look on her face, the sheer horror of it, had frozen Kormak for a second.

The Mayor's knife buried itself in Kormak's side then. If it had gone in a quarter of an inch higher, the rib would not have deflected it and he would have died instead of the Mayor. It was not a mistake he would have made ten years ago. He was getting soft.

The city watch had come bursting through the door in answer to the man's terrified screams, but by then Kormak had spoken the sentence and done his job, despite the little girl's howled protests from the cupboard in which he had locked her.

He had thrown the Mayor's severed head at the guards and cut through them while they were distracted. A dive through the window and into the cobbled streets and he was racing through the town gates while the alarm bell was still being rung. He had thought he had made a clean getaway till he heard the pounding of hooves on the road behind him later that day and realized that he must flee.

The youngest boy returned and moved over to a place by the fire, kneeling, warming his hands though it was not cold outside. His sister hunkered down beside him, hands on his shoulder, looking up at Kormak with big, wide eyes. They were both blond like their parents, their hair rough cut. Their eyes were blue and innocent.

"My father says you are a soldier," said the boy. "You must have seen many wars."

Only one, Kormak wanted to say, *and all the other wars you have ever heard of are merely part of it.* Instead he said: "Yes. I have seen wars."

"Have you killed anybody?" asked the girl.

"I have killed too many." He was going to say *too many to count* but somehow the words would not come out properly. The witch-root must be getting to him.

"Have you ever killed an orc?" asked the boy.

Kormak nodded.

"He would tell you he had killed anything you ask about," said the eldest son. The sneer was there still, the fear, too.

"I have killed a full-grown Orc Tyrant," Kormak said. "I slew it at the field of Aeanar while men around me fled in terror and crows feasted on the eyes of the fallen."

The witchroot must have been stronger than he thought or he was more tired and had slipped into a waking dream. For a moment he was back on the trampled field, dancing over the corpses, the dwarf-forged blade singing in his hand. The great orc, half again his height and many times his weight, loomed over him, the scimitar of black iron, large enough to hew through a tree, poised to strike down on the neck of the fallen king.

Perhaps that day he had been the man the boy he had once been had thought he was going to be. Perhaps, but by then he no longer believed in honor or wanted to be a hero. He had seen too much corruption and too much treachery and too much death.

He shook his head and concentrated on drinking the soup right from the bowl. It was hot, and full of potatoes and carrots, with some meat and some fat to add taste.

"Good," he said to the wife of the house, hoping she would offer him more. She did not, so he began wiping the bowl with a chunk of bread.

"Could you kill a troll?" said the girl. There was an odd note of hope in her voice.

"Gerda," said the woman, "it is best not to speak of such things lest the Children of the Moon hear you."

"I was only asking, Mother, and if this man could save me…"

Kormak's heart sank. He had been half expecting this ever since he had heard the father's words at the door. He did not want to go out into the night and face the monsters once more, but he had sworn an oath long ago, when he was still a boy and had wanted to be a hero. They had put a bright sword in his hand that day, and told him that he was one, and for a brief, shining instant he had believed it was true. There were times when he thought he had lived his whole life in the long shadow cast by that one incandescent moment.

"Save you from what?" he asked.

"Something out there in the dark," said the mother. "It took some of our cattle and we can hear it prowling in the night. Sometimes it calls to us. Telling us to send Gerda out. It says if we send her it will leave and let the rest of us live."

Kormak stared into the fire, thinking of the other eight-year-old he had seen today. She had seen a monster. He kept his mouth firmly shut.

"How old are you, soldier?" the farmer asked.

"Thirty-five. I will retire in seven years."

"What?"

"Nothing." Kormak regretted his words immediately. Less than one in ten of his order lived through the long years of their term, and most of those were the crippled veterans who taught the next generation. The odds against his own survival were long and grew longer every year. Most likely he would never see the cloisters of Mount Aethelas again. So many from his oath year were already gone. Maera, with her golden hair and lovely smile. Grim Solian. Snub-nosed Rurik, who had wanted so hard to be brave and had been, right till the end....

And those were just the ones he knew about, for he had been sent to reclaim their swords, to take up their burdens, to kill the things that had killed them.

"You must be good with that blade."

"I am." And why should he not be? He had paid with his whole life to be good with it.

"Could you defeat a troll?"

Kormak considered the matter. Trolls were among the toughest of the Moon's Children. Some were tall as a house and could kill a bull with a single blow of their fist. Their skin was as hard as stone.

"I don't know."

"Most men would simply say no."

"I am not most men."

The farmer looked thoughtful. "I heard a tale once—of an order of knights sworn to oppose the Shadow. It was the mark of their order that they carried a dwarf-forged blade—on their backs to symbolize the burden of their oaths. They were supposed to have the Dragon tattooed over their hearts, as well."

So he had seen the tattoo when he was looking at the wound. Kormak cursed the fact he had adjusted his sword belt so that the scabbard hung from his shoulder, but then, after all these years, he never felt comfortable carrying it in any other way. An unspoken question hung in the air but did not hang for long.

"Do you carry a dwarf-forged blade, warrior?"

Kormak knew he could simply say no. The moment would pass. These people would most likely be safe anyway behind the Elder Signs on their walls. They would never give up their daughter to make the thing in the darkness go away, would they?

And he was tired, weary from the wound. More than that. If truth be told he was tired of fighting, of killing. Mortally tired. If he said nothing, he could stay here by the fire for the night, and quietly slip away in the morning. Nobody would be any the wiser, except himself. For a moment that's what he wanted to do that more than anything in the world, but the oath held him, the words of a boy stronger than the fear and weariness of a man. "I do."

"Then I ask of you this boon—protect us from the terrors of the night. Watch over us while we sleep. Guard us, the Children of the Sun, from the Children of the Moon."

All their eyes were locked on him. Fear and hope shone in them. The words were spoken according to the rite. He could not refuse. He gave the ritual reply.

"I will guard you," he said. "This trust I will keep or this burden die carrying. Should I fail, my brothers will take it up. On this I give my word."

He finished bandaging his wound and, weary though he was, picked up his sword once more. "I cannot stay to ward you so I will rid you of the monster this night."

As soon as he stepped into the wood Kormak knew there was something wrong. The quiet was menacing. He felt the presence of something *other*. By an effort of will he kept his hand away from the hilt of the broadsword. He wished he were wearing his mail of truesilver, which would burn the Old Ones with its touch.

Might as well wish for the sun, he thought, and it was just past midnight. The full moon beamed down through the trees. He thought he saw the cold glitter of tiny beady eyes. He heard the sound of small things moving away through the underbrush, but when he turned, there was nothing there. Mice, he told himself, but he knew they were not. Something stirred in the branches overhead and that was not an owl. This whole wood stank of the Old Ones. It had their signs all over it.

A dead tree stood, half-toppled, nearby. One branch pointed back along the path toward the farm, to safety. Go, it seemed to say. Flee while you can.

He strode deeper into the woods. With every step the feeling of menace increased. With every step he sensed hostile eyes upon him from the dark. At last, he found what he wanted. He came to the clearing, saw the symbol the moonchild had carved on the tree stump. He stood in the middle of the glade and shouted: "Speak. I know you are there."

Kormak held himself absolutely still. Something massive closed with him, coming through the trees, something pale and chill as the moon, mostly obscured by the branches of the trees. Were those teeth? Was that an eye? By the Sun, he thought, the thing was huge.

"You should not have come here, daychild." It was not remotely like a human voice. It was too low and too powerful, and its tones were too strange. There was a hunger in it. It was the voice of a great predator. If a lion could speak, thought Kormak, it would have a voice like that.

"You have broken the Law," said Kormak.

"It has been a long time since one of your kind has remembered the Law. Who are you to speak of it?"

"You know who I am. You know why I have come here."

"Where is your mail of truesilver? Where is your white horse? Where is your lance with its dragon pennon fluttering in the breeze?"

"I left them behind. I thought I would give you a sporting chance."

"You stand there wounded, with that accursed sword on your back, daychild, and you do not draw it, although I stand close enough to reach down and tear out your heart. Are you really that good?" There was amusement and contempt in the voice.

"If I draw this blade, I must kill you. I thought it better to give you warning first."

A roaring sound emerged from the blackness, the thunder of a pride of lions that have heard prey. It took Kormak a moment to realize it was laughter. Sniggers and shrieks echoed it all the way back through the forest. The laughter was horrible, the mirth of things old and cold and deadly. Were there really so many there? Kormak wondered.

"I ask you again, are you really that good with the blade?"

"There is only one way you will find out. Do you wish to test me?"

"I know that sword, daychild. I know what it is. Do you?"

"Yes."

"So if I kill you there will be one less Guardian of the Dawn."

"If you kill me, two more like me will come. If you kill them, four. If you kill them, twice as many again. And on and on, until you are dead. The Order is a great machine. Behind it stand all the Armies of the Morning. But first you will have to kill me and I am not a peasant or a little girl."

"Let us talk while I make up my mind about killing you."

Kormak stood ready. He recalled Master Ibrahim's words: *Show no fear, no weakness. The Children of the Moon will respect that.*

"By all means. We have all night."

"I remember that blade," said the leonine voice. "Areon the Bold carried it at Brightmere."

A faint shock passed through Kormak's mind. Areon had been in his grave for a thousand years.

"He killed my brother Masarion with it."

A clue there, Kormak thought, although the conclusion it led him to was not a bright one. The thing out there was something infinitely worse than a troll. "I give you greetings then, Telurion," he said.

"You know your history," said the moonchild. "Perhaps you are what you say. Since you know my name, it is only polite for you to give me yours."

"I am Kormak mak Kaine."

"I have heard that name. They say you are the best to bear that blade since Areon. Myself, I do not see it."

"They say you are not what your brother was, so perhaps we will prove well matched."

Again that thunderous laughter rang out. It went on for a long time. He knew he was being tested and that the Old Ones did not judge as humans judge.

"I smell blood on your hands and I see men on your trail."

How did he know that? Kormak wondered. The Sight was not known to be among Telurion's gifts. Perhaps he would have something to add to the Records if he lived through this night.

"I killed a Son of the Shadow back in Sturmgarde."

"And they hunt you for that? I would have thought they would be grateful."

"Unfortunately, his fellow citizens were not aware of the nature of his crimes. The city guard found me as I passed sentence on him. I was not gentle with them as I made my departure."

"You skulk in the dark and murder your own kind where once you would have rode openly forth to battle. Your order seems greatly diminished these days. Are you sure you are worthy to uphold the ancient Law?"

Kormak was no longer sure, but he said: "To end the long wars between our peoples the Children of the Moon swore to keep to their lands and leave my people unmolested. Do you foreswear that oath?" Kormak steeled himself. Swift death could be the only outcome if the answer was the wrong one.

"Your people no longer respect the ancient borders."

"And your people can and have punished them for their transgressions. As I will punish you for yours, for that is the task of my order. These are not your lands."

"Who are you to speak to me of punishment, mortal? I was old when this land was young. I have lived ten thousand years and will live ten thousand more after you are gone."

"Not unless you respect the Law."

"Bearing that blade does not make you Areon. You must know how to use it as he did."

"I can use it well enough. I ask again, do you foreswear the oath?"

The bushes bulged outward as if displaced by a great weight. He waited for the monster to loom into view but it did not—although it was closer now than before, still partially hidden by the leaves.

"I do not fear that blade."

"You fled from it once. You abandoned your brother's body on the field of Brightmere as you ran from its wielder. Will you leave these lands or must we fight?"

"I have always regretted leaving my brother behind that night. You mortals cannot understand how much I do. We attended the court of the Lady together before she turned her face from us. We roamed the Wildwood before the coming of the Elves and strode across the great ocean before ever the ships of your ancestors sailed it. We composed poems to the beauty of the Stormfangs before the Dwarves tunneled there or the first citadel reared its dark towers over the deserts of ash. We fought in battles the likes of which you will never see in this diminished age—when the Powers uprooted mountains and boiled lakes in their fury. All of that ended on Brightmere Field."

"I am sorry for your loss. Had your brother not chosen to steal the Sun King's daughter perhaps you need not have suffered it."

"I have long thought about that blade you bear, mortal. I have long considered what it means to my kind."

"It means death."

"I have lived long, and I have seen your kind drive my people into the wastes of this world. I am tired of running. I am tired of being driven forth by your sorcerers and your spells and your cold silver blades."

"You have made your choice then and we must fight...."

For a long time there was no answer. Kormak raised his hand to the hilt of his sword. The silence deepened. Then it seemed like the night sighed. He sensed another presence, heard words hissed in the Old Tongue so quickly that he could not make them out. What was being said there? he wondered. What news had been brought to Telurion?

"We will not fight tonight, mortal. I will leave these petty farmers you guard in peace."

"You swear it in the name of the Lady and your hope of forgiveness?"

"I swear in the name of Our Lady of the Moon and my hope of her forgiveness that I will not trouble them for as long as they live."

That was not an oath any of the Old Ones would foreswear but Kormak did not like the wording of it at all.

"Then go in peace, Child of the Moon."

"We will meet again, you and I. That night I may not be so friendly."

"Nor may I."

"Go in peace, Guardian of the Dawn."

Mocking laughter followed Kormak as he strode from the woods. He was certain he knew why. It took all his strength of will to keep him from running.

The farmhouse was silent. Kormak could hear the neighing of many horses in the stable. He could smell something on the wind that he had smelled before. The stink of burning human flesh was not something he could ever forget.

He moved closer to the door and heard the men inside. There were a lot of them. A quick glance at the stables told him at least ten, judging by the number of horses. His pursuers had been determined. They had ridden on even under the full moon's light. He supposed weight of numbers must have given them confidence.

Kormak slid closer to the door. They had left no sentries outside. No man wanted to wait outdoors, alone, when the Children of the Moon were abroad.

Light shone through the doorframe. They had kicked the door in. The farmer had not been as hospitable to a large group of armed men as he had been to Kormak and he had paid the price. High-pitched, near-hysterical laughter echoed within the cottage walls. He steeled himself and stepped through the door.

They were a group of rough-looking men in the garb of the Sturmgarde city watch. Kormak recognized one of them, a brawny fellow with a bushy mustache and a bald head. He had a bandage tied round the bicep that Kormak had pinked earlier. In the gloom it took them some time to realize he was there.

The little girl was dead on the floor. Her mother lay close by, hands stretched out in death, trying to reach her daughter. There was blood pooled in one of her eyes. It had overflowed and dribbled down onto the earthen floor. It was easy to see what had happened here. His experienced eye read the signs as if they were the pages of a book.

The guardsmen had burst in. They had started to question the family. The farmers had not answered to their satisfaction. One of the intruders had seized the girl and threatened her. That was when the boy had run forward and had his brains smashed out by a panicky man.

Fear and anger had gotten out of hand, and there had been a bloodbath. The old farmer lay near his wife, a massive hole gaping in his chest. The eldest son was sprawled near the fire. His face was burned. His pitchfork lay close at hand. He must have taken half a dozen wounds and fallen into the fire. The guard had dragged him forth. That was what the smell of burning was.

It could have been worse, Kormak thought. When the stink had hit his nostrils, he had expected torture. The old man's words came back to him. *Dead is dead. It does not matter how it happens.*

All this had happened while he was standing in the woods, debating with the moonchild. And Telurion had known. This was the news he had been brought. He had sworn his oath knowing that it was already past the point where he would ever have to keep it.

The city guards noticed him then. Their leader looked up from where he sprawled in the chair. "I knew they had hidden you somewhere," he said. "You were stupid to come out of hiding, but no matter. We would have found you in the morning."

"You should not have come here," said Kormak. "You should not have done this."

"And you should not have killed our Mayor—he was a fat greedy bastard, but we can't have people going around murdering whoever they like. It sets a bad example."

"One it seems you have followed."

The captain had the grace to look ashamed for a moment. "Things got out of hand."

He glanced at the rest of the guard and they, too, looked ashamed. Kormak knew that their shame was his death warrant. They would not want to leave anyone alive who had witnessed this.

"Who killed the girl?" Kormak asked. "Who started this?"

"What does it matter?" asked the captain. He stood up and drew his sword from his scabbard. He was a big man and he wore chainmail.

"It matters to me."

"I did, then, if it will make you happy. Consider your last request granted before we take you out and hang you. She gave us some cock and bull story about you going off to save her from monsters in the dark. She would not change her tale, even when I cut her."

Kormak looked at the small corpse. I am sorry, he thought. The monsters came from the dark and I could not save you. They came looking for me and I was not here, so they killed you instead. The man with the wounded arm interrupted his train of thought.

"Hanging's too easy for this bastard. He almost killed me today. He should pay for that in blood."

"I was trying not to kill you," said Kormak softly.

They laughed as if he had made a joke. They were still laughing as the first of them died, still amazed by the speed with which the blade had appeared in Kormak's hand. He slashed the next nearest guard across the belly. Dwarf-forged steel ripped chainmail as if it were wool. A man's stomach opened. His entrails spilled forth.

They looked at him, astonished, not quite understanding what was happening, that one man was attacking them all. Three more died before they could react—skull split, heart pierced, arm severed at the elbow.

One guard brought a horse axe sweeping down toward Kormak's head. He took the man's hands off at the wrists, turning his head slightly to avoid the blood gushing from the stumps. He buried his blade up to its hilt in the captain's stomach, passing it right through his body, and then pulled it free, twisting it on the way out. The captain fell to the ground screaming.

Kormak turned and saw the rest of the soldiers fleeing out into the night.

The full moon beamed down. When he heard the roaring of the Moon's Children, Kormak took a chair by the fire and waited, doing his best not to look at the corpses of the people he had failed to protect.

It took a long time for the screaming outside to stop.

Ed Greenwood

Years ago, Ed Greenwood entertained himself by writing short fantasy tales in settings he devised to "feel like" the worlds of iconic fantasy authors. (He recalls doing Burroughs, Dunsany, Howard, Leiber, Lovecraft, and Tolkien pastiches.) He was literally trying on various literary costumes to see which ones he enjoyed enough to explore further.

"How Fear Came To Ornath" began as a Burroughs pastiche, and was published in *Magic Casements* under the title "Sky Pirates of Shiningstorm." So far it's the only story written about the cities of Shiningstorm Deep. Greenwood enjoyed writing it, but saw "like my trying-on-Tolkien attempt, I had limited my storytelling options too much by bringing the reader to a ringside seat of a great epic struggle that was going to change the setting. I decided I wanted a more Leiber-like background for my stories, where the action seen in the tales I wrote would have more localized impact. In other words, I'd started right off with royalty and the clash of city-states, whereas I'd have more room for characterization, setting detail, subplots, and fun if I started with simple stablehands or peddlers, and worked up to the Big Stuff. It's hard to spend time on intrigue and making the reader really *feel* a character's rage and thirst for revenge when skyships are crashing, swords are plunging into shouting, screaming warriors, and the world is being shaken."

Greenwood feels that Shiningstorm is far narrower in scope than a well-established fictional shared world, one that serves as the backdrop and impetus for many stories told by many writers, as opposed to a single tale or story sequence from one pen. Although it's far more detailed than what a reader can see in this brief glimpse, Shiningstorm is also less deep and colorful than a setting properly prepared for use in fantasy roleplaying, where players can literally try anything. Greenwood believes neither shaping a world to suit story purposes, nor detailing a world then telling stories that arise out of those details, is inherently superior or preferable—both are "simply different approaches to spinning a good yarn to entertain around a fireside."

Greenwood is a Canadian librarian, writer, and game designer best known for creating the Forgotten Realms fantasy campaign setting. He has written or co-written more than 100 game sourcebooks and adventures; over 1,000 articles, short stories, and magazine columns; and some 30 fantasy novels. He has won several Origins awards, been a judge for the World Fantasy Awards, and had his work nominated for the Nebula Award. He is currently writing fantasy series for Wizards of the Coast (the Knights of Myth Drannor Trilogy), Tor Books (the Niflheim saga), and Solaris (the Falconfar Trilogy).

HOW FEAR CAME
TO ORNATH

BY ED GREENWOOD

HIGH IN THE heart of Ornath, the royal castle soaring at the heart of Sarandrar, the peaceful, empty room was pleasant enough.

It might have been a dark cavern, had its polished rock walls, floor, and ceiling not been so glossy-smooth and bright. Beige, white, and sandy in hue they were, great sheets of mottled and banded beige stranthadun, glowing honey-bright in the dancing flames of float-braziers that hovered here and there about the great chamber, each near a soft, dark cradle-couch.

In midair in the center of the room, a spell-spun image slowly and continuously shifted, melting as it turned from a scene of a tall tower atop a stone spire surrounded by dark, towering old harthask trees, to a god's overview of the great bay of Shiningstorm Deep girt about by the tiny, glittering spires of the proud port cities that ringed its shores. Then the bay slowly became the tower again… only to turn into the bay once more. And so on.

Sarandrar was one of those Shiningstorm cities; one of the score or so that flourished, each preening and sneering at the others—except when they made war on each other, which was often.

Now, for instance.

Wherefore the stillness of the deserted room was broken by a sudden fury of thuds upon one of its doors, as if someone was being thrown or thrust against it.

Those deep blows erupted into the louder sounds of that door bursting open, and six struggling hojands striding into the room, scabbarded swords bouncing at their hips. They held the cause of their struggles firmly between them.

Firmly but not securely. Though she was ringed by armed and armored warriors who matched her in height but had shoulders twice as broad and thick as hers, the lone captive tugged and twisted in their midst like a mad Deep eel or a raging snake of the Dreen jungles. She wasted no breath on sobs or curses or spitting, but fought silently, seeking to tug the burly hojands into overbalanced collisions and awkwardnesses that would let her win free. And though they were veterans who'd fought and slain scores of foes, their wide, sneering smiles had long since gone hard and then faded entirely.

They had forcibly measured the worth of their foe, and were grimly continuing to do so. Princess of Belmoar this wildthorn in their midst might well be, but she was no languid, scented and painted weakling. Nor a weeping, pleading one, either. Battling in silence, relenting only briefly in ruses, she fought her hopeless fight as if sheer determination would win victory. Thrice she'd had one or more of them on their knees or flailing helplessly for balance—and once, despite iron-hard fingers clamped about her wrists, she'd plucked a hojand dagger from a sheath that had strayed just close enough, and almost driven it into a warm and waiting home ere it was smashed out of her grasp.

She was covered with blood, none of it her own, and her eyes blazed like two storm-whipped torches as a seventh man strode into the room, the bloodied leathers he'd worn during the raid cast aside in favor of a shimmering open shirt. He'd shed his great-gauntlets, too, and rings now shone on his fingers. At the sight of them the fiery eyes of the princess went hard and flat.

With those, he could enthrall her utterly, turn her into a flopping fish or a mute groundworm in an instant, or blast her to ashes. Every time one of them spat out magic, it drank one of the distant lives it was linked to, draining a poor chained slave to a shriveled husk. Probably a Belmorn slave.

Struggling in the bruising grip of too many hojands to wrest free of, Tasmra Hawkharl glared at the gleaming rings.

One of those finger-bands promptly winked back at her—and the fate she'd expected seized her, whirling her up off her feet into a brief, shuddering whirlwind of searing pain, leaving her writhing limbs no opportunity to deal harm to the hojands as she was torn from their ungentle hands.

They melted away like spell-chased shadows, to leave Tasmra facing that seventh man in a room that suddenly seemed to hold no hojands. A man whose butter-brown eyes were gloating as he sketched a mocking court bow.

"Be welcome in Sarandrar, Princess of Belmoar. I am your host, and am known here as Brightlord of Sarandrar. Prince Marask of Sarandrar am I, heir to the greatest city in all Asmarand—just as you are the last of the blood of Belmoar. We are... of like breed, you and I."

The magic of his ring had returned Tasmra to her feet, but still tingled like ghostly flames about her wrists and ankles. Ready to harden into chains if she made a single movement not to his liking.

Coward.

A moonset ago she had hated all sneering, swaggering Sarandrans, with their rings of spells and haughty decrees and treacheries.

Now she knew very well whom she hated most in all Asmarand.

This Marask was the foe she most wanted dead. This prince who showed cold ruthlessness in his gloating eyes as he stared into hers, smiling his broad and cruel smile at her as he stood in his finery from swordbelt up, but below that still wore breeches and boots drenched with the blood of the Belmorn knights who'd died trying to save her from his clutches.

"And... so?" she asked, making those two words a regally calm challenge.

"And so you are well won," he replied smoothly, "that the safety of your fair person may now compel an end to the long and fruitless bloodshed between our two fair cities, so that Belmoar and Sarandrar may be joined. To tower over Gaurokh, Telvair, and Zirthran; lesser cities that will ultimately bend the knee before our bright throne—or be hurled down, set afire, and left as scorched ruins to teach the defiant prudence. Sarandrar is ever victorious."

Gods, how she hated that last, boastful sentence. This prince and his younger brothers loved to roar it out at the end of their fist-waving speeches, to goad their well-trained knights and hojands into thundering it back at them.

Sarandrar is ever victorious, my left earlobe, she fumed. *Not against Belmoar; never against Belmoar....*

Until today, when they'd boldly smashed holy law by mounting a raid in the midst of High Princess Norlaurine's funeral, using spells to whisk themselves from graveside to the guarded altar where Tasmra, as sole surviving heir of Belmoar, was confined. To sword they put weeping ladies-of-court and shouting knights and hojands alike, using dark magic to overwhelm valor and pluck her own ceremonial steel from her—and her from the heart of grieving Belmoar, casting a cloak of serpents in their wake to sow shrieking terror among the fair ladies of Belmoar, as the dark snakes of their conjuring coiled and struck and slithered in all directions.

Wherefore she was here, facing the slayer of two of her older brothers across a room that would probably become either her tomb or her prison in short order. A scoundrel whom, despite her complete lack of weapons, she would now spring at, seeking to slay even if the cost would be her own swift and painful death, if it weren't for those moon-bedamned *rings* so abundantly worn on his fingers.

A dozen of them, or more, winking and glowing. Cowards' weapons, magic that perhaps only old Lord Toraun, in all Belmoar, could overmaster.

And this grinning snake knew it.

"Princess?" he drawled now, a fresh sneer rising in his eyes and about his mouth.

"Even now, Brightlord of Sarandrar," she made reply, keeping her voice soft and calm, as if this were all happening to someone else and she were only mildly interested in the passing proceedings, "the gods frown upon this city for the sacrilege you and those you commanded have done this day, and gather their anger for your suitable reward. Your hand is around me, yes, but do not presume to think you thereby hold the house of Hawkharl, or compel anything of the behavior of Belmoar—or of its king and queen. As it happens, I know my father and mother rather better than you do."

Something like fire flickered briefly in Prince Marask's eyes. He took a slow, almost menacing step forward, holding up both hands and idly moving his fingers like a high lady languidly drying fingernail-glister. The rings adorning them winked and sparkled merrily, in a none-too-subtle reminder of the power that could strike her down.

"You are both courteous and loyal to Belmoar," he replied politely. "I expected no less. Yet, Princess, consider: you must in the fullness of time wed *some*one, and what better match—to the waxing strength of Belmoar in years upon years to come—can you find? Whose might, and wealth, and armed vigilance can better serve the home of the Hawkharls?"

"The might, wealth, and armed vigilance of one who obeys divine custom, and demonstrates both wisdom and mercy," Princess Tasmra replied, just as politely. "Something the deeds of Marask Ornlar and all his kin thus far demonstrate not at all."

The Brightlord's voice softened into warning anger. "In the judgment of a sheltered Princess of Belmoar, perhaps. We of Sarandrar see things rather differently."

Tasmra shrugged. "It matters not what Sarandrans see and think—nor, for that matter, what we of Belmoar or any of the other Shiningstorm cities believe. The *gods* see all, and know your pretty but empty words and self-serving excuses for what they are."

"And now your mask of civility slips," Prince Marask said sharply, "which can only betray how tired and overwrought you are. You need time to rest and reflect—not to mention recollect your courtesies."

He gestured, more lazily than grandly, and added, "You'll find a bedchamber beyond that door, and a bathing-room behind that one. I shall leave you now, until your mood is improved—and bright word comes to us from Belmoar from your right royal

parents, regarding your hand in marriage and their own abdica-
tions in light of the glorious victory of Sarandrar."

"Word that shall never come," the princess flared, even as he
waved a hand and the air between them glowed with sudden
phantom, rushing flames—tongues of fire that shone white and
threw forth a deadly chill that made her shiver where she stood.
She fought not to retreat, and found herself frost-covered and
trembling as Prince Marask Ornlar gave her a last sneer, turned
his back on her, and strode grandly back out the door his hojands had dragged her through.

The flames faded even as they followed him, but Tasmra marked
how they raced upon and around the closing door. She made no
move to follow him or seek to open it. Rather, she turned to a
nearby couch, knowing unseen eyes would be spying on her every move, and firmly quelled a sigh.

Patience. Darangar, mightiest knight and Champion of Belmoar, would come with sword and fury to deliver her from this
imprisonment.

And if the risen might of Sarandrar arrayed against him held
him back overlong, there was still the magic slumbering in her
skin-rune.

The last gray tatters of cloud fell away, leaving the towers of Sarandrar bare to the burning glare of the armored knight standing
in the forepeak of the slender-prowed *Warserpent of Belmoar.*

Fastest skyship of the fleet, racing under full sail and riding
favorable winds, it was slicing through the skies far too slowly for
Lord Darangar's liking.

They could have done *anything* to her by now.

Had done it, if he knew Sarandrans.

And he knew Sarandrans, all right. They died, on the point of
his sword, like *this*....

His snarl was silent, his mind bent on bloody memories, but
Darangar had survived many battles; he heard the faint sound
behind him even in the whistling winds. He spun around as
swiftly as the beast for which the speeding skyship was named.

Gloran, best of his knights, flinched back and raised empty hands. "Easy, lord," he murmured. "I'm no Sarandran."

Darangar nodded. "News?" he asked curtly.

"The men are ready, and no sign of ships readied against us. The helm asks if it's Ornath itself we're to head for."

Darangar nodded. "Of course. They're probably too busy gloating, thinking we're a day away or more."

He turned back to the spires of Sarandrar, for the first time glaring not at the tallest central towers of Ornath, but at the slender dock-towers along the city walls and the floating skyships moored to them, riding the air. There were men aboard some of them, but no flurry of a crew making ready for voyage, no sails being let out and rigged.

"No flame-hurling, and no noise," he ordered. "We go in fast, swinging swords. You stay aboard, in command. Loop back up into this cloud, sailing down again when you think best to come nigh Ornath's battlements, and then right back up into cloud if we're not waiting to be taken aboard. Away and back, away and back, with no noise and no banners. I want Sarandrar to drink and crow their triumph as long as possible, not straightaway see and know that Belmoar is come to snatch their princess back."

Gloran's smile had fallen off his face at hearing he was to stay aboard the *Warserpent*, but a trace of it returned as he nodded. "I hear and obey. We shall triumph, as we always do!"

Darangar nodded. "As we always do."

The *Warserpent* banked as the helmsman obeyed his orders, and picked up even more speed as it started to dive. A few last wisps of cloud vanished in damp and chill moments as the skyship sped through them, heading for Ornath.

Then they were out over the city of the foe, with the royal castle seemingly rushing up to meet them. Darangar turned from peering at this tower and that, to see if his knights were ready, and found them striding silent and soft-booted up the forepeak ramps to join him.

He gave them a silent nod, raised his arm, and awaited just the right moment.

The battlements loomed. Bare of sentinels, it seemed; Darangar's lip curled. Sarandran fools.

Now! Let it be now!

The helm threw out an anchor-sail and turned the main sails sidewise; the *Warserpent* slowed with a lurch, so suddenly that Darangar's gorge rose. He was pleased to see that every knight had hold of a rail, and no one plunged overboard or even stumbled.

Darangar nodded approvingly and brought his arm down. The anchor-sail was cut, the skyship under him bobbed up and started to gain speed again—and they were scudding over the rampart wall, with an easy drop down onto the battlements of the tallest tower of Ornath.

His knights leaped and sprang, and he followed them, landing hard and rolling to his feet, to peer all around as his sword sang out into his hand.

Which is why Darangar had time enough to see the ruthless grin Prince Marask of Sarandrar was wearing as three rings on his fingers flared into sudden life, the spell-darkness that had enshrouded the Brightlord fell away—and swords with no one wielding them came spinning and lancing and whirling up out of every guard-way to butcher all the knights of Belmoar.

Swords that glowed as they came, and sliced through armor as if it were but feather-web, hewing down every last man from the *Warserpent* in a sobbing, shouting trice.

Including Darangar, mightiest knight and Champion of Belmoar.

Darkness rushed in on him, and he found himself sprawled on cold, hard stone, armless and legless, afire with greater agony than he'd ever known in his life, as he saw Marask Ornlar's grin widen into a bared-teeth sneer. The prince strolled forward, heading right for Darangar.

As the greatest knight of Belmoar struggled to choke down enough blood to gasp aloud, "Sorry, Princess. By the brand you bear, may the Sky Pirates deliver you, where I have failed."

Then darkness came and took all Asmarand away, leaving Darangar never knowing if he'd got those words out in time.

There had been a time, not so long ago, when Tasmra had worn only skirts, and kept to the shadows. Her older sister Norlaurine had been the Belmorn princess folk round Shiningstorm talked about—when they remembered that Belmoar had princesses at all.

For in those days Tasmra had walked demurely behind eight brothers, eight strong princes whose swords were as sharp as their wits, whose daring deeds were cursed in Sarandrar fervently and often, and retold excitedly—and daily—in all the other cities around the Deep.

Sarandrar's royal castle had been rather more crowded with princes then, too.

Yet princes who make war on princes have a habit of killing princes—and being killed by princes.

Battle after battle had spilled royal blood, until now Sarandrar had but three princes, two of them rash younglings, and Belmoar had none.

No heir of the Blood Royal still strode Asmarand but its last princess, Tasmra. There were no hidden Hawkharls she knew of, and she could not imagine her mother and father keeping any child secret or birthing a new prince or princess without her knowing. She, Tasmra, was the last Hawkharl.

Which meant that for the sake of Belmoar, she dare not take her own life to spite this sneering Brightlord of Sarandrar.

Three sleeps ago, he'd come to taunt her with a severed head, claiming that her vaunted Champion of Belmoar had perished trying to rescue her. Cut down by this preening Prince Marask himself.

He'd held the pale, blood-drained, blindly staring thing in her face and shaken it, to try to make her weep or scream. It had been Darangar, right enough.

It had been nine sleeps, or more, since she'd been brought here, and she'd seen Marask just once since his visit to taunt her with Darangar's head.

Before then he'd visited daily, all gloating courtesy and sly words. He'd come just the once after she'd stared him down, eyes glimmering with tears but mouth grimly silent, until he stormed out in shame, kicking the head down the hall.

That last visit, he'd come in a savage temper, and without any courtesies had demanded her surrender, to wed him without delay. When she'd spat at him, he'd threatened to use "these," his rings, to compel her. Whereupon she'd shaken her head and silkily reminded him that he didn't know just what protective spells had been cast on her. Spells that would likely bring most of Ornath down upon his head at the touch of his ring-magic, to say nothing of causing scales and worse growing all over his body.

He'd called her liar, bitterly and then fearfully, and stormed out again. There'd been something added to her food to make her sleep very soundly then, when all the furniture but her bed had been carried out of her rooms, and all the candles, too.

Arising chilled in the empty dark, Tasmra knew why he'd been so furious. Word must have come to him from her royal parents. Their answer to his threats, holding her hostage to coerce the surrender of Belmoar, would have been cold, disgusted renunciation.

She also knew, from the skyships bustling with armed men that raced away from Ornath and never returned, that the war between Sarandrar and Belmoar was raging on. Moreover, as her wine disappeared altogether and her meals went from sumptuous dishes to sops and stews, she understood that its fortunes were not pleasing Prince Marask Ornlar.

This morning, the covered bowl that had replaced her domed platters was itself replaced, by a battered warriors' plate strewn with table scraps, some of them a-crawl with maggots.

Her goblet, too, had become a tankard full of someone's foul wash-water.

She had not been surprised when the door of her chambers had been thrust open without warning, and the largest men she'd ever seen had streamed into the room, ten-and-four of them, and laid large and hairy hands on her. The hands that weren't carrying knotted clubs or flailing lengths of chain.

With brutal efficiency they'd literally torn the clothes from her body, and manacled her. Ankles, knees, wrists to throat, and throat to a wall-sconce that had seemed oddly massive at her first sight of it.

So Prince Marask Ornlar, Brightlord of Sarandrar, had done this a time or two before.

Bare and shivering, but defiant, Tasmra stood staring at nothing—for what else could she do?—after the men had just as suddenly departed again, leaving her alone in the darkness.

The princess waited for the door she was facing to open again. She knew she'd not have to wait long.

"We are *not*," the King of Belmoar said severely, "going to call on *pirates* for aid. Why have laws, and a crown, if we turn to outlaws whenever the needs of the moment press us? I can father new princes for Belmoar. Or princesses, if it comes to that."

"May I remind you, dearest," his queen said in a fierce voice that trembled on the edge of tears, "that we yet have a daughter? Tasmra—"

"Is in the hands of Marask of Sarandrar, and lost to us. She might as well be dead."

"Gods in the sky!" Queen Narazra seethed. "Have you no heart, Aldaer? Where is the stormlion I wed, all those years ago? When did you become as cold as a warserpent?"

"When I put on this crown," her husband snarled, thrusting his face close to hers so she could see the fire in his eyes, "and took on the cares of Belmoar, not merely my own. I *want* to storm Sarandrar and snatch Tasmra back—gods, how I want to!—but Marask knows that, and is expecting it, and is waiting for us, all prepared. How, then, does that help you, Naz, if I lose you Aldaer and crown and all hope for Belmoar, and leave you all alone? Do you think Marask will fancy your charms enough to keep you alive after he's savaged you one triumphal time and then thrown you to all his men to use? Do you really?"

Queen Narazra went white. "That's what he's doing to Tasmra right now."

The King of Belmoar turned away. "Has done, more like. And for that I'll have his life, or die trying. Yet I'll not try to take it until I can survive my avenging, for the sake of Belmoar—and you."

He took two steps along the battlements, and then turned and asked quietly, "Do you really think what Marask has done to her is any worse treatment than she'd get from the Sky Pirates? Or did you not think at all?"

His queen stared at him for a long, silent time, her face as white as bone, and then announced softly, "I *think*, Aldaer, that the usefulness of this converse between us is at an end."

The door swung open unceremoniously, and the Prince of Sarandrar strode in. He was alone, wearing his usual confident sneer and carrying only a small coffer in his hands. He spoke no greeting. No servant announced him, so Tasmra did it for him.

"Behold," she told the dark room around them, "Prince Marask Ornlar, Brightlord of Sarandrar. Fair greeting to you, Prince."

He crooked an eyebrow. "You are strangely insolent, for a woman chained naked to a wall."

"I would have thought, this particular woman being of royal blood," she replied calmly, "that the insolence was yours. You deepen the doom of Sarandrar by treating me so."

Marask's sneer widened. "Empty threats are poor, pitiful entertainment." He set the coffer on the floor. "I know full well that you're no sorceress, and so can work no harm when stripped and chained." He smiled and let his gaze travel slowly up and down her body. "As you are."

Tasmra stood proudly facing him in her chains, stirring not at all. He let out a little crow of laughter at the mark he saw high on her right hip. "So you were a Sky Pirate slave, were you? Well, well! The adventures you've had, my little beauty! You must tell me all about it, some time...."

Tasmra said nothing. Marask lifted both brows in a mocking, silent inquiry, and then shrugged and took a slow step closer.

He took another, hand going to a knife at his belt. Then his hand drew back.

"No. Not yet," he said aloud, his gaze lingering on the skin-rune. "Not when there just might be a magical reprisal. Yet your magics can hardly work on a bare and gentle hand—or how would your maids ever dress you?"

He reached out a hand to fondle her chained body, running his fingers over her, smile slowly widening in the face of her steely glare. When he brought them up to stroke Tasmra's cheek, she turned viper-swift and bit down, hard.

Snatching his hand free, he cuffed her across the jaw even harder, leaving blood in his wake, and snarled, "I'll be back to taste your charms—when you beg me to do so."

"Empty threats are poor, pitiful entertainment," she replied, in perfect mimicry of his own sneering tones.

Prince Marask gave her a glare as venomous as her own best. "We'll see how soon hunger and thirst break you, Princess."

He turned away, striding for the door, and then stopped and turned to face her again, his gloating smile back. "Food and wine and myself—"

He used his foot to flip open the coffer lid, letting half a dozen lean, dark, hungrily squeaking rats stream out of it in all directions, and added, "Or nothing at all, until the rats nibble your eyes and the name of Tasmra Hawkharl is forgotten."

The Princess of Belmoar yawned. "I rattle my chains in your general direction," she drawled, turning her head to one side to let her glorious fall of hair swirl and sway over one magnificent breast.

Giving him a sweet smile, she added as breathlessly as any empty-headed princess at a revel, "Pleasant plundering and butchery, Prince!"

"This is our *last* ship," Sir Haeldron snarled, waving at the empty mooring-balconies all around them. "'Tis utter folly to sail off to attack Belmoar once more, and leave Sarandrar unguarded!"

"You tell me nothing I do not know already," Sir Larrask replied heavily, drawing on his great-gauntlets. "Yet the Brightlord's orders are short, clear, and admit of no misinterpretation nor yet reinterpretation—and they *are* the Brightlord's *orders*. Myself, I'd prefer to leave Ornath aboard a ship, not hurled over the side to my doom. Our prince is not very *patient*, just now."

Haeldron stared at him and then turned away, shaking his head. At last he bellowed, "Make ready to sail! Stations, all! Helms on!"

Jamming his own warhelm onto his head, he gave Larrask another baleful look and muttered, "We'll be getting into pirate season, soon, and how will Sarandrar fare then, with nothing to defend it but the Brightlord's orders? *We'll* all be dead, and our ears to hear his commands with us!"

"The fate of us all, in the end," Larrask murmured. "Or had you forgotten that?"

Tasmra listened until she was quite sure the prince was gone. Then she moved for the first time, twisting in her chains to thrust her right hip out from the wall, turning her head back until her chin was poised above it. Her mouth was full of her own blood from when he'd struck her. She let that blood dribble out of the corner of her mouth, slowly and carefully, moving her head until the pinkish stream spattered the rune tattooed into her flesh.

So the high-and-mighty Prince of Sarandrar knew a Sky Pirate mark when he saw it, did he? Yet not well, or he'd have known that slaves are branded; a tattoo meant a trusted member of the Sky Pirates.

He was quite correct about one thing. She was no sorceress at all.

Then again, she didn't have to be. The magic of the tattoo had been put there by Dajarra Thorn, the old Witch of the Winds, matriarch of the Sky Pirates.

When Tasmra's blood touched the rune and the right word was murmured, the magic would awaken, alerting Sky Pirates who bore the same tattoo to her need and location.

Now, dashed in her blood, the mark was beginning to burn, warm and deep. Fire that told her it was working, holding out to her hope she dared not trust.

Yet found herself seizing upon, almost grinning at the watching walls.

They will come, she mouthed, making no sound at all lest spying spells listened to her every word. *Yes. Fear will come to Ornath.*

Durlan Feeral crouched low to avoid any flying knives, his smile widening. "Fear!" he could hear the Sarandrans shouting, sounding, yes, fearful. "Fear is come!"

Under his boots, the *Dusk Dagger* quivered and shook, lurching sideways for a moment, and then sweeping on. Only to quiver and shudder again.

He'd helmed his sleek raiding ship low across the decks of the Sarandran war-freighter, and its slicing hull-blades were now shearing through its rigging.

The *Dagger* quivered again and, in its wake, a Sarandran outrigger half-mast toppled.

The Sarandrans were leaping for their lives, now, as his own men made pincushions of them, aiming and loosing their dart-bows with quiet, calm precision.

Soon this freighter would be helpless, adrift in the skies the moment his men let loose their lines—or he decided to tow it away for refitting. Not that the Sky Pirates had much use for such a lumbering hulk as this.

Nor did one Durlan Feeral—better known from one end of Asmarand to the other as simply "Fear"—see any way that bringing in such a prize could enhance his reputation. No, better to dispose of it in some jesting manner, a mocking wave into the teeth of the Ornlars of Ornath. Perhaps—

Feeral stiffened, his eyes rolling up in his head, and swayed like a dead man at the *Dagger*'s next lurch.

Then, slowly, the whites of his eyes disappeared again, and he was blinking around at the scudding clouds and starting to grin.

"So it has happened at last!" he announced happily, to no one at all. "The proud princess has landed in need great enough to spurn me no longer!"

Two swift strides brought him back to the helm, where he spun the wheel that turned the great vanes and rudders, sending the *Dusk Dagger* suddenly banking away from the freighter, banking and climbing.

"Full sail!" he roared, waving at his astonished crew, as he aimed the prow of his beloved ship east to the Shiningstorm Deep and the distant, soaring spires of Sarandrar.

Frowning pirate faces stared at him.

When they saw Fear's fierce, flashing eyes, they lost their looks of concern.

Belmoar was broken—must be, by now—and not another city of the Deep would dare send skyships against proud Sarandrar.

Prince Marask Ornlar stood on the empty, bloodstained battlements of his many-spired city, stared out across the clear skies of the great bay and down at its endlessly restless waters, and allowed himself a real smile at last.

His title of Brightlord of Sarandrar was about to become shining truth. In time to come, scrolls would laud him as the brightest emperor over all the Deep. One by one, the proud cities would fall to him, or be dashed down into rubble to serve as grim warning to all who might dare to defy—

Marask frowned, and peered hard to the west. There was something on the horizon—a skyship, scudding fast toward Sarandrar. Just one, dark and slim and unfamiliar. A private vessel of some wealthy Belmorn family, fleeing to the victor to beg shelter and acceptance? Self-styled royalty of some other lesser city, hurrying to sue for peace ere Sarandrar brought war to them? Or—?

The ship came in fast and low, under full sail, disdaining the mooring-balconies. He knew it not.

Lips thinning as he heard laughter from the vessel, as it descended and slowed—was the helmsman mad enough to try landing on the battlements, like a pirate?—the Brightlord strode swiftly to a stair-head, readying his rings.

Only to be shaken by something bright and impossibly fast, that spat through the air to smite him a numbing blow to his left hand. The impact spun him around and sent him staggering.

Prince Marask found himself blinking at a bloody ruin where his hand had been. Rings and all, it was gone, and—

"Greetings to Sarandrar! Fear has come calling!" a merry voice rang out behind him.

The Brightlord whirled with a snarl, lifting his right hand to deal doom to the strange ship.

He knew—all the Deep knew—who Fear was. Durlan Feeral, master of the *Dusk Dagger*, deadliest of the Sky Pirates! A—

Marask found himself staring up into the mocking gaze of a man who wore rings of his own. A handsome man at the bow-rail of his looming ship, whose rings were already brilliant and alive with shimmerings that were racing to cluster around Marask's own hand like swarming fireflies, quelling his magics. He could see surging power wrestling in the air around his wide-flung fingers, could—

The *Dusk Dagger* grounded on the broad stone battlements of Sarandrar with a shrieking, booming grinding that clawed at Marask's ears.

Then the skyship struck him with bone-shattering force, and never slowed.

"The brand beckons, and we answer that call," Durlan said lightly. One of his rings shone and a needle of ruby fire sheared through heavy chain.

Tasmra Hawkharl, Princess of Belmoar, tossed her head as if she were defying him before the throne of Belmoar, tall and terrible in all her finery, rather than standing nude and chained, clad in her own sweat and tangled hair. Fixing him with a very direct gaze, she asked calmly, "And so—?"

"And so you are now my captive," Durlan Feeral replied with that wry smile she had hated for so long, "or my equal in the Sky Pirates. The choice is yours. You can lie bound in my cabin as I fight the ships of Sarandrar until they are all flung down out of the sky, or fight alongside me, to smash Belmoar's foe."

Tasmra's face was unreadable, but her voice was calm and cool. "And after?"

Durlan shrugged. "Though kings and brightlords may disagree, there are never enough pirates. The Brightlord of Sarandrar, by the way, is now a smear upon his own battlements."

Slowly, the Princess of Belmoar nodded.

"I'll need a sword," she told him, "some thigh boots, and a sunset to sail off into. With you."

Fear's smile, then, was as dazzling the sun itself.

J. Robert King

"The Admiral's Reckoning" is set in a near-future earth universe that J. Robert King created for his first published short story, "Death of a God," which appeared in *Amazing* in 1992. King has continued to develop this universe so that he can write hard SF. Most of his shared-world stories have been traditional fantasy (Dragonlance) or exotic fantasy (Magic: The Gathering), so he enjoys having a venue for exploring science and technology frontiers. Two other published short stories, "Jovian Dreams" (*Journal of the Travellers' Aid Society* #25, 1997) and "A Tooth for a Tooth" (*Troll* #2, 1998), are also set in this universe. Each of these stories centers on Dr. Gheist, a cyberpsychiatrist called in to assist patients who are part human and part machine. The Gheist stories deal with the ever-thinning line between intelligence and artificial intelligence, between biological life and digital life.

For "The Admiral's Reckoning," though, King kept Dr. Gheist on the sidelines so that he could explore a different character—a young hot shot becoming part of the old guard. When he wrote the story, King himself was undergoing a similar, less-than-glamorous transformation. He had joined the staff of Write Source, a publisher of writing instructional materials, as a multiply-published 36-year-old editor surrounded by 50- and 60-something colleagues. Within three years, many of his mentors had retired, a group of younger folk had joined the staff, and King, nearing 40, was suddenly editor-in-chief. In three years' time, he had gone from being the wily wunderkind to being the irascible old guy.

King has written 20 published novels, most recently the hardcover Holmesian mystery *The Shadow of Reichenbach Falls* (2008) for Forge and a hardcover Arthurian trilogy for Tor: *Mad Merlin* (1999), *Lancelot du Lethe* (2000), and *Le Morte D'Avalon* (2001). He wrote his three most recent novels on his lunch hours, sitting on a rock behind the St. Charles Cemetery and smoking cigars to keep the mosquitoes at bay. King has since given up cigars due to fears that local kids would report a weird man smoking something strange in the woods behind the cemetery. King has also contributed over 2,000 pages of material to the writing instructional series *Write Source*. In his spare time, he takes to the stage, appearing in such productions as *The Complete Works of William Shakespeare (Abridged)* and *Arsenic and Old Lace*.

THE ADMIRAL'S RECKONING

BY J. ROBERT KING

As he watched his gunboats drift in stately majesty across the dat screen, Admiral Davies had only one thought: *I've got a bunch of good boys and girls*.

Davies snorted. He'd always hated when a ranking officer called him a boy. Now, at thirty-five, Davies outranked everybody, and he committed the same offense. He shrugged. It was true. With these good girls and boys, he'd won the Vangosian War.

Davies took a long draw from his maduro cigar. Tobacco was outlawed in space, of course, but war heroes were allowed their excesses, especially here in the admirals' room. The Scotch, too, was an excess—single malt and deep, here a hundred million miles from any pool of peat. Even the chamber's artificial gravity was needlessly grave, adding weight to the overstuffed chairs and helping velvet drapes properly pool across mahogany floors. Such luxuries repaid Davies for his sacrifice, and he appreciated the cigar and the Scotch, if not the extra gravity. The last was only a reminder of legs that could no longer stand.

Davies wheeled closer to the wide window. It was in fact a dat screen, pixilated so tightly that its images seemed more real than real. Just now, Saturn dominated the view, its surface draped in bunting of purple and pink. The gas giant reached out icy arms as if to grasp Space Station Roosevelt and the Solar Armada. A thousand ships had gathered to celebrate the annual Saturnine Regatta. This year's regatta was special, commemorating the end of a bloody war by reenacting it in bloodless panoply.

Gunboats paraded past the dat screen. Every last blast point had been patched, every fire-blackened crystal replaced. Even the laminar scoring of space dust had been polished away. No longer war craft, the gunboats were now showpieces. They sported ancillary fins and false bridges. Five-man fighters had been refitted to look like thousand-man cruisers. Each crew-member represented twenty of his or her fellows. In miniature, they would reenact the glorious victory of the Solar Armada over the Vangosians. It would be a glad regatta....

Especially for Admiral Davies. At last, he would get the recognition he deserved. Though he'd won the Battle of Delgoth and the Vangosian War, only he and his folk knew it. Admiral Belius had taken the credit. Davies had led his squadron on a suicide attack of the enemy base, had destroyed it, had forced an unconditional surrender, and in the bargain had sacrificed the use of his legs. He would have willingly sacrificed his life. No one seemed to care. Belius wore the medals. He hadn't even flown at Delgoth. He hadn't fought. His legs worked just fine, though his breathing was a little labored under all those medals—Admiral Belius, the Hero of Delgoth.

That title would not last long once the other admirals saw what happened today. Davies's boys and girls would make sure the whole fleet knew how the battle had truly gone, and who was the real hero of Delgoth.

"Hello, Davies," said the old bastard himself, appearing out of the crowd of admirals that filled the room. Belius carried a file folder next to his chest—paperwork was his shield—and he slapped his supposed protégé between the shoulder blades. "Damned glorious day, what?" The man was the quintessential old guard admiral—white mustachioed and pompous. His generation and their imperialism had begun the Vangosian War. Davies's generation—clean-shaved and black-haired—had had to put an end to it. Still, Belius and his cronies took credit for the whole damned thing.

"A glorious day, yes," answered Davies. His hands clenched into fists within the wide sleeves of his dress uniform. "Just like the last. It'll be just like it was last time."

Belius studied the dat screen, and his nostrils flared. His mustache began an easy inch up those monstrous cavities. "You've not fielded all your gunboats," he said, blinking beneath flocculent brows. "You've twice the complement present here."

"*Now*, I do, yes, sir. But not then," replied Davies. He stared proudly at his gunboats. Twelve ships, decked out with miniatures of the precise arms and armaments of his twelve cruisers—plasma cannonades, temporal repulsers, titanium rams, and flack countermeasures. Antique stuff. With that ancient equipment, the seventh fleet had battered the Vangosians into defeat—with antique equipment and sheer guts. Admiral Belius's ships had had sixth-dimension guns and time-slip armor. It did them little good. His crew had no guts aside from Belius's own infamous paunch. His fifty battleships had lingered on the verges of the dogfight, all twisted metal and bluster, while the true heroes won the day. "Or don't you remember the fight?"

"Of course I remember it," Belius replied. "I won it."

That was almost more than Davies could bear. Yes, at the Battle of Delgoth, Belius had commanded Davies, who was a new admiral. And, yes, Belius himself had advocated the promotion. But neither fact gave him the right to steal his protégé's glory. The old skydog had left him dangling in the breech, left him to die. When Davies had in fact prevailed, Belius robbed him of the victory.... Davies's fists almost rose from their sleeves, but this was neither the time nor the way to teach Belius his lesson. The regatta would do that, in front of the whole armada.

"Take a seat," suggested Davies, gesturing to a brocade chair nearby, "so we can be on the same level."

Nodding, the old man pulled the chair toward the dat screen and its swarming ships. He set his file folder on a nearby side table. Cocking an eyebrow at Davies, the old man said, "These days, the cybergeneticists have engineered gams that could stop a cruiser. How long before you get your new legs?"

"Never," Davies replied.

"Never?" spluttered Belius. "Don't you want to walk again?"

"I don't miss walking. I miss flying," Davies said flatly.

There seemed nothing more to say after that. While the other admirals mingled, Davies and Belius watched the gathering ships. They glowed beautifully before Saturn, massive and languid. It was the perfect backdrop for the reenactment. Its pink and purple clouds were so bright, its rings so vibrant, they dimmed the stars, which shone everywhere else like the lights of an endless city. To those who had not been at Delgoth, Saturn might have seemed a gaudy prop, but for Davies, the planet looked eerily like the home world of the Vangosians.

They were a species spawned in oceans of liquid hydrogen, pieced together under pressures and temperatures utterly beyond the predictions of terrestrial science. As it turned out, life hadn't merely a single, carbonic path into being, but thousands of routes through dozens of elements. Life was the overwhelming organizing principle of the universe. The reason that quantum mechanists had never found the Unified Field Theory was that they had approached the problem from the standpoint of physics. Instead, they should have used biology.

Vangosians were a perfect example of biological diversity. They had no eyes, for their very skin was retinal, absorbing liquid hydrogen vibrations more precise than any reflection of light. They had no arms except those they willed from their protoplasmic forms—pseudopods large enough to grasp and digest ten humans. They had no need for instrumentation, for EVA suits, for thrusters. Their interstellar craft were merely extensions of their own all-seeing skin. Vangosians swam through space like carp through water. They ate human spacecraft as though they were hard-shelled prawns.

Even now, their part in the regatta was taken by great balloons of mercury, shimmering and silvery, able to break upon a Solar craft and course eagerly along its every conduit. For ten years, the Vangosians had done just that, overwhelming the fleet.

Until Delgoth.

From that single, massive base, they had launched all their attacks. They had hid the station well among the icy rings of their home world. The Solar Armada had pounded site after site on Vangosia only to be repeatedly trounced by swarms from Delgoth. When at last the station was discovered, Admirals Belius and Davies had been sent to destroy it. They had. It was that very battle, in miniature, that would play itself out today.

Vangosian balloons hovered in a vast cloud at the center of the dat screen, mirror bubbles that wore the black of space on their glowing hides. To either side waited Belius's gunboats, menacing and beautiful with their bristling arms. Directly before the Vangosians, though, hovered Davies's ships—small, few, but tenacious. It was so familiar a scene, it took him back to that horrible, glorious day.

He was not supposed to command from here, from within a flack ship, but Davies was a new admiral, not about to fight this battle from some coffee-sipping command chair. Besides, the aching sky beyond, the reeling stars, and the gas giant Vangosia called to him. This would not be battle, so much as festival.

No command chair fit Davies like this piloting harness. At his literal fingertips were fire controls for antimatter torpedoes, lightning salvoes, and beam cannonades. His arms defined the attitude of wings, his legs the throttle of thrusters that propelled him across the sky. No human could be closer to flying than the pilot of a flack ship, and though Davies had been promoted, he was not about to give it up.

"Keep the ring tight," Davies instructed over the com line. He sensed the presence of his squadron in a warm buzz around his ship. "Target the center. The crossfire will rip apart any Vangosians near enough to strike and open a corridor up the middle." He led the way, his ship skipping out across the icy rings of the gas giant.

"Aye, Admiral," came the response from a number of voices. Davies's wingman, Lieutenant Jenkins, went on, "What do we do once the middle's open?"

"Keep it that way. We've got to make a corridor for Cruiser *Gigliousi* to get near enough to blast Delgoth Station. Once it's gone, the Vangosians will be stranded in the rings and we'll mop them up.

Davies sent his flack ship into a light dive. He pulled out, strafing along the icy lanes. His approach drew out Vangosian sentries like schooling piranhas. From amid tumbling ice chunks, they rose.

The beasts came like amoebae, formless and fierce. They flooded up as if on a single wave. Light from the gas giant poured through their translucent bodies and gave them a peptic hue. Their skins, forged in furnace heat and impossible pressure, were proof against cold and vacuity. The gelid beasts swarmed toward Davies.

He was ready. Ring fingers depressed the pressure pads on their tips. With a thump, a pair of net capsules sprang from the ship. The pods hurtled out and split open. Titanium mesh spread across two square miles of space. Nets enmeshed the nearest Vangosians. The metal filaments themselves could not have contained the beasts, but the lightning pulses within the fibers scrambled neural impulses. Wobbling piteously, the Vangosians were dragged away by the nets.

More titanium mesh ripped from the rest of the squadron. The devices spread in a wide circle of destruction before the slanting ships. One square mile at a time, they opened the way toward Delgoth Station.

It was a spiny structure, seeming almost a sea urchin as it clutched one of the largest and most ferrous of the ring's asteroids. Any Vangosian who brushed against the needle-sharp spines could be absorbed into the inner sphere, there to rest and replenish in the well of shared essence. Any Solar ship that approached too near these spines would be ripped apart. Once Cruiser *Gigliousi* could draw a bead on that urchin, though, it would be gone, and the Vangosians would be obliterated.

Davies ignited his rocket cannons and watched as Vangosians before him spattered like water droplets.

"Clear the way," he shouted to the others. "Here comes my cruiser."

"There goes my cruiser," Admiral Belius announced with satisfaction.

He and Davies had been watching the regatta progress. Tiny disarmed heat bombs had jittered among the silvery balloons in imitation of Davies and his flack ship brigade. Now, the way was open for Davies's cruiser to punch through—only it wasn't Davies cruiser that advanced, but Belius's.

The old admiral watched gladly as the gunboat that represented his counsel ship penetrated the wall of gasbags. "There goes my cruiser!"

"Yes," Davies replied, fairly hissing, "*your* cruiser. You ignored the battle plan we had laid out."

Belius puckered his face, eyebrows and mustaches almost meeting in a scowl. "No, I did not ignore the plan. I modified it on the field."

Heat entered Davies's voice. "It was to be my flagship—*Gigliousi*—that took the lead, not yours. I had left strict orders. You pulled rank on *Gigliousi*'s captain so that your ship could steal the glory."

"The moment was too critical to be handled by a mere captain," Belius replied offhandedly. "It needed a ship with an admiral—"

"*Gigliousi* had an admiral—me!"

"No, *Gigliousi* had a captain. Your flack ship had an admiral."

"Yes, and with those flack ships, we won the battle!" Davies shot back, wheeling so near the dat screen that the chrome of his seat rattled on the glass. He jabbed his finger toward the images. "See!"

The heat bomb that represented Davies's flack ship took on a sudden, amazing life. It and its squadron whirled through space like spinning fireworks, circling and protecting Belius's cruiser—in fact, a massively armed and armored gunboat. In their midst, the huge ship seemed dark, inert, like a giant stopper shoved in the center of the sky. It was Davies's squad that pierced the quicksilver balloons, that slew Vangosians in their gleaming hundreds—just as it had been in the real Battle of Delgoth.

"What the hell is he doing?" Davies raged into his com line. With the precise motion of a man standing to peer out over a crowd, Davies extended his legs and triggered a massive afterburn from his flack ship. The vessel leapt across the sky, a lightning jag following an ion trail. Davies's squadron charged in his wake. They lanced toward a new swarm of Vangosians that threatened Belius's cruiser. "That idiot! What the hell is he doing?"

Belius had forgotten how to fight. He had never known how to fight Vangosians. If it had been *Gigliousi* in the breach, Davies would have taken the battle to Delgoth Station. With Belius's cruiser, he'd have to fight sheer defense.

Davies's flack ship roared down an aerial canyon of mercurial droplets—the drifting protoplasm left by the Vangosians he'd already killed. He angled toward a huge sphere of mercury. In that ball he saw his ship's own reflection. It was as bright and sharp and fast as flame. All around the image loomed the black shadow of Belius's cruiser. Davies attacked the Vangosians as if he attacked Belius himself.

His fists clenched. Fingertips depressed the fire controls of antimatter torpedoes. With a mechanical glee, fat canisters chucked free of their barrels. They tore across empty space and ripped into the mirror face of the Vangosian. It was just like shattering a Christmas ornament. The silvery orb cracked. The warped image of the flack ship and the cruiser splintered. Within lay darkness, the syrupy heart of these horrid beasts. The antimatter torpedoes had opened a door into blackness, and through that door soared Davies.

His flack ship plunged into the meat of the monster. Muscle like mercury parted before the prow. The blood of the beast, a plasmic stuff somewhere between metal and electricity, coursed across the lines of the flack ship. This was how Vangosians killed. They swarmed their foes amoebically—surrounding, absorbing, digesting. Davies's flack ship was just another meal, except that it had been shot into the beast's mouth with the momentum of a rocket.

There was a moment in blackness—while acids etched the screens and Vangosian neurology synapsed through the flack ship's conduits—when Davies wondered if he would live or die. There, in his piloting harness, cinched into the heart of his ship,

Davies was in one-to-one contact with his foe. He sensed its hatred of him and of all things human, and then its shock that this microbe was tearing its way through, and then the thrilled agony of a mortal creature glimpsing its end.

This was why Davies flew. This was why he would always fly. This was when he was truly alive.

Shrieking like steel on glass, Davies's flack ship cracked out the other side of the Vangosian. He roared across the emptiness and dragged the shimmering guts of the monster in his wake. All around him, more flack ships tore from the bellies of more Vangosians. They smeared the things through space like slugs on cement.

Davies whooped, "Great flying, kids! Belius won't have to fight after this. He'll just take aim and shoot!"

The moment the words skated away across the com line, Davies knew they were wrong. His aft view ports showed the admiral's cruiser retreating back through the hole that Davies had carved.

"You coward!" Davies hissed under his breath. He stared in disbelief at the aft screens, watching the huge ship retreat. "*Gigliousi* would have destroyed the thing by now, and you withdraw. Coward!"

Mercury balloons disintegrated spectacularly under the assault of heat bombs. Meanwhile, the gun ship that represented Belius's cruiser made a slow retreat. The regatta painted a giant eye upon the looming blackness of space. Davies's flack ships spattered Vangosians into a spreading iris, and Belius's cruiser formed the empty pupil at the center.

"I'm surprised you had the courage to let them see what happened," Davies said, the giant eye reflected doubly in his own. "To let the whole fleet see how the battle played out."

Admiral Belius had obviously had enough. He was done allowing his honor to be so often, so completely impugned. "Everyone knows what happened. Everyone here knows. Only you seem to be surprised."

"You blocked *Gigliousi*'s entrance into combat, only to withdraw, yourself," raged Davies.

"We had received a surrender signal. You could not have known it in your flack ship, but my cruiser had received a signal suing for peace."

"Peace!" growled Davies. "What did Vangosians ever know of peace? You didn't feel their hearts. You didn't sense their hatred—"

"Nor did you feel their hearts. You felt *one* heart. It was one warrior, one whom you slew, that felt that way—not the leaders. Not the nation."

"The surrender was a ruse. A feint. You fell for it, and I didn't. You withdrew, and I completed our objective. Watch!"

The heat bombs that represented Davies and his crew converged in spinning fury on a new figure.

It was a mercury balloon, as had been all the others, but this one was different—twenty times the diameter of the rest, bloated and spiked like a blowfish. The giant sac loomed up with such sudden malevolence from behind the shattered Vangosian balloons that all conversation in the admiral's room fell silent. Every eye turned to the dat screens, every mind considered the brave line cut by one flaring heat bomb.

"If Belius won't finish the job, we will," Davies shouted over the com line. It crackled furiously. Streamers of dead Vangosians ripped apart the electromagnetic field. Even now, Davies's flack ship dragged what was left of his slain foe across the sky. "We destroy Delgoth just as we destroyed its defenders."

"What do you mean—" shrieked his wingman, Lieutenant Jenkins, only belatedly adding "—Admiral? You mean a ramming assault?"

"This is the Vangosians' Pearl Harbor, except that the destruction of Delgoth will end the war, not start it. And what did the Japanese do at Pearl Harbor? They made their planes into bombs."

"Admiral, you can't command us to do this," Jenkins replied. "You can't order a suicide strike."

"I'm not ordering anything," the admiral said, keeping his eyes on the station that swelled out before him. "I'm not back in some cruiser somewhere telling you to die. I'm out here. I'm flying. I'm fighting, and I'm asking you to fly and fight beside me. If we die, we die together, but the world lives."

There was a long silence after that. Space scrolled by. Stars stared in avid disbelief at the surging flack ships. They seemed as small and furious as gnats before a giant.

"I'm with you, Admiral," came Jenkins's response. "You're one of us."

Davies did not even smile. He only nodded in appreciation. He'd expected no less from his wingman.

One by one, the others in his squad added their assent. Every last one. *What a good batch of boys and girls....*

There was time for no more. Delgoth had swelled outward to eclipse Vangosia. There were no stars anymore, no chunks of ice or spinning rock—only that huge station, echinodermatum and iron.

Davies's fists clenched, unleashing every last payload. Anti-matter bombs blazed away first. They pocked the mirror edge of the station and ripped holes through its fuselage. Then beam weapons stabbed out, reflected along the shimmering spikes, and slammed, multifarious, into the blackened holes left by the bombs. Pure energy gashed them wider. Next, lightning reached craggy hands toward the station. White-hot energy leapt gladly to the metallic spikes and mantled them. Millions of gigawatts of electricity fried what would fry and scrambled the rest.

The last and most brutal weapon of all were the ships. Davies's flack ship struck the station like a dagger. His nosecone augured through living metal. Delgoth gave way, as soft as flesh, as hot as blood. Davies's fighter plunged through protoplasm. Beams glowed through the dark heart of the station and boiled the goo. Lightning strikes rolled out in eerie pathways of red, like the blood vessel in an egg. Heat bombs jagged out to detonate nearby with a sucking roar. Davies's fingernails cut through the control gloves and into his own palms. He emptied his arsenal into the murderous beasts.

That was what the liquid was, incubating Vangosians—some fetal, some wounded, some resting. Soon, all were dead.

Davies killed them with fury, not just because he remembered the massacres at Titan and Europa, not just because of the Martian atrocities, but also because he now knew what this station was. He couldn't help knowing. The beasts he killed screamed the truth through the piloting harness. Their dying flesh clove to the outside of his ship, telling him who he was killing.

Delgoth was no mere station. She was the fecund queen of the Vangosian hive. She was no military base, but a huge entity, the mother that gave birth to all the others, that healed their wounds and succored their weaknesses. She was their goddess, their only hope for survival, and Davies was killing her—Davies and his good girls and boys.

Through the dying body of the Great Vangosian, Davies glimpsed his squad. They chopped their way through the goddess's flesh, just as he did. They burrowed, chiggers through muscle. They were the worst parasites—voracious and relentless. Their beams and bolts and bombs riddled the heart of the goddess. Just like Davies, every last flier knew what he or she did.

This was worse than a suicide mission. They would all live through this. They would all have to live with what they had done.

Beyond the dat screen, the spiny balloon collapsed upon itself. Fires flared fitfully where there was oxygen to fuel them. Mercury gushed like blood from the shattered form. From the far side of the deflating figure burst heat bombs—one after another. They represented Davies and his squad, hurtling out of the dying goddess.

In his wheelchair, Davies jabbed an emphatic finger toward the dat screen. "Look at that, Belius. Get an eyeful! Did you have any idea what that station was?" he raged. Every admiral in the room listened to him. This was his moment. This was when he could nail Belius to the wall. "Did you have even the first notion why the Vangosians had hid that station so well, why they had fought tooth and nail to keep us away from it, why they had surrendered the moment we approached it? It was no station, Admiral. It was a being, a goddess, forever creating the Vangosian race. Do you realize what we did in destroying that creature? We committed genocide. We destroyed the future of an entire sentient species! Without her, they could not reproduce. But you couldn't have known that. You came nowhere near them. You never fought them. You never felt their minds crawling through yours. You never engaged. Of course you didn't know what Delgoth was—"

"Of course I did know," replied Belius flatly, interrupting the rant. It was not the stuttering response Davies had expected. The old admiral was stern-eyed and utterly sober. Gone was the lint-haired dolt that Davies had so despised. Beneath the softness of age shone a steel-edged warrior who had once been no different from Davies. "Of course I knew what that station was. I read the confidential reports filed by the scout ships."

Davies stared in bald-faced disbelief at the old admiral. "What?"

"I knew Delgoth was the Vangosian breeding mother, their goddess. I knew that once we had her cornered, the Vangosians would surrender. Our attack was never meant to go to comple-tion. It was meant to be a checkmate, stopping short of taking the final piece. We wanted to end the war with the Vangosians, not to wipe out their species." From beneath stormy brows, Ad-miral Belius glared at his young protégé. "But that is what you did, isn't it, Davies?"

The young admiral's jaw hung open. "If you knew all of this, why didn't you tell me—?"

"I *did* tell you, but you didn't listen. I said that Delgoth was the key. I said they would never allow us to fire a shot on her. I said we wanted to force a surrender, to drive them to their knees."

"You said nothing about a goddess—"

"You received the same reports I did. Why didn't you read them? And the word *goddess* appeared countless times in my briefings. But you care nothing for reports and briefings. You think bureaucracy is a waste of time. You weren't even in your command seat when I signaled the rest of the fleet to cease fire. You were out flying, out fighting, so mantled in Vangosian dead you couldn't hear the order to retreat. Even if you had, though, I'm sure you would have ignored it."

Admiral Belius dragged Davies's wheelchair to face him. He stared levelly into the young man's eyes. "You think you should be the Hero of Delgoth—I know you do. But let me tell you why you are not. You didn't fight like an admiral at Delgoth. Not even like a captain. You fought like a gunner. You wanted to feel every bolt leave your fingertips. You wanted to sense Vangosian claws through your piloting harness. Unless you killed it with your own little ship, it wasn't dead. And look what you killed with your own little ship, Davies. Look!

"Admirals cannot fight that way. We must consider our whole fleet, and the enemy's whole fleet, and the nations that send these fleets. We cannot afford to attack every planet and fight every foe. Memos, reports, meetings, maps, rosters, schedules—these are our eyes and ears. Without them and the distance to interpret them, we fly blind and deaf and dumb. That's how you fought at Delgoth. Blind and deaf and dumb. Yes, Davies, you had courage. Yes, you had will. And look what they brought you." He gestured at the dat screen.

Davies stared at the great, burning balloon. It flailed piteously in its death throes—what once had been a goddess and now was but a collapsing membrane. Vertigo laid hold of him. The stars spun violently. Davies had arrived in the admirals' room hoping for recognition from his peers, from his nation. He had thought he needed to educate them about the sacrifice he and his boys and girls had made at Delgoth. Now he realized that they needed no education. They recognized all too clearly what had happened.

Davies looked beyond Belius to the silent room of admirals. One by one, they nodded grimly. Their eyes were not accusing. It seemed each man and woman there had made similar mistakes. It was part of the rite of passage from captain to admiral. It was equally obvious that no man or woman there had made the mistake of slaying a species and its god.

Davies began a retort. His voice was low, like the growl of a dog. He wasn't sure what he would say until he opened his mouth. "I have made mistakes, surely—most grievous mistakes. I recognize that. But they were honest mistakes, made out of courage, honor, and self-sacrifice—the virtues of a warrior. I've lived by those virtues all my life. Yes, sometimes, they have led me down destructive paths, but all in all, they are the best counselors of my soul. I cannot for one moment believe that paperwork can replace courage, that meetings can replace honor, that bean-counting is better than self-sacrifice. Bureaucracy does not win wars, does not protect freedom, does not save lives. Warriors do that. I cannot believe the best admiral is not a fighter but a bureaucrat...."

Belius replied in a firm voice. "Yes, you can believe it, and you do believe it." Deep sadness filled his tone.

Davies's face swelled with blood. "How can you know what I believe?"

Belius reached to the table beside him and lifted the folder he had brought. "Paperwork—my eyes and ears. It is how I know." From the folder he slid two slim reports. The first had been dictated by the fleet neurosurgeon and signed with his voice imprint. The second was a longhand note from the imperial cyberpsychologist, Frank Gheist. "These reports indicate there is nothing wrong with your legs... except that you are unwilling to use them."

Davies snatched the pages from the man's hand. "These are confidential! Where did you get these?"

Ignoring the question, Belius said, "And the reason you are unwilling to use them is that you know, as an admiral, you cannot fly, cannot fight as once you did."

"God damn you, Belius!" hissed Davies, lunging for him.

Belius retreated, just as he had at Delgoth.

Davies landed, panting, in a heap on the floor.

Belius continued, "It's why I didn't have you demoted, because you knew you needed to change—"

"God damn you!" Davies barked again. He brutally swung his fists.

The old man caught both strikes. "I didn't demote you, Davies, because you are a good man, and because I knew it was only a matter of time before you stood up and joined us." Gritting his teeth, Belius lifted Davies slowly to his feet.

Once-dead legs twitched with pain. Flesh shuddered. Bone engaged bone.

On limbs that creaked like old timber, Davies stood. His hands were still clenched within the grip of his mentor. His face was still swollen with blood. But now, the fury—and even the humiliation—were gone. His eyes were filled with a look of strange triumph.

"Yes," said Admiral Davies as he stared at his shaking, living legs. "It was only a matter of time… till I stood up… and joined you."

Monte Cook

The Lands of the Diamond Throne were created as a setting for *Monte Cook's Arcana Unearthed* (2003), a fantasy roleplaying game, and later fully incorporated into the more elaborate book, *Monte Cook's Arcana Evolved* (2005). The goal of the setting was to create a robust fantasy landscape without using some of the more familiar fantasy tropes—no elves, dwarves, and so on. To help give life to this new setting, numerous talented authors were commissioned to write stories for two anthologies, *Children of the Rune* (2004) and *The Dragon's Return* (2005). "Memories and Ghosts" appeared in the latter.

The region now known as the Lands of the Diamond Throne once teemed with dragons who ruled over the realm for countless centuries. However, it was enslaved by hideous dragon-spawned demons called the dramojh who ruled over the lands once the dragons had left for the mysterious West. Defeat came to the dramojh only when they were discovered by a race of noble giants that came from across the eastern sea. The giants waged a terrible war that eventually liberated the humans and other races subjugated by the dramojh. The giants have ruled over the land ever since, for the most part fairly and justly, from the seat of power called the Diamond Throne. But now the dragons have returned after a millennia-long absence to find their former realm a very different place. "Memories and Ghosts" highlights the dramatic conflict that then arises, personified by the meeting of two of the mightiest individuals of each mighty race.

Cook is a longtime game designer and writer with well over a hundred credits. He was one of the co-designers of the third edition of Dungeons & Dragons, worked as the managing editor for the Champions and Rolemaster game lines, designed the popular Marvel and DC HeroClix superhero collectible miniatures games, and recently brought us *Monte Cook's World of Darkness* (2007) from White Wolf Publishing. Through his own game company, which he runs with his wife Sue, he has released award-winning products such as *Ptolus, Monte Cook's City by the Spire* (2006). A graduate of the Clarion West Science Fiction and Fantasy Workshop, he has published a number of short stories as well as two novels, *The Glass Prison* (1999) and *Of Aged Angels* (2001). Two of his serialized novels, *The Shandler Chronicles* (2002-2004) and *The Saga of the Blade* (2005-2006), appeared in *Game Trade Magazine*. He's also published dozens of articles and essays, and scripted the *Ptolus* series for Marvel Comics. His work has earned him 14 ENWorld RPG Awards, an Origins Award, the Nigel D. Findley Memorial Award, an InQuest Gamer's Choice Fan Award, numerous Pen & Paper Fan Awards, and more.

MEMORIES AND GHOSTS

BY MONTE COOK

WHEN RE-MAGUL FOUND the master dragonstone, he sat down upon it. After a while, he stood again, drew *thu-terris* from its sheath, and resumed his position with the bared blade lying across his lap. The stone was red, although patches of a dark lichen grew on its surface. Its top rose up from the ground about five feet and was about seven feet long.

He waited.

When Re-Magul's jaw began to hurt from being clenched in anger, he stood and performed an ancient giantish ceremony, taught to him by his father, designed to calm the spirit. While the rite did not grant him serenity, at least it gave him something that some might call patience. Others would say that *patience* is too gentle a word. "Grim determination," they would say, or perhaps just "tenacity."

On the third day, a rainstorm rolled in over the Bitter Peaks and drenched the area surrounding the hill where he sat, a place the locals called Draconhill—although none of those Re-Magul had spoken with knew why. The giant warmain appreciated the rainwater, which replenished his own dwindling supply. He caught the big, heavy drops in his helmet to refill his leather waterskins.

When the rain ended, he waited some more.

Nithogar had departed from the host three weeks ago. He had not needed to give them a reason why, but he did mutter something to the elders about checking some of the ancient sites. Which, of course, was the truth.

"A useful tool, the truth can be," he had once told his lair-mate, Jelissican, "but that is all it is—a tool. Not an ethic. Not a goal unto itself."

She never liked it when he spoke that way, so he learned to avoid doing so. Of course, that was lifetimes ago. Dragon lifetimes. When Nithogar had lived in the Land of the Dragons.

When he—and the other elders of the Conclave—had ruled it.

His survey of the ancient sites had borne no fruit. He felt despondent at the sight of so many places his people had once revered and used now fallen into ruin. In fact, *ruin* was not a word that performed its job adequately in this case. The ancient dragon sites were no longer sites at all. They were nothing. An anonymous spot in the woods here, an unnoticed end of a ravine there. Even the topography had changed in the time the dragons had been gone. Rivers had carved new courses, mountains had toppled, and even the coastline had taken a different curve here and there, like the face of a long-lost love, now held tightly in the talons of age.

Nithogar was a stranger to age. The sight of even the land itself changing upset him greatly. He had dwelled upon the world for more centuries than had passed here before his birth. Yet, he had spent most of that time away from this, his ancestral home. There was a crime in that—and, worse, those of his kind who still lived no longer remembered this place. To them, the Land of the Dragons was a tale told in the hatchling dens and dreamed of in monthslong slumbers deep in subterranean caves and high in floating castles. And Nithogar knew he was to blame. But truth was not a goal unto itself, and thus dwelling upon it served no purpose. Guilt was an emotion for lesser beings, a pitfall to be avoided by those with the power and intelligence to reach for the stars.

There were still great deeds to be done, and only those with the will to persevere could accomplish them. He had been granted—no, he had earned—immortality, or something very close. It was not something to squander in regret or remorse. The threat of future regrets was no barrier to stop one such as he.

It had indeed been dragon lifetimes since he had been to this realm. Jelissican's lifetime, to be sure. Thoughts of her urged him onward.

Nithogar drew upon the power of the land around him. It felt warm and familiar as its essence flowed into his outstretched wings. After a savoring moment, he channeled that power into his tired muscles to grant himself speed. There was one more site to visit. It was perhaps the most vital, and thus the most dangerous.

At first, it was just a black spot in the sky. Re-Magul had no doubt as to what it was. He kept his seat upon the reddish stone atop the hill. His shaggy black hair showed tufts of gray, both on his head and in his beard. His helmet lay on the ground next to the rock, but the rest of his towering form was clad in articulated armored plates—except for his hands. He eschewed gauntlets so he could hold *thu-terris* with his bare flesh. That was the way he had entered battle since landing at Khorl, some five hundred years ago.

His steely eyes focused on the ever-growing shape as it approached. Its form grew steadily more distinct, but its color remained black. Wide, sweeping wings were visible, propelling the thing at great speeds. Soon, its long serpentine neck and terrible reptilian head became clear.

A dragon.

Re-Magul resisted the urge to stand. This was what he had been waiting for.

The dragon flew directly toward him, or, perhaps more accurately, toward the master dragonstone upon which he sat.

The huge creature circled Draconhill in a wide arc, its head turned inward as it rounded the giant, studying him. Its shuddering black wings and back, covered in black scales tipped with red, glistened with rainwater. It made the dragon's scales gleam as if they were metal, a dark reddish bronze. It kept its four massive legs tucked loosely under its immense torso as it flew, its belly scales showing more red than black, though its claws were ebon. Of its entire body, easily one hundred feet from nose to tail tip, only its pale teeth and fiery eyes—the color of the hungry desert sun—were something other than black or red.

Finally, the dragon descended, landing quietly in the grass on the side of the hill that the giant warmain faced. It folded its huge wings and took a few steps forward with its head low—right at Re-Magul's eye level, in fact.

"I know who you are, worm," Re-Magul said through teeth clenched so hard that his jaw again ached, but the pain helped him focus his anger. His deep voice sounded weak from disuse.

The dragon cocked its head slightly. "I have no idea who you are, giant," it—or rather *he*—replied with a gravelly voice that, while soft, betrayed its ability to become louder. Much louder. It was as though he were speaking to a child.

Re-Magul could not resist the urge to stand in the face of the creature's obvious contempt. He gripped *thu-terris* so that his knuckles showed white. He arched his back so that he stood at his full eighteen-foot height, stiff bones crunching loudly in his back as he did. His massive chest, like the prow of a mighty ship, thrust toward the dragon. "I am Re-Magul, warmain in the service of Lady Protector Ia-Thordani; oldest of the Hu-Charad; slayer of the dramojh fangmaster Villithiss at the Battle of the Serpent's Heart; commander of the Knights of Diamond; and wielder of the Blade of the East: *thu-terris*, the sword-that-severs-with-icy-flame-as-it-dances."

Nithogar stared at him in silence, without the twitch of a draconic muscle. Eventually, he spoke. "I have no quarrel with you, giant. Remember what your grandfathers must have told you of the ancient pacts, of which their own grandfathers must have spoken before them."

"I have no wish to speak with you of pacts," Re-Magul said, still gritting his teeth.

"I would think not. Those ancient pacts made between your people and my own lord, Erixalimar, the dragon king, forbade you from even coming to this land. Yet here you stand."

Now Re-Magul only stared, his eyes narrowing.

"And it is my understanding that you have been here for some time."

"We came here—" Re-Magul took a breath, then continued "—because this land was in peril. A peril you had wrought, then fled from."

The muscles around the left side of Nithogar's wide mouth twitched.

"You said," the dragon noted, raising its head higher, "that you know who I am."

"Oh, yes. Perhaps you thought that such lore had been lost, but the akashics have made sure your crimes would always be remembered. I know who you are, Nithogar the Wicked. Nithogar the Hated. Nithogar the Despoiler."

"These are epithets I must have earned after I left."

"Then how about this one, dragon: Nithogar, creator of the dramojh." Out of habit, Re-Magul spat as he said both "dragon" and "dramojh."

Nithogar flexed his wings. "You know nothing of it, Hu-Charad."

"Nothing?" Re-Magul's eyes flared. "You are ancient, it is true, but I am no mere youth. I was there when the stone ships arrived on these shores, one of the first off the boats. I remember the battles with the dramojh—the so-called 'dragon scions.' I battled their dark sorcery and demonic powers. I saw friends and relatives die in their claws and teeth. They scuttled out of the shadows and they raped this land like nothing before them or—thank all the singers in the Houses of the Eternal—since."

"So your kind dealt with the dramojh. I am aware of that. And you were some kind of leader in your campaign against them. What do you want from me—gratitude? So be it. Thanks to you, giant, and to all your kind."

And with a sneer, he added quickly: "Now be on your way."

Re-Magul recoiled. No one had ever spoken to him like that regarding the hated dramojh.

The dragon pointed to the east with a long, sharp claw. "Your ancestral home lies in that direction." He lowered his talon and added, "I trust your vaunted sailing craft still work."

"I know where my homeland lies, beast! I left everything and everyone there to come here to deal with the chaos you created."

"Really, giant. Is that so? And what made the dramojh your problem? I recognize that they were an abomination, but why do you, hailing from across the boundless sea, care about such matters?"

"We are the wardens of the land!"

"We *are* the land!"

The shouted words of both giant and dragon echoed dully across the landscape. Each could feel the fevered breath of the other. Re-Magul trembled with anger, while the only change in the dragon's demeanor was an intensity of color growing behind his narrowed eyelids.

The dragon's words were not without their own truth, Re-Magul knew. This was once the Land of the Dragons, and the creatures held a mystical tie to it that even today sages wondered at.

But that was no excuse for their crimes, particularly not this dragon's crimes.

Nithogar spoke again. "You came here because we had gone, and you assumed we would not return. You saw a chance to rule yet another land, under the guise of your vaunted stewardship."

"Lies!"

"You serve the land. You protect all who live in it—as long as they submit to giant rule, is that not so? You are the guardians of all, as long as they obey the will of your sacred Diamond Throne!"

"I'll kill you where you stand!"

"You think you can do what time itself cannot?"

This gave Re-Magul pause. He raised *thu-terris* so that its point—a full twelve feet from its pommel—pointed at the dragon's neck. "Why *are* you still alive, worm? Even dragons grow old and die. Why have you not? Are you so base, so vile, that you have given in to the Dark? Have you succumbed to undeath?"

"There are secrets to magic that you cannot comprehend, giant."

Oh, how he hated dragons. Re-Magul had always felt so, for as long as he had been aware of their existence. Dragons were arrogant, self-serving monsters with no concern for how they might affect the land around them. So powerful and yet so careless with that power. How could he not despise them and all they had wrought?

Especially what they had wrought. Especially what *this* dragon had wrought.

"Like the secrets of magic that allowed you to give birth to the dramojh? That's a secret I don't want to comprehend, monster. That's a secret that resulted in the deaths of thousands and the enslavement of many more. Your actions brought this land to its knees. And yet you claim ties to it. If that's so, why were you not ravaged as it was?"

"Impudent giant. Do you really think the failure of the dramojh did not harm us? *We left our homeland because of them!*"

"You fled in fear of your own creation. You took no responsibility for your actions. You—"

"Enough!" The dragon's roar, issued from his upraised head far above the giant's own, shook Re-Magul's very bones, but he fought not to show it. It resonated through the silence that followed, drifting amid the stones that littered the surrounding hills.

Nithogar's gaze fell upon the red master dragonstone behind the giant.

"How…" he began, lowering his head. "How did you know I would be here?"

Re-Magul smiled mirthlessly. "Perhaps there are secrets to magic that you do not comprehend, dragon. Do not think that your scaly kind has a monopoly on arcane lore and magic spells. Your coming was foreseen by our magisters, and your presence by those who have bonded with the Green. True, not many had the power and insight to see it, but some did, and when I learned of it, my path was clear."

"Your path?"

"I am here to kill you, Nithogar. *Thu-terris* does not leave her sheath lightly."

Nithogar studied the giant standing before him. It had been centuries since the dragon had engaged in physical combat. And even then, he was used to fighting creatures far smaller than this giant. True, in the past, there had been reason for dragon to struggle against dragon, but those days were long gone and better forgotten. Re-Magul was large, even for a giant. The sturdy warrior held his blade in a way that suggested not just skill, but intimate familiarity. And Nithogar could see the arcane power seething within the sword as easily as he could see that it was made of finely tempered steel. The sword had all the markings of something giant-made and ancient. Probably something the giantish armies had brought with them from their own homeland across the Great Eastern Sea. Maybe something brought by Re-Magul himself. He claimed to be that old, but Nithogar had not known that giants were so long-lived. There was much he did not know about giantkind. Why would he? For so long, they had simply been the folk of distant lands, of little concern to him and his kind after the pact wrought by Erixalimar ensured that they would never come to these shores.

But now they were here, entrenched in the ancestral homeland of all dragonkind. They had broken the pact. Perhaps they had done it in the name of what they saw as a good cause, but that was irrelevant—particularly now.

"You have threatened me with death twice now, giant," Nithogar said softly but without a mote of gentleness. "I can look at you and tell that you are prepared to stand behind your words. You want to slay me with every fiber of your being. So why address me at all? Why not await me here with an army to sling stones and arrows into the sky at my approach, with a phalanx of your so-called warmains ready to charge when I landed?"

How much could he know? the dragon wondered. The folk of the realm seemed to have forgotten the ancient sites of dragon power, each centered around one of the magical, reddish dragonstones. Perhaps not all had been forgotten. But did this giant know the significance of this site above all the others?

As if he had read Nithogar's mind, Re-Magul responded, "Before you die, I want to know why your kind have returned." He took a step backward and pointed his sword at the dragonstone. "Does it have something to do with this?"

Nithogar could not help betraying his dismay with a gasp.

"It's of obvious value to you, dragon. But is it why you have returned?"

Nithogar regained his composure, reminding himself that surely the giant's blade could do no harm to the magical stone. "You don't realize it, giant, but you ask two questions, not one."

Re-Magul stared back at the dragon without a change to his angry countenance.

"You ask why my kind has come back, and the answer is simple. This is our land. Our time of self-imposed exile has reached its end. The Dragon Conclave is composed of different dragons now—except for me. Those who led us out of this land are gone and, in fact, even their children are gone. Time has a way of..." Nithogar readjusted his wings uncomfortably, "changing things.

"But," the dragon continued, "you also ask about the stone, and why I have come back. That is a very different question with a very different answer."

Nithogar examined Re-Magul for any sign that might betray what he knew about this particular site, then said, "And it is an answer I have no intention of granting you, if for no other reason than you threaten me with your paltry weapon."

The insult seemed to shake Re-Magul, but he clearly possessed more self-control than the dragon had given him credit for.

"You asked me why I did not bring an army with me," the giant said. "I could ask the same of you. Where is the draconic host that, I have heard, darkens the sky with its numbers? Why are you here alone? Is it because this place—this rock—has something to do with the creation of the dramojh?"

Was he really asking, or did he already know? Nithogar mused.

The dragon sighed. "I wonder," he said, "will every dragon find a giant with a sword wherever he goes in this land? Must there be war?"

"Answer my question, dragon."

"Perhaps, after you answer mine. Why are *you* here alone?"

Re-Magul ran a hand through his beard, letting the tip of his sword almost touch the ground. He worked his jaw slightly.

"No. War is not inevitable. I do not speak for all giantkind. I do not even speak for the Lady Protector in this instance. You are the progenitor of the dramojh, Nithogar. I cannot abide you in the land I struggled and bled for. I came here, alone, of my own will and no other's. You are the root of virtually all this land's shadows. I could, perhaps, permit the dragons to return. But not you."

"Permit?" Nithogar spat. "I called you impudent before, but I was wrong. That is arrogance. Misplaced arrogance. We are dragons. This is our land. You permit or deny us nothing."

"Things have changed, dragon. This *was* your land, but you abandoned it. We are its stewards now. Were it not for us, it would be a wasteland: barren of life and broken forever from the Green."

Nithogar raised a massive claw, blocking the rays of the setting sun as it sank to the tops of the distant Bitter Peaks. Re-Magul was cast in shadow. The giant responded by raising his sword with both hands above his head.

With a roar that shook both the warmain and the hill upon which he stood, Nithogar brought his talon down upon the giant. Re-Magul called upon the power within *thu-terris*, and the blade flared with blue flame. With a mighty swing, he deflected the dragon's strike and cut into the scaly flesh of the claw.

Nithogar did not utter a sound with the wound, but he did rear his head back in surprise.

The giant stood his ground and gripped his sword tightly, holding it low to the ground in a hunched, defensive stance.

"I wondered how long it would be before you came to blows," a voice said.

Both dragon and giant turned toward the sound. Standing on the north end of the hill was a reptilian creature covered in scales: yellow-gold on its back and brownish-copper on its belly and limbs. It was not as large as Nithogar, but it was thick and broad where he was thin and snakelike. And the new creature bore no wings on its back.

Another dragon.

Re-Magul was ready to fight one dragon, but two? His hopes for surviving until nightfall diminished to nil. Still, he stood firm.

"Afraid to face me alone, Nithogar?" Re-Magul taunted. His mind raced for some strategy. Perhaps angering the dragon further might buy him some time.

The black dragon ignored him, however, and spoke to the newcomer in Draconic. Re-Magul had studied the ancient language of dragons, however, and understood the words: "Who are you?"

The yellow and brown dragon's voice was gruff, sounding almost like stones rattling around in an iron bucket. "You don't remember me, I'm sure. I was very young when you left. My name is Cohalisaram, or… it was. No one has had cause to use that name in five thousand years or more. Yes, Nithogar, I am one of those you left behind, and I still live. There are a couple of us still here, and a few children and grandchildren of those who stayed when the dragon host left. I may not have the power of the tenebrian seeds to give me long life, but there are other means."

Then Cohalisaram turned to Re-Magul and spoke in Giantish. "Greetings, Hu-Charad. I have taken great pains never to meet one of your kind in person, until today, of course."

"How—?" Nithogar began.

"Did I approach you," Cohalisaram interrupted, "without you seeing or hearing me?" The dragon gave a gruff laugh. "I'd like to say it was because the two of you were too busy posturing for one another's benefit, but the truth is that—like those few others of our kind who remained in this realm—I have adapted to a life of secrecy. I have learned to step between the moments. I hide within time itself."

Re-Magul had no idea what that meant, but it was nonetheless true that a dragon like Cohalisaram, who must weigh at least one hundred tons, should not have been able to approach the hill undetected without the aid of some kind of magic.

"And what," Nithogar said, "is your business here? Have you come for the stone?"

"I have had millennia to access this stone. Why would I come for it now?"

"So you have come here because of one of us," Nithogar stated, cocking his head to one side ever so slightly.

Re-Magul stood tall and held his sword before him in a new but still fully defensible stance.

"Both of you, actually," Cohalisaram replied.

"Explain," was all Re-Magul could manage. He reflected back to his ceremony of calming to keep his rage in check. His hatred for dragons made it difficult to concentrate on their words. And he had not come here to talk.

Cohalisaram took a few steps closer. "I suppose, in the tales of old from the Denotholan, I would be the threat that provides a reason for you two enemies to work together. That, however, is not my intent. I have no desire to enter combat with either of you. Frankly, I have no doubt that either of you could best me. I have spent eons perfecting ways of avoiding fights, not winning them."

Re-Magul shook his head with distrust.

Cohalisaram turned his attention to the giant. "You knew Nithogar was coming, and you knew who he was, but do you know his purpose here? Do you know the stone's significance?"

Nithogar gave a low growl.

"This specific stone?" Cohalisaram asked.

The answer was no, but the giant did not care. His mind was focused only on slaying the dragon he had come here to slay and avenging the dead he had come here to avenge.

Cohalisaram did not explain further. Instead, he turned his wide head back toward Nithogar. "And do you know who Re-Magul is? Even I, cloistered away, know of this hero and his position as the eldest of the giants."

Nithogar spat something like a laugh. "Like that means anything to me, the eldest of the dragons—"

"You forget yourself, ancient one. I may not be as old as you, but I am old enough to remember great Erixalimar, who still lives."

Nithogar shook his head at the mention of the name, as if shooing away a buzzing insect.

"So an old giant and an old dragon meet..." Re-Magul said, rubbing his beard.

"Two old dragons," Cohalisaram added with a lilt to his voice that seemed strange coming from the massive creature.

Re-Magul smiled in spite of himself. "Either way," the giant said, "it sounds like the beginning of a joke a faen would tell."

Cohalisaram laughed loudly and long, showing teeth that looked like sharp stones.

"Very well," Nithogar said when the other dragon had finished. "Evening comes and with it more rain, most likely. You have stopped our battle before it really started, which is fine with me. Why don't the two of you move along somewhere else now?"

"Oh no, Nithogar," Cohalisaram said. "We haven't even told the giant about the dramojh within the rock."

Re-Magul stared at the master dragonstone, then back at Nithogar. He once again gripped his weapon in both hands, as though readying an attack.

Nithogar wondered at the other dragon's motives for causing him this trouble. He had no problem slaying the giant if he must, but Nithogar did not have the stomach for fighting another dragon this night—particularly one that seemed to have honed his draconic nature in new and unknown ways.

As the sky darkened, Re-Magul finally broke the uneasy silence. "Dramojh? In the rock?" He prodded the stone with his sword. "Impossible."

"Once again," Nithogar replied, "we find your knowledge of the possible to be sorely lacking." The dragon tensed, raising his head high. "What my... brother says is true."

"That cannot be," Re-Magul said softly, more to himself than to the dragons. "The dramojh are all dead or driven from the world. We saw to it. We were thorough."

"Indeed," Cohalisaram agreed, his manner betraying a respect for the giants that Nithogar did not share.

"Calm yourself," Nithogar said. "The dramojh are all gone. If there is a dramojh within the stone, it is dead."

Re-Magul's brow furrowed in confusion and perhaps distrust. Cohalisaram looked at Nithogar expectantly.

Nithogar sighed and glanced around distractedly before speaking. "I put a spell on a number of dragonstones and sent them to sites important to us. The spell was a contingency, so that if ever the dramojh were destroyed, some of their essence would remain preserved within them. Time has worn away the enchantment on the other stones. This is the last one, but it is the most powerful."

"And here," Cohalisaram said, "the spell remained and performed its function."

Before Nithogar could ask the other dragon how he knew this, Re-Magul shook his head, his eyes wide. "Why? By all that is holy, *why*?"

Lies filled Nithogar's head, but his anger wouldn't allow him to speak them. "Because I wasn't done with them, giant! There was still work to be done!"

"Work? Those... demonic things..." Re-Magul sputtered.

As the giant and dragon faced off in rage once again, Cohalisaram opened his mouth wide and, from deep within his throat, a thin stream of silver and green energy poured forth. It did not move in a straight line, nor was it necessarily quick. It danced and meandered through the air. Re-Magul cried out and lifted his sword defensively. Nithogar just stared.

The energy worked its way around the giant and instead struck the dragonstone. The rock glowed silently with the stream's silvery-green essence. The surrounding hills had grown as noiseless as the three of them standing there, looking at the stone.

A creature stepped forth from the glow. It was dark but glistening, like the web of a spider, and translucent. Nithogar had seen such a creature before. "A ghost..." Its body was like a scale-covered mockery of a spider, too many legs splayed out from a twisted form. It had a long, serpentine neck and a demonic face that seemed to be all teeth and eyes. Fluttering, nervous wings like those of a bat curled on its back. The thing did not move, it seeped, as if it were oil and the air a sieve.

It was a dramojh.

No," Re-Magul said, "it can't be real." He looked to Cohalisaram for some kind of explanation, but somehow the dragon was gone. Just gone.

The dramojh was a liquid shadow. Each second that passed seemed to cause a ripple to move along its surface. It looked around, as if attempting to gain its bearings.

Every nightmare that had ever haunted Re-Magul's sleep or shook his waking thoughts had suddenly come true. Like so many of his brethren, the giant had sworn to never rest, never allow himself to exit the Wardance, never stop hating, until the demon-dragons were gone. Now, one stood in front of him, dripping darkness like a festering cancer. His soul cried in anguish at the sight of it, but his determination fought to keep his mind clear.

This thing was a dramojh, but it was different, too. Ephemeral. Ethereal. Like the dragon had said, a *dead* dramojh. This was not one of the creatures Re-Magul had struggled for so long to destroy. It was the shadow of one of them, preserved by perverse magic—a crime against the land, to say the least.

The shadow of the dramojh focused its gaze on Nithogar, ignoring the giant.

Father/Betrayer. Kin-Abandoner. Maker/Forsaker. Scion-Slayer. The shadow's thoughts were Re-Magul's thoughts—and Nithogar's as well, presumably. Re-Magul had experienced telepathy before, but this was different. There was no other voice in his head. The ghost spoke to him with his own mental voice.

Left us alone. Left us to die.

"We had to leave," Nithogar whispered.

Fearful. Distrustful. Incapable of dealing with the consequences.

"No," the dragon shook his head ever so slightly. "I was going to come back. Sooner. Much sooner. But the West. It held... things... unknown to the Conclave. Matters became very complicated."

Nithogar seemed to shrink.

We are forsaken. We are gone.

"Damn right!" Re-Magul said, pointing the tip of his sword at the creature.

The shadow turned toward the giant, looking him in the eye for the first time. *Slaughterer. Murderer.*

"Of horrors like you? Yes!" Re-Magul launched himself at the ghostly dramojh and swung *thu-terris* in a wide arc. This must end. The shadow had already contaminated the world too long with its unexpected presence.

The warmain's magical blade flamed through the shadow, tearing at it like a hand splashing through greasy, thick oil. And, like oil, the blade slicing through it did not seem to affect it at all, except to cause its surface to ripple slightly.

Worse, *thu-terris* clouded over with a darkness that oozed into its blade like blood into water. Without warning or threat, *thu-terris*, the Blade of the East, died in Re-Magul's hands.

Nithogar saw the light fade from the giant's sword like a candle snuffed. He watched as the shadow dramojh focused its dark abhorrence toward the giant, and imagined that, hundreds of years ago, such a scene would have been commonplace in the land where they now stood. The dragon wondered at his creation.

Even as he watched, he could not help but remember his last experience with his scions. His plans to wrest control of the Conclave from those dragons who opposed him had reached its fruition. Dramojh by the tens of thousands swarmed over their mountain palace. Dragon fought against dragon, but the sudden appearance of the squirming horde of the dramojh made the outcome of this final battle a foregone conclusion. Scales were torn from dragon flesh, and flesh was rent from dragon bone. Dark, thick blood, rich with power, flowed down the mountainside in grisly torrents. But even as victory belonged to Nithogar, he saw his creations turn against him and his allies. Like an infection, the dramojh suddenly had no cause to discriminate—they swarmed over all dragons.

Nithogar surveyed this scene, even now calmly monitoring the unplanned contingency, wondering how to control the new situation, or at least turn it to his benefit. But then he saw her.

Jelissican.

The dramojh, born of a fusion of his own essence and the dark but potent magic of the tenebrian seeds, the result of his matchless intellect and dauntless pursuit of power, swarmed like hungry locusts over his lair-mate. In his mind's eye she fought valiantly—Jelissican's physical power matched or exceeded his own—but the dramojh were numberless. For every five that fell with a sweep of her rending claws, ten more took their place. For every dozen consumed in the fiery blasts of her breath, two dozen more swarmed over their remains to renew their sorcerous attacks.

Nithogar did not see Jelissican die. Her green and golden form was buried in black dramojh bodies, spreading over her like the darkness spreading into Re-Magul's sword.

There was no way to turn this situation to Nithogar's advantage. Somehow, just as all his plans had reached fruition, everything that mattered died.

He had heard much later that the day of his would-be triumph ended with Erixalimar's arrival on the scene with a host of celestial beings who, together with the dragons' lord, eradicated the dramojh horde and sent the last few survivors squirming into deep holes in the Bitter Peaks, from which they would eventually emerge to blight the land once more. But Nithogar was long gone, fled to the West.

He could not speak for the dragons who'd come with him, but he knew that with every beat of his wings he'd been fleeing from himself. Fleeing from what he had wrought.

And now, after millennia, he stood before his progeny again.

Hate. Revulsion. Disgust. Contempt. Loathing.

With a taloned claw, the dramojh reached for Re-Magul. *Thuterris* was cold and dead in the giant's hands, and he could not move it to block the strike. The shadow's hand seeped through his armor as effortlessly as it seeped through the air, and the giant felt a coldness—felt a *darkness*—enter him. He cried out.

"After all these centuries," Nithogar whispered. "Guilt is an emotion for lesser beings." His voice grew louder, but he spoke as if reciting a mantra. "Truth is not a goal unto itself."

The dramojh shadow continued its attack upon Re-Magul. The giant quivered, helpless to act, engulfed by the cold and darkness only a dead demon could wield.

"I was wrong," Nithogar said.

The shadow ignored him.

"I should have known then, as I watched her last moments. Passion served nothing, I thought. Revenge, guilt, anger—these could not serve me, I said. I only had to forget. I had thought I could exorcise these feelings through absence, but I was wrong. After so long, I know now that I must remember."

Nithogar rose to his full height. He seemed to draw power from the hill itself and fill himself with it.

"You were a *mistake!*" Nithogar's front claws, shimmering with a power all their own, came crashing down upon the specter. Out of the corner of his eye, Re-Magul saw the glistening fire, and recognized its color and texture. He had seen it before, in the pattern deep within the rune of every runechild and the heart of every spell. It was the power of the land itself, and it tore through the shadowy demon, spattering darkness and defilement across the hill and across Re-Magul.

The ghost wavered and drew away from the giant, whirling like a vortex of black water to face Nithogar. It hissed within his mind incoherently.

Re-Magul lay in the grass, blackened and charred from the dramojh's eldritch power. His sword had been torn from his grasp. He fought to remain conscious, his heart and lungs so cold that he could not breathe; his blood had almost stilled within his veins.

Dragon and dramojh clashed in mid-air, like a moth crashing into a flame. But which was which? Re-Magul shielded his eyes from the brilliant blaze of power and darkness—a conflagration that both lit up and dimmed the twilight upon the hill.

And then he was alone.

Nithogar and the spirit had vanished. The dragonstone was sundered into two halves, although Re-Magul was unsure how it had happened.

But no, he was not alone.

Cohalisaram once again stood on the hill, also gazing at the stone. His massive form looked almost like part of the hill.

Re-Magul said nothing. He struggled to his feet and walked to where he had dropped *thu-terris*. A dark streak still cut across the silver of the blade, but it had stopped spreading. The sword still felt cold and heavy. Lifeless.

The giant felt likewise.

"I'd like to hear the ending of that faen joke," Cohalisaram said, lowering his body to the ground, resting his head on his folded forelimbs.

"I am a very old giant," Re-Magul said quietly. "And still I have never taken the time to learn the art of jokes."

The giant continued to stare at his sword, and Cohalisaram did not reply. The hilltop was silent for a time.

"I have been sustained by anger and hatred," Re-Magul said finally. "A need for revenge. My hatred for dragons—for dramojh—seems to have sustained me as clearly as Nithogar's magic sustained him."

Cohalisaram snorted. "And I by my fear. My need to hide.

"But now," he continued, "I believe that need must pass. Perhaps I should no longer hide between the moments, but become a part of them. It is time I came forward, as I did today."

Re-Magul studied the dragon. "Are you saying we must change? Adapt to the present... or the future?" The giant sheathed his dead sword on his back. "I think I am too old to change."

Cohalisaram laughed. "My friend! Have you paid no attention at all? You may be the oldest of your kind, but did you not watch, as I just did, one of the oldest beings of all recognize his mistake and decide to change?"

"And it killed him." Re-Magul gestured at the empty air.

"Oh, I don't know about that," Cohalisaram said. "From the tales I've heard, it might take a lot more than that to kill a dragon like Nithogar. Whether he is gone or not, I am heartened by what I saw."

"And you think a giant can learn from a dragon?"

Cohalisaram raised a claw as if to mirror the giant's gesture at the empty air. "Two dragons."

Now it was Re-Magul's turn to laugh, something he had not done for a long time.

"Perhaps you are right," Re-Magul said, still laughing. "Perhaps I have it in me to change."

"I have it," Cohalisaram said, his monstrous visage brightening. "A dragon and a giant meet on a hill. A dragon and a giant leave a hill. But it's not the same dragon—and it's not the same giant."

"I'm no faen, but that's not very funny."

"Perhaps it's more of a proverb then a joke, then. You giants like those, don't you?"

"Dragons teaching giants proverbs," Re-Magul said, laughing again. "What could possibly come next?"

"I, for one, will be interested to see," the dragon said.

Lisa Smedman

Lisa Smedman is an accomplished writer and game designer, with 15 novels published to date. In February 2004, her novel *Extinction*, set in the Forgotten Realms shared world, made the *New York Times* bestseller list. Her non-shared world novels include *The Apparition Trail* (2004), an alternative history set in the Canadian west of 1884, and *Creature Catchers* (2007), a children's fantasy set in an alternative Victorian England with mythological creatures. She has designed adventures for the Advanced Dungeons & Dragons game, as well as for the Indiana Jones and Star Wars roleplaying games. She has also written three one-act plays that were produced by an amateur Vancouver theater group, and is the author of numerous short stories. A journalist for more than 20 years, she currently splits her week between her "day job" as an editor and columnist at Vancouver's third largest newspaper and writing fiction. She was one of the founders of *Adventures Unlimited*, a magazine for roleplaying game enthusiasts. She facilitates a bi-weekly writers' workshop and has been active in organizing science fiction conventions.

When not writing in franchise settings like the Forgotten Realms, Smedman most often crafts alternative historical fantasy. Her favorite starting points are the Canadian west of the 1880s and the Bronze Age. She views writing historical fantasy similar to writing in a shared world: The settings are fixed (although often mutated, hence the "alternative"), as are the names and general attributes of many of the real-world historical characters she uses. The fun part for her comes in playing with the "what ifs" of history. Smedman also creates settings entirely of her own devising, from fantasy to cyberpunk. The joy there is not being bound by any existing rulebooks and having the freedom to come up with a future or a magical system entirely of her own. "The writing," she notes, "is much quicker, if you don't have to stop to look everything up!"

About "Three Impossible Things," Smedman explains: "The story is too short to claim to detail a 'world,' but it is an original setting. The work was the result of an exercise my writing group did, in which we all endeavored to write a 1,000-word story from the same illustration. We chose an Arthur Rackham illustration of goblins. The starting point for the exercise was the old expression 'a picture's worth a thousand words.' None of us quite managed to keep our stories within 1,000 words, but it was fun seeing the wide variety of worlds that came out of the exercise, each as different as its creator, even though we all started from the same 'scene.'"

THREE IMPOSSIBLE THINGS

BY LISA SMEDMAN

THE GOBLIN'S EYES glowed yellow with reflected moonlight as it stared down at the supplicant from atop the ruined stone wall in the forest. It raised a small silver bell in gnarled fingers and cocked a pointed ear.

"Ye be not brother to her, then?" it asked. "Nor uncle, nor cousin?"

The supplicant—a slender human with tousled brown hair and bare feet, dressed in knee-length trousers and a baggy peasant shirt—answered clearly. "I am none of those things."

The bell pealed once, a thin silver note in the darkness.

"Do ye love Madiline?" the goblin asked.

"I love her," the supplicant replied, eyes suddenly glistening. The bell pealed again.

Low chuckles gurgled in the forest around them, indicating they were not alone. The goblin waited until they fell silent. "This one speaks the truth," it pronounced. Then, to the supplicant, "Know ye this. To claim Madiline, ye must perform three impossible tasks, without the aid of magic. Fail at any one, and ye will die."

The supplicant nodded.

"If ye succeed, Madiline is yours," the goblin continued. "But ye must swear an oath: the first child from any union of ye and she is ours, upon its thirteenth year. Do ye so swear?"

"I do."

The goblin chuckled, then glanced at a bucket that sat on the wall next to it. With a smirk that revealed pointed yellow teeth, it kicked the bucket to the human, who caught it deftly. "There be a stream, a short walk to the north. Ye must use this bucket to empty it. We will return, at Fullnight on the morrow, to see if the task be done." Then it hopped backward off the wall, disappearing from sight. Chortling laughter followed in its wake, along with one word, whispered on many tongues. "Impossible."

The supplicant stared at the bucket for a long moment, then grimly nodded as an idea sparkled in dark brown eyes. "Nothing's impossible."

The supplicant knelt, exhausted, arms and legs smeared with mud and hair limp with sweat. The bucket lay next to an empty streambed whose rocks still glistened in the moonlight. The stream itself now flowed through a channel that had been scraped in the forest floor. It poured with a loud gurgle down the steps of a ruined tower, into its dungeon.

"Very clever," the goblin said, leaning on a broom as it surveyed the rerouted stream. "But when the dungeon be full, the stream will seek its course again."

"You told me to empty the stream," retorted the supplicant, standing wearily. "You didn't specify for how long."

"Hmph," the goblin snorted. "The task be done, then."

From the darkness behind it came disappointed grunts and the soft slither of steel, as its fellows slid swords back into scabbards.

The goblin tossed the broom it held at the supplicant and pointed at a tree with a trunk so wide that two humans—or three goblins—would have been hard pressed to encircle it. "The second task is to fell that tree, using this broom." It spat in the empty streambed, and smirked. "Dig all ye want, this time; it won't help ye none. The roots be as deep as the moon is high."

As the goblin slipped away into darkness, the supplicant picked up the broom and hefted it like a lever, eyebrows knitted together in a frown, then stared at the clump of dirty straw tied to one end. "Who said anything about digging?"

When the goblin saw what the supplicant had done, it broke two teeth, so fiercely did it gnash them. Spitting out the jagged bits, it glared at the roaring fire that blazed brightly around the charred and smoking stump. The rest of the tree lay beside the fire, on a bed of smaller, splintered trees that had been knocked down when it fell.

"Ye cheated!" the goblin snarled. "Ye used fire."

This time, its fellow goblins were visible in the firelight, their skin made even ruddier by the licking flames. They stood no taller than the supplicant's waist, but like a pack of savage wolves, were capable of swift destruction.

The supplicant glared back at them, eyes bright in a soot-smudged face. "I used the straw as kindling, and the handle and string to make a fire drill. Without the broom, there'd have been no fire. The broom felled the tree."

"That be true," the goblin leader said grudgingly. Then it leered. "The third task be the most impossible of all." It stalked toward a weed-choked staircase that led up to a ruined manor and pointed at a loose stone, about the size of a loaf of bread, at its base. "This stone must be moved to the top of the stair," it announced, "without ye touching it in any way, or using any object to touch it."

The supplicant counted the stairs—fully thirty of them—then turned to the goblin. "If it can be done, you will honor the oath we swore?"

"*If* it can be done."

"Then bring Madiline to this spot tomorrow night."

The goblin nodded, then pointed a gnarled finger at one of its companions. "Watch this one," it ordered. "Be sure there is no cheating."

Madiline staggered through the forest, compelled to follow the goblins by the leather thong around her wrists and the spear point at her back. They jerked on her lead and prodded her with the spear, then dabbled dirty fingers in the blood that trickled down her bare back and sucked its potency from their finger-tips. The girl's blond hair, which had hung to her waist two years ago when her father honored his oath on her thirteenth birthday, had been shaved from her scalp. Her bare feet were blistered and cracked, her dress reduced to a rag that hung in tatters from her hips. As they led her to the supplicant, who stood at the bottom of the ruined staircase, her eyes widened in recognition.

The goblin leader noted this—and the pained look the supplicant returned to the girl—with a leer. Then it glanced at the loose stone, still lying unmoved at the base of the staircase.

"Ye have failed," it told the supplicant. "Ye will die."

The goblins behind it licked their lips and wrenched swords out of scabbards.

"Wait!" The supplicant pointed up at the moon, which was just rising above distant hills. "It's not yet Fullnight. I have some moments yet to complete the task."

Muttering, the goblins looked to their leader, who rolled yellow eyes, then nodded at the stone. "Move it, then, if ye can."

Ignoring the goblin, the supplicant stepped toward the girl and reached out to tilt up her chin. "Madiline, are you still strong?"

"They use me poorly," she answered in a strained voice. "But, yes, I am still strong."

The supplicant's voice dropped to a whisper. "Strong enough to...?"

The girl's eyes widened as the supplicant whispered in her ear, and she nodded.

Even as the goblins strained forward to hear what was being said, the supplicant wrenched the thong away from the one that held it and knocked the others away from Madiline with a flurry of kicks and blows. Madiline, suddenly free, seemed poised to run away into the night. The goblin behind her leaped forward, blocking her way, but instead of trying to pass her captor, she stooped and picked up the loose stone. Grunting, she lifted it despite her bound wrists, and staggered up the stairs. The goblins tried to grab the thong that still trailed from her wrists, but the supplicant pushed them back. A moment later, a panting Madiline dropped the stone a heartbeat before four goblins who'd surged up the stair grabbed her. The stone struck the top stair with a loud thud just as the moon climbed fully above the distant hills, marking the dawn of Fullnight.

"The third task is done!" the supplicant cried, half-buried under a swarm of goblins. Then, "Let me go!"

A furious look in its eye, the goblin leader beat its fellows until they fell back from the supplicant. "Ye did not complete the task," it howled, pointing at the spot where Madiline stood. "She did! Ye are *mine* to kill."

The supplicant, nose bloodied and arms and legs bruised, struggled to rise. "You said I couldn't touch the stone or use any object to move it. I didn't. I used a person, instead. You must honor your oath and set Madiline free."

The goblin's eyes narrowed to mere slits. It glanced up at the stone—and at Madiline, whose eyes shone with triumphant hope and love for her rescuer. "Very well," it answered, in a voice grim as disease. "Ye have won the girl. But ye must honor your part of the oath, as well, by gifting us the first child of your union, upon its thirteenth year." It crooked a gnarled finger at the goblins who held Madiline, indicating they should escort her down the stairs, then turned evilly gleaming eyes back upon the supplicant. "The pact will continue, as it has done these three hundred years, since the kingdom of humans fell."

"No, it won't," the supplicant answered.

"Eh? What do ye mean by that? Ye swore ye were fertile, and your words rang true."

"I am fertile," the supplicant said, taking Madiline's hand. "I am also a girl. I'm Madiline's sister."

"No!" the other goblins howled. "A trick! Kill her!"

Fury blazed in the goblin leader's eyes, but at the same time it whirled on its fellows. "Stop!" it ordered. "I swore an oath, by the Foul One Below. Would you face his wrath?"

Grumbling, the goblins shook their heads. One or two spat on their blades, cutting their words.

"Farewell, then," Madiline's sister said. Grasping Madiline's hand, one wary eye still on the goblins, she led her older sister away.

"Hrmph," the goblin leader spat. Then it glanced around at the ruins that dotted the forest. "We set him—her—three impossible tasks. And she succeeded at four. I fear these humans are becoming too clever, by far."

Greg Stafford

Greg Stafford's mythic tales of Glorantha began as short stories and novels during late nights in his freshman year at college. "I had run out of mythology books and stories to read, and began my own to fill the gap," he says. "This was before I discovered Tolkien, Moorcock, or any fantasy or science fiction at all. I naively thought I was the first person to create an entire fantasy world."

Stafford wrote considerable background for the world over the years, punctuated by lacks of time or energy to work. Glorantha became a game setting in 1975 with the publication of *White Bear & Red Moon*, the first professional fantasy board wargame. Stafford describes the project as a "do-it-yourself novel," where the game provides the setting and characters, and each play of the game determines the plot. A few years later Glorantha became the setting for the revolutionary roleplaying game RuneQuest (1978), and the two have been associated ever since. Glorantha has been the subject of other board games and roleplaying games, as well as a highly regarded computer game, with 1999's *King of Dragon Pass*. "Near the End of the World" was first published in issue #43 of the semiprozine *Space & Time*, published by Gordon Linzner in 1977. It appeared again in *Book of Drastic Resolutions, Chaos* in 1998.

Stafford is quick to note how the participation of other creative people has been vital to the setting's growth and success. "I am one of the luckiest guys alive," he explains. "Hundreds of people have helped to facilitate the manifestation of my vision. Even at the time I wrote the first Glorantha short story, back in 1966, I thought it'd be great to eventually have a whole bunch of people working on the world. I saw that it might be too big for just me."

Stafford was one of the key publishers and authors during the earliest days of the roleplaying game industry. He's the designer, co-designer, or developer for five groundbreaking RPGs—RuneQuest, Pendragon (1985), Ghostbusters (1986), Prince Valiant (1989), and HeroQuest (2003)—the computer game *King of Dragon Pass*, five board games, and innumerable supplements, including *Cults of Prax* (1979), *Trolkpak* (1982), and *Thunder Rebels* (2001). He founded and led the seminal game company Chaosium, Inc. during the height of its creativity, when it published Call of Cthulhu, Thieves' World, Ringworld, Elfquest, and many other trendsetting titles. You can visit his webpage at www.weareallus.com.

NEAR THE END OF THE WORLD

BY GREG STAFFORD

The Slime Deer

THE PRAYERMAN WAS on his way to help the Old Lady when he discovered the slime deer. He heard a peculiar barking sound up ahead, an alien noise like nothing he'd heard before, and cautiously made his way forward. He fingered his holybeads and said the proper prayers as he went, aware that he was sweating, that his cloak itched, and that his knuckles were white from clutching his prayerstick. But he went on, for facing the unknown was part of his calling. He topped a knoll and looked down at the fight.

They appeared to be headless, but the prayerman noticed the hunk of rotted flesh and bone hanging from the shoulders, where a neck should have been; instead, in that place, was an opening that barked out a jet of greasy slime when the creatures attacked. They knelt with their front legs, rumps raised high, and exposed the neck valve to aim. There were up to a dozen kneeling at a time, with dozens of others circling clumsily on their decaying legs.

They fought a red man who was no easy prey. He was surrounded by a ruddy aura, which meant that the fire gods were among his ancestors. When the slime touched this flame it sizzled and made a thick green smoke that slid down the aural shield. Clumps of this smoke dotted the hollow like poisonous ghosts of dead bushes. Along with butchered pieces of the slime deer, they marked the path of the fight.

The prayerman was fascinated with the perfection of the fighting man's attack. He had several short spears made of pure fire metal. These were threaded like needles to a rack of spools about his belt, and unwound perfectly or wound back up again at the man's cast or pull. A thrown spear passed through is target, but the barbed tip embedded in the ground behind the deer. As the man leapt around, the spools kept the wires taut so that the thin, jerking thread cut the slime deer to pieces.

The prayerman looked upon the innards of the dead animals. The whole body had been changed, and its organs were now made of the same sickening slime that covered its once-sleek coat. A shudder of disgust and horror shook the prayerman. But he had little time to dwell on his reaction.

From the knoll he could see that the warrior was being contained to a small area. His attacks were successful, leaving many pieces and puddles of slime behind. But these fragments were not more dead than alive, and continued to move as if possessed of some grotesque intelligence. They formed a mass, a rolling marsh of decaying, corrosive green-black slime. It moved, like a giant melted slug, to encircle the fighter.

That was how Chaos had looked when the prayerman encountered it before. Despite the thing's familiarity, he knew he would never get used to the sight. It was never easy to look upon something that would sear your soul with the touch of the Abyss, then swallow even that tainted remnant. But the prayerman looked, for he had chosen that calling, and he acted.

He ignored the bushes that tore at his ragged cloak as he made his way closer to the mass and the slime deer. One of the beasts stumbled in trying to turn and reach him, and spewed a puddle of ooze over itself and the ground. The prayerman decided he was close enough and held his prayerstick above his head with both hands as he yelled. Fear, as well as faith, added to his voice.

"This is the Cloak of the Law! This is the Standard of Being! I am the Order, and this is the Way! All Chaos fades before me."

The quivering mass did not slow, nor turn away. Necrotic heads loomed from the mass in meaningless inquiry. Shattered bones thrashed wildly as it crept closer. The prayerman stood his ground. Off to the side the slime deer fell back from him, and the fiery warrior began carefully making his way toward the newcomer.

The deer crept to within a foot of the prayerman; they stank like the offal of the demon gods. He trembled and prayed and held on to his faith. The forward edge of the glob seemed to gel. By the time the warrior reached his side the quivering mass was covered with a thin shell of gum, like a bubble of pus. The men looked at each other once, then turned and ran. Behind them the bag burst as a slime deer stumbled into it, and spread a widening pool of thick yellow tar.

The men ran together, the warrior in the lead. They were no longer strangers, but comrades in war. They didn't speak until they reached a muddy stream, where they washed off their fear and the dirt, and decided to spend the night.

The Left Arm of Dehore

"What *were* those things?" asked the warrior. He was red, as if he'd lingered in the sun too long, and completely hairless. Over his armor he wore a fine embroidered shirt, which was faded by age, but untorn.

"Part of Chaos, though I don't know their origin," said he prayerman. "I'd hoped you would know."

"I know nothing of this," said the other. "I was a recluse in my mountain before the increasing snows drove me out. I hunted the mountain deer, until one day they were all, every one of them, blotched by that slime."

"There were certainly many," said the prayerman. "Perhaps that herd ate some corrupt bushes, for it is certain that creatures do not just become part of Chaos by themselves."

"Then all the deer food in this country is tainted," said the warrior. "I have not seen one, not a white-tail or black-tail or four-horned deer that was not slowly turning to grease."

The red man looked uneasily about him, at the seemingly normal rush of life on the riverbank. The prayerman looked, too, finding an immense calm in the minute details of each perfect leaf. He knew they might be the last ones in the world, and so he loved them as if they were.

"It makes me feel ill at the prospect of eating," continued the warrior. "Can a man know what is tainted when a beast of the wild does not?"

"I can ease that pain for you," said the prayerman. "Refresh yourself in the water; it is pure, I assure you. I know that poisoned water is unable to stay in its bed and drifts as much up into the air as down to the ocean. While you do that, I must pray."

The prayerman had few tools, but his skill with them was great. He placed the prayerstick upright on the ground and laid his newly scrubbed cloak over it. Then he knelt, praying and giving his word, heart, and all to the gods. The warrior sat, watching and soaking his feet in the stream. Finally the prayerman was done, refreshed and cleansed deeper than any water can touch. He picked up his cloak and revealed a dozen assorted bottles of various liquors. The warrior looked amazed and pleased.

"I never hoped to fall in with a drinking man," he said, smiling.

"This is not for me," said the prayerman. "I need no drink or food, but when the gods can, they deliver what is needed by others." He looked at the bottles and the warrior, then allowed himself a small smile, too. "Although you are the first man I've met who *needs* liquor before food."

"It must have been Dehore, my god, who determined my needs," said the warrior. "The battle has left me cold and sober, and I wish to drink and forget what I've seen today."

"I am a prayerman," said the other, "but I have yet to learn of this god Dehore. Is he numbered among the gods of drunkenness, as are many others?" He watched the warrior nearly finish the first bottle, which took only a moment.

"Have you tried this Uxoriag beer?" The red-skinned man offered the bottle to the prayerman, who shook his head. The warrior smiled and finished the last drops himself.

"You're a smart one," he said as he opened a second bottle. "Most men would grab the first drink that came their way, but that was the worst-tasting beer in the world. I can see that you're going to wait for the better brews, despite those horrors we fought."

He didn't seem especially pleased with this, but ungrudgingly offered the prayerman a mouthful from the second bottle.

"As I said, I don't drink." At this the warrior grew unbelieving. "I swear it," said the prayerman. "I enjoyed it once, but simple discipline helps give me inner strength."

Convinced at last, the warrior smiled broadly, sending wrinkles around his bald head and over his scalp.

"I'm glad," he said, hefting the container. "This gives me *my* inner strength. And somehow, I've got a feeling I'll need every bit of that I can manage for the days ahead." He finished the second bottle, opened a third.

"It's truth enough, though," he added sadly, "that I've always needed all the booze I could get a hold of, and it still wasn't enough to hide the sorrow." He turned his glazing eyes to his friend. "I've seen more sorrow than a sea of wine could drown. I don't need to see any more."

"It is up to the gods," said the prayerman softly. "Surely you have faith in the gods."

"How could I not? All of us Dehori are gods. Don't you know of our legends? We haven't been extinct that long."

"I know little of the ways of men. I am of the gods."

"As am I. I am the left arm of Dehore, who carved himself to pieces in the War of Creation, and thusly saved himself from his enemies." He opened a fourth bottle. "Dehore, with the knowledge of the Trickster, carved his limbs from his torso. Thus there were five of us to meet the foes, and the one holy temple of the body. I was the left arm, the shield arm, and so the military. The right arm was the artisans, while the legs were workers and farmers. We were ruled by the heads, and we reproduced by the body." He finished the fourth, opened another.

"You were many?"

"Me? Thousands, a head once told me. I never counted, of course. We were many, yet one. But a head told me once that just us lefts numbered in the thousands."

"And what happened?"

"You men took us. Your type: you with the sexes. We were prized for our mental abilities. Men treasured our mindspeak, just as they prized us for our blood, which many of them relished." For the first time anger crossed his face. "A man once kept me, this flesh, in his cellar for special occasions. He opened my veins to impress his intoxicated guests. He called me Dehori Rosé." He spat and opened another bottle. "After I freed myself my right hand sewed the copulator to the bottom of a wave, then left him adrift in the sky. We Dehori naturally fought back, and because of our mindspeak, we could outfight three times our opponents.

"But you got us all eventually. We, like fools, would try to gather and perform the sacred Rite of Sewing, hoping to reunite ourselves with our god. But sworn enemies joined hands to cut us from ourselves forever. They formed the Alliance of Scissors, which destroyed the holy torso. We could not replace ourselves again." He opened another and wiped a tear from his cheek. He was flushed even darker now, like a man about to burst from blood. But his speech was still clear. "That was the end. We died, one by one. I am the last." He opened another bottle, a clay jug, and was nearly weeping when he faced the prayerman. "For a thousand turns I have cursed your type. You are unique, prayerman, in helping me. And in being my friend."

"Perhaps," said the prayerman, "it would have been better to join your spirit sooner." His tone was guarded, testing. "Just end your wretched life."

"I cannot, any more than you would cut off an arm because of a splinter. I am in perfect health, and that is the curse of my loneliness."

"I am glad to hear that you will not give in," said the prayerman. He watched the warrior empty the clay jug and pick up his ninth bottle. "These are evil times, and each small surrender takes us closer to Chaos." He held the Dehori's shoulder to comfort the drunken man. "The gods move in strange ways. We must put our faith in their wisdom, for it is plain that the ways of men are inadequate." The warrior opened the tenth flask, whose odor nearly broke the prayerman's sober discipline. The warrior smiled, stuck the neck in his mouth, then fell on his back to guzzle it. Shortly afterward, the prayerman knelt over his unconscious friend.

"I shall pray for you."

The Old Lady

The nearest ocean was a thousand miles away, but the land looked like it had been washed by a tidal wave. Debris was scattered everywhere. Only the stoutest of life remained, surrounded by pools of yellow pus or green filth.

Only corpses that were surrounded by their own blood had remained intact. Gray powder made a line where blood and slime touched. Men and horses lay in heaps, covered by flies and condors. The prayerman watched attentively as a condor, bloated from its meal, lumbered along to get aloft. But the air was still, as if even the sylphs had been crushed, and it ran far beyond the circle of dried blood.

"Let us hurry," said the Dehori. "I don't want to spend the night in the open."

"Wait," said the prayerman. "Look."

The condor's feet were dissolving into stumps, and the tips of its wings smoked where they had brushed the slime. It slipped, shrieking in terror as it rolled and flopped about. Its cries were audible even over the distance. Upon a closer look the men saw that there were several corpses of birds, taken over by the slime as the deer had been, thrashing about and moving toward them. The whole lake of filth, in fact, seemed to be pulsing and moving slowly in their direction, drawn the way opposites are always drawn together.

"I am glad those poisoned condors cannot fly," said the warrior. "Let us be off from here." They began trotting then, but everywhere they went were corpses and slime, making their path very difficult. The gruesome sight and smell seemed to shake the Dehori from his surliness. The prayerman, too, was shaken enough to crack his enigmatic shell with an attempt at joking.

"I'm certainly glad," he said, "that I believe in all the gods. It is plain to see what happens when you believe in none."

"One is enough," answered the warrior, "when you are his only worshiper and body."

"That's how it has been with the Old Lady," said the prayerman. "She worships a deity called the Hell Terror, a thing from the Pits. When the Sword Kings took over they outlawed its worship and turned the last heretics into stone. Except for the Old Lady. Yet rather than ask that god's help, men said they'd prefer to die." He gestured about them. "She sent me word that she is its last worshiper."

"From the looks of the land hereabouts," said the Dehori dryly, "she must certainly be the only one nearby."

"Not with me here," said the prayerman. His beads, each a part of a god, clattered and clacked as he walked. He felt one obsidian bead start to warm as they closed with a distant ruin.

The black tower, which had withstood gods and men since the instant when time was born, looked as though it had exploded. Chunks of stone lay scattered about in the dirt. But there was no slime there, and the interior of the temple was intact. Its heart was an altar on the brink of a pit, surrounded by a ring of ten-foot statues, the petrified remains of the Hell Terror's former worshipers.

The Old Lady greeted them at her broken doorway. For the first time in history she looked her age. For centuries she had thrived, stealing sacrifices when they were not given. Thus, she was eternally young and powerful, even after the Sword Kings began worshiping their weapons instead of the fickle gods. But since the people had fallen to Chaos there were no more sacrifices and the Old Lady had to feed the Hell Terror with her own being.

She was a skinny mummy of a woman, with ragged hair and a toothless mouth. But her eyes were as black as the obsidian tower and as sharp as the broken fragments of the ruins. They flashed with excitement and hope at the arrival of the two men.

"Welcome," she said. Her voice was like grinding glass between your teeth, and she moved her hand toward them as if for support. "The Hell Terror welcomes you. I welcome you...."

"And I thank you for it," said the prayerman as he pulled the Dehori back. "But don't try to fool me with your old tricks. I know the ways of the gods, and I know you will steal from us and kill for your god. It won't work."

The Old Lady's face fell, and little brown flakes of skin dropped from her wrinkles.

"You have," she noted, "brought a victim. That is good." The warrior, whose steady gaze hadn't shifted from her yet, slid his eyes sideways to watch his new friend.

"No," said the prayerman. "That is not the way for the faithful, though I might think differently if we had a godless Sword King here."

"A sacrifice is the only way to appease the Hell Terror," whined the lady. "Last night I sent him two skinny children that had been entrusted to my care. He was weak, though, and you can see what the slime things did to us." She gestured toward the open sky. "But with the strength of a warrior like this—"

"No."

"Perhaps," said the warrior slowly, "she is right. With your prayers my soul would go to Dehore...."

"No," repeated the prayerman. "The world is a being, just as each being is a world. You cannot sacrifice yourself, even to yourself, any more than we can sacrifice the world to itself to fight Chaos." He stared into his friend's bloodshot eyes. "I am sure that is not the fate your god has planned for you."

"We need some god present," said the warrior. "It grows darker even now, and you yourself said we can't withstand Chaos alone." The Old Lady smiled wickedly.

"We must pray," said the prayerman, "each to his own god."

"The Hell Terror will not come. Pray yourself immortal, but he will still need a body to materialize here."

She eyed the men coldly. "I will not sacrifice myself to save you, either."

"Then we will find another," said the Dehori. "We must do as the war god's children do—sacrifice an enemy. When the attackers come we will give one of them to the god."

"I know the gods' ways," smiled the prayerman. "They will thrive, and grow, if Chaos is slaughtered for them, just as Chaos grows upon devouring us."

They all agreed that the Dehori's was the best plan, and the Old Lady's stooped gait straightened as she crooned happily to the statues of her friends.

The Hell Terror

The slime deer approached as night, lit by a few dim stars, closed down. The corrupted animals had a mobility denied to more degenerate forms and so led the attack for the Chaos thing. The prayerman knelt behind a stone, mumbling need-prayers for the coming fight, hoping some god could spare a blessing or luck for them. The Dehori half frightened the prayerman to death when he screeched his battle cry and leapt at an enemy scout that had come creeping.

The slime deer halted and bowed, then barked a jet of slime at its target. The warrior burst into flame and the slime crackled into green smoke. The thing tried to leap away, even after the spear passed where its heart had been.

The Dehori pulled gently on the wire so he wouldn't slice up his prey, but the animal stumbled and the hulk of its head, which dangled between its forelegs, got caught on a rock. The creature's delicate balance, never secure, was lost. It stumbled, and the wire cut itself loose. The warrior cursed its escape.

Then the prayerman leapt atop the retreating slime deer. He held his cloak out for protection and encircled the beast with the magical garment. The Dehori joined him as the animal struggled, and used his weapons to sew the cloak tightly closed. Still struggling, the animal was carried into the temple.

"Your prayers were of little help," said the warrior. "But your bravery is undisputed. As is the quality of your cloak."

"My need-prayers only produced those barrels of wine," said the prayerman, gesturing to a stack of casks out in the temple's yard. "And in the end, there is only one god I rely on: that one within me. The garment, as my oath states, is truly the Cloak of Law. Even this atrocity can't break it."

"Then let's bring in those barrels," said the warrior, "and have a drink while there is still time."

"You're going to get drunk now?" said the prayerman, incredulous. "Now, before the mass of our foes strike? I swear, even with this sacrifice and my prayers, this Hell Terror will need help against Chaos tonight."

"The wine is my fuel. It makes me burn," said the man, then added, "and even if it weren't, I'd rather be drunk than not tonight."

The prayerman used his sacred chant, calling upon the Cloak and Standard of Law, to clear a path between the barrels and the temple. As the warrior rolled the casks to the interior, he watched the horizon, where the sickly green-purple glow of the Chaos forces heaved slowly toward them. To the three people in the temple it seemed that all the world had fallen, save them. The warrior sat and drank, while the naked prayerman knelt and prayed his strength to the god who would materialize before them. The Old Lady danced and knifed out her ritual on the sacrifice, screeching in joy as her youth returned. The Dehori felt himself sobering, despite his best efforts, as her ritual ended. With a shout of triumph she pushed the wrapped corpse into the pit at the temple's heart. A hoarse bellow answered. The warrior leapt to his feet in surprise as the statues all about them moved.

The Old Lady screamed. The warrior cursed, snatching at his weapons. The prayerman opened his eyes and looked up. He had seen hellish things before. He was ready for the bloody claws and the gaping maws that had appeared on the now-animate statues of the old worshipers. But he was not ready for the dripping ooze of their faces, or for the gout of slime that one of the statues retched up as it closed on him.

Before the statue could reach the prayerman, a spear pierced its legs and cut them off. As the huge body fell, the wire sang back and forth, slicing it to pieces. The prayerman rose and ran to the warrior's side, calling for the Old Lady. Ice filled his bones. He thought his heart would burst with the agony of his realization.

"Chaos overtook the old god," he said.

The Dehori lashed out at another pair of the things, already sliding into piles of mush, and cut them to immobile chunks that slowly melted into a slithering mess. The Old Lady pinioned one statue temporarily with a stone, and tried to make her way to the men. She was still human, fighting her god and the already-corrupted parts of herself, to remain free of Chaos.

"She's a strong woman," said the prayerman. "We can save her." Then a gout of greasy fog bellowed from the pit behind the altar, enveloping her. She screamed, trying to tear herself loose. But it clung to her, thickening. The Dehori hurled three spears into the smoke, and the prayerman threw his staff. It struck her head with the liquid sound of a melon dropped in a tunnel. There was a white flash, then more green smoke swirled within the fog. A tentacle writhed over the altar, while others secured a grip on the edge of the pit.

"Even Death is a god of ours, and better than Chaos," said the prayerman. He thought the Old Lady lucky and almost hoped for the same fate himself. But he fought on.

The statues that had survived the warrior's attack now joined the grotesque parade of creatures that surrounded the temple in an undulating wave. The mass grew higher with every moment. The prayerman spun his beads over his head as a weapon and faced the nauseating thing rising from the pit. The Dehori, his eyes glazed with drink but still somehow sharp, grinned with clenched teeth and spoke: "Dehore laughed as he dismembered himself!"

The prayerman wanted to reply, but the best the man could manage was a ghastly smile.

Looking the prayerman in the eye, the warrior lifted a short dagger to his own armpit. "Do as I say. Knock holes in the kegs and let the wine flow all about. Leave one full and climb in. Hold your breath and pray, friend."

"I won't desert you," said the prayerman through clattering teeth. "Not to Chaos."

But the warrior seemed not to hear. "Hold something for me, would you?" he asked with surprising calm. With the dagger he cut his left arm from his body, and thrust it into the prayerman's hands. As if he did not notice the loss, the Dehori kicked over some barrels and advanced toward the thing rising from the pit. It slobbered over the edge now, making a sloshing sound as its unstable body oozed out.

The prayerman watched, stunned. The arm in his hand flexed, making mystic signs over a barrel. The prayerman stared stupidly at the limb, even as the Dehori warrior leapt at the monster, shouting defiance in his old secret language. The arm grabbed the barrel rim. The warrior's yell stopped, absorbed into his being. The arm pulled itself and the prayerman into the barrel, submerging them, even as the prayerman caught a glimpse of slime overhead; he held his breath and prayed to Dehore. An instant later, the warrior detonated his own body. The concussion split the keg's seams, but the prayerman kept his head under the leaking wine, even though he thought his lungs would burst with pain. At last he blinked wine from his eyes, licked his lips with a parched tongue, and emerged.

A dull gray powder covered everything, save for the space around him. Wine, the color of a rich rosé, still dripped from the limb in his hands. Everywhere else the liquor had been changed, as always happened when living blood met the slime. The arm had consecrated the wine, and the furious self-ignition of the warrior had scattered blood and Chaos everywhere. It had spread far, or else had been strong enough to set off a chain reaction. The lands all around were the same gray under the dim starlight.

The prayerman reconsecrated the altar, and as the dim sun rose he burned the warrior's arm. Only the arm, the seat of the man's soul, was important to Dehore. The prayerman made certain it reached the god properly. He watched, praying softly, as pieces of flesh peeled off like burning paper and drifted languidly upward with the wind sylphs.

At the edge of the ash-clogged pit he threw the black stone bead from his string away, followed by a part of a deer's antler. He knew that both were worthless now, their gods destroyed.

He knew where the slime had come from, too. The mystery had been solved for him when the Hell Terror accepted Chaos and was transformed by it, then passed on the evil to its followers. It was plain then to the prayerman, who was knowing in the ways of the gods, that the great god Deer, the soul of all deer, had succumbed and passed on its evil to its followers, too.

He walked away slowly, praying that the whole world might turn to ash rather than Chaos. But he knew it would not be so. The gods themselves were falling, as were their mortal cousins, men.

"But there is something I am doing right," said the prayerman aloud. "There is something, and so I must continue." He prayed aloud as he walked, fondling the new bead on his chain: a single red thumb joint of an otherwise forgotten deity. Cloakless and staffless, he shivered under the cold sun. But his voice was strong, and that was all he needed that morning as he traveled, filling the world with his strength.

Paul S. Kemp

"Confession" illustrates the moody, dark tone typical of Paul S. Kemp's fiction. It owes much to the standard tropes of sword and sorcery fiction, but where a typical sword and sorcery tale is a high-action affair, "Confession" is a more introspective work. The story's action takes place in the minds of the protagonists, not on the field of battle.

The tale is set in the world of New Dineen, a bleak, unsavory setting suffering through the political, cultural, and magical churn associated with the fall of its continent-spanning Imperial Magocracy. Kemp's short story "The Spinner," which appeared in *Sails & Sorcery: Tales of Nautical Fantasy* (2007), is also set in the world of New Dineen and shares this tale's dark tone.

"Confession" was Kemp's first creator-owned publication. It appeared originally in *Dragon* #356 (June 2007). The expletives in the story (particularly the first line) elicited some pre-publication discussion among the magazine's editors and the author. Were the words appropriate, given *Dragon*'s demographics? Ultimately, everyone agreed that the story's tone called for the expletives and they were retained. After publication, some readers found the language offensive and both Kemp and *Dragon*'s editor-in-chief participated separately in a discussion on the publisher's website, explaining their respective reasons for the creative choices they had made.

Kemp lives in Michigan with his wife and twin sons. He is a corporate lawyer by day, and is therefore evil. (He is sorry about that.) But when he's not doing evil, he writes. Kemp has published eight novels and several short stories with Wizards of the Coast, including a *New York Times* bestseller. He is best known for his Forgotten Realms fiction featuring his signature character, the shadowy assassin-priest Erevis Cale. While his work in the Forgotten Realms will continue, Paul has begun to expand his writing into creator-owned short fiction. Check his writing blog for recent news and publication announcements at paulskemp.livejournal.com.

CONFESSION

BY PAUL S. KEMP

The First Epistle of Malkiir Zhorne, the twentieth day of Urkan, the Year of Flames:

I SLOSHED THROUGH shit up to my ankles. The rains from the previous week had caused the sewer's main channel to overflow. A soup of water, urine, feces, and rubbish immersed the walkways on either side of the channel. I held the lantern high and kept my eyes from the sludge.

A few paces ahead, my brother Kazmarek limped forward, unperturbed by his twisted leg, the stink of the sewers, or the immorality of what he planned to do. We might have waited a day before venturing beneath Dineen's streets. The overflow would have drained into the bay and the evening's high tide would have scoured the tunnels clean. But Kazmarek would not hear of delay, not of a day, not of an hour, even if it meant coating himself in the city's dung.

What an arrogant ass he was.

I knew that if we accomplished what we intended, neither the high tide nor the spring rains would wash us clean. Yet I kept my misgivings to myself. Raising them with Kaz would have been futile. Kaz had heard the call of his only mistress—power—and I knew better than to dispute with my brother when the mistress called.

"Kaz, we must stop for a moment."

Kaz did not so much as turn around. He answered my words with a grunt and a dismissive wave of his casting effigy. The effigy, despite the fact that it was inanimate, managed with its frozen features to communicate Kaz's contempt for my weakness. I hated the effigy. In form it looked like a miniature human, but made from bone, cloth, leather, and bits of gemstone instead of flesh. I thought it a little devil who whispered depravity in my brother's ear.

I can admit now that my brother was mad. Madness had led him to take the Thaumaturgic Oaths and craft the casting effigy symbolic of a thaumaturge's art. For my part, I could never have made the sacrifices required by the Oaths. I remained only a minor practitioner—a hedge wizard, my brother called me. In truth, I often thought myself little more than my brother's familiar, a filial imp. In my more generous moments, I thought of myself as my brother's conscience. But conscience or no, when Kaz had told me what he had learned, even I had heard the tempting call of power, albeit distantly.

"Kaz...."

He turned to face me. His one good eye burned red in the lantern light. The other socket was an empty hole.

"We're near. I can feel it."

I could feel it too: a heaviness in the air, an oiliness on my skin—evil given corporeality. It had been hours since we had passed beneath a street sewer grate, hours since we had seen any light other than that of the lantern. We were in a part of the sewers beneath Old Town, an area the city's channel-sweeps had long ago surrendered to the rats.

And to the demon.

Kaz had learned of the fiend by accident. He had been researching a ritual in a Plague Era tome in the dusty shelves that stood idle near the back of Dineen's High Library. While Minnear—the green moon of mages, for the unlearned—leered gibbous through the library's high windows, a yellowed piece of parchment had fluttered to the floor from between the tome's pages.

Inked in blood, the page described a demonic cult and showed the location of an unholy shrine in the city's sewers—even provided a rough map. Further research revealed unsettling rumors: it was said the cultists had lured human sacrifices to their dark lord in exchange for his blessings and the power he offered.

Kaz had seen the possibilities immediately. He'd shared his find with another thaumaturge of his order, but the colleague had laughed at Kaz's claims. So Kaz turned to me. When he had told me of the map, of his plan to summon and control the demon, I had—Alethan forgive me—flirted with the thought that Kaz meant to sacrifice me. After all, Kaz likely had sacrificed others as part of the rituals associated with the Oaths. Criminals and slaves, no doubt, but still men who would have screamed at the sight of the knife.

In the end, though, I couldn't believe that my brother would harm me. Call it self-delusion, if you will, but I wouldn't believe it. Instead, I tried to dissuade Kaz by echoing the warnings contained in some of the magical tomes I had read through the years—in all but the rarest of circumstances, consorting with demons led to insanity and soul death. Kaz, of course, had dismissed my caution as cowardly. How wrong he had been.

At length, we found a corridor that opened off the main sewer channel. Kaz did not consult the map. He did not need to by then. He could smell the power.

"We're near now," he murmured, and I did not know if he was speaking to me or that damned effigy. "Near now."

I followed, the thickening essence of evil slicking my skin like sweat. I swear the substance still lingers in my lungs.

The corridor narrowed and sloped upward. The walls smoothed. Our footsteps echoed off the dry floor. Ahead, an archway loomed.

Unable to control his enthusiasm, Kaz hurried forward, giggling the while, shaking his effigy. "Here. This is it."

An open archway stood before us, a wide black maw exhaling the breath of evil. The elaborate jambs seemed the embodiment of madness: carved in relief from the stone, the fanged faces of demons leered from the stone, snarling, promising.

I shudder even now. I must pause, reader. My hand shakes....

The lantern light did not reach beyond the doorway guarded by those diabolical visages. An impenetrable curtain of darkness blocked it.

"Warded," Kaz said, as though I couldn't see that for myself.

Kaz held forth his effigy while he hissed the words to a counter-ward. Moments passed. Kaz continued to intone. Sweat beaded his brow, then—

"There!"

The ward of darkness blocking the archway gave way with an audible pop. All at once, the magical darkness dissipated and the demonic faces built into the jambs became flesh. Long necks stretched as the creatures tried to lunge from the stone. Fanged maws snapped at Kaz; forked tongues hissed; slitted eyes glared. Kaz bounded backward, nearly bumping into me. Unable to escape their stony prison, and just unable to reach us, the demons screamed in futile rage, their unholy voices echoing back down the sewer, echoing toward infinity. Kaz grinned and incanted another counterward—as suddenly as they had formed, the demons retracted into the stone and the jambs reclaimed them once more.

"Burn me," I oathed, and tried to control my hammering heart. Kaz turned to me and smiled; he looked as feral as a moor tiger.

"We go," Kaz said.

We stepped through the door, past the inert demons and into the round chamber that lay revealed beyond. A domed ceiling soared above us beyond the limits of our light. Runes of power were etched deeply into the otherwise smooth stone of the floor. The runes faced this way and that, with no discernable order to their placement, the inscrutable scrawl of a mad demonologist. Kaz knelt over each in turn, running his fingers over the power-laden lines the way another man might lightly brush the skin of a lover. Lacking formal training, I could not read the runes and was glad of it. For me, they called to mind the blood channels in a butcher's slaughter block. I could not have been more correct.

In the center of the room stood a featureless block of obsidian: the binding altar. The demon—I will not poison this page by here recording the fiend's name—was bound within an extra-dimensional space represented in this plane by the magical altar. Atop the altar sat two wrist-thick candles, their gray wax no doubt made from melted human flesh.

Kaz stepped to the altar, gingerly, as though it were an easily startled animal. He sighed and ran his hands along its smooth surface. He spoke a word of command and the candles flared to life. They sputtered, spitting rancid black smoke.

"This is where he sleeps," Kaz said. My brother's eye had that distant look that I knew well. Already Kaz was planning what he would do with the power granted him by the demon.

I swear by Alethan's name that I wanted to scream for him not to do it, but I swear equally that my mouth, clotted with the very essence of evil, could not form words. Instead, I simply stared, listened to the gonging of my heart, and did nothing.

May Alethan forgive a coward.

Kaz took his casting effigy in hand—even the inanimate little man managed to look eager—and began the ritual.

The spellchant filled the room and rang off the walls. The moment Kaz began the casting, the hairs on my arms stood on end. I struggled to draw breath. I backed away from that foul altar as far as I could. When I felt the cold wall against my back, the strength left me and I slid to the floor. My vision began to grow blurry.

"Do not do it," I finally whispered, but knew it was already too late.

Kaz's voice grew in volume as he moved through the spellchant. The runes in the floor began to glow, then to move. To move! For an instant, I thought myself mad but not so!

The runes propelled themselves along the stone surface of the floor like waterstriders on the surface of a pond, undulating toward the altar, vanishing under it. As the altar swallowed each of the dire characters, the darkness above it grew. The air thickened. My ears felt pressure. Gradually, the darkness above the altar clotted into a shape—smooth black skin lined with red veins, sinewy muscles, membranous wings, and unforgiving coal-black eyes.

I will never forget those eyes. I met them for only an instant, and that was enough to test my sanity. I cradled my knees to my chin and rocked, as helpless as a babe.

I promise that you would have done the same.

"Do not, Kaz, do not," I repeated, my own incantation an ineffective counter to my brother's spellchant.

Kaz's voice rose in ecstasy as the demon manifested fully. The creature issued a challenge in a tongue so vile it struck me like a physical blow. When my brother answered with his own commands in the same tongue, I vomited down the front of my robe.

How could my brother speak such things? What had he become?

Then something happened, something unexpected. I heard the most terrible sound that I could have imagined.

The demon laughed.

Kaz answered with a shouted command. I heard the desperation in it.

More laughter from the demon, louder. My bowels turned soft.

The demon mouthed more vileness, its tone commanding. Kaz, his arrogance gone, began to plead, then to whimper. I covered my ears; I had never before heard my brother make such sounds. I glanced up to see Kaz slumped on the floor before the demon, gibbering nonsense. His effigy lay on the floor beside him, staring at me. It had lost an eye somehow, and its leg was bent askew, nearly torn off.

I clamped shut my eyes. My mind ceased to function and the series of events that followed are a blur. The next thing I remember, I ran out of the summoning chamber and down the sewer tunnel, screaming. The demon's laughter chased me the while.

Abadon stared at the stone of the meditation cell. The candle behind him cast his shadow on the wall. It looked exaggerated, deformed.

He choked down the disappointment. He had failed—again.

Once more his entreaties had not reached his god; once more he had failed to achieve the soulbond. He remained only an aspirant—a half-cleric, separated from the grace of Alethan.

"Forgive me," he whispered, and meant it. He needed forgiveness. He had transgressions unnumbered in his past. He could not even remember all of his sins. He knew only that he wanted to be absolved of them, to efface the past.

The stone wall held its silence. So, too, did Alethan.

Other aspirants of the Order spoke of sometimes hearing Alethan's soft voice in their ears; it was known that senior priests routinely heard the guiding voice of their god. Abadon never had. He feared he never would.

Anger rose in him, frothy and hot, and he knew it was that very anger—a remnant left over from the man he once had been—that prevented the soulbond. For Alethan was a god of peace, a gentle god, but Abadon was a man of war. Or had been, once. And he had never been gentle. That fact was the divide that separated man from god, the chasm that kept Abadon from the soulbond.

A soft knock on the door ended his recriminations. Abadon stood.

"Enter."

The door opened, flooding the cell with the light of the setting sun and framing the thin, stooped body of Prior Nis. As always, the elderly prior wore his blue robes, his gray beard, and his soft smile.

Abadon bowed his head in deference, as was the custom in the priory.

"Forgive me for intruding, Abadon," the prior said. "I heard speaking and assumed you must have completed your meditations."

"Yes," Abadon answered, and offered nothing more.

The prior regarded him. The silence stretched.

At last the prior said, "The soulbond eludes you still?"

His words were barely a question.

Abadon's jaw tightened. "It does."

The prior stepped into the small cell and put a gentle, fatherly hand on his shoulder.

"The soulbond eludes you because your past and your guilt anchor your spirit to your flesh. Before Alethan can offer you forgiveness, you first must forgive yourself. You will not progress in the faith otherwise."

Abadon felt his cheeks flush, nodded. The prior had said such things to him before.

"I am guilty of things, Prior. Terrible things. You know what I was."

The prior's eyes held no judgment. "I know what you told me when you arrived. You were a dreamleaf addict and a onetime soldier. You killed, sometimes without justification. But all men are guilty, Abadon. All men. Soldiers and cobblers, even priests. You must release your guilt and approach Alethan with nothing hidden. Only thus can your soul soar to grace."

Abadon nodded but only to please the prior. He knew his flesh wrapped the guilt in his spirit as tightly as his fist once had wrapped his sword hilt. He could not release it.

He remembered scattered images—murders, rapes. His past was a beast within him, squirming, creeping up his throat to try and get out from behind his teeth. But he refused to let it out. Its darkness was too black to put before Alethan. He wanted—needed—his god to absolve him sight unseen; he could not bring his sins into the light, not even to the god of forgiveness.

"I do not know if I can do it, Prior," Abadon said. His eyes welled and he did not fight the tears. He wished he could reach down his throat and pull out the guilt, stinking and squealing, and throw it into a hole where no one would ever see it.

"You can do it. You will do it." The prior took him by the shoulders and looked at him with soft eyes. "Hear my words—one has come seeking, Abadon."

It took Abadon a moment for the import of the ritual words to register. When it did, Abadon's legs grew weak. Trials were reserved for only senior priests.

Abadon looked up into the prior's face. "A Trial? But I am only an aspirant, Prior. I—"

"One has come seeking, Abadon," the prior repeated, more forcefully.

Abadon's mouth went dry but he managed to speak the ritual answer. "And in seeking one has found. How may I be of service?"

The prior smiled, gave him a nod.

"You are different than any of our other aspirants, Abadon. More burdened. I think a Trial may free you to let go of what is within you. It is unusual for an aspirant to take a Trial, true, but not unknown. Follow me. A man has come. He asked for you."

That froze Abadon. "Asked for me? By name?"

The prior nodded. "He says he knew you before… before you came to the priory. That is why I think this might be good for you."

Abadon's heart thumped. He had no desire to confront ghosts from his past. He imagined a brother of some forgotten man he had killed, some terrified woman he had violated.

"Prior, I cannot—"

"It will be all right," the prior said. "You must face your past. Here is an opportunity to do that."

The two men stared at each other. Finally Abadon nodded.

"Very well, Prior."

Prior Nis led Abadon through the monastery to the small waiting room off the worship hall. With each step, Abadon's heart beat faster; his body grew heavier. By the time they reached the door of the waiting room, he felt as though he were made of lead. He put a hand on the prior's shoulder for support.

The prior patted his hand and opened the door.

The First Epistle of Malkiir Zhorne, the twentieth day of Urkan, the Year of Flames:

I ran for a time that felt like forever. By the time my fear began to dissipate, I was covered in sweat and stink. But as the moments passed, a peculiar exhilaration came over me. Kazmarek was dead, presumably consumed by the demon. I was alive. Kazmarek had failed and I was alive.

You consider me horrible for thinking such things, no doubt. But you must understand that I had stood in the shadow of my brother for a lifetime. To exult in his failure was human. Or so I told myself. I would learn of my error soon enough.

I emerged from the sewers a changed man. Free of my brother's domineering presence, I felt free, and the sudden rush of freedom led me to indulge hugely in the pleasures of the flesh. My appetite for all manner of vice grew and grew. Once starved, I now feasted on life. Within a sevenday, I considered myself a hedonist. Within a month, others considered me debauched. Within two months, even criminals considered me depraved, and still my appetites knew no satiety.

Finally, my desires turned from sex and narcotics to blood. So I joined a mercenary unit—me, a hedge wizard!—and tried to find satisfaction in the violence of war and pillage. Yet even war did not satisfy me, though it came closest. I will not here pen the bloody details of those days. I will write only that my puissance in the violent arts surprised both myself and my fellow soldiers. My surprise soon turned to dismay.

A bald man with the ochre robes and amber ring of a thaumaturge waited at the polished wooden table. His dark eyes scoured Abadon's face and flashed recognition. A smile split his thin lips. Abadon did not recognize the man but that meant nothing. He had spent years in a dreamleaf haze.

Abadon cleared his throat. "Greetings, seeker. You are to be my Trial. I, your servant."

Prior Nis excused himself from the room and closed the door. Abadon had almost asked the prior to remain but by custom seeker and servant always spoke in confidence, and the communications were never shared.

Abadon stepped to the table. The seeker's eyes never left his face. He still wore his smile, though there was something behind it that made Abadon uneasy.

"Abadon?" the thaumaturge said, as the aspirant sat at the table. "I have been looking a long while for you."

Abadon's stomach churned. As he feared, the seeker must have known him when he had done… dark things.

"You know me but I do not remember you," Abadon said. He fell back on ritual to hide his discomfort. "Tell me what you seek. I am here to serve."

"You do not know me. But you knew my brother. And that was a few winters ago. Do you remember? In Dineen?"

Abadon shook his head. The air was close, thick. It was hard to breathe.

The thaumaturge nodded. "You are far gone. As for what I seek, I have found it." He leaned forward and his eyes burned when he whispered his next words.

"I know what you are."

Abadon's skin went gooseflesh. The guilt within him, the thing he kept hidden, began to pound against the bars of its prison.

The seeker took something out from under his robes and laid it on the table. When Abadon saw it, the world fell in on him.

From the Second Epistle of Malkiir Zhorne, the fifteenth first day of Coram, the Year of Flames:

I already had begun to suspect that much of what I thought I remembered was false. My First Epistle may be a lie. Be warned, reader.

My memory began to fade soon after I exited the sewers, replaced by new knowledge. Fearful knowledge. The process was gradual but inexorable. I began to know things that I should not have known—how to wield a blade, advanced necromantic arts, how to prolong the torture of a whole host of beings. I feared I was going mad. The truth was worse.

On the streets of Dineen, near the bazaar, in the early evening hours of the fifteenth day of Thulsil in the Year of Plagues, I learned all of it.

Someone was following me—a bald thaumaturge in the ochre robes of Kazmarek's order. I knew his face, but his name was lost to me. He bore his casting effigy on a necklace about his neck. It reminded me much of Kazmarek's.

I ducked into an alley and lay in wait for him. When he turned into the alley, I pounced, slamming him against the wooden wall of a building. I held him by his shirt and he clutched at my hands.

"You are following me," I said.

I saw fear in his eyes. He stuttered and I shook him to show my strength.

"Is this about my brother Kazmarek?" I demanded.

The fear in his eyes turned to puzzlement.

"Your... brother? Your brother, Kazmarek?" He studied my face. "Do you... know me? My name is Toorgan."

I did not, and indicated as much. His face was familiar but I did not remember his name. Given my failing memory, it was possible that we once had known one another.

He continued to stare at me and I saw realization dawn in his eyes.

"What is it?" I asked, but already a chill was sneaking up my spine.

He looked me in the eye. "What is your name?"

The question made me pause for some reason but I finally managed, "My name is Malkiir Zhorne. Brother to Kazmarek, once of your order."

"Malkiir," he said, testing the word. "Well... Malkiir, the Arch Magister of the Order wants to question you."

I had heard stories about how the Order "questioned" people. I declined but he insisted. He tried to force me but I resisted and we scuffled. I was the stronger and threw him to the ground. My bloodlust rose in me, then. I drew my eating knife and resolved to split him from groin to gullet.

He tried to flee but I kicked him until he was out of breath, then knelt on top of him.

"Who are you?" I asked. "What do you want of me?"

I put the knife to his throat and that pried loose the truth. At least I think it was truth.

He said, "You told me of me of your planned trip to the sewers. I followed you. I saw the ritual. I know. So does the Order. And the Arch Magister wants what you have."

"What I have?"

I stood and stepped back from him. The knife fell from my hand. My mind whirled.

"What you have," he said, standing. He stepped toward me.

I shook my head. "I told no one of our trip to the sewers. Kazmarek would have taken my heart had I betrayed his secret."

The thaumaturge smiled and there was something evil in it. He held the effigy about his neck up for me to see. I saw then that it was Kazmarek's effigy. His next words hit me with the force of a mace.

"Your memory is a lie. *You* are Kazmarek. *You* summoned the demon."

My world spun. The words echoed in my head. I could not see clearly. "No. My brother summoned the demon. I escaped the chamber. I escaped. If you were there, you saw."

I backed up but the thaumaturge followed me, his words a relentless series of hammerblows.

"You are a thaumaturge like me. Malkiir was the name of your effigy. *This* effigy. You did not escape. You fled past me, screaming. I entered the chamber after you were gone. The summoning chamber was empty. The runes were gone. The demon was gone."

"That is not possible," I said feebly.

He pressed. "You invented a past to wall off the truth. Somehow it is also walling off the demon. We can free him, Kazmarek. We must free him."

I stumbled on something and he lunged for me. Instinct—or something else—took control of me.

I grabbed him by the robes and spat denials into his face. I threw him to the ground and punched him, bit him, kicked him until he was insensate. Finally I retrieved my knife and cut his throat. I do not know if anyone saw me.

After that I fled that place, fled the Order, fled Dineen.

A small effigy lay on the table. Made of magically bound cloth, bone, leather, wood, and gemstones, the chip of its single onyx eye stared accusingly up at Abadon. One of its legs was bent askew.

It was one-eyed and crook-legged. Like Kazmarek.

Like Kazmarek?

How did he know that name?

"Do you remember?" the thaumaturge asked, an eager gleam in his eye. "He is exactly as you remember him, no? My brother was Toorgan. Do you remember that name?"

From the Third Epistle of Malkiir Zhorne, the first day of Fel, the Year of Flames:

This is the last I will say on this matter. I write it down because my memory continues to fade and I cannot trust what I do remember. I see in my mind everything that I have written as though it happened, but I do not know if what I remember is truth.

What I did know was that I was possessed. A demoniac. That explained my fading memory and burgeoning knowledge of forbidden things. Strange that I had not realized it, but that is nature of possession. It is subtle.

I eventually learned the demon's name: Abadon.

For months I sought solace in all manner of mysticism to help combat the evil within me. At first I thought to have the demon exorcised, but I feared what might befall the world should he become free. For a reason I still cannot explain, the demon was literally bound within me. My spell had forced him from the prison of his altar and into the prison of my flesh. Perhaps, back in the stinking sewers under Dineen, I repented of my course and resisted his attempt to possess me; instead, I possessed him, or we possessed each other. That is what I prefer to tell myself.

His desires manifested sometimes in my proclivities and tastes, but I could control them. I came to realize that I could never be free of him, not without loosing his evil upon the world. I resolved then to bear him and to find help in controlling the unholy appetites he caused in me.

I had never been a religious man, but I finally found that help when I committed myself to a faith. I hoped to find forgetfulness in faith, too. I write these words now to capture my memories as they exist as of this date, for I expect them to fade just as have all others. I also write these words as cautionary tale to others, or to myself.

Be warned, reader.

Abadon could not breathe. Memories returned to him, at least snippets. The haze that lingered over much of his past vanished, leaving behind sharp, clear images of blood, sex, violence, and death. He saw further back, to the day he traveled alone into Dineen's sewers to summon Abadon, the demon that now writhed within his soul, the demon he had thought to be merely his own guilt.

He was Kazmarek Zhorne, a thaumaturge. He had no brother, only a dark past, a darker soul, and a mind full of memories, some real, some false, some of his own creation, some those of the demon.

"I found your letters in the High Library of Dineen. Your effigy I found among my brother's things, along with his notes. I wondered: Why would you write those letters and leave them in the High Library if you did not want to be found? Then I realized it: Abadon wanted to be found, to be freed. I can free you," he said, and he was not speaking to Kazmarek.

Kazmarek clutched the table. Abadon writhed within him, trying to squirm free, trying to squeeze through the cracks of his will.

"I see him behind your eyes," said the thaumaturge, leaning across the table. "Let him out." He pushed back his chair and lurched to his feet. "Let him feed. Here, Kazmarek. Now. This entire monastery. Let him out! I can bind him to my will. To our will."

Abadon snaked up Kazmarek's throat, past his tongue. He was... emerging.

Kazmarek thought of Prior Nis, the aspirants, the clerics, the monks. He fought. He remembered the blood he had spilled when taking the Oaths. He remembered that he was a thaumaturge. Those memories served him and he held the demon in.

"No," he said through gritted teeth.

Within him, Abadon railed against his bonds.

Kazmarek calmed the demon with a promise, a promise that pleased Abadon.

When Kazmarek had recovered himself, he leaned forward and in a conspiratorial whisper said, "I did want to be found. I have been waiting for one like you to come. We can free him, but it will take two of us to bind him. We cannot do it here."

The thaumaturge breathed heavily, visibly deflated. Still, ambition gleamed in his eyes. "I know a place of privacy," he said.

Men blind for power always show the same failings. I did. The brother of Toorgan did. We believe that others see the world the way we do, through the lens of our ambition. So when I intimated that I wanted the demon out and bound to our service, he believed me. He could believe nothing else.

I took the thaumaturge unawares in his summoning chamber and there kept my promise to Abadon. The demon served me well: I caused the thaumaturge pain until he told me the location of my letters and those of his brother. After retrieving them, I burned house and man in a conflagration that left both in ruins. That sin, too, I will bear. For a reason I cannot explain, I returned the letters to the High Library.

I still feel Abadon within me. I still use his name rather than my own; it reminds me of my purpose. I reside still in the monastery, praying, meditating, trying to forget. The monastery is my home, the abode of my guilt. I know I will never experience a soulbond with Alethan. The darkness within me prohibits it. My god will remain forever separate from me. I try to convince myself that there is nobility in what I do but I know that is a lie. I do it because I can do nothing else.

I have come to believe that my real intent in writing the letters was not to warn others but to save myself through confession. It failed of its purpose, of course. Some transgressions cannot be absolved through confession, and some sins can never be expiated. In the end, some men are meant to bear burdens. I hope there is salvation in that.

There are times, however, when I feel Abadon squirm within me and sense that he is laughing. His laughter reminds me of the words of one of my letters, words that haunt me still, words that make me wonder who controls whom:

Possession is subtle.

Be warned, reader.

Elaine Cunningham

A love of history, including the cultural history expressed through myth and folklore, infuses Elaine Cunningham's writing. She approaches shared-world books as she would historical fiction: an excuse to read far too much in the name of research. A fact geek by nature, this former history teacher considers the fictitious nature of shared-world "histories" to be interesting, but irrelevant. Facts are facts, whatever their origin. And when Truth is needed, she turns to myth.

History and legend play primary roles in Cunningham's creator-owned fiction, as well. "Lorelei" is set in a fantasy-touched Germany, on the banks of the Rhine River, long before the coming of the Romans. Originally sold to *Troll* magazine, which ceased publication before the story saw print, "Lorelei" was first published in 1999 as "River War" in the short-lived e-zine *The Dragon's Scroll*. Her other history-based fantasy tales have explored such diverse settings as 18th-century Rhode Island, medieval Tuscany, and Arthurian Britain. Her first editorial project was *Lilith Unbound* (2008), an anthology of tales based on the Lilith mythology, from Popcorn Press.

Cunningham's shared-world fiction includes the *New York Times* bestseller *Dark Journey* (2002), a Star Wars novel in the New Jedi Order storyline, and three related short stories published in *Star Wars Gamer*. She is perhaps best known for her work in the Forgotten Realms, which to date includes 13 novels, short stories in 11 anthologies, four stories originally published in *Dragon* magazine, and the reprint collection *The Best of the Realms: The Stories of Elaine Cunningham* (2007), which included three new tales. She has also written a novel set in the world of EverQuest (2006's *The Blood Red Harp*), a short story for *Tales of Ravenloft* (1994), and a story for *Tales from Tethedril* (1998), an anthology set in a world created by R. A. Salvatore. In 2008 Cunningham scripted the adaptation of her Forgotten Realms story "The Great Hunt" for the *Worlds of Dungeons & Dragons* comic book anthology. She is currently at work on a serial fiction project for Pathfinder, Paizo Publishing's RPG setting.

When it comes to novels, Cunningham's original work focuses primarily on contemporary fantasy tales. These include two books in the Changeling Detective series from Tor, *Shadows in the Darkness* (2004) and *Shadows in the Starlight* (2006), and "Beyond Dreams," a novella in the paranormal anthology *Beyond Magic* (2008). "Raven," a short story published in the illustrated anthology *Modern Magic* (2005), is being reworked and expanded into an urban fantasy novel.

LORELEI

BY ELAINE CUNNINGHAM

NIGHT CREPT SOUNDLESSLY down from the forested mountains, unnoticed by the dirge-singing river and the people who
had fought along its banks. Mist rose from the river, for the night
was chill and the water was warmer than many of the folk who
had fought that day. Tangible as a wraith, the mist clung to the
river folk and ran in rivulets down their faces, darkening as it
licked away the dried blood of their wounds. It glistened on discarded weapons and darkened the stones the survivors heaped
high upon their fallen kin.

A few stars shone listlessly overhead as the exhausted river folk
trudged up the hill toward their camp. One of the last to climb
the hill was Hronulf the Cooper, an unassuming little man who
had not expected to survive the day's battle. He eyed the summit,
where fires blazed, promising warmth and comfort. The sharp
scent of healing herbs rose from steaming soup caldrons.

He drew in a deep breath, and to his great surprise found that
he was ravenous. It seemed to him that his stomach should rebel
against the very thought of food. Hadn't it roiled and clenched all
day at the sights and the sounds and the stench of death? How
could his body forget so soon what it had endured—and what it
had avoided?

The answer came to him, simple and straightforward: Food
was life. His instincts served him as well, whether at the campfire or the battlefield. A small revelation, perhaps, in a day that
had forced upon him so much new and disturbing knowledge,
but he marked it as a thing important for a warrior to know.

Odd, to think of himself as a warrior. Hronulf had never thought
to wear that particular mantle. He was a cooper and a brewer,
justly proud of his skill at those crafts. His barrels held tight, his
ale seldom went sour. The clan valued him for these things, and
for his way with a clever tale or bawdy jest. Granted, there were

times when Hronulf wished for shoulders like those of Berk the Chieftain or the knotted forearms of old Yusteff Boarslayer. But for the most part, he was content.

He picked up a wooden bowl from a tilting stack and joined the group gathered around the cauldron where Betya, the chieftain's wife, dipped up the soup for the warriors.

Hronulf observed her with wistful pleasure. The daughter of a chieftain, now the wife of one, Betya was the sort of companion the gods granted only the greatest of warriors. Three sons had she given the chieftain, and trained them all to hunt so well that there was little left for their father to teach them. Betya was swift and strong, and she carried herself always with quiet courage. For all that, she was among the first to laugh at a good tale. Hronulf often found himself glancing her way when he told his jests and stories—and if truth be told, at most other times, as well. Betya was beautiful, though she had seen every one of his own thirty winters. Many women of the clan grew thin and stringy with years, but her sturdy form was still pleasantly rounded and her nut-brown hair held the gloss of ripe acorns.

With each bowl she filled, Betya spoke the ritual blessing offered to battle survivors. But her voice was as dull as oak leaves in winter, and her gaze followed Berk—clung to him with a fierce mixture of hatred and love. This day a thread that bound them had been broken. Their firstborn son had followed his father's call to battle. The lad would sleep this night beneath the cairn.

Hronulf's heart ached for Betya, but she would not thank him for speaking of her loss. It was not the clan way. So he merely watched her, and endured his own quiet heartache.

Standing a pace or so behind Betya, as silent as a shadow, was the clan shaman. The wizened old man did not search the faces of the returning warriors for surviving kin, as did most of the old folk and the children. He studied the cauldron, as if a surer tale could be read from the small bones that tumbled in the simmering broth.

When Hronulf's turn came, he held out his bowl for Betya's broth and blessing. To his surprise, the shaman abruptly ceased his contemplation of the cauldron and lifted his gaze to Hronulf's face. A strange expression filled the old man's rheumy, almost colorless eyes. The shaman inclined his head to Hronulf—a tribute more fitting to a chieftain than to a cooper—and then touched his ear.

It was an odd gesture, one that held the power of ritual and the portent of augury. Betya saw it, and a lightning-flash of panic lit her stoic features. For his own sake as well as Betya's, Hronulf brushed aside his dismay and gave the woman a broad wink and a smile. "The old man's powerful fond of my ale."

Betya rewarded him with an uncertain smile and an extra ladle of soup. But the cooper could not easily dismiss the strange little occurrence. He pondered it as he slurped up the broth and sucked the marrow from the small bones that flavored it. Giving a chieftain's tribute to a newly blooded warrior was an ill omen. Berk the Chieftain lived, as did many of the clan's best warriors, but there would be battle tomorrow. If the shaman was looking to Hronulf as Berk's successor, he was dipping his cup in the dregs of a nearly empty barrel.

Hronulf set aside his empty bowl and watched the shaman. The old man had taken his accustomed place at the council fire. He sipped from his bowl and watched with unreadable eyes as the younger men strutted and shouted, shaking their fists at the stars and setting improbable boasts adrift on the night breeze.

Thus did the clan ready their spirits for the next day's battle. The fighting would be fierce. That knowledge was written in the anxious lines creasing the faces of wives and mothers, sung by the rasping sound of weapons against sharpening stones, celebrated in the wild war games that the children, only half understanding, played in the flickering light of their fires.

Hronulf wondered, briefly, if the shaman saw what was to come, if he knew which of the boasting warriors would live and which would fall.

He quickly thrust this thought aside. It was less troubling to watch Berk move about the encampment. Despite his own losses, the chieftain exuded strength as surely as the fires gave off light and warmth. He made the rounds of the fires, exchanging a few words with each warrior.

Berk was a good leader, Hronulf acknowledged, a man that others followed as naturally as spring follows winter. When the sun rose, every man who could still lift a weapon would gladly fight beside his chieftain. And fight they would—there was no question of that. They all knew the clan needed to regain the river.

But why?

The question came unbidden to Hronulf's mind, startling him with its blasphemy. The river was theirs to hold against the many who coveted the fertile valley, the fine fishing. Though, come to think of it, the clanspeople were hunters, not fisherfolk. The forest was their life, the river merely the boundary of the lands they hunted.

Why, then, did they fight and die for the river?

On impulse, Hronulf rose and made his way to the shaman's side. He squatted beside the old man and stared into the fire as he sought words that fit the shape of his thoughts. "Berk is a great man," he ventured at last, thinking it best to begin on solid ground.

The shaman glanced in Hronulf's direction. "He does not understand, but at least he hears. That is more than most men can do."

This faint praise—or was it condemnation?—startled the cooper. Chieftains were heroes, battle-proven and worthy of praise. Skalds and shamans spoke of them in extravagant terms. It was the clan way.

"Strange words, old man. Dangerous words."

"Dangerous words," the shaman repeated with a small, wry smile. Once again he turned that odd, colorless gaze upon Hronulf. "That is the way with truth. If I told the clan half of what I knew, if I tried to explain the songs carried by the night air, I would be branded moon-mad and cast out into the forest to die." The shaman made an impatient gesture toward the council fire.

"All I can do is tell fireside tales, and hope that some might have the ears to hear."

Hronulf waited for the old man to continue. The shaman merely held him in his unblinking, colorless gaze, waiting expectantly for something that Hronulf could not name, much less provide. For lack of better inspiration, he clapped the man on the shoulder as he had seen Berk do. "The time for tales will come soon enough," he said in a bluff, hearty voice. "See that you gird the men for battle to come!"

The intensity faded from the shaman's eyes, to be replaced by the resignation of the very old. "That I will, boy. That I will."

Later that night, when all had eaten lightly of broth and flat cakes made from ground nuts, the warriors gathered around the council fire. It was custom to hear tales of heroism and valor on the night before battle. The stories inspired the men to greater deeds, and reminded them all that they would live beyond the coming day in tales of glory and honor. Despite the disturbing words he had exchanged with the storyteller, Hronulf awaited the tales with as much anticipation as the whispering, jostling children who gathered at the edge of the firelight circle.

But the shaman did not relate the expected stories. There was no ode to those who had fallen that day, not even to Wulfghard, who had fought more battles than the old storyteller had teeth! There were no tales of the wolf-folk, the shapeshifting people of whom they knew, though none had seen. No stories of past river wars, no legends of the clan's heroic ancestors, no tales of the exploits of the Elder Gods. Instead, the old man spoke of something called a mermaid, a ridiculous half-fish, half-woman creature whose songs lured seagoing men to hurl their ships upon the rocks, and so die.

It was an odd story, but the novelty of it seized the attention of the clan. "Why does the mermaid wish to kill these men?" demanded one of the children—a son of Berk and Betya, still too young to join the battle. "Is the sea her clanhold? Does she keep it safe against the men who would sail and plunder it?"

Hronulf saw the chieftain lift a hand to his mouth to cover his proud smile. Those were worthy questions. He suspected the answer would be less pleasing.

"The sirens of the sea know no clan," said the shaman.

"No clan?" The boy was incredulous. "Then why does she do this?"

"No one knows for certain. I can say only this: The mermaid sings, and those who hear her voice and follow it will die."

Several of the listeners shuddered, and one of the children—a tiny, browned-eyed lass named Wren, the much-indulged child of a man who had fallen that day—began to weep softly.

Her mother gathered the little girl close and sent the storyteller a reproving look over her daughter's head. "Why do you frighten the children needlessly? We are many days from the sea. There are no such creatures here. Tell them so!"

But the old man shook his head. "In truth, there are tales of similar creatures in these lands. The wolf-folk are not the only magical beings in these forests. I have heard tell of the lorelei, beautiful women who dwell in the rivers. Their voices are magical, and they lure men into the water, where they are drowned."

Berk scoffed. "That is even more foolish than your talk of mermaids! At least *that* tale makes some sense, for the sound of a woman's voice singing from a rocky shoal could carry far on the night wind and fool sailors into thinking the shore nearby. Ships could be lost, and the men with them. But what fool would leave the land and drown himself?"

"Foolish indeed," the shaman said in a soft, sad voice, "is the man who hears, but does not understand."

A long silence followed. Several faces furrowed as the people of the clan searched for meaning in the old man's words.

The chieftain snorted and tossed the dregs of his ale into the fire. A searing hiss greeted the offering, and steam rose into the night.

"I'm for sleep. Have you heard enough nonsense for one night, Betya?"

His wife rose from the women's circle and followed him to their shared bedroll. The others soon followed, drifting off until the fireside was deserted except for the cooper and the old shaman.

For many long moments, Hronulf stared into the dying flames of the council fire. The shaman's words disturbed him, leaving him feeling as if he'd glimpsed the edge of some long-forgotten dream. The old man sat at his side, patiently awaiting Hronulf's questions. But the younger man's courage deserted him, as it had not done on the battlefield. This particular dream, Hronulf suspected, was best left unexamined.

He hauled himself to his feet and sought out his bedroll. But sleep was long in coming. His blood sang in his veins, and the beating of his own heart sounded in his ears like the pounding of a battle axe on a shield in the moments before the charge. He'd often heard warriors say the night before battle was like nothing else—at no other time did a man feel so completely alive—and now he knew it to be true. For him, this feeling was inspiration enough, but he was sorry that the young men would go to battle without the songs of their ancestors echoing in their hearts. What was the shaman thinking?

He pondered this a while, then shrugged it away as beyond his ken. The morning would come, and with it the battle. And so he willed his battle-song to lull him into sleep, and tried not to think on this night as his last.

When the sky was just beginning to fade toward silver, Hronulf rose from his sleeping place and joined the rest of the warriors. They crept through the fading darkness to the edge of the hill, where a smooth, steep incline swept down to the river valley.

The valley was filled with Northmen, most of them taller and broader than even Wulfghard, the clan champion. They were fair haired and fierce, and there were far too many of them. Yesterday's battle had thinned their ranks, but new fighters had joined the invaders.

A guttural roar, too low to have come from a human throat, rose in challenge to the approaching clansmen.

"Look!" Hronulf breathed, pointing toward a large, dun-colored beast among the gathered Northmen. It was pacing about with barely contained fury.

"A bear," Berk said grimly.

A ripple of consternation passed through the warriors. These invaders had powerful magic indeed, if they could summon and command such a beast. Or perhaps—and this was more frightening still—the bear had been with them always, walking among them as man among men. Hronulf had never quite believed the stories of shapeshifters, but for the first time in his life, he sensed the cold, compelling touch of magic at work.

There was magic, and there was the river. In the swift-flowing days of spring, the river's song was wild and sweet. Surely no man alive could fail to hear its voice, and answer its call.

"The river!" shouted Berk, raising his sword.

"The river!" echoed the clan, their voices sounding as one.

Hronulf shouted as loudly as any. The river belonged to the clan. They would drive the Northmen away from the valley or die trying. In this moment, the matter was that simple. The song of the river sounded clearly in his mind, drowning his fears.

Berk led the charge. The warriors of the clan thundered down the hill after him, and the Northmen ran to meet them.

A tall man with long yellow braids came at Hronulf with lowered pike. Hronulf dug in his heels and raised his wooden shield—a small, round targe he'd made in his cooper's shop. Though sturdily built and boasting a central spike of sharpened iron, it offered scant protection against the oncoming charge. Hronulf knew it well, and so did his enemy. Smug triumph lit the northerner's ice-blue eyes, and his wolfish grin anticipated an easy kill.

But Hronulf held his ground. At the last moment, he dipped the shield down, just a bit, and leaned his body to one side. The pike tore through the upper part of his shield, the weakest part, almost as easily as a stooping falcon might penetrate a cloud.

Too late the Northman saw the danger. Before he could halt his headlong charge, he stumbled and plunged into the targe. The center spike sank deep into his fur mantle.

At once Hronulf released the shield and lifted his wooden cudgel. He swung as hard as he could, smashing into the targe and driving its spike deep into his enemy. The Northman stiffened in shock. Hronulf caught a glimpse of crimson foam at the corners of the man's mustache before he pitched forward like a falling pine.

Hronulf stooped to claim his enemy's pike and ran to meet the next foe. From him, he claimed a fine iron sword. So he continued, playing one trick after another, long after he was deaf to everything but the pain singing in his shoulders and the song of the river beyond.

Long and costly was the battle, but the clansmen pushed the northerners back to the river, wading into the water itself and fighting until the swift-flowing course ran crimson.

At last the clatter of weapons faded into silence. Even the riversong seemed muted. Then ravens gathered like black clouds, and their strident voices were answered by the call of hungry, forest-dwelling wolves.

The clan would not yield up their dead to this grim feast. Women wandered among the fallen warriors, stoic and silent as ghosts as they sought the fate of husband or son, father, brother, lover, friend. They worked long after the night had fallen, building fires to light the battlefield and to hold back the wolves. Betya moved dry-eyed through the carnage, torch in hand and arms bloody to her elbows as she sought to piece together something that had once been her husband. But Berk was not to be found.

Finally the slain were gathered, and stones piled overtop in a mighty cairn to mark the battle and honor the slain. It also gave warning to those who might wish to take the river: Those who held it would not yield it lightly.

As for the northerners, the clan merely tossed their bodies into the water to wash downriver. Not for them the honor of burial upon clan-held land. The bodies of the invaders would come ashore where they may, even farther from their cold homelands than they had any right to be.

That night, the fireside stories rivaled the best tales of the clan shaman. The old storyteller listened in silence, and his sad, strange eyes seemed to measure each of the survivors. It seemed to Hronulf the shaman's eyes lingered on him too long and too often for comfort. He schooled himself to ignore the old man, and listened instead to the tales of valor.

Jorgen and his brother Sveniff had killed the bear. They claimed they'd skinned the beast after the battle and hung the hide over a limb to dry. Upon their return, they had found not the pelt of a bear, but a thin, nearly hairless hide.

A moment of stunned silence greeted this tale. Shapeshifting was the stuff of many stories, but this was the first time such wonders had actually touched the clan.

Yusteff Boarslayer, their oldest surviving warrior, spat loudly into the fire. "Should have kept the hide and tanned it for boot leather!" he roared. "Even a Northman's got to be good for something!"

Rough, exhilarated laughter rolled through the small groups of survivors, and the next warrior rose to tell his tale. When his turn came, Hronulf told his story of the pikesman's defeat against a barrel-bottom targe, and he showed them the fine, rune-carved weapon he had gained from his trick. Amid murmurs of admiration, Hronulf rose to his full, if meager height, and concluded with a broad wink and the observation, "Proof that the length of a weapon is not the truest measure of its worth!"

His bawdy jest brought more laughter and lifted the survivors' spirits one step further from exhaustion and despair. Hronulf continued to talk, and words poured from him as if from some hidden spring. He spoke of the clan's triumphs over the many long years they had held the river, and his clever tongue turned the old stories into ribald tales, shapeshifted the invaders into comical bumblers. Though the clan knew the truth of the matter—they had measured it with each stone they'd heaped upon their warriors' cairn—they took courage from the tales. Laughter rang out again and again, and their eyes shone with the vision Hronulf's words shaped for them, *of* them.

Their celebration lasted long into the night, as those who had cheated death raised their voices and their tankards in defiance.

The fires had burned to ash and silence blanketed the camp, but sleep would not come to Hronulf. When the setting moon was impaled upon the highest trees of the forest, he slipped from camp, compelled by the desire to stand at the banks of the hard-won river.

He was not altogether surprised when a thin, faint shadow approached from behind and mingled with his. He had over-spoken himself with his tales and jests, and the clan storyteller had come to put him back into his place.

"Greetings, shaman," he said with resignation.

The old man was silent for a long moment. "You know what the new day will bring."

Hronulf turned a puzzled frown upon the shaman.

"The clan will choose a new chieftain. They will look to a man who fared well in battle, for this is the way of the clan and the old customs run deep and strong. But he need not be the greatest of warriors, so long as he can hear the song of the river and sing it back to them in a voice they can hear and understand."

His meaning slowly came to the little cooper. "You cannot think they will choose me!"

"Can I not?" The old man gestured to the dark water. "What do you see? What do you hear? Tell me I'm wrong about you, cooper, and I will thank you for it."

"I see the river," Hronulf stammered. "Only that."

"Shall I tell you what I see?" the shaman said in a strange, soft voice. "I see a woman emerging from the moonlit river, rising up from the water like a maid enjoying a summer afternoon's bath. She is young and very beautiful, with the fair, freckled skin of my mother's folk and hair of a glorious red-gold that gleams in the light of the dying moon."

"I see no such woman," Hronulf said, wondering if the old man had gone mad.

"Nor would you. More likely, she would appear to you as brown and buxom as a woman of the river clan, just as she would wear sun-colored braids and eyes the color of a winter sky to entice a northerner."

Hronulf shook his head, not understanding. "A shapeshifter?"

"Lorelei." The old man stooped and dug his fingers into the clay of the riverbank. He said a few strange words in a singsong voice and then rose and advanced on the puzzled cooper. Before Hronulf could anticipate his intention, the shaman touched his clay-streaked fingers to Hronulf's ears, and then again to his forehead.

"See," he admonished. "And do not merely hear, but *listen*. If you cannot, you are no better than Berk."

Suddenly the murmuring of the wind and the river exploded into a dizzying roar, like a hundred unseen spirits shouting for this attention. Hronulf fell to his knees, his hands clamped to his ears. After a time, the tumult began to ebb, and a woman's voice emerged from the chaos.

Her song had an immediate, soothing effect on him. He felt strangely content, yet as disconnected from himself as if he had drunk a barrel of his own ale. All he could do, all he wanted to do, was to listen to the woman's song.

In a strange, sweet voice she sang in an almost-forgotten tongue—the language of the ancient, haunting lullabies of Hronulf's earliest memory.

No, not his memory, Hronulf realized with absolute certainty, but the shaman's. The old man had been captured many years ago during a raid on an eastern tribe. Rumor claimed he was druid-trained, and certainly he seemed to know things the very gods had forgotten. To Hronulf's amazement, he realized he was hearing what the old man heard, seeing what he saw.

The woman standing in the shallows of the river was just as the shaman had described her. She was as slender and white as a birch tree, beautiful beyond compare. Never had Hronulf seen hair of that bright red-gold hue. He could not look away, though he seemed to remember there was reason why he should. A faint voice in some small corner of his mind implored him to remember the shapeshifting warrior his clan had slain. It reminded him that worse dangers existed. It shrieked at him to flee.

But Hronulf stayed and listened as the lorelei sang songs of such poignant beauty he was certain his heart would burst from joy.

Time passed, a moment or an eternity, and suddenly Hronulf realized that he was standing ankle-deep in the cold water. The lorelei, still singing, eased her gown from her shoulders and dropped it into the river. Moonlight lingered on her pale skin.

It had been many years since Hronulf had wanted any woman but Betya, and he had banked that particular fire long ago. As if she sensed his longing, the beautiful apparition shifted form. She became shorter, darker, with a hunter's thick and sturdy frame. Her hair was still gloriously unbound, but it held the nut-brown gloss of Betya's hair, and her face was dear and familiar— Betya's face, but more beautiful than any human woman could be. She held out her arms to Hronulf, and all other thoughts deserted him.

He was one step away from claiming her when his foot hit something both hard and yielding. Instinctively he kicked out, and he felt the tear of fabric. The body of a large brown-haired clansman bobbed to the surface, freed of the submerged limb that had held it under the water. Hronulf glanced down into the unseeing gaze of Berk the Chieftain.

As the current swept away Berk's body, it seemed also to take the strange thralldom that held Hronulf. He did the bravest and most foolish thing he had ever done in his life: he lifted his eyes and gazed straight into the lorelei's face.

"You have claimed victims enough for one day," he said softly. Then he turned and strode for the shore, surprised to find he had the will and the strength to do so.

The lovely creature's cries of protest, her pleas, her promises— all these he ignored. Her voice followed him onto the shore, growing strangely louder and more insistent as he left the river behind.

As he climbed the hill toward the silent campfires, the shaman fell into step beside him. The old man began to speak, telling Hronulf the stories he had denied the clan the night before—tales of the wise chieftains of times past. He spoke with great urgency and told Hronulf things he would need to know. He spoke as if he did not hear the imploring cries of the lorelei.

"Berk heard the siren's song and thought only to fight for the river. The Northmen's leader also heard, but to him the lorelei sang of conquest and pillage. And you—now that you have seen and heard, and what will you do?"

I will tell them the truth.

The words sprang into Hronulf's mind. Just as quickly, he dismissed them. The shaman had been right—the clan would think him moon-mad.

"Do all men hear the lorelei's voice?" he asked tentatively.

"All," the shaman confirmed. "Some more than others. Men follow those whose vision is clear and hearing is keen—as long as these leaders do not sense, or at least do not speak, too much more than the followers' own eyes and hearts can perceive."

"I will lead them if I must," Hronulf said slowly, "but not to war. I know the lorelei for what it is."

The old shaman nodded and fell silent, but the expression on his weathered face was one of deep contentment.

Hronulf felt no such ease. Though he knew he should not, he cast a glance over his shoulder. The spirit of the river knelt on the bank, still wearing Betya's beautiful face. She wept over him as real Betya would no doubt weep private tears over her lost husband.

His heart ached with the knowledge that the lorelei could be his, if only he would lead men into battle to feed her incomprehensible hunger. Perhaps the real Betya could be his as well, for did she not also hear the siren's song? For the price of blood, would the river spirit lure Betya into the new chieftain's arms?

He could have it all. On the morrow, the clan would make him chieftain. The shaman had said so, and Hronulf had reason to believe the old man's vision.

Just as he had reason to fear his own.

"I cannot do this," he whispered.

The shaman gave him a sharp look. "That may be true. The clan will not thank you for ignoring voices all men can hear."

They walked the rest of the way to the camp in silence and parted in silence, for what more was there to say? On the morrow Hronulf would take up this burden. He would bear as well as he could the terrible temptation that came with it.

And so the future chieftain wrapped himself in his cloak, and fell asleep at last with the sound of the lorelei's beautiful, pleading voice in his ears.

James Lowder

James Lowder's dark fantasy tales of Janus the Undying were originally planned as part of a shared world fiction line. As he worked on the novel intended to introduce Janus, the corrupt Lord Ebonacht, and the nightmare-haunted island of Thran, Lowder realized that his plans for the characters and setting conflicted with the shared world's precepts and the book line's general direction. Rather than contort his creations to fit the shared world, he withdrew the novel and, after a long tug-of-war with the original publisher, secured the right to develop the material in creator-owned projects.

"The Unquiet Dreams of Cingris the Stout" first saw print in *Gaming Frontiers* magazine in 2002 and is the earliest existing Janus story, in terms of chronological reading order. The story also serves as a direct prequel to the first novel of the Ebonacht Trilogy, *The Screaming Tower*, which is set for release from Elder Signs Press in the fall of 2008. A number of Lowder's other published tales have featured or at least referenced Janus. The character has appeared—as Janus or Edward Janus—in settings as diverse as the medieval fantasy world of Thran ("Heresies and Superstitions" in *The Leading Edge* #39, 2000), an alternate history Victorian-era Sudan ("The Price of Freedom" in *Troll* #2, 1997), and the gangster-plagued streets of 1920s Chicago ("The Night Chicago Died," originally in 2003's *Pulp Zombies*, but most recently reprinted in *Thrilling Tales* #1, 2008).

Lowder has worked extensively on both sides of the editorial blotter, with both shared world and creator-owned projects. He's authored several bestselling novels, including *Prince of Lies* (1993) and *Knight of the Black Rose* (1991), short fiction for such anthologies as *Truth Until Paradox* (1995) and *Shadows Over Baker Street* (2003), and comic book scripts for DC, Devil's Due, Moonstone, and the city of Boston. He's written hundreds of feature articles and book, film, and game reviews for such diverse magazines as *Dragon*, *Sci-Fi Universe*, and *The New England Journal of History*, and published roleplaying game material for AD&D, Call of Cthulhu, Marvel Super Heroes, and the World of Darkness. As an editor, he's directed book lines or series for TSR, Green Knight Publishing, and CDS Books, and has helmed a dozen critically acclaimed anthologies, including *The Book of All Flesh* (2001), *Path of the Bold* (2004), and *Hobby Games: The 100 Best* (2007). He's been a finalist for the International Horror Guild Award and the Stoker Award, and is a multiple Origins Award winner. While he cannot claim to have written the book on shared world fiction, he can at least say that he penned the entry on the subject for *The Greenwood Encyclopedia of Science Fiction and Fantasy* (2005).

THE UNQUIET DREAMS OF CINGRIS THE STOUT

BY JAMES LOWDER

CINGRIS HUDDLED ATOP a spire of polished black rock. Overhead, swollen thunderclouds moved in bleak procession across a sky the color of freshly spilled pig's blood. He knew, and loathed, that particular shade of crimson from the hours he'd spent as a boy in his father's butcher shop. It didn't seem odd that the sky had taken on that precise hue, any more than it struck Cingris as unusual that the sea pounding the spire's base quite clearly boomed and hissed the word *death* with each pulse of the tide.

This was, after all, a nightmare, and a familiar one at that.

Two creeping steps brought Cingris to the edge of the small, level spot that was his sanctuary. He looked down the face of the spray-slicked spike, and his stomach heaved in protest. Groaning, he forced himself to stare down the rock face in the hope of spotting some half-hidden escape route. As on each of the three previous nights, Cingris found only a featureless spike of stone that fell away to roaring darkness.

A screech filled the air. The noise drowned out even the rumble of the unseen ocean. There was no need to look up; Cingris knew the face and form of his adversary. Memories of the thing haunted his days, just as the thing itself haunted his nights. Yet curiosity had always been one of Cingris's faults, and now it goaded him until he stared skyward with wide, fear-filled eyes.

The beast tore through the air like a feathered and furred thunderbolt, a terrifying mixture of eagle and lion, four times the size of even the largest hunting cat. Round eyes, as yellow and lifeless as lumps of sulfur, fixed on Cingris. The griffin spread the talons on its forelimbs, flexed the clawed pads of its leonine rears. Folding massive eagle's wings to gain speed, the beast became a blur against the blood-red sky.

"Appear," Cingris whimpered. His gaze darted along the edges of his cold, stony perch. "Please..."

As if in reply to the trembling plea, a picket of rowan stakes burst from the ground to form a defensive square around the dreamer. The griffin slammed into the palisade, and the sharpened spikes gouged its shoulders and wings. A cry went up again from the hunter. This time pain overwhelmed the chords of anger in its screech.

Cingris cowered at the center of the tiny rowan fort. Feathers and steaming blood showered down on him, and the musky stench from the beast filled his nostrils. Choking, Cingris shrank back. But the griffin pressed closer. As it did, it impaled itself inch by awful inch upon the picket.

On the previous nights, the dream had ended here, with Cingris and the griffin locked in a violent tableau, their conflict unresolved. Tonight, though, the beast forced itself down the stakes much farther than it had managed before. For the first time Cingris could see the tatters of old flesh clinging to its beak. He could feel the griffin's pyre-hot breath. Each puff seared his face as the hunter closed in for the kill—

Cingris awoke screaming. Sweat beaded his pudgy face. Quivers of fear rippled his jowls. The guts of his shredded pillow floated around him, feathers lofting lazily in the moonlight.

The bed frame creaked as Cingris rolled his not inconsiderable bulk onto the floor. He rushed to the window. A hiss of pain escaped his lips as a cool night breeze slid in through the tall, narrow opening and slipped across his face. He tentatively raised blunt fingers to his cheek and tested the skin. Burned.

Cingris clenched his teeth to hold back the scream scrabbling up from his chest. He tried to cobble together a rational explanation for the burn, but the truth would not be denied: The griffin's breath had scorched him. The hunter in his dreams had the power to inflict real harm.

For a time Cingris stood at the window, staring with unseeing eyes into the night. He half-expected the griffin to appear over the town square and dive toward his second-story room. But the attack never came and the captured scream bled from the inn-keep's locked jaw as a pinched groan. Dread dulled the edge of his terror, replacing it with clarity of thought.

The griffin was a magical assassin, a dream stalker. And if Cingris remembered the old stories correctly, the dream stalker's form revealed its master.

He looked across the small, dusty square that lay between his inn, the Silver Plow, and the ramshackle hulk of his only competitor, the Sleeping Griffin.

A lowlife gambler named Deema had opened the Griffin less than a month ago. Cingris had dismissed the venture as a certain failure; the crossroads town of Kiran played host to the Giant's Feast twice a year, but it could scarcely support one taproom in the off-season. Besides, Cingris's own inn had been the uncontested center of Kiran's meager social life for more than six generations. The Griffin wouldn't change that.

Time had seemed to prove Cingris correct. Few in Kiran trusted Deema and fewer still would frequent his seedy bar. The regulars at the Plow only mentioned the brutish gambler as a punch line. Eisirt the Tailor had even started a pool to predict the hour and date of the upstart taproom's demise. Now, apparently, Deema had found a way to beat the odds and rid himself of his conquering rival.

Cingris considered the possibilities. The gambler could have offered a bloodbond to the Strangerfolk; loosing a dream stalker was well within the power of the Twilight Court. Or he could have forged a bargain with the wild things that lurked just beyond the town limits, the goblins and redcaps and imps that made the nighttime forest so perilous. The right wage could persuade even the most horrific of those creatures to work its magic for a particular end.

Cingris's mind raced. Deema must have offered something of great value to gain the use of a dream stalker. A sweet young girl tended the Griffin's customers, when there were any. Her unstained soul might be valuable enough to pay for the assassin. Cingris had no prize to equal that. He was a widower, with no children. There was Belle, the inn's serving wench, or Janus, the orphan boy who worked the kitchen, but their souls were far from spotless....

Cursing himself, the innkeep dismissed the idea. He knew that it was wrong to drag others down with him. Besides, to forge such a pact was madness. There were more terrible fates than death on the Isle of Thran, and bargaining with the Strangerfolk was a certain way to discover just what those fates entailed.

Sudden sounds drew Cingris's attention back to the town square. The door to the Sleeping Griffin was opening to admit someone. Cloaked in black, the shape crept haltingly past the oak platform at the square's center, toward the inn. In his left hand the stranger clutched a yew staff topped with three metal rings. The rings chimed brightly each time he planted the staff, a sharp contrast to the grinding hiss of his crippled footfalls.

As the black-clad man reached out to the doorframe to help himself across the threshold, Cingris glimpsed an elaborate silver gauntlet that glowed with reflected moonlight. This time the cry of fear could not be held back; the shriek burst from Cingris's throat. The cloaked figure paused, then turned toward the open window. Slowly, he held out his silver-gauntleted right hand in an arcane sign of malediction.

Cingris gaped, horrorstruck, as the figure disappeared into the Sleeping Griffin. That gauntlet was the centerpiece of a hundred Thranian tales of horror, its owner someone who made all the innkeep's earlier dark imaginings seem foolishly hopeful. His nemesis hadn't bargained with the Strangerfolk or the goblins to loose the dream stalker. He'd forged a pact with Lord Ebonacht.

"That's quite a welt you got there." Eisirt gestured with his brimming mug toward Cingris's red cheek. "You been chasing Belle around after closing again?"

A burst of ale-strengthened laughter rang through the common room at the Silver Plow. Cingris forced a smile, an expression everyone misinterpreted as a conspiratorial leer. As for Belle, she shook her head and let the comment pass unchallenged. The tailor was wrong about Cingris chasing her, but a reputation as someone who could defend herself helped keep the rowdy farmhands and lecherous merchants at bay.

"I'd like to be here the next time she puts you in your place," Eisirt pressed happily. "You deserve it. You're old enough to be her father—" he gulped down a mouthful of ale and winked at the shepherd slouched at his side "—and heavy enough to be the rest of her family!"

Cingris had made an art of dealing with friendly barbs about his weight, so the whole taproom fell silent in anticipation of the host's witty retort. But the near-sleepless night had jumbled his thoughts, and a churning dread was working him to distraction. He heard the griffin's hunting call in the patrons' laughter. Their pipe smoke became the beast's breath, the amber ale in their glasses myriad reflections of its sulphur-colored eyes. And every silver coin slapped onto a tabletop strengthened the image of Ebonacht's gauntlet gleaming in Cingris's mind.

At the thought of the gauntlet's infamous owner, Cingris silently repeated a prayer against evil for the hundredth time that morning. Lord Ebonacht spun necromancies so hideous they supposedly terrified even the Strangerfolk's mightiest princes and sent goblin lords scurrying to their barrows, their teeth chattering all the way. Nightmares were Ebonacht's coin. He trafficked in them the way inns trafficked in ale.

"Nightmares," said a voice in the taproom, as if it had pulled the word from Cingris's troubled thoughts.

The innkeep looked up to find Janus standing in the kitchen door. The young man's eyes were fixed on Eisirt the Tailor. "Nightmares," Janus repeated. "That's what caused the welt. Cingris hurt himself falling out of bed after a bad dream."

In most places, such a revelation would have prompted mocking laughter, but not on the Isle of Thran, where superstitions about bad dreams and dire omens ran deep. And not when it came from the lips of young Janus, who alone of his countrymen held those superstitions in open contempt. From him the statement was a challenge, one that both infuriated and frightened the locals. To let it pass in silence might be construed by the minions of the Twilight Court—perhaps even now hidden among them at the Silver Plow—as a sign of rebellion. But to confront the outrage might require someone to speak the names of those same minions of the Strangerfolk aloud. The rituals for doing so were so complicated that it was better not to utter the names at all.

Janus understood their quandary and counted on it. The web of competing superstitions was so complex it paralyzed most Thranians. They couldn't even raise a hand against him for fear of foiling the terrible supernatural revenge that the Twilight Court must surely be planning for him, just for showing the phantom kingdom such disrespect. "You all tremble at shadows," he said, reveling in the men's self-enforced impotence. "You quake for fear of things you've never seen."

"Because we can't see something don't mean it's not there," one of the shepherds ventured. "Like air. Can't see that, can you?"

"You can feel it fill your chest each time you breathe," Janus shot back. "What evidence do you have of the Strangerfolk? Can any of you prove you've seen a creature of the Twilight Court, or that Lord Ebonacht is some undying sorcerer and not just the latest in a long line of very mortal recluses?"

The answer the young man expected, and received, was silence. No one had any evidence to support these beliefs—at least evidence of the sort that Janus had not easily, and rightly, dismissed before. Yet still they clung to the centuries-old stories of Thran's dark heritage, and let those tales color every aspect of their daily lives.

Janus crossed his thin arms over his chest. "Fools," he spat.

"The only fool here is you," Eisirt said, though it was unclear if the bitterness edging those few words was born of Janus's comments or his own inability to muster a better reply.

"And perhaps Cingris," one of the shepherds added. "For letting a bad bit of work like you stay under his roof. My sleep would be the poorer having you in the next room, too."

A sneer curled Janus's lip. "He's a better, braver soul than any of you lot."

"That's enough, boy," Cingris warned at last.

Janus readied a sharp-tongued reply. Though Cingris had raised him for almost all of his fifteen years, Janus was more than willing to argue with anyone. Yet the haggard look on the innkeep's face, the withering terror in his eyes, was so extreme that it left the retort stillborn. In its place, Janus murmured a surprisingly meek, "Yes, sir," and retreated to the kitchen.

A disheartening silence smothered the taproom until Belle thumped an empty glass onto the counter next to Cingris. "Nightmares and such are off the menu. Time for you all to chase a new topic," she said with a brightness she did not feel. "You've run that one to death."

"Besides, there's better conversations to be had about other things that go on in bed, eh?" someone called.

A flush colored Belle's face as crimson as her employer's scalded cheek, and she cast her gaze to the floor. The timing and execution of both displays of feigned embarrassment would have awed the most veteran thespian. With an equally practiced sway of her hips, she exited to the kitchen, intent on giving Janus a piece of her mind. Her departure would also allow the patrons to sweep away the gloom by pursuing the topic at hand with bluntness they would never use in her presence.

Yet the conversation floundered in Belle's absence, with Cingris's grim mood overpowering even the few futile attempts to wallow in jovial obscenity.

"Split seams and tangled thread," Eisirt muttered after a few uncomfortable moments. The tailor rolled to his feet and made his way rather unsteadily toward Cingris.

Oblivious to all but the fearful thoughts fogging his mind, the innkeep mechanically moved a rag over the glass clutched in his fat fingers. "Eh? You dry again?" Cingris asked when finally the tailor shook his arm. "Belle, get Eisirt another—" He looked around. "Where's she gotten to?"

"Back to scold that monstrous ward of yours," Eisirt said. He rapped the ale-stained bar in a pattern meant to hasten a wish's fulfillment. "May she employ the sharpest knife in the kitchen to make her point."

Cingris set aside the glass and sighed. "Concede, at least, that the boy has reason to be bitter. An unknown father, a mad mother—and the whole town's malice simply because those unfortunate events suggest some awful fate still in store for the lad. If it weren't for your son, he'd have nary a friend in the world, besides me and Belle."

"If I had my say of it, he'd have you two alone," Eisirt grumbled. "But I've no more mastery of my boy Dob than you do of your foundling." The tailor repeated the patterned tapping on the bar, though this time he did not speak his wish aloud. Cingris knew the man well enough to guess it had something to do with Janus vanishing from Thran forever.

"See here," the tailor said after a moment. "I hope you're not letting the boy's ignorance stop you from taking care of your problem."

"I—I don't know what you mean," Cingris replied.

"The nightmares." Eisirt leaned closer and lowered his voice to a conspiratorial whisper. "There are ways of dealing with such things. People who can help you."

Cingris glanced around nervously. "That's illegal."

"I worry about my soul first, the laws second, even if it puts my life in danger."

To dabble in magic was a dangerous business on Thran. The Ebonacht family had outlawed sorcery decades past. Most thought the ban was intended to prevent anyone for challenging Lord Ebonacht, rather than protect his subjects, but the superstitious farmers and craftsmen were eager enough to deal with any suspected wizard or witch that came their way. Each village had its own method of dealing with such threats—a deep and swift stretch of river, a specially built rowan scaffold, or merely an old and trustworthy axe. The laws against consorting with a sorcerer were only slightly less severe than the ones against being one.

The innkeep turned away from his old friend. "I don't think we want to be discussing this."

"I trust you, Cingris, and I know you aren't afraid to deal with outcasts. You shelter one under your own roof." Eisirt looked over both shoulders to be certain no one had ambled up to the bar. "I've heard that the tinkers have set up shop an hour or so down the Forest Road. The old woman, Fea, helped me when that ache crippled my fingers. Turned out it was a curse, and—well, it wasn't luck that lifted it."

Had he not seen the silver gauntlet, Cingris never would have dared to defy the edict against sorcery. But Lord Ebonacht was already acting against him, already helping Deema achieve his destruction. He was surely doomed if he did not find his own help.

"All right. How do I find them, and how much money should I bring?"

Before another hour had passed, Cingris closed up the taproom and sent his patrons on their way with a final drink on the house. Belle and Janus looked on in confusion as he hurriedly filled a small sack with coins. His distraction had metamorphosed to resolve somehow, but that left him equally unresponsive to questions. He departed without any leave-taking or explanation, though the rowan staff he carried suggested a destination outside of Kiran. Such staves had long been believed to be proof against the bloody-minded goblins, thieving bogels, and shape-shifting waffs that lurked in the surrounding woods.

As he emerged from the Silver Plow, Cingris gripped that staff tightly and paused to glower in defiance at the Sleeping Griffin. Deema had just emerged from the inn with a rickety ladder and a bucket of tools. Even as Cingris watched, the rival innkeep leaned the ladder against the building's weatherworn facade and went to work on his sign. It looked as if someone had taken an axe and a paintbrush to the carved griffin; its wooden shoulder was splintered and its breast was spattered with crimson.

Cingris gaped at the sign. Its wounds matched those the picket in his dream had inflicted upon his would-be assassin.

"Hurry up, Gerthec!" Deema barked. "I need to get this done before nightfall."

Deema's dim-witted assistant staggered out of the inn hauling another, larger sign. This griffin was nearly twice the size of its predecessor, with talons of hammered brass and a beak of black iron. Glassy yellow eyes stared from beneath heavy lids. Those eyes were sightless, unblinking, but Cingris could feel a palpable wave of malevolence strike his back as he turned from them and hurried north toward the Forest Road.

The tinkers' camp was easy enough to find; it was the one built from human bones.

Tables and torch-posts and tent pegs were all constructed of them, as were the four small wagons in which the tinkers wandered the island. Cingris stood at the road's edge, stunned. The stories he'd heard, told in whispered voices late at night, described the tinkers' camp as terrifying. He had steeled himself accordingly, ready to confront a sight to chill the blood in your veins. Now, as he looked around him, the innkeep struggled for a word to describe the camp. Whatever that word was, it wasn't *terrifying*.

Perhaps the bright, late afternoon sunshine robbed the place of its menace. Perhaps it was the way in which the tinkers seemed so comfortable with their surroundings. Not far from Cingris, an old man dozed in a chair made up of some unidentifiable leather stretched between human femurs. Near the wagon, a girl whistled cheerfully as she attended a half-dozen wild forest fowl crammed into a coop with ribs for bars. A little boy sat upon the ground at the very center of the clearing. A ragged cloth bear snuggled beside him, he played jacks with a red ball and a scattering of finger bones. Their utter disinterest in the ossuary thrown up around them made it seem to Cingris more squalid and unfortunate than frightening.

"You bring us work?"

Cingris started at the sudden, shouted question. The woman who had asked it stood next to the rear-most wagon, hands on her hips, foot tapping with impatience. Cingris realized that this must be Fea, matriarch of the tinkers. Like the camp itself, she had little in common with her counterpart from the night tales; she more resembled the sturdy farm wives that came into Kiran's monthly markets than the spite-hardened old crone of the stories.

"Uh, right," Cingris stammered. "Work." He took a step forward, then backed up, waiting to be formally invited into the camp. As he did, he stumbled over an exposed tree root and nearly fell.

"In with you, then," Fea said with an enigmatic smile. "Before you hurt yourself."

That odd half-smile lingered about her lips as she waited for the innkeep to cross the camp, a trek he made with painful care and slowness for fear of bumping against some weird table or washtub. The other tinkers spared him only the briefest of looks as he passed.

"What do you have for us?" Fea said without preamble, when Cingris finally reached her side. She nodded at the small sack he carried. "Metal mending, is it?"

"No, no," Cingris blurted. He hefted the sack of coins with fat fingers. "That's what I can pay—if you get me what I need."

Fea studied him for a moment, her appraising eye only making him fidget and fumble all the more. "I want some, uh, *special* help," he stammered.

"You want some company? You'll have to wait for my daughter. She's—"

"No. Not that," he said. "You misunderstand."

Fea's eyes narrowed. "Out with it."

"A dream stalker," Cingris whispered. "I need you to free me from a dream stalker."

Her smile suddenly gone, the tinker rumbled, "You'll find no help of that kind here."

"Please," Cingris cried. "There's no one else."

"Do you know magic's price?" Fea hissed. She swept an arm wide. "All this. Our dead surround us because of magic. One of my ancestors so lusted for the power that she paid the goblins whatever they wanted in exchange for its secrets—secrets so foul that the earth itself refused to accept her corpse when she finally died, or any of her blood after her. The Grim Tailor's needle and thread couldn't sew their eyes closed. It's either carry them with us forever, or face them when their graves shove them out and send them in search of us."

Cingris opened the sack and emptied it. Coins cascaded into the dirt, all the profit he'd ever made from the Silver Plow. Finally he took a simple gold band from his finger and dropped it onto the pile. "I'll not ask you to harm anyone," he said softly. He'd meant to say more, but the words wouldn't come.

Fea retrieved only a single silver coin from the heap, then motioned for Cingris to follow her around to the other side of the wagon. The innkeep barely noticed the skulls grinning at him from where they'd been worked into the wagon's design, or the oddly beautiful arrangement of vertebrae that made up the small table to which the tinker led him. Before she sat down, Fea tossed the coin into the shadow of a nearby oak, where it was lost in the gloom. Cingris guessed that this must have been a gift to the Strangerfolk, who were said to travel through shadows to the Twilight Court, but he couldn't understand the invocation Fea spoke next. The language was unknown to him. The sounds of the words were inhuman, bestial.

The tinker continued to mutter in that same strange tongue as she poured a red liquid into a wide silver bowl, then sloshed the contents onto the ground in a line between the table and the shadowed oak. "A silver coin to loosen the tongue of the shadow walkers," she announced. "The juice of the rowan berry to keep them at bay."

Fea fixed her dark eyes on the dregs remaining in the silver bowl. She studied them for a moment. Then she leaned slightly to one side, as if she were listening to some quiet voice from the oak shadow, a voice that Cingris could not hear. "Yes," she said, "a dream stalker. Sent by a rival."

"A man named Deema, I think," Cingris offered. "He opened an inn across the town square from mine."

She nodded and cocked her head, listening intently again. This time Cingris thought he heard a whisper from the wood, but it might have been nothing more than the wind. "It is the one you suspect," Fea said in a dreamy, distant voice. "But you have foiled his plans. The assassin cannot reach you. Why is that?"

"A rowan picket springs up around me in my dream."

"Your bed frame is rowan, then. An heirloom carved long ago," Fea said. "Yes, that would be the reason the sending cannot reach you. Rowan is proof against such things and will keep you safe from evil sent against you as you sleep. Do not sleep elsewhere."

"And to stop the dream stalker?" Cingris asked eagerly. He leaned forward to peer into the silver bowl at the rowan dregs. The shapes were as mysterious to him as Fea's incantations. "Does that tell me what I can do to destroy it?"

"I can make a talisman to defend you, but there is no certain way to stop a dream stalker, short of evil of a greater kind directed against the sender. That I will not help you do."

Cingris's shoulders sagged and he scrambled in his thoughts for some solution they'd missed. "The sign outside his inn was damaged in the same places as the monster in my dream was wounded by the spikes. Maybe if I chopped up the sign, burned it—"

"The sign is merely a guide for the sorcery. It's a shape the sending can borrow," the tinker interrupted. "This Deema could simply get a new sign or assign the stalker another form. So long as you sleep only in your bed, the thing cannot reach you. Take comfort in that."

The innkeep buried his fat face in his hands. "Is killing Deema the only way to stop this?"

"Death will not stop the sending," Fea said angrily. "And I will not help you in the things that would end it. Besides, this Deema has allied himself with someone quite powerful, someone whose power is beyond mine to counter."

"Lord Ebonacht."

"What?"

"Lord Ebonacht," Cingris repeated, his voice as dead as his hopes. "I think I saw him at Deema's inn last night."

"Get away from here!" Fea shouted. She grabbed the staff from Cingris and hit him with it. "Get away before you destroy us all!"

The first blow struck Cingris on the shoulder, but he ducked the next two clumsy swipes, then pulled the staff from Fea's hands. With a gasping sob, the tinker collapsed to her knees. "Not him," she pleaded. "Not again."

Cingris heard a sound at his back, one he'd heard in his taproom more often than he cared to admit: the hiss of a long-bladed knife leaving its sheath. He turned to find the old man holding a saw-toothed blade in a fighting stance, expertly flicking the knife so that its edge flared in the sunlight and flashed in the innkeep's eyes. Cingris raised one hand to shield his face and bulled ahead. He felt the old man fall away before him. As he rounded the corner of the wagon, he tensed for the bite of the blade, but the blow never came.

"Here," said a small, high voice. "Take him."

Cingris looked down at the boy standing before him. The grubby child, no more than five or six years old, held a patchwork bear in his hands. He shook it slightly and said, "I heard you tell Nana about your nightmares. I had them, too."

"Go away," Cingris said, glancing over his shoulder. He could hear Fea and the old man, but they were still on the wagon's opposite side. He'd be able to get away, if he ran. But when he took a step forward, a surprisingly strong hand on his leg stopped him.

"Nana made him for me," the boy said, round face pale with remembered fear. He thrust the bear up again. "To protect me from the nightmares Lord Ebonacht sent to get me after I stole some apples from his trees. It worked, so I don't need him any more."

Fea finally rounded the wagon, the old man limping at her side. "No, Tomari," she cried. "Don't help him! You'll bring his curse down on all of us!"

Cingris snatched the bear and ran. Had he been allowed even a moment at the camp to consider Fea's warning, to ponder what grief he might cause the child by accepting his aid, he would not have taken the poor little boy's toy. At least, that was what Cingris told himself later, as he wheezed and puffed at the side of the Forest Road, unable to waddle one step farther. By the time the stabbing pain in his chest had subsided enough for him to walk again, he'd convinced himself that there was no point in taking the thing back. The vagabonds hadn't come after him, so it couldn't have been all that serious. Or perhaps whatever peril he'd exposed them to couldn't be undone by the bear's return.

"I'll make it right tomorrow," he said, one eye on the darkening sky. "At least now I have a fighting chance to see tomorrow."

With the motley, moth-eaten bear clutched to his breast, Cingris set off through the growing twilight for the Silver Plow and the safety of his bed.

Janus stood in the doorway to his guardian's bedroom. The young man frowned at the floor, staring at the scuffed wood as if searching there for the right thing to say. Cingris saved him the struggle. "I know you're sorry, boy," the innkeep said. "You're always sorry after you start trouble in the taproom. I just wish for once that you realized it was the wrong thing to do *before* you opened your mouth."

"I—I didn't think you were coming back," Janus noted, after clearing his throat twice to drive back his tears.

"No fear of that," Cingris replied kindly. "Not even you could drive me away from the Plow for long." Before his ward could ask again, he quickly added, "And it's none of your business where I went. Off to bed with you."

Janus lingered for a moment in the doorway. "You know I don't believe in—" he began, then shook his head and started again. "If it would help you sleep easier, I'd stand watch over you."

Fiercely Cingris hugged the boy, then turned him around and pushed him toward the stairs. The innkeep usually avoided such open displays of affection, but his ward's offer was so unusual that it called for nothing less. "Thank you," Cingris said. "But I can deal with any more bad dreams by myself. After all—" he patted his gut and forced a laugh "—I'm a big boy now, eh?"

After listening to be certain Janus had made his way down the creaky stairs to his bed near the taproom hearth, Cingris locked the door, undressed, and struggled into his nightshirt. He recovered the bear from its hiding place in his clothes chest. The innkeep felt distinctly foolish kneeling beside his bed to pray for a safe night's sleep with a child's stuffed animal in his arms, but he did so anyway.

With an exhausted sigh, Cingris pushed himself up from his knees. He rolled onto the bed, unafraid of sleep, hopeful that this night would see the dream stalker's demise. But as he settled in, he found that the bear had snagged on the wooden frame. A jagged splinter had pierced the talisman through one leg. The crude stitching there threatened to come undone, so Cingris had to work carefully to free it. He managed to do so with enough dexterity that the bear was left with only a small hole to mark its misfortune.

The innkeep drifted off to sleep wondering if that wound might prevent the talisman from doing its duty. The answer came quickly enough. As on the four previous nights, Cingris found himself huddled atop a spire of black stone, beneath a ghastly red sky. Only now a bear towered beside him. The beast was twice Cingris's own considerable bulk, with paws as large as the man's head. Its hide was still the motley of its smaller counterpart, and a fist-sized hole gaped high on the bear's hip.

Cingris scarcely had room to move. For some reason, the rowan picket stood ready, even before the arrival of the dream stalker. There was little enough space for him within the defensive spikes, and the bear was so large the innkeep was pressed against the barricade's interior.

When at last the griffin appeared, Cingris saw that it now resembled the larger, more ferocious creature on Deema's new sign. The beast flexed its talons and gnashed its black beak, then swooped lower. At the sight of the bear, though, it slowed its descent. It hovered, great wings flapping, and glared down at the defenders in anger and confusion. The griffin dove again, but pulled up at the last moment and retreated to the crimson sky.

Cingris patted the bear's motley hide. "Safe. I can hardly believe—"

The rest was lost as the bear roared once, a bellow that shook the spire to its roots, then buried its bright silver teeth in Cingris's throat. The griffin caught the headless body that the bear tossed out of the defensive square; it toyed with the corpse for a time, but soon grew bored and let the remains of Cingris the Stout plummet into the dark sea far below. At the tiny, sullen splash, the pulsing tide ceased its call of "death" and hissed a sigh of satisfaction.

A small, high voice called out in Kiran's town square. It spoke a single word in a language not meant for human tongues, and in reply, something appeared at a second-story window in the Silver Plow. The motley bear braced itself in the narrow frame, cheerfully waved its paw, then leaped into the night. With a soft thud, it struck the hard-packed earth before the inn. As it rose and waddled toward the little boy waiting for it with outstretched arms, the thing limped only a little. Not from the fall, but from the wound inflicted by Cingris's rowan bed frame.

Tomari took up the bear in his arms and squeezed it so tightly he hurt his own ribs. Then, pouting, he prodded the little hole in its leg with one finger. "Nana will fix that," he said. "Don't you worry."

The boy padded across the square to the Sleeping Griffin and slipped unnoticed through the open door to the taproom. He found the inn's owner counting out money for his grandmother.

The man grimaced as he slid each coin across a greasy table, as if he were slicing off bits of his flesh and giving them away.

"And the coins you can pry off this thing should settle it," Deema said, dropping a glove onto the table. The leather was studded with silver pieces and fake gems so that it resembled, at least from a distance, the gauntlet supposedly worn by Thran's mysterious ruler.

"Not enough," Fea replied. "We don't expect the rest now, of course. You'll pay us this much—" she indicated half the heap of coins before her "—on each full moon."

Deema cursed and spat on the filthy floor. "If anything, I should be getting something back to pay for my new sign. Those things aren't cheap, you know."

"Had you done as I asked and found out about the man's bed first, we all would have been spared some expense," Fea said as she gathered up the money. She tapped each coin lightly against her bracelet before dropping it into a small, velvet-lined chest, listening for the sour note of a counterfeit. All the while, she continued to explain how an ancient blessing on the wooden frame had kept out the dream stalker and had almost been strong enough to spoil their second sending, even though Cingris himself had carried the talisman into the bed. "I want you to get that bed frame," she said at last. "You can make it part of your next payment to me."

"Fine. I'll wait until the town lynches that ward of his for the murder and take it then."

A coin slipped from Fea's fingers and clattered to the floor. "Do not rely upon your neighbors to deal with that one," she said. "No, that young man has another, more terrible fate in store." She tried to shake off her discomfort, but the topic clearly bothered her. "A few silver will be enough to gain the bed. He'll need money now that his guardian is gone. Beyond that, I do not want him involved in our business."

"Fair enough," Deema said. "I'll buy the bed. Will that settle things?"

"The fee is not negotiable." Fea swiped her hand across the tabletop, sliding the rest of the coins into the chest. Only the false gauntlet remained on the oak plank between them. "But if you care to argue further, perhaps we can bring this dispute before Lord Ebonacht. Ask him to settle it. I'm certain he would be interested in hearing how you impersonated him in order to frighten Cingris into visiting our camp."

"At your direction!" Deema shot to his feet. A nasty-looking knife appeared in his hand and thudded into the table, pinning the glove, before Fea even had a chance to react. "I've run this same game on rubes myself, so spare me the demonstration. You want to play power against power? The mayor will happily call Ebonacht's men to escort us all to the manor for an audience. I don't know what the laws say about play-acting, but I do know what they say about sorcery."

"'Scuse me," Tomari said. When Deema turned to the little boy, he saw only a vague form in the darkness. "You have a little girl," the shadowy figure continued. "You don't keep her with you, but you send her and her mum money."

"How did—?" The gambler flashed a look at the tinker matriarch, searching for some sign that this was just another move in the game, but Fea was staring at the child. She obviously hadn't heard him come in either. And her face was pale, her hands clasped together so tightly that the knuckles had gone white.

Deema turned back to Tomari, but the child was gone. He peered around the large room, but could see no sign of him. He listened for the telltale creak of a floorboard, the sound of a footfall; he heard only the sputtering of the lone candle on a nearby table and a strange whispering, as of many muted voices speaking at once, coming from the darkest, most shadow-draped corner. The whispering stopped abruptly, and Tomari spoke from that same corner. "It's a secret. Nobody else knows the money comes from you—not even them. That's nice of you."

Tomari emerged from the darkness, passing in front of the open front door just as the clouds parted above the square and a shaft of moonlight streamed into the room. "Maybe she'd like this," the boy said. Before him he held the tattered bear. Its blood-flecked silver teeth flashed in the ghostly light.

Deema shook his head and retreated up the stairs. Fea smiled her gratitude to her grandson, but when he came close, she couldn't bring herself to pat him on the head. Instead, she busied her hands with the leather straps she needed to secure the chest of coins to her back for the long walk home.

For his part, Tomari waited patiently for his nana to be ready, passing the time by hugging his bear and reassuring it that its hurt would be mended soon. He missed the ragged thing when they were apart, and slept better when it was by his side at night. The little boy knew that terrors really did lurk under your bed, and they always had sharper claws and bloodier fangs than the ones you imagined. He knew that there were things in the darkness, creatures far more monstrous than the winter-starved wolves or even the goblins and walking dead that stalked the unwary.

It never occurred to Tomari that there was a reason these terrors did not threaten him, a reason they confessed their frightful deeds and shared their secrets, whispering endlessly to him in lightless corners and lost woods. For the night things could see him as clearly as he saw them, and they recognized a truth the little boy had yet to discover—that he, of all the horrors haunting the Isle of Thran, was among the very worst.

Will McDermott

Will McDermott specializes in game-related fiction. He's written two novels and more than a half-dozen short stories set in the world of Magic: The Gathering, most recently a tale for the anthology *Shadowmoor* (2008). In addition, he wrote the definitive novels for Games Workshop's Warhammer 40,000 antihero, Kal Jerico—*Blood Royal* (2005), *Cardinal Crimson* (2006), and *Lasgun Wedding* (2007). These gritty novels set in the Hive city on the world of Necromunda give a glimpse of both the seedy side of the lower reaches, where a quick trigger finger and a quicker wit are the only things keeping you alive, and the political backstabbing that runs rampant in the top of the Spire.

More recently, McDermott has taken his distinctive style of dialog and storytelling online. He has spent the bulk of the last two years writing for the Guild Wars MMORPG. His words are now read by millions of gamers around the world as they play *Guild Wars Nightfall* and *Guild Wars: Eye of the North*. He is now hard at work on *Guild Wars 2*.

"Off-Ramp" is one of several short stories that McDermott has written over the years for anthologies set outside the strange and wonderful world of game fiction. He was asked by editor Eric Reynolds, on short notice, to provide a work for an anthology that had as its central conceit stories written as if the last 50 years of science had never happened, penned as if by authors living in the 1950s, peering into the future.

Thus "Off-Ramp" is set on a space platform above an Earth that was visited a hundred years ago by aliens. However, those aliens didn't come to share technology, or overthrow humanity, or even serve us up at a buffet. No, they simply wanted to build a truck stop on the Intergalactic Superhighway. And it's not even a big truck stop. "The Earth's stuck out in the boonies of the universe," McDermott explains. "We're Muncie, Indiana."

The story was a huge departure from McDermott's franchise work. "There is no real villain and no big fight scenes," he notes. "It's a simple tale of a boy overcoming his fears and insecurities by getting himself into a lot of trouble. The story's core concept came to me while brainstorming ideas for the anthology on a long road trip, late at night, driving home from a party at the penthouse apartment of Canadian SF author, Rob Sawyer. When asked 'What do you see?' by my wife (and creative director), I replied, 'Tail lights. A long line of tail lights.' That started a conversation that ended with the creation of this fun and interesting future where Earth has been turned into one giant truck stop."

ON THE OFF-RAMP OF THE INTERGALACTIC SUPERHIGHWAY

BY WILL MCDERMOTT

FRED WIPED DOWN the counter for the umpteenth time that morning. It wasn't that the counter got dirty. It was just that Fred was bored. There hadn't been a truck in the station in days. The diner was spotless. Old Marge, the station's cook and resident mother figure, had made him mop the floors twelve times this week, and yesterday he'd spent three hours cleaning the grease traps.

What Fred really wanted to do was spend more time in the garage. George had said last week that he'd start teaching Fred how to tear down and rebuild a sub-light thruster. But as soon as George realized how slow they were, he'd taken the week off to go fishing.

Fred didn't blame him. George had been on duty at the station for over a month and hadn't been Earthside since before Fred had arrived six months ago. Still, that meant there was nothing for Fred to do but wipe down the counters and wait for a customer... any customer.

Just as Fred was about to volunteer to mop the floors again, Marge stepped out of the kitchen followed by a gangly kid wearing a broad grin on his sunburned face.

"Hey, Fred," said Marge. Her eyes crinkled almost shut on her pudgy face as she smiled. As usual, that smile made Fred want to help her in any way possible. It's how she'd gotten him to clean the grease traps. Still, he was wary of what was coming next.

"This is Roy," she said. "He'll be helping out around here. He came in on the bus that took George planetside. He just finished his orient-ation."

Fred smiled at how Marge said the word, as if the training took place somewhere in the Eastern Kingdoms.

"You show him around the station while I go clean the grease traps."

Fred wanted to argue that he'd done that yesterday, but knew that his idea of clean and Marge's idea of clean were about as close as the station was to Earth.

After Marge banged through the swinging door into the kitchen, Fred took a long look at Roy. He stood well over six feet tall. His sandy hair all seemed to grow straight out from the center of his head, cascading down past his ears. He wore ratty jeans and a white shirt with ripped sleeves to allow more room for his bulging biceps.

Fred smiled at the newcomer. It would be good to have someone his own age to talk to. "So, Orient-ation," said Fred. "You come up from China then?"

It was the same joke George had told Fred on his first day. They'd had a good chuckle about Marge's lack of worldliness despite the fact that she was chef to denizens of the entire universe.

Creases formed on Roy's sunburned forehead as his ear-to-ear smile turned into a sullen frown. "Naw," he said. "I'm from Muncie, Indiana."

Great. Another yokel. Fred wasn't any jetsetter either, but he'd grown up in Portland, Oregon—a decent-sized city with ties to the aerospace industrial complex of the Northwest. And he had dreams. Big dreams. Sighing inside, Fred decided to give Roy a chance and started the tour.

"Welcome to station eleven twenty-seven," he said and extended his hand. Roy grasped it in a crushing grip, shaking his hand so hard, Fred almost lost his balance. Afterward, he flexed his fingers to make sure they still moved before continuing.

"Let me show you around," he said and led Roy around the counter toward the door. "This is the diner, obviously. Marge makes everything from a mean omelet to some nasty-looking dishes with things that squirm. But the customers from Antares seem to think they're the best squirming worms they've ever eaten, so I guess she must be a pretty good cook."

Fred palmed open the door and a whoosh of air escaped into the cavernous repair bay as the air pressure equalized. George would have to look into that when he got back. There was either a problem with the compressors or another micrometeor had made a pin-sized hole in the repair bay again.

Spotlights illuminated circles of floor in the bay far into the distance, showing hydraulic lifts, coffin-sized metal boxes full of tools, and a few repulsor carts. These sounded more glamorous than they looked, being nothing more than raised metal grating that lay dormant until flipped on. At each station, hoses of numerous colors extended into the blackness above. To the side there was a bank of five-story-tall glass-pane doors that led to the landing pads and the filling stations.

"This is the repair bay," said Fred, spreading his arms out. "This is where George works doing odd repairs on the trucks that come to our station."

"It's kinda small, isn't it?" asked Roy. The crease on his forehead had returned. "I mean, ain't no way a spaceship's gonna fit through those doors."

Well, at least he isn't too easily impressed. That's something. "Any trucks—" started Fred "—we call 'em trucks; sort of tradition. Any trucks needing major repairs land at one of the Earthside stations." They sauntered down through the circle of lights, alternating from hot white light to pitch blackness. Fred knew every step of the station, and never slowed once.

"George and his crew, who are all still sleeping on account of George being fishing, do mostly minor repairs here—sub-light thrusters, guidance systems, solar panels—anything that can be brought into the bay on one of those repulsor lifts."

"You're not part of the repair crew?"

"I'm working on it," said Fred. His lips quivered a little as he tried to suppress a pout. "I wanted to go into mining, but I stink at tests and bombed the entrance exam. I'm a repair tech trainee, which is just a glorified term for gopher...."

Fred stopped talking. They had entered one of the pools of light and, glancing over at Roy, he detected something amiss. The kid's eyes were wide and his jaw had dropped, turning his mouth into a cavernous hole.

"You wanted to be a miner?" he said after a moment. "Isn't that like the most dangerous job in the system? Why on Earth would you want to be a miner?"

"I want to see the stars."

Fred's ears popped. As he stretched his jaw to equalize the pressure, he heard Marge's voice, loud and shrill, echoing across the repair bay.

"—hot one, Roy!" he heard her yell. "Get a move on!"

"What?" he called back.

"I said we've got a hot truck. Get your butt to the tower!"

"Oh, Christ," he said. He grabbed Roy by the elbow and pulled him into a run. "Come on!"

The two ran back to the diner and Fred led them to a door marked *Tower—1127 Personnel Only.*

"What's a hot truck?" asked Roy.

Fred ignored him and palmed the access panel. The door swung open, and Fred hardly slowed down as he raced up the circular staircase. He took two steps at a time, pushing off the outside wall as he went, to turn his body around three complete circles on the way up.

A second door stood between them and the tower. This one had a keypad attached below the palm panel. Fred pressed one hand on the panel as the fingers of his other hand blurred across the nine-digit keypad.

"What's a hot truck?" asked Roy again.

The door opened and Fred rushed into the tower. The circular room had computer panels at waist height, beneath reinforced glass panes, around the entire perimeter. Fred pointed at one of the chairs dotting the room. "Sit there and do exactly what I tell you," he said. "Or we might all die."

Fred sat and began pressing buttons at the terminal in front of him. "When trucks land, the station takes control to guide it into a berth. It's automatic and foolproof—most of the time."

"Except when truck comes in hot, right?"

The screens flared to life in front and to the side of Fred's terminal. One showed a three-dimensional representation of Station 1127 and the space around it. Another showed the readouts and options for the automatic berthing system. The last one showed a dial marked out in megahertz.

"That's right," said Fred. "Each station operates on a specific wavelength. Normally, the truck's computer connects to the station's computer and the two systems synch up."

"But not this time?"

"It happens," said Fred. "Old trucks don't synch up right sometimes or the drivers screw up. Then it becomes our problem. Key on that terminal and type in *1127* and *access*. I will need you to—"

Fred glanced over at Roy, who already had the station guidance system up and running on his monitor. "Good," he said, halfheartedly. It had taken George half a day to teach him how to access the various routines up here. Was this kid some kind of idiot savant? "Now scan the hot truck and call out the wavelengths. They'll fluctuate, so we'll have to work together to get both systems synched up."

As he waited for the first set of numbers, Fred glanced up at the light flooding through the bank of windows. It was always daytime on the station. He'd been told in orient-ation that there were five hundred foot candles of light on the deck. He had no idea what that meant, but it was damn bright. So bright that if you looked up all you saw was light until you saw dark. No light from outside the station ever made it down to the deck. Only the moon, the Earth, or an incoming truck with its flare of burning fuel could penetrate that light barrier. He couldn't see the incoming truck yet, so they must have some time.

"One seventeen," called out Roy.

"Well, no wonder they didn't synch," said Fred. "That's not even close." He flipped a few switches on his console to set the ABS to manual and traced his finger along the dial on the screen to reset the receiver.

A sudden roar above him made Fred look up. A mile-long stream of flame spread across the inky blackness outside the station's light barrier.

"Good God," said Fred. "They're just now firing their brakes? What the hell is wrong with this driver?"

He turned to Roy. "Quick, we need to fine-tune the wavelength down to the thousandths. I'd say we have maybe a minute and it's a five minute job manually."

Roy got up from his chair. "We don't need to do that," he said as he stepped across the small room. He leaned over Fred's shoulder, tapped a few buttons, and then leaned back.

"There," he said. "All synched up."

Fred felt his jaw slacken as he stared up at Roy. "What the hell did you just do?"

Roy smiled that big, disarming smile of his and wiped a lock of hair back from his forehead. "I just re-engaged the ABS. Once you get it close it can do the rest—and do it at the speed of a billion calculations per second."

"George never told me you could do that," said Fred. "Where'd you learn that?"

The roar of the truck drowned out Roy's reply. Fred looked out the window. With thousands of these stations spilling light into Earth's night sky, he'd never seen the stars. Heck, he hadn't seen the moon until he got to the station, but the sight of a truck entering the station almost made up for it. Almost.

A fountain of flame washed over the deck, turning the docking bay into a roiling sea of fire. Great clouds of bright, smokeless heat billowed and grew, pushing and shoving each other as they rushed toward the edge of the deck.

The fountain continued to flow into the deck as the truck descended into view. The crimson flames gave way to a white-hot circle at the base of the truck that left a purple afterimage on

Fred's retina. He grabbed a pair of protective goggles from the panel and slapped them to his face.

"Don't look directly into the sub-light thrusters!" he called out.

In stark contrast to the fiery maelstrom on the deck, the truck seemed to float down toward the station. Fred had always been amazed at the utter silence of truck arrivals and departures. It seemed completely unnatural.

Six fins of varying sizes and shapes jutted out from the base of the descending cylinder. Three perfect triangles were spaced around the base. In between were three more fins with odd shapes Fred had never seen in geometry class.

Little flares shot out here and there along the fins, seemingly at random, as the truck floated down. Fred had heard George talk about the purpose of each fin and their respective flame jets, but much of it hadn't sunk in. It all had something to do with maneuvering and stability during arrivals and departures.

As the truck settled to the deck it triggered huge clamps that swung up and grabbed it between the fins. Most of the truck still loomed above the tower, reaching out into the inky blackness past the reach of the lights. It was a stark white cylinder, like one of the long, narrow sausages Marge served to the Andromedans.

Fred felt a rumble and the truck began to descend again; this time under the power of the station. With the truck firmly cradled in the clamps, a large section of the deck descended to bring the cab doors down to the diner level. He and Roy would have to raise it back up again for fueling, but the truckers were first priority on the station. They had the money.

Three more triangular fins stuck out around the truck about halfway up. These were much larger and broader than the lower fins and actually folded down as the truck descended into its berth. According to George, the jump engines were housed inside these fins. One more set of fins protruded from the top. Just two this time, one to either side of the cab doors. Fred had no idea what these were for, but he'd often seen truckers grab hold of them as they climbed into and out of their cabs.

All the fins were red. This seemed to be an intergalactic standard. Although Fred noticed that the fins on this truck were a subtly different shade; almost rust colored or the color of dried blood. Perhaps the ship was just old. There were a number of nicks, dents, and scrapes all along the side of it.

Fred glanced at Roy to explain what was going on, but the newcomer didn't seem fazed at all by the sight of the arrival and the descending deck. He was busy switching off the automatic berthing system and bringing up fueling specs and dietary requirements from the truck's database on his screen.

Fred shook his head. *Who is this guy? And what's he doing in a truck stop?*

He looked back just as the cab doors opened and the truckers dropped to the deck. Half a dozen space-suited bipeds piled out of the cab and began walking toward the diner door. They had an odd gait like there were several more joints in their legs than they truly needed.

Fred couldn't place the race, but even in their spacesuits, something seemed oddly familiar about them. But he'd have to figure it out later.

"Come on," he said, turning toward the door. "Marge will need us for sure. That's two or three trucks' worth of diners there. We just got busy."

The next few hours were a blur. First there were dishes full of foul-smelling, nasty-looking food served to customers Fred could only describe as squid-faced, multi-jointed ogres who smelled worse than the food. He couldn't shake the feeling that he'd seen them before, but he was sure nothing like this had been on the station in the six months he'd been there. He must have seen them in one of his schoolbooks.

Neither Marge nor Roy seemed put off by their strange appearance. Of course, it had been drilled into all of them during orient-ation that staring at the customers was impolite in many alien cultures. In fact, some aliens considered staring a direct challenge, and the last thing you might see in this life would be a tentacle hurtling straight at you. Keeping your eyes down not only kept them safe from the blinding lights of the station, it could keep your head attached to your body. So maybe he was just being paranoid. He shrugged off the feeling and got back to work.

After the aliens ate, Fred spent another hour cleaning dishes as well as the huge mess they left on the tables and his clean floor. Then he and Roy finally donned their suits and headed out to refuel the truck while the aliens spent some quality time in the rec rooms behind the diner.

Fred uncoupled the fuel hoses and clomped across the magnetic deck to the truck. "This is how you attach the hose," he said as he turned toward Roy, but the new guy was busy punching in the fuel formula back at the pump, a process Fred hadn't learned until his second month at the station. Fred sighed and finished the coupling job himself and walked back to the pump.

Checking the gauges, Fred finally thought he had found something the new guy couldn't do. "That mixture is way too rich," he said. "You must have set it wrong."

Roy shook his head inside his helmet. "Nope," he said. "That's what they ordered." He showed Fred the readout on his datapad. "I thought it was off, as well, so I triple-checked."

"Weird," said Fred as he scanned the order. "I've never seen a mixture that strong. Why would they need it so rich?"

"You want the long answer or the longer answer?" asked Roy. The smile that Fred was beginning to truly despise had returned to Roy's boyish face.

Fred shook his head. "Never mind," he said. "Just start the pump. I assume you know how to do that ... and how to uncouple the hose and stow it away." He turned toward the diner. "I'll go see if Marge needs help with the grease traps."

Fred sat in his bed, a Captain Galaxy comic on his lap. He'd read it so many times the corners of the pages were rounded and torn.

—329—

George had promised to bring the last six months' worth of issues back with him from Earthside. Fred couldn't wait. Comics were about as close to adventure as he would ever get, especially with Mister Perfect in town now.

Roy sat on his own bed across the room, reading a technical manual. What was with this guy? "You get all that knowledge of yours from books down in Muncie?" asked Fred.

Roy smiled. "Books, school, work. Everything is a learning experience," he said. He closed the book and turned toward Fred. "By the way, thanks for showing me the ropes today."

"Yeah. No problem."

"You never did tell me why you wanted to become a miner," said Roy after a long pause. "Something about the stars?"

Fred fumed a little longer before deciding to give the big farmboy with the big brain another chance. They'd have to live together a while, so no use staying mad.

"Well, I never was any good at school. I preferred reading space stories to textbooks. I guess I had my head in the stars even as a kid. But nobody on Earth's seen the stars in almost a hundred years."

He dropped the comic on the floor and shifted around to sit on the edge of the bed. "Intergalactic travel takes money or power," he said ticking it off on his fingers. "Truck driving takes lots of math. Heck, even planetary couriers are the cream of the crop Earthside. My only option was mining. At least out around Venus or Jupiter, I'd be away from all these damn lights. And they always need more miners—you know, to replace those they lose. All they require is a good head and a strong back."

"What happened?"

"I froze," said Fred. He kicked the bed frame with his heels. "I never tested well. That's probably why I hated school so much. It's all about testing. I know the stuff. It may take me a little longer to get there, but I know it. I just could never prove it to anyone."

"So you came here, instead?"

"Yeah. My old man doesn't have the kind of clout you need to reach the stars, but he's still got connections. So even after I threw up on my instructor during the zero-G tests, he was able to get me a post on a refueling station. My only hope now is to prove myself here and maybe learn enough astro-mechanics to make my way to the outer planets as a technician."

"That's great," said Roy, his smile beaming across the space between bunks like a beacon. "We'll be working together. You see, they just hired me as George's new tech trainee. I already know all about sub-light engines. I did my master's thesis on propulsion systems for the new millennium. But I still have a ways to go on guidance systems and navigational controls..."

Roy chattered on about a childhood spent fixing machines on his daddy's farm; days working at the Muncie filling station, puttering around with engines to make money for college; and then studying mechanical engineering at Purdue University. But Fred hardly heard any of it.

George had hired a new tech trainee. The enormity of that statement had not escaped him. Fred would not be learning about sub-light thrusters anytime soon. It would be endless days of slopping wriggling food, mopping dirty floors, and cleaning grease traps for him.

Fred glanced down at his comic book, thinking he might pick it up and begin reading again to drown out the noise of his dreams slipping away through Roy's charmed life of technical expertise and training. But that would be rude. He simply had to listen and nod and try to smile at all the right times.

It wasn't Roy's fault anyway. Fred was the one who couldn't take a test. No, that wasn't it. He'd always had his head in the stars, but for some reason his heart just could never make the same leap. He choked at critical moments, perhaps out of fear. Fear of success or fear of failure, he never knew which. But his stomach knotted up. His breath came in gasps and his palms began to sweat every time.

As Roy continued talking about his thesis and the preparations for coming into space, Fred noticed something on the back cover of his comic. He'd read this issue a zillion times, but for some reason the advert for the next issue caught his eye just then. The title bored itself right into his brain: *Stowaway*.

This is crazy. This is crazy.

Fred's mind was screaming inside his head as he pushed the repulsor cart back into the repair bay. With George gone, it had been easy to convince Marge to let him handle the night shift. Then, once everyone else was asleep, he'd loaded clothes, food, and air canisters onto the lift, hauled them out to the truck, and deposited them into a dead space behind the cab.

God! Dead space. That sounds bad.

He shook the doubts from his head as he started back toward the truck. This would work. There was a false floor between him and the cab, behind the seats. The cab floor was not airtight, so he'd get air. It would work. He was determined not to choke.

Stop saying things like that!

Fred pulled himself back up into the cab and crawled through the panel behind the seats. It was cramped and dark. He had a flashlight and all his comics to help avoid going stir crazy, plus enough food for several weeks of travel. The rest of the space was jammed full with empty bottles for waste.

The air canisters were in case he had to hide. The crawl space had an airlock—emergency access to the cargo hold. Fred planned to keep his rations and his used waste bottles back there.

Fred opened the airlock and moved the supplies inside. He palmed the door closed, rechecked the seals on his helmet, gloves, and boots, and then cycled the air. It seemed horribly loud to him. During the trip, he'd have to quietly lift the panel a crack and check the cab to make sure the truckers were asleep before cycling the air. That should help minimize his chances of getting caught.

He grabbed a crate of food and gave it a gentle shove through the airlock into the darkness below. A ten-gallon bottle of water followed into the black hole at his feet. One by one his supplies disappeared into the cargo hold. Once the airlock was cleaned out, Fred grabbed the edge and swung himself through.

As he floated down, it felt like he was sinking into a huge bottle of ink. It was oppressive. The knot in his stomach grew several inches before he remembered the flashlight. He switched it on just as his feet touched down. One foot landed on a water bottle, which sent him off at an angle. Fred caught the handle with his toes and pulled himself down next to his supplies.

"Now, to stow these out of the way," he said, more to steady his nerves than anything else. But Fred's legs wouldn't obey. His flashlight beam had landed on the side of one of the crates netted together below him, revealing the shipping label and a large, red symbol.

The label was printed in about a hundred different languages, from a hundred different worlds. But the symbol was universal. It showed a black cloud erupting on a blood-red diamond. Explosives. The size of the cloud indicated the strength. This one dominated almost the entire diamond.

Fred willed himself to move closer. He dug his toes into the net, leaned down, and pulled his face close to the label. Scanning down the list past all the weird symbols from far-off worlds, he let his eyes fall toward the bottom where the English line always lay. The knot in his stomach tightened as he read the single, hyphenated word: *Hydro-Gel*.

"What the hell are they doing transporting Hydro-Gel in an unmarked truck?" asked Fred.

He didn't remember much from high school chemistry, but the unit on explosives had been pretty fun. Plus, the villains in his comics used a wide variety of explosives, which had given him an added incentive to learn the names. Hydro-Gel was the single most potent explosive in the known universe. It was basically just hydrogen concentrated into a viscous matrix.

He remembered in one issue, Dark Raven spread a thin layer on the door to an office building. The resulting explosion leveled a city block. A crate this big would take out the entire station and maybe the three closest stations, as well.

"God, if this truck had crashed yesterday, we'd all be little flakes of flesh floating amid metal fragments right now."

Fred found it hard to breathe inside his mask as the knot in his stomach seemed to jump up into his throat. The impact must have jarred something loose in his brain, though, because he finally remembered where he'd seen the alien truckers before, at least their species. And if he was right, Fred had to get out of this truck immediately.

He waved the flashlight around, looking for his satchel among the haphazard pile of supplies, but instead the beam landed on more and more crates with the billowing cloud symbol.

"Holy crap," he moaned. "How much do they have here?"

As he scanned the hold around him, crate after crate came into view. He couldn't see below the first layer, but he assumed that if all of the ones on top contained Hydro-Gel, the rest of the hold must be full of the stuff. They weren't hiding anything worse, that was for sure.

He tore his eyes away from the crates and back to his supplies. Finding the satchel, he opened the flap and pulled out all the comics. He had to know if he was right. He flipped through them, tossing one after another aside, looking for a specific cover. The comics floated in the air around him like a flock of deranged butterflies.

"There it is!" he said, finding a cover with a supernova engulfing an Earthlike planet. He thumbed through the pages, hunting for the intergalactic zealots who had blown up the star. And then there they were. The squid-faced ogres from the diner. Zealots from one of the Megallanic Clouds—he was never sure which—who had some grudge against the residents of the other cloud.

He remembered reading an article in the back of the issue describing the tactics of the real-life Megallanic zealots. They had blown up ships, space stations, even entire planets to terrorize their sworn enemies, and thus prove their superiority.

Looking at the dozens, if not hundreds of crates of Hydro-Gel beneath his feet, Fred knew there was enough firepower here to blow up a very large planet.

"Time to go, feet," pleaded Fred. He managed to swallow part of the knot and flexed his knees to launch himself toward the airlock. But before he released, a loud click echoed through the hold. Fred flashed his light up toward the airlock to reveal his worst fear yet—it had closed.

Either an automatic system had cycled the lock in preparation for departure or one of the aliens was heading down to check the cargo. Either way, Fred needed to secure himself in a corner, hidden from view and safe against acceleration. There was no time now to choke. No time for regrets.

He grabbed the floating comics and crammed them back into the satchel. Then, after shoving his belongings to the side of the hold, Fred pushed everything into nooks and crannies around the Hydro-Gel crates. He pressed his body into the last spot and switched off the light. A few minutes later, he realized he was holding his breath, and almost passed out before he dared the deep intake he knew was coming.

But nobody came through the airlock and Fred began to breathe normally again. At least until a vibration in the side of the truck threatened to shake his bones right out of his skin. The truck was moving, but there were no G-forces. Just a horrible rumble and the sense of movement. The hydraulic lift must be raising the truck into departure position, he realized.

A few minutes later, after the rumbling ended, a thought occurred to Fred. Someone must be operating the hydraulics. Roy was in the tower! He keyed on his radio. "Roy," he whispered. "Roy. Can you hear me? Help. I'm in the truck."

A long moment passed with the knot pushing its way back into his throat with every beat of his heart.

Then came the answer. "Hello?" said Roy's voice in his helmet. "Is someone there?"

Roy hadn't understood him, probably could barely hear Fred over the noise of the truck. And why was he whispering? There was an airlock between him and the truckers. Plus, there was no air outside his suit to carry the sound waves anyway. He was flunking another test, and this one would cost him his life.

Fred screamed into the microphone. "Roy! Help Me. I'm in the tr—!"

The crushing weight of full thrust drove the rest of the sentence out of Fred's mouth, along with most of the air in his lungs. The rumble from the hydraulics earlier felt like sitting on a vibrating chair in the rec room compared to the nine-point-five earthquake he now experienced.

For the next few minutes, all Fred could do was try to re-inflate his lungs and hang on to the supplies that threatened to jiggle free and fly around the hold. All the while, the com signal in his helmet blared static. This was why they used computers communicating on microwave bands to land the trucks. The vibration of the engines created too much interference in the radio wave range.

Fred could only hope Roy had heard his plea for help and would alert the authorities. They might be able to stop the truck before it fired up its intergalactic engines.

That hope flared briefly a half-hour later when the sub-light thrusters shut off. But a moment later, Fred felt an entirely new sensation and the knot in his stomach was now the least of his worries. At first, he thought his head would explode as pressure built up inside his ears. Then his entire body began to feel bloated, as if he were being filled with helium.

Fred switched on his flashlight, but then wished he hadn't. The light flashed out only a few feet before it bent to the side. Pieces of the beam seemed to flake off the end, and he watched as bits of light whisked past him. He switched it off, but the beam didn't fade immediately. It just continued to shred and zip past him until all the pieces were gone.

They'd engaged the IG engines. Fred was now leaving the solar system and, probably, the Milky Way galaxy. He was trapped in a truck with enough high explosives to destroy a planet, perhaps even a star. He was going to die, and he doubted he would even get to see the star before they dove into it.

Fred wiped down the counter again and refilled the glass in front of him with some green, bubbling liquid. He pushed the glass over to the alien trucker sitting across the counter.

The trucker grabbed the glass in a red claw and lifted it toward his chitinous mouth. A thin, forked tongue slithered out and into the liquid, which began to drain away.

"Great story," said the trucker in a clicking voice after draining the cup. The translation came from a speaker mounted on the counter. "Then what happened?"

"Two weeks of nerve-racking boredom," said Fred. He rinsed the glass and placed it back on the shelf before continuing. "I huddled in the crawlspace or down in the hold, never knowing whether the zealots would find me or not, and assuming I was dead either way."

"And then?" clicked the trucker. His eyestalks waved around in a way Fred assumed showed rapt interest in his story.

But Fred was tired and just wanted to hit his bunk and get some sleep. "With my nerves shot and my food running out, I screwed up. I cycled through into the hold before checking if they were all asleep. They caught me and tossed me into the exterior airlock. What followed was a moment of pure terror that will surely dwarf any test anxiety I ever encounter in the future."

"How did you survive?" asked the trucker, his eyestalks waving even more frantically now. "Did you overpower them?"

Fred just shook his head. "No," he said. "My dumb luck kicked in to save me. That and Roy figured out what was going on. Apparently he got suspicious about the rich fuel mixture and the strange ABS frequency and did some checking. He figured out they were Megallanics and alerted the authorities in … I'm sorry, which cloud are we in here?"

The trucker clicked his response. "Large Megallanic Cloud."

"Yeah, that's it," said Fred. "Roy alerted the LMC police and they arrived just before the airlock cycled me out."

"And here you are," said the crablike trucker.

"And here I am," said Fred. "Too poor to buy a trip home. Stuck working in another diner until I can bum a ride home."

He poured the trucker another drink. "On the house," he said. After a moment, Fred leaned forward. "You wouldn't happen to be going near the Milky Way, would you?"

The noise that came through the translator sounded like laughter. "No. Sorry," the trucker said finally. "Not much need to go way out there. Hardly even civilized."

"Yeah. I get that a lot. Well, thanks anyway."

Fred returned to cleaning the counter. As he turned to move down to the other end, the trucker chattered through a series of clicks and gulps.

The translation came a moment later. "Did you ever get to see the stars?"

The trucker gestured back toward the front door of the diner with his huge claws. The glaring, star-obscuring white light of the truck stop practically poured through the window.

Fred nodded. "Standing in the airlock, gasping for air as the atmosphere drained away, I saw the stars against the backdrop of the cloud. It was quite... breathtaking."

"Was it worth it?" asked the trucker. "Almost dying. Getting stranded. Losing everything. Just to see some little points of light?"

Fred didn't hesitate a moment before replying. "Yes. Yes, it was." He smiled and got back to work.

Gary Gygax

Beginning in the 1960s, Gary Gygax wrote or co-authored over 80 games, game-support products, and books. His first professional gaming work saw print in 1971, shortly before he co-founded the publishing company Tactical Studies Rules (later TSR, Inc.) with his longtime friend, Don Kaye. He is best known for co-creating and authoring the original Dungeons & Dragons roleplaying game, and creating both the AD&D game and the World of Greyhawk fantasy setting, which provides the backdrop for "Twistbuck's Game."

On the Dragonsfoot website (www.dragonsfoot.org), Gygax explained the origin of the game referenced in the story's title: "I confess to having lifted it from actual experience. When in England Don Turnbull introduced me to the game as we were driving from place to place. He knew the pub signs and would cheat outrageously by altering the route so as to pass by a sign with many legs on it when it was his turn...."

The adventures of Gord the Rogue have been chronicled in several works, beginning with the 1985's *Saga of the Old City* and the short story "At Moonset Blackcat Comes" from *Dragon* magazine #100, also in 1985. *Artifact of Evil* (1986) was the last Gord novel published by TSR. Three subsequent Gord titles saw print in 1987 from New Infinities (*Sea of Death*, *Night Arrant*, and *City of Hawks*), and another two in 1988 (*Come Endless Darkness* and *Dance of Demons*). Gord also made the jump to the multiverse of Michael Moorcock's Eternal Champion in "Evening Odds" in the anthology *Pawn of Chaos* (1996). The most recent original Gord story—"The Return of Gord," co-authored with K. R. Bourgoine—appeared in 2006, in *Dragon* #344. An additional tale of Gord and Chert from Gygax and Bourgoine, "A Wizard's Thief," is due for publication from Flying Pen Press in 2008. Troll Lord Games will be re-releasing the entire Gord cycle in hardcover, with the Troll Lord edition of *Saga of the Old City* hitting shelves in 2008. Gygax's other fictional works include a trio of fantasy-mystery novels featuring the Ægyptian wizard-priest Magister Setne Inhetep: *The Anubis Murders* (1989), *The Samarkind Solution* (1993), and *Death in Dehli* (1993), all of which are available or forthcoming from Planet Stories. In 2008, Planet Stories also released Gygax's previously unpublished novel *Infernal Sorceress*.

In their "30 Most Influential People in Gaming" article series, released in March of 2002, *GameSpy* magazine placed Gygax at #18, tied with J. R. R. Tolkien and just after George Lucas. In 2005, *Sync* magazine placed him at the top of their list of "The 50 Biggest Nerds of All Time." The same year, a new strain of bacteria was named after him—*Arthronema gygaxiana*.

TWISTBUCK'S GAME

BY GARY GYGAX

THE LAST TIME it had happened Gord had run for his life, laughing all the while. This time the reaction was the same.

"Treacherous little trickster!" the big barbarian bawled. "I'll split that scheming skull of yours in two!"

As Chert charged headfirst, elbows tight at his sides and fists raised, the supple young thief flipped sideways, avoiding the rush. The barbarian thudded into the wall, rebounded, and fell sprawling over the table. No construction of mere wood could withstand such an impact. With a groan, the table's legs spread outward and its top split with a sharp crack. Chert's roar of outrage as he struck the floor drowned out the cracking and splintering noise of the sundered oak, but Gord's laugh pierced the din.

"I think I'll go out for a while, old comrade!" the young thief called loudly, still laughing uproariously. "After all, I have a few coins to dispose of now, thanks to you!" So saying, Gord danced nimbly over to where two stacks of copper and silver coins were piled, scooped them off the top of the tall chest, and sped out the door of the dwelling. As he went down the lane, Chert's roars could clearly be heard despite the closed door. Exactly what the brawny Hillman was threatening, Gord wasn't sure, but it undoubtedly concerned the young thief's limbs—and anything else that could be chopped or torn off.

"Such a poor loser," Gord clucked in mock disgust as he clacked the coins together in his palm. The amount of money was paltry, a mere hundred bronze zees in total. But the wager had been fair, after all, and it wasn't Gord's fault that Chert had been too slow-witted to detect his friend's ruse. "Well, no matter. By the time I finish spending the winnings," the crafty thief assured himself, "he will have cooled off, I hope." At the cost of one zee for a small mug of beer, the money would soon be gone.

And since wine was even more expensive, and he fully intended to drink some now that he could afford it, his winnings would dwindle even faster. "If Chert had any sense of humor, I would have allowed him to help drink my winnings," Gord said, shaking his head as he carelessly tossed a coin in the air and quickly retrieved it. "Oh, well. More for me." Whistling a jaunty tune, the young thief strolled off to see what was going on along the Strip.

Meanwhile Chert was grinding his teeth and surveying the wreckage in the small quarters he and Gord shared. They had recently acquired an abandoned shop on a disused lane in the trade sector of the River Quarter. It had been easily converted into lodgings by expending a few silver nobles for labor and materials. The shutters chosen for the front windows made the place seem deserted still, a definite necessity for someone in Gord's and Chert's line of work. After making a few additions to the furniture that had come with the place, the two had themselves a fine apartment. Of course, Gord talked Chert into taking the third floor while the young thief had installed his sleeping quarters on the second. The ground floor was their lounge, with the little back room serving as kitchen and dining room in one. Neither of them cooked nor ate at home often anyway.

"It's the principle of the thing!" Chert exclaimed aloud, talking to the walls. "A friend shouldn't use sharper's methods to win bets from a pal!" *Screw it—let Gord clean up the mess*, the big Hillman told himself as he stomped up the narrow steps leading to his quarters. The wooden planks groaned and creaked in complaint at his weight and the force he angrily put into each step, but Chert ignored the warnings and the worn steps somehow managed to withstand the assault. At the top of the long flight, the still-fuming barbarian slammed and locked the door that made the upper story his private domain. "At least that foxy little thief doesn't steal directly from me," Chert said as he went to the place where he hid his wealth. "But then again, he doesn't exactly know where I keep it."

The incredibly strong Hillman extracted a wall beam as easily as if it had been a splintered piece of wood waiting to be peeled.

Behind the beam was a space large enough to contain a long, narrow iron box. Therein Chert kept his ready cash and a small fortune in jewels. He peered into the container and breathed a sight of relief. A sprinkling of gold orbs, a handful of electrum coins called luckies, and a fair quantity of silver nobles, copper commons, and other smaller coins lay scattered around a small sack of soft suede leather. Chert shook the container so that the coins made a pleasant jingling sound. Then he opened the small leather sack and took out the little silk parcels inside it. Each square piece of cloth encased a bright gem, a dozen in total.

These precious stones were his mad money, so to speak. If he ever needed to leave town in a hurry, the gems and gold would not only provide ample means to do so, but would see to his needs for a year of travel, as well. Unlike Gord, the barbarian Hillman managed to hold onto his money carefully. He never admitted this to anyone, let alone Gord. Thank heavens the sums he had invested in various places in the city were bringing him handsome returns! At the rate the miserable thief he associated with was skinning him of funds, he was adding barely a silver noble a day to his balance.

Chert chuckled softly as he played with the stash and it occurred to him that Gord would be buying meals for him for the next few days, since the troublesome trickster was working under the assumption that he had won the last of his friend's meager holdings. "This is going to end up costing him much more than he stole from me!" Chert proclaimed loudly, and then he fell back on the bed and erupted in a fit of thunderous mirth.

"Perhaps I need a little sport myself," he mused, running the coins through his huge, thick fingers. "I should only spend the extra money earned from 'activities' with Gord, but what the devils!" With a careless motion, the Hillman plucked several of the coins from his hoard and placed them in his purse—a noble, a pair of coppers, and twice as many bronze zees. "That's enough for a fair night on the town!" he exclaimed happily to himself. With that, Chert clumped downstairs, taking the steps three at a time. He'd head for the Toad on a Toadstool. Taverns in the University District were far more reasonable than ones outside its confines, and their clientele included a goodly number of impressionable young females.

"Top of the evening to you, Chert. What's your pleasure?"

The big barbarian put a zee on the counter. "A jack of that brown ale you serve, Paddy," he said to the fat barkeep. "I'm in a mood to drown my troubles tonight!" Tankard in hand, Chert went to an empty table and sat down to ponder. How was he going to get even with the rascal he lived with? Some time passed. Another brown ale and then another went down easily. Chert was finishing off his fourth when the place began to fill up.

The crowd was a happy, amiable bunch, mostly students from a nearby college, a few locals, and Chert. The huge Hillman stood head and shoulders above everyone else in the Toad, and his thick body was broad enough for two of the smaller men to hide behind, had there been a need. Naturally, such a figure attracted considerable attention—especially after things loosened up as the drinks began to flow.

"Where have you been lately, Chert?" It was a young scholar asking the question, a lad of about eighteen years who openly worshiped the barbarian. He eased his own considerable frame into a chair at Chert's table, setting a large pitcher of ale and his jack down as he did so. "Have one on me!"

Chert happily complied, filling his bumper full to its rim and swigging down half of it immediately before replying. "I've been busy—taking care of duties in the High Quarter, you know."

It wasn't a lie, but from this and remarks the barbarian had made in previous conversations, the student thought Chert to be some sort of special guard and consultant to those wishing protection against danger—and loss of goods. "How did it go?" he asked admiringly.

"Well enough, Budwin," the barbarian said with a slight frown to indicate things didn't work out as well as hoped for, "save for the loss of a large chunk of my all-too-meager holdings. But what the hells, live and learn, right? Your good health!" With that

Chert drained off the remainder of the flagon and refilled it in one continuous motion.

"Don't tell me—you got stiffed!" the student exclaimed, noting the huge barbarian's sour expression. "I can get a few friends together, and we'll help you get things straight, what say?"

Budwin was well over six feet tall and weighed in excess of fifteen stone. Chert knew his college associates were likewise large—for city-bred folk anyway. It was a sincere offer and the lad was anxiously searching Chert's face for a reaction, to see if he should jump up and begin gathering a gang. "Relax and drink the brew, my friend," Chert said with a nugatory tone. "I need brainpower, not muscle and brawn, to set this little matter straight."

Budwin drank and scratched his head. His thinking ability in no way matched his strength of limb, but he was willing to try. Just then another student came to the table with three twittering girls in tow.

"Hey, my men! I'd like you to meet—"

"Shut up, Lloyd!" Budwin ordered. "We're thinking. If you bring another ewer of brown ale here and be helpful, maybe Chert and I will let you join us." The newcomer nodded, left the girls standing in silent confusion, and went off to fetch more drink. Budwin eyed the trio, smiling lecherously at them, and said, "Sit down, cuties. Lloyd will bring us refreshment in a trice." They sat.

One of the girls, a blue-eyed blonde, was very attractive and met Chert's gaze boldly. "Hi there, darlin'," he said to her. "My name's Chert."

"I am Holly," she said with a smile. "Are you—?"

"We have a problem to solve," Budwin interjected. "Tell them about your problem, Chert," the young scholar said ingenuously.

The Hillman frowned in irritation and resisted the urge to cuff Budwin on the ear for thoughtlessly spoiling his play. Then the barbarian shrugged his massive shoulders, deciding to clear the matter quickly and get on with the pursuit of the tender morsel sitting across the table from him. "I have an... associate... who continually plots and schemes to dupe me. He throws off outrageous statements, claims so fabulous that no one in his right mind could believe them. When I rightly object to the outlandishness of his assertions, this sly trickster suggests a wager as to right and wrong. Invariably, by the most outrageous of twistings and machinations, this devil wins! I must devise some problem or trick that will best him. Otherwise I will never see an end to his trickery."

"Has he won great sums of money from you thus?" Holly asked with interest.

"It isn't the amount of money lost," Chert lied, "but the very principle of the skullduggery involved which galls me so. I won't rest until I turn the tables on the little devil and stop the bull he throws at me!"

Lloyd arrived with the fresh supply of ale, and for a time they drank and bandied ideas about. There wasn't one really good one brought forth in all that time. Chert decided to make a serious attempt to separate himself and Holly from the crowd. Then Budwin slapped the big barbarian on the back and nearly shouted.

"Say, look! See that tall, kind of paunchy fellow who just came in?"

Chert, who was attempting to empty his ewer of its contents, nearly choked on the stuff when his young friend hit him. The barbarian again stifled a desire to throttle the bumptious chap. "Yeah, I see him! What of it?" Chert asked angrily, wiping some of the spilled drink off his face.

"That's Twistbuck, a don of Counts College. Everyone says he's the cleverest man around. I'll wager he could solve your problem!"

Chert was about to dismiss the suggestion in the rudest of terms when Holly jumped up. "You're in luck. He likes me!" she exclaimed happily. "He's always flirting and trying to get me to…" Her voice trailed off but a wave of crimson spread quickly across her face, telling all. "I'll get him over here."

Before Chert could object, she was heading toward the professor. The scholar seemed more than happy to see her and, after some reciprocal eyeplay, the couple began looking in the barbarian's direction. Holly seemed to be doing all of the talking and, finally, the man issued a hearty laugh that could be heard across he room. Then she had him by the arm, and the don was dragged over to the group.

After introductions and a brief statement from Chert regarding the problem, Twistbuck gave Holly a pinch on her round bottom and smiled at the unamused Hillman. "Must you actually win the wager from this antagonist?" he asked. "Or will a loss to me, for instance, serve your needs?"

This sounded too good to be true. The brawny barbarian could easily ignore the affront of the scholarly fellow molesting the girl he had his eye on in exchange for the promise of beating Gord at his own game! "Your emptying the purse of the cheating jackanapes would serve splendidly!" Chert said with eager enthusiasm. "But it must be a hefty and thorough trouncing!"

"Yes," the college don said contemplatively. "I think I can just about guarantee that. Are you willing to put up a fair sum to back me on this? The stipend paid to even a headmaster is insufficient for this undertaking, if I read you right, barbarian."

Chert looked skeptically at Twistbuck. "How much should I be prepared to furnish?" the Hillman asked unenthusiastically.

Twistbuck eyed Chert in return. "A pittance for one of your obvious means," he said after his assessment. Sliding an arm familiarly around Holly's waist, the don added, "Let's say a thousand zee at worst, but it is far more likely that I'll win that and more from the knave!"

"Do we share winnings?"

"Certainly not!" Twistbuck said indignantly. "It will be through my wit, and the clever game I have devised, that I will bring a return to your honor. Surely, should not my efforts then bear a return of the monetary sort? Or is your honor not worth so slight a risk as a mere gold orb?"

"You have a deal," Chert said, trying to keep the sourness he felt from creeping into his voice. An orb was far more than he cared to hazard, but all this talk of honor made it impossible for him to back out now. "Give the details to me now, Master Twistbuck, whilst Lloyd fetches us more ale—take care of it, Budwin," he added, seeing Lloyd searching his flat purse for odd change. As soon as Lloyd got up to do his duty, the hulking barbarian moved to his spot, thus placing himself between Holly and the college don. Then, leaning in front of her in a feigned effort to grasp every detail of Twistbuck's plan, Chert began to make his own move upon the sandwiched Holly. The rest of the evening was sheer joy.

"You're remarkably cheerful and forgiving this morning," Gord noted as his companion slapped bread and cheese on the table across from him. Tossing a sliver of cold chicken beside the young thief's other viands, and helping himself to the remaining half, Chert sat down with a grunt and tore into the breakfast, humming with his mouth full. After demolishing several additional slices of bread and all of the cheese, as well, he wiped his mouth with the back of his hairy arm, belched, and washed the food down with a final gulp of pungent goat's milk.

"Why not, old chum? It's a fine, bright morning!"

"But last evening you were ready to kill me. I'll swear to it! You never forgive and forget so easily. Why, last time I took you in a stupid bet you didn't even speak to me for a week, and this morn you're happy and even feed me breakfast. What gives?"

"Well, I'll admit I was slightly peeved. But that was yesterday. What matter you managed to dupe me for a few coppers? Ire is a thing of the past when one has a means of regaining one's losses."

Gord couldn't believe his ears. "What? You want to take me on again? I've already won the piddling amount of money you had to lose. What do you propose to wager this time?"

"Well, dear friend, it just so happens I have been saving for a rainy day for some time now. But I won't be giving you a chance to rob me. No sirree! I have a sure thing in mind that is going to make me a rich man!"

The combination of learning about his friend's hidden resources and his plans to build on them was too much for the greedy thief. Gord began demanding the full story, in detail, while Chert coyly avoided telling much. After a fair time, however, he fully consented. "I am loath to give you such a mark, Gord, for I intend to take the fellow by myself. You are my friend, though, and this idiot has enough to make us both rich ten times over, so I guess I should let you have a crack at him, as long as we split the winnings and you put up the capital."

Gord bridled at the last stipulation. "Why not split the capital, as well?" he asked suspiciously.

"Because you won my share from me last night and I'm doing you a favor as it is—one you hardly deserve, I might add," Chert said, putting heavy emphasis on the last part of the statement. Then he added, in a somewhat gentler tone, "This will work out for both of us. We'll both get a large sum and I won't have to touch my savings while I earn it." The barbarian's tone convinced the usually cautious thief that his friend was sincere.

"Then tell me, and be done with this ambiguity!"

"It's a game of this college don's own making, and one I think you could most definitely best him at," Chert replied, a little too eagerly.

Gord began to sniff the odor of a setup. "And what made you think you could get the best of this college professor?" he asked, one eyebrow raised in telltale uncertainty. "Or were you planning on drawing me into this all along?"

The usually slow-thinking Chert had been prepared for this question, and he answered posthaste. "All right, so I set you up. But what of it? At least you come out better when I trick you than I do when you pull the same stunt! If you pull this off, which I think you can, then we both win. So what can be wrong with that?"

Chert's response was so vehement that Gord felt a little sorry for him. "Why didn't you just ask me to help you out on this, instead of trying to dupe me?" Gord asked gently.

"Because," Chert sighed, "if the truth be known, I wanted to pull a trick on you for a change."

"I hate to have to be the one to tell you this, poor fellow, but you couldn't fool a fool, let alone anyone of my intellectual caliber." Gord issued the insult in a matter-of-fact tone of voice.

"Well, it was worth a try," Chert said humbly. *And still is*, he thought, smiling inwardly. "So, will you do it?"

"How can I resist?" Gord eagerly agreed. "It will be fun taking money from someone other than you, for a change." And with that he planted a hearty slap on the Hillman's broad back. Chert had all be could do to keep from pounding his egotistical friend into the floorboards.

"So tell me, when do I get to meet this soon-to-be-broke professor?"

"Tonight you'll accompany me to the Toad, and there you can get the details directly from the man himself. Then it will be up to you to set the time and the stakes—should you opt to game. Oh, and one more thing," Chert added in as offhand a tone as he could muster, "we split the winnings evenly. But should you lose, you're on your own, pal."

"Agreed. I have no fear, for I know not the meaning of the word *lose*!" the overconfident thief boasted.

Chert simply nodded his agreement. If things worked out to his satisfaction, Gord would soon become well acquainted with the meaning of that particular word, as well as a few others. The barbarian fairly shook with repressed laughter.

"I hadn't recalled the Toad on a Toadstool being this far," Gord said as the two made their way to the tavern.

Chert gleefully noted his friend's obvious attempt to hide his eagerness to get to the game that was promised. The challenge, as well as the prospect of wining, was an apparent sauce to his appetite for chicanery and wagering. "Hmm. I thought you said you had gone to the University and lived around here," Chert said in a perplexed tone.

"Yes, there! Isn't that the sign?"

In a minute they were seated comfortably at a table in the establishment. Chert, much to Gord's delight and amazement, volunteered to buy the first round. He purchased good wine for the young thief and heavy, black-colored milk stout for himself.

"Drink up, Gord, for the fellow will be here soon. To your health and our imminent wealth!"

Gord drank to that, of course, and bought the next round. Those drinks, too, were history a few minutes later, and Gord was soon starting to fidget. "Where is this Twistbuck? Are you sure he'll be here?"

"Relax. This round is on me, old chum. I'm not willing to stake my life on it, but he said he would be likely to stop in here when we parted company yesterday. Let's kick back and enjoy the evening."

After a couple of hours, Gord began to suspect that he was being had. But the fact that Chert was buying the majority of the drinks was at least a saving grace, so the young thief decided to take it as it came, enjoy the moment, and see what happened. *Let Chert have his fun,* Gord thought to himself. *He probably thinks he's getting me back for last night.*

Then, when it was close to eleven o'clock, the Hillman reached over and nudged Gord.

"There, you see? The man who just came in is Twistbuck. But now I'm wondering, Gord; maybe it's unfair to get him in a game against you...."

"Oh, no, you don't! You're not getting me to back out of this now!" the nearly salivating rogue cried. "This is too good an opportunity to pass up."

Chert shook his head in mock sorrow. "I really do feel bad about this, Gord. We aren't in the habit of stealing from honorable men."

"If he desires it of us, what can we do?" Gord asked with mock sincerity. "C'mon, Chert. If bringing me here and getting me all excited about the prospect of adding to my holdings and then letting me down is your idea of a joke, then the joke's on you! I insist on being introduced to this gamester or I'll make my own introduction!" The tone in the young thief's voice left no room for doubt.

"Very well. You are forcing me into this, Gord. I can see that you have no intention of sparing the fellow, so I'll go fetch him.

You get another round—he usually drinks a decoction of lingon-berry spirits and barkwater, by the way." With that, Chert stood up and went over to where Twistbuck was involved in conversation with several other scholars.

After signaling the barmaid to take a fresh order, Gord eased back in his chair and waited. The drinks arrived and a moment later so did the barbarian and the professor. Chert introduced Gord to him, and soon the two were chatting.

"Chert tells me you once attended the University," Twistbuck said with an inquiring smile.

The young thief nodded. "Yes, I did manage to spend some time studying at Ganz, but I didn't stay long enough to be graduated."

"What courses did you pursue?"

"Some of this, a bit of that," Gord said impatiently. But the scholar pressed him, so Gord mentioned the more interesting classes. There followed some banter concerning the instructors and relative merits of the various colleges. Eventually the young adventurer managed to steer the conversation onto the subject of betting and games. "Is it true that you have devised an amusing game, Professor?"

"Oh, you must be referring to 'Legs.' It's a silly little pastime, really, nothing more. I can't understand why it seems to have piqued anyone's interest, and calling it 'Twistbuck's Game' is annoying! It is beneath my dignity and station, after all, to have so foolish a thing bearing one's name."

"On the contrary! Chert says it sounds quite exciting and very sporting, too," Gord said ingratiatingly, and then he leaned close to the professor and said in a low tone of voice, "In fact, my barbarian pal was so intrigued by the game that he was considering placing a wager on his ability to best you at your own creation! I told him it would be an insult for someone in your position to be challenged at your own game by someone with Chert's, ah, shall we say, low standing in the community of scholars? So he dragged me in here to do his dirty work for him. I'm going along with this just to humor him." Gord put away the rest of the drink and issued a self-satisfied belch. Then he loudly prompted the professor, "Do be so kind as to explain this 'silly little pastime' to me."

Twistbuck concealed his fury, all the while consoling himself with how much fun it was going to be helping Chert get even with this arrogant rogue. With an airy wave of his hand, Twistbuck explained, "It is so simple a child can play. Why, I think even you could catch on in a matter of minutes." Gord ignored the insult, and the processor continued: "One simply notes the names or depiction, or both, on the sign about an inn, tavern, or drinking house. If legs are implied in the name, then one counts them, modifying the count upward if the depiction on the establishment's sign should show a greater number." Gord looked puzzled, so Twistbuck further explained, in as condescending a tone as possible. "Let's suppose there is a tavern called the Fox and Hounds. A fox has four legs and hounds, being plural, implies two dogs and eight legs. Therefore, the minimum score of legs for such a place would be twelve. Am I clear so far?"

"Yes, I can see the game scoring clearly now," the young thief said enthusiastically.

"That's not quite all there is to it. Suppose the sign showed a single hound?" Before Gord could answer, the fellow went on impatiently, "It wouldn't matter a whit! *Hounds* is plural, so that calls for a score of eight legs. However, should it happen that the sign showed three or four hounds, then the score would be twelve or sixteen for the canines, plus the fox, naturally."

"That's all well and good, sir, but knowing how to count legs doesn't actually tell me how to play your game."

"It is a matter of alternate occurrence—mere child's play. Two individuals engage in a contest. Each alternately counts the legs, if any, on the sign encountered during his turn. There is usually a time or distance limitation so that the game lasts a reasonable period and has a conclusion. Of course, the player with the highest leg count wins." Twistbuck paused to finish his drink, and Gord immediately ordered a fresh one to replace it. Thanking him for his generous consideration, the professor decided that an example of the game might serve to illustrate the whole thing clearly and completely.

"Chert and I might, for instance, decide to play a game." Twistbuck paused, looked at Chert for effect, and shook his head in disbelief. The barbarian cast him a menacing look, and Gord found the little interlude amusing and made no attempt to hide his reaction. The professor continued: "So anyway, we decide that we will walk outside, move randomly, and alternately count the legs that appear on signs along our path. Each of us gets one sign, legs or not appearing on it, the occurrence of a sign ending one player's turn and beginning the other's.

"Suppose we walk out the door now, and Chert is given the first sign encountered after leaving, but I choose what direction we take. Now, after an inn, tavern, or drinking establishment is encountered, legs are counted and scored, and a running total maintained on paper. The person awaiting his turn can select the next direction of the route of the game, as long as it does not go back over territory already covered. After some set limit—say an hour's time, five signs each, or whatever—the total scores are compared. The person having the higher total of legs wins. Simple. To add zest, the loser might have to buy drinks or perhaps pay a small sum for each leg his opponent had counted above his lesser score."

Despite the somewhat-convoluted explanation, Gord grasped the game easily. "What a delightful pastime indeed," he said with admiration oozing from his voice. "Do you ever actually wager on the play?"

"Certainly," Twistbuck replied. "Didn't your gigantic comrade here tell you that? However, I don't waste my time playing for small stakes."

Gord could hardly conceal his enthusiasm. "Let's play a game now! It would be quite exciting to learn from the one who invented it, you know—quite a feather in my cap!"

"Well…"

"Of course, I'd be willing to place a small stake on each leg. Would a zee be too little for a man of your talents?"

The professor slowly nodded. "Too little by far. A common is the least I'd be interested in wagering."

"A man after my own heart! If you're going to wager, you might as well make the stakes worth winning. What say you to a silver noble a leg, then?" Gord asked, brimming with uncontained eagerness.

"Done, young man. It is nearing the witching hour even now, and I must repair to my chambers for study and rest. Tomorrow is a day of classwork, you know. May I suggest that we play at noon on Starday?"

Gord was delighted at the stakes and the time, for the delay would enable him to do some scouting beforehand. "That seems satisfactory, although I'd hoped to play sooner," he told the professor, allowing false disappointment to enter his voice as he did so. "No matter. I defer to your wishes, sir. May I select the starting point?"

"Of course, my boy," Twistbuck agreed heartily. "But it must be somewhere within the southern half of the city, and it must also be at an intersection with three or more possible directions to choose from."

That sounded reasonable. "I agree," Gord said, his mind racing. "But who shall go first? And what length of game will we play?"

Twistbuck considered the questions for moment, then suggested, "You take the first sign, and we'll just alternate back and forth from then on. In the case of two signs on either side of the route, the one on the left shall be taken first, the one on the right considered second. As you shall have first count, you will also pick what direction we go from the starting intersection, I'll pick the next direction, and so forth. Alternating choice prevents any pre-selection of a route—that would be cheating, now, wouldn't it? Signs off the direct route are not allowed as proper for either contestant, even if the sign is clearly visible from the artery being traveled. That is all, save for us to set the limit on play."

"Time could allow one or the other player to gain an advantage by having one or more signs than the other fellow, as would distance traveled. I suggest that we each be allowed a set number of signs," Gord said thoughtfully.

"Of course! Now do be so good as to set the number, and I'll bid you good night!"

Gord arose as Twistbuck did, shook his hand, and said, "A noble a leg to the winner, game to commence on Starday noon, each counting a dozen signs before total score wins."

"Indeed, and I look forward with pleasure to the amusement my little game will provide to such a bright, enterprising fellow as yourself. Good rest to you all!" So saying, the don took his leave, and Gord and Chert left the tavern soon after.

Chert was sound asleep when Gord went out the next morning. He had much to accomplish in the little more than twenty-four hours left before the game would begin. The young thief was suspicious. Twistbuck seemed too casual about the stakes involved, too willing to let Gord determine the details of the arrangement. Gord was going to carefully go over the area he would choose for the game to start in, familiarize himself with the signs around it, and be fully prepared when they began. Perhaps this was unfair, but the verbal rules set down by the game's creator held no provisions for or against such conduct. Planning and preparation were smart steps, and Twistbuck himself had set the day and time. If that gave Gord an edge, it would be foolish not to utilize it! What worried him most was the possibility of some variation of the rules that the professor had neglected to mention.

"Where have you been?" Chert asked as his comrade returned to their domicile near sundown.

"Taking care of some business and walking a bit. Nothing important," Gord replied carelessly.

Turning away to hide his smile, the giant Hillman asked Gord if he should fix something for them to eat.

"No, let's go out for a bite—my treat. How about the Toad again?"

"Sure, pal, whatever you say, if you're buying, but the food there isn't very good. What about—"

"Hey! I'm buying, so we go where I choose!"

"Okay, if it means that much to you. I just thought you might like a good meal." Chert wasn't about to argue when the ride was free.

"Well, in all honesty, I'm hoping your professor friend will be there. I need to ask a couple of questions about our game tomorrow."

"Oh," said Chert, dropping the subject.

They had eaten and were sipping drinks when Twistbuck came in. As soon as he saw the two, he came over to their corner and sat down. After pleasant greetings were exchanged and Chert had ordered and paid for the professor's refreshment, Gord began to grill the fellow.

"If I were playing this 'Legs' game of yours, and I came upon a placed called the Boot, would I count a leg?"

"Hardly, old chap," Twistbuck replied with disdain. "It's a game of legs, after all, not footwear."

"Doesn't a boot imply a leg to go onto?"

"Phis! Does a horseshoe imply the leg and hoof of a horse?"

"Well, then, how about an octopus? Does that merit a score of eight?"

"Never!" Twistbuck cried in mock horror. "Tentacles are also referred to as arms. Must I constantly remind you that the game is 'Legs'?"

"A table has legs."

"Of course."

"And a chair or stool likewise?"

"Certainly. The legs need not be those of a living thing."

Now Gord smiled triumphantly. "What of a wine bottle? It is said that wine has 'legs,' you know?"

Twistbuck's reply was dished out with a large helping of scorn. "You are reaching for very silly meanings to this straightforward game, young sir. A wine bottle has no legs, and the name of the establishment, or its sign's proper designation by name, demarks the limits which are allowed."

"What?" Gord asked, somewhat puzzled.

"Should a sign state the establishment is known as Zygig's Arms, and should the arms thus being displayed show various things with legs upon them, there would be no counting of such legs. The proper name of the establishment mentions a person or thing with arms, not legs. Furthermore, should the sign not bear writing, the picture displayed would still have an implied name; that of Zygig's Arms, in my example. Ergo, other things shown would not allow the scoring of legs."

"But what if a place called the Ship showed several crewmembers aboard the vessel painted on the sign?"

"That, Gord would absolutely be irrelevant to the game. No score!"

"Hmmm..." said the young thief, feeling a bit foolish but still highly suspicious that he was being duped. "How about a game or a race? Either can have legs as part of them."

"A point I can concede. I shall leave it up to you whether or not to score legs for the occurrence of such signs—providing, naturally, that nothing indicating the contrary appears on the sign in question. If a tavern was called Chequers and showed a game of that sort, or the Game and showed chess, chequers, or some other game having no legs of play, then no score, obviously. In other cases I would allow scoring of two legs, if you wish."

"I do wish it," said Gord, feeling any point was a victory after the rude handling Twistbuck had given him in this matter. That concluded their discussion and the evening.

It was high noon on Starday; Gord and Twistbuck were at a six-point intersection in the Low Quarter. Chert was there to assist in keeping count in case of disagreement, although the university don also had a bit of parchment and quill to mark totals. Gord was pleased that his comrade was there, for marks could be added or forgotten in the excitement of play. The young thief had selected the site with care. He knew the drinking places for a mile in any direction and when turns were made he would be aware of what lay ahead. He would then have several choices of direction and would choose the route that promised him the highest gain. It looked to be a solid win, and Gord was wondering if Twistbuck's earnings would be sufficient to pay the losses the don would incur when the total was discovered.

"You count first, so what route would you like to take?" the professor asked Gord.

"I believe we should follow that route," he replied, pointing to the northeast. They walked up Tosspot Lane and almost immediately came to a small tavern.

"The Blue Elf. I score two," Gord said with artificial disappointment. It was one of the least desirable shops around, but he knew what came next, in any of the optional directions.

"Let's continue along this route for now," the professor said. They followed the curve of the lane uphill and soon came upon another sign.

"The Castle. Pity. I don't have any legs at all and it's now your turn again, Gord."

The young thief whistled as they walked along. Two signs down, two and twenty to go, and an intersection lay ahead. "I say we go right along Uskbarrel Road," he informed the others, and headed off due east thereon. Soon he came to the place he knew was there. "What luck!" Gord called happily to the pair trailing him. "Here's the Stag and Wolves, and I note that there are fully four of the latter painted on the sign, too! Twenty legs for me then, plus the two before. I lead two and twenty to naught, I believe."

Twistbuck nodded glumly, but then pointed to a narrow opening to the left. "There is a new intersection and I choose to follow it." He peered nearsightedly at a small, filthy plaque high above the brick wall of the building whose shoulder stood next to the passage. "Rag Alley, it says. Let us see what lies along this way."

Gord was disconcerted, for he'd missed this narrow place. No help for it now. There was a dingy drinking house there, too, but it didn't help the professor at all.

"It is a place called the Crock," he lamented, holding his head. "I seem to be most unfortunate this day!"

"Cheer up, good don," Gord said with merriment oozing from his every pore, "for such ill luck must surely change." He still led the way, and very soon the alley debouched on a broader thoroughfare, a street named Felbo Close. Gord had never seen or heard of it, but it didn't matter. It ended to the left, so he had no real option but to turn right, and they were walking eastward again. "Does that count as a choice?" he inquired.

"Yes, any intersection is counted, but what matter? It is now my choice at the next joining, but your sign comes next."

It turned out that the next place was a tavern named Rose in Ice. It was irritating, for Gord had hoped to build his lead further, but twenty-two was still commanding.

"I say! My turn, and what do I have but the Hungry Bear! Four, and your lead is cut to only eighteen legs, my boy!"

There was a very little triumph, even though the place stood on a corner, and Twistbuck opted to continue along toward the east. Gord was up again in both sign and intersection direction, and he knew the area now. "A crossroads!" he said as happily as the don had exclaimed when he scored the four count. "Let us turn to the right here, and see what lies southward along Hothand Street." He knew very well and soon added eight legs for coming along the inn of the Double Dragon. He led by six and twenty now. Chert was beginning to get agitated. Gord was not supposed to be enjoying this little exercise.

A mile farther and seven signs passed, Gord had scored a total of ten more legs to the professor's two. That gave him a round six and thirty, less Twistbuck's mere six, for a lead of fully thirty legs! The poor professor was going to lose the equivalent of six hundred bronze zees, thirty silver nobles, at that rate! Even the fact that they had passed out of the Low Quarter and into the Halls District didn't trouble Gord now. Chance dictated a win of from twenty to forty legs in his favor. Chert was not at all pleased.

The Avenue of Fountains was not a place for drinking, and Twistbuck had the option of direction at the next intersection. He selected Scrivener's Crescent, which curved off southeastward. The professor did not add to his score when they came upon Iggy's Inn. Gord was pleased to see that there was a tavern a little further along with a sign showing a wispy maiden in green and brown garb. "I score another two for the Dryad," he noted reflectively, not bothering to name the lead he now held.

"What miserable luck I am having today," Twistbuck lamented in earnest. "Now you are up by thirty-two legs. I have no idea what direction to take," he added miserably, indicating the lane that ran into the crescent at an odd angle. "Well," he said in a resigned manner, "I don't wish to go back to the fountain area again, so I guess I choose Haven Lane for my next route." They walked some distance, and then Twistbuck clapped his hands in glee.

"My luck is changing!" he caroled. "This is my sign and I count two legs!"

"How so, Twistbuck?" Gord demanded. The tavern had only a piece of metal above its door, a chime to be struck to indicate meals or some like event.

"Surely that is an iron triangle, is it not?" When the young thief concurred, the professor nodded and said firmly, "Triangles are figures composed of two legs!"

"How do you figure that, or are you beginning to grasp at straws here, Professor?" Gord was more than a little perplexed.

Twistbuck grinned. "In my lexicon the legs of a triangle are two sides, as distinguished from the base or the hypotenuse. Therefore I score two, and your lead is cut to thirty!"

Gord shrugged and let the new totals stand. After all, he was still incredibly ahead. They zigged and zagged and passed two more establishments that had permissible signs. Gord's was Web and Spiders for twenty-four, since the sign depicted three of the arachnids; Twistbuck's was the Xorn and Gems. Since that creature had three legs, the total lead now enjoyed by the young thief was fifty-one.

Gord began to feel a bit sorry for the unfortunate professor, for he could never afford to pay over such a sum as that lead would demand. Chert had long since begun to trudge along in a dejected manner. He was, of course, feeling sorry for himself, but

Gord took his demeanor as an indication that Chert felt the same way he did about taking such great advantage of the professor. But Gord shrugged off his pity abruptly; after all, a game was a game, and old Twistbuck was responsible for his own decisions.

"Perhaps we should stop where we are," Gord ventured, for he glimpsed a sign ahead that would aid Twistbuck. If it were counted, Gord's lead would be sharply cut.

"Never!" the fellow shot back. "How dare you attempt to cheat me of my rightful opportunity to win!"

"As you wish, as you wish," Gord reassured the angry professor. "I simply thought it might prove expedient considering the high losses you might suffer, but I will abide by the number of a round dozen each, so set when we began."

"As well you should," Twistbuck countered, "and I make my new score to be up by a figure of twenty-four, for there is the tavern called Six Mastiffs!"

"That reduces my lead to but seven and twenty—slender indeed," Gord replied dryly. Twistbuck ignored the sarcasm.

"You are next, and it is your choice of direction, as well," he told his opponent flatly.

"Then let us follow Harper Street here," said Gord. He had been in this section of Clerksburg before, and he thought he remembered a tavern that would seal his victory and teach the pedant a sharp lesson. Sure enough, they came upon the place after a short walk. It was called the Loyal Company. Twistbuck started to protest loudly, but Gord pointed to the illustration on the sign. Although only some of their legs were shown, the sign clearly depicted a score of men. "Forty legs, I am certain, and a lead of sixty-six. You have two signs to go, and I one," he added with a small but triumphant smile.

"So I am foredoomed, it appears. No matter, we shall proceed straight along this route to the next establishment."

Had he noted the sign ahead? Gord thought so, but it didn't matter. "You gain six for the Blind Basilisk," Gord said smugly, "cutting my lead down to only sixty-seven with that coup." Twistbuck started to say something, then clamped his mouth shut. The young thief stole a glance ahead. They were coming to another crossroads, and far ahead he could make out another sign. "I approve of your selection, Sir Don. I, too, shall march straight ahead... What's this? The Hornets' Nest! Do I see ten of those angry insects there? Yes, I do! Sixty legs plus sixty make a lead of one hundred and twenty, Twistbuck, and you have but a single sign left to count!" Chert moaned under his breath, and Gord continued to taunt his opponent. "Shall we end the charade now? I'll be kind, allowing you twenty off the total I have, so that you need pay over but a hundred good nobles."

"Your generosity is monumental, my young fellow, but I prefer to allow the game to run its full course. I shall take my last sign no matter what the outcome, and I shall also choose the direction here. I think we will pass down Inkwell Lane to close the game."

A little time later they came to the end of the passage. There was a tavern there, and Gord turned pale at the sight of its sign— a very clear depiction of three red centipedes.

It was almost two weeks before Gord would exchange anything approaching friendly conversation with his huge companion. In fact, for several days he wouldn't speak to Chert at all, and thereafter he had merely grunted replies when necessary to do so. Finally, the pain of having lost a hundred and eighty nobles, almost four gold orbs, wore off sufficiently for the young thief to resume a semblance of his former swagger and assurance.

"You noted, didn't you, that never once during the course of playing that stupid game did we encounter a felon or ruffian? They feared to accost us, for it was evident that I was there to protect the scholar from harm," said the thief.

Chert flexed his arm, looked at Gord, and said nothing.

"Of course, your being along as a backup was of benefit, too. But tell me, did you set the whole thing up?"

"Gord, I am thunderstruck at such a suggestion," the barbarian said, shaking his head in hurt disbelief. "You insisted on going to meet Twistbuck and you alone determined you'd play against him!"

"True, true. Still, I am troubled. There has to be a logical explanation for the professor's victory over one with my capabilities. It just doesn't make sense. Do you know what position the man holds at Counts College?"

"He professes."

"Of course," the young thief snapped irritably, "but what does Twistbuck profess?"

"Architecture."

"And?"

"Someone mentioned cartography, I think."

"That wouldn't have been a factor. Is there anything else that you heard about Twistbuck that would have contributed to his win?" Gord demanded.

"Well, there is one minor detail that might have made a difference in the game. But I don't know, maybe it's nothing," Chert said hesitantly, while concentrating on stifling the grin that wanted to spread from one cheek to the other and back again.

"Let me be the judge of that. Tell me, what do you know?" Gord demanded.

"Oh, just that your worthy opponent also specializes in history and city planning. Knows Greyhawk like the back of his hand!" The barbarian allowed the insistent grin to have its way and then broke into a fit of uncontrollable laughter.

"Aaargh!" Gord roared in absolute rage. It would be some time before the furious rogue would send another word in Chert's direction.

Collect all of these exciting Planet Stories adventures!